LIGHT
in the
DARK

THREE RIVERS BOOK TWO

New York Times and *USA Today* Bestselling Author
Jasinda Wilder

LIGHT
in the
DARK

THREE RIVERS BOOK TWO

THREE RIVERS

LAKE MICHIGAN

CINEMA

BOOKSTORE

GROCERY

The Cellar

COOPER'S HOLLOW

MAIN STREET

FIRST STREET

N
W E
S

1

Felix

I CURSE UNDER MY BREATH, STICKING MY THUMB IN my mouth like an idiot for a split second before yanking it out and shaking it—also idiotic. I hadn't burned it, I'd smacked it with a fucking hammer. Sucking on it and shaking it weren't going to do anything for the pain. Instincts are stupid sometimes.

I look at the injured thumb—it'll bruise like a bitch, but whatever.

Annoyed, I tossed my hammer onto the ground and stood up, taking a second to let my temper cool off. Working angrily leads to mistakes. If I make a mistake here, it could mean days, weeks, or even months of setbacks to correct—I'm building this place by myself, no crew I can bitch out and order around. Just little old me, building a house from the ground up with my own two hands. Well, and generous use of heavy machinery—it's sorta impossible to raise framing by yourself.

I've made good progress in the last few weeks—I'd actually taken a long weekend, putting Riley and Bear in charge of my crews; I was able to get the driveway cleared so I could start getting the machinery back there.

Yes, I know, I'm nuts. Building a house from scratch with your hands is sort of nutty, I get it. Back in the day, it meant cutting down trees, splitting, sawing, all that. A whole hell of a lot of insanely hard work, sure, but doable. A modern house? That's a whole other beast. And I'm not building a thousand square foot cabin, I'm building a Crowe construction special—the kinda thing you'd see in a neighborhood downtown, just...way out here in the middle of nowhere.

So here I am on a Saturday morning, putting framing together. I'd dug and poured the foundation last weekend, and now, while it cures, I'm putting the framing together. Again, I'm doing it the hard way. You can get preassembled framing, but not only is this cheaper, I'm determined to do every last lick of work with my own two hands, concrete, plumbing, electrical, the whole fucking kit and kaboodle.

Because I'm a crazy man.

My phone rings, jarring me out of my idle reverie. I step over the piles of lumber and boxes of screws and nails and other odds and ends to where my phone sits on the tailgate of my truck. It's stopped ringing by the time I get to it, of course. The notification reads: "Missed call: Bear."

Fuck, that's not good. Bear doesn't call on the weekends. He doesn't call period—he hates cell phones. It rings again immediately, the photo of Bear with Noelle popping up on the screen.

I swipe to answer and put it on speaker, taking a long slug of lukewarm water before answering. "Bear, what's up?"

His deep voice is troubled. "Sprung a leak out at Aspenview Lane."

"Fuck me, what? A leak? Which house? How bad?"

I hear sloshing. "Bad, boss. Real fuckin' bad." I hear a grunt, a curse, a splash. "Jesus. Got the main shut off, but this basement is a swimming pool."

"Goddammit, how the fuck did that happen. Which one is it?"

"Nine-one-six-one. The one that was almost fuckin' done."

"Shitting Moses," I mutter. "Fan-fucking-tastic."

"I got Reggie, Alvarez, Tom, and Dominic on the way. Reggie's cousin runs one'a them emergency restoration companies, I guess, so he's got his cousins bringing pumps and fans and whatever else."

"I'll be there as soon as I can," I say.

"Sorry, Fee. I don't know what happened."

"We'll figure it out. Mistakes happen." As I talk, I round up my tools one-handed.

"I just—" By the growl in his voice, I can tell Bear is on his way to taking the responsibility for the situation on himself.

"Bear," I cut in, "I know better than anyone how seriously you take your job. Mistakes happen. You can't watch every guy do every job all the time. I ain't mad atcha. You're good."

He sighs. "Supervisor's supposed to supervise."

"Were you off playing hooky or some shit when plumbing went in?" I ask.

"No."

"New crew? New guys?"

"No."

"So you were doing your job, to the best of your knowledge?"

"Yeah."

"Then let it go. We'll handle it. It'll cost time and money, it'll suck, we'll all sacrifice our weekend, but it ain't on you, buddy. I'm the boss. It's my name on the door. Buck stops with me, not you. Yeah?"

He sighs, a big, blustery sigh of acceptance. "Yeah, I got it. Just sucks."

"I ever tell you about the time a new guy tried to show initiative and accidentally burned down a build we were four days from turning over to Mackenzie?"

Mackenzie Laird is our broker, in charge of selling our builds—she was a marketing and sales guru who could sell water to a fish.

"How the hell?"

I chuckled. "Investigator said he was trying to do something with the wiring that never got finished, something shorted, sparked, caught, and he barely got out alive."

Bear snorts, and the sound is decidedly ursine. "If y'ain't got the training, you don't touch plumbing or electrical."

I consider my own intention to do the plumbing and electrical work here myself. "That is true. And since then, I've made a point of making that clear to all my newbies. Stay in your lane. If you don't KNOW you know how to do something, don't fuckin' do it."

I make sure the keys for the cherry picker are safely locked in the glove box of my truck, double-check the site to make sure I haven't forgotten anything, and then slam the tailgate closed.

"A'ight, Bear, I'll see you there in fifteen."

"Yes, sir. Sorry to fuck over your Saturday."

"Quit fuckin' apologizing, man, Jesus."

He lets out a grunt that sounds like a growl. "Whatever. See you." I laugh as he hangs up on me.

One last glance at my site—my hammer is still where I tossed it after smashing my stupid thumb. I grab it and chuck it into the orange 5-gallon bucket of frequently used tools I keep strapped into the front left corner of my bed, smack the white cap in place, and take off.

I arrive at Aspenview Lane and park in the street behind a line of pickups, a battered blue late 90s Suburban, and a cube van with the rolling door open to reveal emergency restoration equipment. I hear pumps going as I approach the open front door, stepping over a mess of cables and hoses on my way to the basement.

"Holy fuck," I mutter as I reach the bottom of the steps.

The basement is unutterably fucked. Water sloshes knee deep. Bear's voice, deep and quiet and rumbling, carries over the rest despite the fact that he rarely raises his voice above a murmur. I rub my forehead with a knuckle, assessing what's gonna have to be done to unfuck this.

All the drywall down here, just completed yesterday, is gonna have to come out. The luxury vinyl plank flooring has to come up—we might be able to salvage it if we get the water up fast enough and get things dry. We'll have to go through all the wiring down here, all the outlets…

the list of items keeps on racking up as I move through the basement.

I find the crew in the mechanical room, several worksite utility lights hanging from the ceiling to illuminate the area. They're focused on a section of plumbing near the water softener.

"What do we got, boys?" I ask, grabbing one of the lights and shining it on the section they're looking at.

"Hey, Boss," Bear says. He points at a junction where the main supply branches off to feed through the softener. "One hundred percent installer error." He points. "Ain't a plumber, but this don't look right to me."

I examine the junction. "Good god almighty," I snap. "What kinda fuckin' glue-sniffing numbnuts did this kindergarten bullshit?"

The guys all clam up, so I look at Bear. "Who was doing plumbing?"

He glances at the ceiling. "Calloway's guys. We've used them for years—you have, I mean. This is my first build with them. I don't know the particular person who did this, though."

"Well, a blind monkey coulda done a better job at this fucking junction." I hand Bear the light and pull out my phone, take a handful of close-ups from different angles.

The next thing I do is take a video of the flooding. I spend the next hour going through the fix process with Bear, making sure he understands what all has to happen. Once I'm satisfied that he's got it, I head back up to my truck, sit on the tailgate, and take off my boots and socks.

I dial Holden Calloway; it rings twice before his gravelly pack-a-day voice answers. "Felix." That's Holden for you—no nonsense, no wasted words.

"Holden, we got an issue, man."

A soft growl, the click-scrape of a lighter, and a breath as he exhales smoke. "Talk to me."

"One of your guys fucked up my build over here on Aspenview."

"Fucked up how?"

"Used the wrong piece for a junction, no glue, I don't know, man, but it's fucked up. Caused a massive flood in the basement. I'm talking weeks to unfuck and tens of thousands of dollars in damage."

He sighs, the sigh turns into a cough, and then he hits his cigarette before answering. "Photos?"

"Incoming." I send him the photos and the videos, put it on speaker, and tug the cuffs of my jeans up to my knees.

He's silent as he peruses the images. "Jesus fucking Christ on crumbling cracker. That's the sloppiest shit I ever seen." A pause, keyboard keys clacking in the background. "Aspenview? Which one?" I repeat the house number for him, and he types some more. "That was...Abel's crew. Abel is one of my best, but he did have three guys quit a few weeks ago. Betcha fifty bucks it was a new guy."

"Well, whoever it was, it's a problem," I say.

"No shit," he says. "We got insurance for this, though. I'll handle it. If you can see your way to trusting me again, I'll give you a break on the next job."

"Just make sure you vet your crews better than this, Holden. This wasn't complicated plumbing. This should *not* have fuckin' happened."

Another snorting exhale. "Yeah, I hear ya, Fee. My agent'll be contacting you. We'll get it fixed, and I'll find who did it and what else he may have worked on. If he fucked that up, who knows what else he fucked up."

I feel like someone slugged me in the gut. "Fuck, Holden. I hadn't considered that."

"Been in business for thirty-five years, Felix. Seen it all."

"'Preciate you, Holden."

"You too, Felix. Later."

"Later." I punch the end call button and only just barely resist the urge to hurl my phone across the lawn—it's in an OtterBox, so it'd survive fine, but I don't feel like slogging over there to get it.

So. Now what? Back to the site? I should, but I'm soaking wet, irritated, angry, hungry, and I just don't feel like it. Fuck it—I'll take a real Saturday. Maybe even go fishing.

I call Riley—he answers right before it would have gone to voicemail. "Hey, bro. What's shakin'?"

"Shitty fuckin' day all of a sudden, Rye, that's what. What are you up to?"

"I'm in Petosky with April."

"Oh. Alright then, never mind."

"What?"

"I just don't feel like going back to the site, so I was gonna see if you wanted to go fishing."

"*Fishing*?" He says it like I suggested parachute-free skydiving. "Fee, my brother, you *hate* fishing."

"Yeah, I know. I just…"

"You suck at relaxing," he says, finishing where I trailed off. "You wouldn't know a real day off if it bit you in the ass."

I chuckle. "You're not wrong. Also, who the hell is April? Flavor of the month?"

"Oh, fuck off, Fee. Don't be a dick." He says something

muffled, then comes back to me. "You need a social life. A girlfriend. Something."

"I know. Well, have fun in Petosky with April. See you Monday."

"I'll be back later. We could grab some brews tonight."

"Sure, sounds good. Hit me up whenever. I'll probably be, I dunno, sorting paperwork or something."

"Felix, if I find out that you spent your Saturday afternoon doing goddamn paperwork, we are gonna be fighting. I swear to god I'll roofie you, take you to fuckin' Vegas, and force you to have fun for once in your Type-A workaholic life."

I laugh, knowing he's in no way joking. "Fine, fine, I'll find something to do."

"Something that isn't *work*. For the company *or* your house."

"Right. That."

"Bye, bro."

"See ya."

I hang up and toss the phone aside with a sigh. What do normal people do for fun on the weekend? I've always worked or found a project. I restored a '69 Camaro, and that took a few years. But then once it was done, I only enjoyed driving it for one summer, and then I sold it. I have a '73 FJ40 in my garage right now, but it's a project I've never really even started. Even the house where I currently live was a weekend project.

I bought this place from the estate of the previous owner, an old widower who'd lived there alone for twenty years after his wife died. He'd been a hoarder, and the estate—managed by a lawyer, since he had no kids or grandkids—hadn't wanted to spend the time or resources to clean it out. So they auctioned it off for pennies on the dollar just to get rid of it. I'd paid less than what the land itself was worth—a bargain and a half since it was on a corner lot with almost two full acres, less than two blocks from downtown.

The less bargain-y part was the state of the place. The old guy had stacked garbage up to the ceiling in an un-navigable maze. The miasma was unbearable—I'd needed full PPE just to go past the front door. And that was *after* the body had been removed.

All told, it took me two months of weekend work to get the shit cleared out. I filled two seventy-five-yard roll-off dumpsters and half of a forty-yard one. The walls were riddled with black mold, the floors were rotting through to the subfloor, and the crawlspace was full of rodents, as was the attic. I'd had to tear the place down to studs just to get to a halfway decent starting place.

I spent two years restoring that house—it was my first solo endeavor. I came up in the business working for Dad, the original owner of Crowe Construction. Back then, I was a bottom-rung rookie, fresh out of high school and just learning the ropes of the construction trade, although I'd spent my entire life on jobsites with Dad. I tagged along as a little kid, got put to work sweeping up nails and whatever, and got paid in McDonald's and ice cream. When I turned fourteen, he officially hired me on the cleanup crew, and I worked after school and on weekends during the football and baseball off-season.

When I graduated high school, I had a D1 full-ride offer from U of M to play ball—both sports. I turned it down to take a position as a foreman for Dad...and primarily because Amy had no intention of leaving Three Rivers. She wanted to be close to her family and friends.

The irony of the thing is that after I drunkenly fucked up my entire life at Ryan Calhoun's party, Amy took a job at a hospital in Detroit, leaving me up here. I don't regret the decision to not go to U of M, but I do sometimes wonder what my life would be like if I'd taken it.

Fuck, I'm maundering. I grab my phone, close the tailgate, and jump into the cab. As I'm easing away from the house to make the U-turn in the cul-de-sac, I pass by a young family coming out of one of the finished and sold homes—the Rogers, if I remember correctly. A young Black couple with a pre-teen son and a daughter about kindergarten age. Sweet family. They're all sporting swimsuits, the kids have swim goggles on their heads, and the mom is carrying approximately seventy pounds worth of coolers, mesh bags full of sand toys, and who knows what else, while the dad wrestles a stubborn back seat down to make room for the gear Mom is carrying.

And suddenly, the beach sounds good. Not the local beaches, though—I've got nothing against tourists, for the most part, but the beaches close to town are swarmed with fudgies this time of year. I'm thinking of what we locals call Secret Beach: a spot a good thirty minutes north of town where I can reliably have the beach to myself, or mostly.

I text Bear: *heading out of town for a few hours and turning off my phone. Please try not to have any more emergencies.*

He gives the message a "*haha*" and then sends a thumbs-up emoji. Yes, a haha *and* a thumbs up. Pro-level texting, right there.

I swing by my house and change into a pair of swim trunks—my favorite pair, mainly because Riley hates when

I wear them. They're super short and tight, as in 70s style. I shrug into a muscle shirt, plop a ball cap on my head, and pack a cooler with ice, a six-pack of Local's Light, and a variety of snacks. As a last-second addition, I even pick up the Louis L'Amour western from my bedside table—despite the fact that I haven't cracked it open in months.

The FJ40 in my garage is a running project—it needs updated tires and suspension, new upholstery, and the engine needs a thorough overhaul, not to mention some minor rust mitigation and fresh paint. But, it runs reliably, and most importantly, I already have a winch system for taking the hard top off from when I owned that CJ. It takes about fifteen minutes since the bolts holding the top in place are stubborn, but I get the top off and the engine running.

Finally, earbuds in my pocket, cooler packed, I head north for a day at the beach.

Alone.

Go me.

2

Ember

I SCRAPE MY HAIR OUT OF MY EYES AND CRANK THE window down all the way as I cruise the beach parking lot looking for a spot to park Pumpkin, my VW bus. The A/C conked out the day after my run-in with Kayce Dutton—I looked up how to spell his name later that same day, because when Dutchie and I watched the show, I'd been envisioning it as Casey, rather than Kayce. Anyway, point being, Pumpkin, the ungrateful bitch, decided to kill the A/C on me right as we enter the hottest days of summer.

Fixing it is beyond my meager automotive repair skills, and certainly beyond my financial means to have fixed. So, I suffer.

And yes, Felix Crowe does look a good bit like Kayce

Dutton, if he was a few inches taller and had a good thirty pounds more muscle.

And a more rugged jawline.

And the most arresting eyes I've ever seen—the piercing, arresting pale blue of the underside of an iceberg.

Maybe it's just the slightly too long, shaggy, unkempt-but-sexy dark blond hair and the heavy stubble that's not quite a beard.

I don't know.

Why am I still thinking about him? I spent ten minutes max with him, and that was what…two, three weeks ago?

Ugh: no spots at this beach either, and this is the third one I've been to. Like, come on. I just want to chill at the beach for a minute before I have to take this online exam for my undergrad program.

Sweating and annoyed, I leave that lot and trundle down Main Street toward the fourth and last public beach within the downtown Three Rivers area.

And that bitch is full too. Wonderful.

Fighting tears—because I'm always on the verge of tears these days, it feels like—I sigh in resignation.

This calls for ice cream. I spot the Korner Kustard down the road a few blocks, and head that way. I have to park a quarter mile down the side street and walk, and then wait in a fifteen minute long line, but I walk away victorious with my M&Ms, Reece's Pieces, and Oreo cement mixer. You gotta take the little victories when everything else is shit.

Losing Dutchie has taught me that.

I blink away tears at the thought of his name and focus on the ice cream. There's a bench across the street from the

Korner Kustard, and my god, I hate that spelling *so much*. I sit on the bench and watch the water ripple and glint in the hot Michigan sun, and wish I was about to go swimming after my ice cream.

I feel the bench dip and hear it creak, stifling a groan at the loss of my solitude. I glance at my new bench-mate.

She's at least six hundred years old, with fat blue veins bulging out of rice-paper skin, white hair sprinkled with pink, blue, and purple streaks, and, I shit you not, a nose-ring. Like, through the septum. She's eating a triple-scoop waffle cone dipped in chocolate, and that old biddy is going to *town* on that shit.

I now stifle a laugh, not as annoyed for some reason. Maybe it's because I have a soft spot for kookie old ladies. They remind me of my GramGram.

She eyes me. "What crawled up your cooter and died, missy?"

I choke on my ice cream, spluttering and coughing. "Ex-*cuse* me?"

She gestures at me with her monumental ice cream cone. "I'm an empath. Felt you stewing from the counter."

I point at the beach with my spoon. "Beach is packed. I've been cramming for an exam for weeks, and I need a break. Thought I'd go swimming. But…" I gesture broadly at Three Rivers in general. "Tourists."

She chuckles. "You're not a tourist?"

I sigh. "I don't know what I am. I'm not from here, no, but I've been here for over two months. I know that doesn't make me a local, but I'm not a tourist. I just wanted to lay out, listen to a podcast, and jump in the lake. But there's literally nowhere to even fucking park. Excuse my language."

She snorts. "Fuckin' fudgies."

I frown at her. "Fudgies?"

She cackles. "What we locals call the tourists. They come up *ooh*-ing and *ahh*-ing about all the fudge." She points at a nearby fudge shop, which has a line out the door. "Case in point. Fudgies."

I snicker, and the snicker turns into a full-blown laughter. "Fudgies. I love it."

She drops a dollop of ice cream down her cleavage, squeals in shock, and fishes it out…and eats it. God, I love old ladies.

"What you gotta do is head north. 'Bout, oh…thirty minutes or so. There's a nice little spot on the left. Big old turn out, looks like one of them whaddyacallits, scenic overlooks. But it's a locals-only secret, so don't go tellin' no fudgies or it won't stay secret."

I blink at her. "What's the secret?"

She snorts, takes a bite, and winces. "Ooooh, fuck, brain freeze. The secret is that there's a path down to the beach near the north end of the turnoff. Bit of a hike to get down there, so don't try to take a whole bunch'a shit, but it's a nice secluded beach. No rocks, nice and wide, and if there's anyone there at all, it'll be another local tryin' to get away from the fudgies."

"Oh. Wow, thanks, that's…god, you're saving my life." I have no clue what comes over me, next. "You, uh…you wanna come along?"

She slowly lowers the ice cream and stares at me. "You for real, missy?"

I shrug. "Sure, why not?"

"You don't wanna drag some strange old lady to the beach. I'll talk your damn ear off." She takes a defiant bite of ice cream, and then launches into hissing and wincing.

"You remind me of my grandmother, and she was my second favorite human," I say.

She gives me a puzzled look. "Second favorite?"

"Husband." It's all I can manage.

She nods, and that's it. I steal a look at her, and she's staring into nothing, her gaze full of memory. Yeah, she gets it.

"Well, missy, if you're serious, and if you've got the gumption to haul my fat ass up and down that trail, I'd love to come."

I grin at her. "I may be short, but I'm strong. And you're a gazelle, so helping you up and down the trail will be no problem."

She cackles. "A gazelle, she says." She slaps her hip. "More like a Greater Kudu."

"A what?" I ask.

"Greater Kudu. Big African deer fella. Spirally horns. Big asses."

"Oh." I stick my spoon into my paper cup-bowl thing and extend my hand to her. "I'm Ember."

"Amber, nice to meet you. I'm Faye."

"Ember," I say, emphasizing the E sound. "Like embers from a fire."

"Ember, huh?" She eyes me. "That your real name, or is that some sort of fuck-the-patriarchy thing?"

I laugh. "I mean, definitely fuck the patriarchy, but no. My mom was a hippie. My full name is Emberly. She thought it was cool and different, I guess."

"You ain't old enough for your mom to have been a hippie."

"Well, she wasn't a hippie, like Woodstock and whatever. She followed Phish around for like…I dunno, years.

Years and years." I shrug. "But she *was* into bell bottoms and free love and peace signs and pot." You can make out my orange bus in the distance. "That orange VW was hers."

"Well, I guess that makes sense." She looks at me again. "So, she followed Phish around, and then had you and settled down, huh?"

It's my turn to cackle. "God, hardly. She took me with her."

This gets me a flabbergasted stare. "On tour? To concerts? With stoners and hooligans?"

"Yup."

"What about school?"

"She had a commune. She traveled with like a dozen people, some of whom were former teachers. I was educated in the back of RVs and busses. But yes, with stoners and hooligans." I shake my head. "It was...nontraditional, sure. But I liked it. Never knew anything different, obviously. There were other kids. They'd park their vans and buses in a big square and we'd all play together while the parents went to the show."

"How'd they make money?" she asks.

I shrug. "Never could figure that out for sure. I know a couple of them sold pot, another sold nitrous or something. Some of them sold shirts and merch, or cannabis pipes and bongs. I don't know what Mom did. She was cagey about it."

She sighs. "Was, huh?"

I nod. "Got cut at a show, developed an infection, and died. I was nineteen."

"Lotta loss for someone so young," she says.

All I can do is shrug. She's right.

We sit in silence, finishing our ice cream.

She points at the street I'm parked on. "I live down that way. I'll just need to grab a few things."

"I'll walk with you," I tell her.

Turns out she lives two doors down from where I'm parked. She pops in and comes back out a few minutes later decked out in a bright purple bikini with a gauzy pale blue wrap around her waist, a straw visor with an oversized brim, and a giant pair of bug-eye sunglasses. She also has a Tupperware container of brownies and an absolutely massive canvas bag which obviously contains a bottle of alcohol of some sort, along with who knows what else.

I grin at her as I lean on the hood of my bus. "Damn, girl, that fit is fire!"

She harrumphs. "What the hell is that supposed to mean?"

I cackle. "It means your outfit is awesome. I fucking love the bikini, Faye. Good thing we're not hitting any public beaches or you'd have the boys swarming around us like flies on honey."

She snorts. "I appreciate the sentiment, Ember, but you need your eyes checked. No boys are gonna be swarming around an eighty-five-year-old woman." She flicks a finger at me. "You got your suit on under there, or what? You can change in my house if you want."

I'm wearing a white sleeveless sundress, the hem flirting with my knees and the neck scooping indecently low. "Yeah, I've got my bikini on under this."

She twirls her finger in a circle over her head. "Well then, let's fuckin' go."

I cackle. "Faye, we're gonna be best friends, I can already tell."

She harrumphs crankily, but I can see her blinking a little too hard as she heads for the passenger door.

A few minutes later, Pumpkin is humming along merrily northward, Simon and Garfunkel singing about feelin' groovy from the speakers, and Faye is, true to her word, keeping up a tour guide-worthy running commentary about the business and homes we pass.

A little over thirty minutes later, we're squealing to a halt behind a vintage red SUV with the top off. Faye carefully lowers herself out of the van and shoulders her bag, stuffing the Tupperware into it to keep her hands free for the climb down.

She leads the way to the far north end of the turnoff, where the guardrail ends. Some enterprising soul built a set of wooden stairs leading down to the beach, some fifty feet below. "Huh," she huffs. "These stairs weren't here last time I was here, but that was…ten years ago? Fifteen? With my daughter and grandkids."

I glance at her as we start down the stairs—she's on the inside, gripping the handrail in her right hand and clutching my arm in her left. "How many kids and grandkids do you have, Faye?"

She sighs. "One daughter, one granddaughter, and one grandson. Tina, my daughter, went through a horrifically messy divorce about three years ago. Her ex was a cheating shitbag, and she'd been a stay-at-home mom their whole marriage. His idea. When she found out he was screwing half of his office staff, she filed for divorce so fast everyone's heads spun. But he had the money, and he knew the judge, so it was a hell of an uphill battle for my Tina. She had to go back to school and get recertified as a CPA and go back to work. She got full custody, child support, and alimony because it turns out he was also a drug addict, secretly." Faye waves a hand. "She got a job offer in California, and she couldn't turn it down, so she moved across the country and now I only see her and my grandbabies at Thanksgiving and Christmas."

"That's rough, Faye, I'm sorry."

She huffs. "Is what it is, missy. I miss 'em somethin' fierce, of course, but I just couldn't see myself moving to California. I've lived in Three Rivers my whole life. My husband Thomas, built the house I live in, and I've lived there for over fifty years. I suppose at some point I'm gonna stop being able to take care of myself and she'll haul my ass out there and put me in some facility." Faye pauses, looks at me thoughtfully. "To be honest, Ember, I guess I hope I die before that. I'd rather die in the bed I shared with my Thomas than in some smelly old folks home where I'm just one more forgotten soul."

She resumes the descent, and I try to figure out how I feel about what she said, and what to say.

She glances at me, cackling. "Not sure how to answer that one, huh, missy?"

"No, Faye, I am not. I understand your position, certainly, but speaking as someone who lost my grandmother, I wish I'd had more time with her."

Faye sighs. "I wish I had more time with them, too. But there's no good solution, Ember. Tina is taking care of an eleven-year-old and a seven-year-old by herself in LA. She can't take care of me too, even if I did move out there. She ain't got room for me, for one. She ain't got the time, for two, and she ain't got the money, for three. So if I went out to LA, I'd have to get my own place or go into a facility, both of which I'd have to pay for since Tina is just barely getting by. And I'd barely see them anyway, since she works sixty hours a week and the kids are in a billion sports and activities to keep 'em busy and supervised while she works and I'm well past the babysitting age."

"That sucks."

She nods. "Yup, it sure does." She shrugs. "But then, that's life. Some things just suck and there's nothing you can do but suffer."

I laugh bitterly. "Wow, that's heartening, thanks, Faye."

She pauses again and gives me a nasty glare. "Oh, hush, you. That ain't all there is to life. The flip side of that coin is the good things that come along are sweeter and deeper because of the suffering. It all balances out in the end, one way or another, I've found."

We descend again, and I can't help a deep sigh. "I hope so. I've had a lot of suffering, so I'm ready for the good."

She squeezes my arm. "It's comin', missy. You just gotta have the gumption to grab it and hold on tight when it does."

We reach the bottom, the wooden plank steps giving way to warm sand. We both kick off our sandals, and I bend and scoop them up. They go into my beach bag, which contains a small umbrella, a mesh sand blanket, a towel, sunscreen, bug spray, my ereader, and a wide paint brush for brushing sand off my feet.

I also have a small cooler with a long strap that holds a few cans of sparkling water, a few individually packaged string cheese sticks, and some jerky.

To either side, the hill slopes to the shoreline; the stairs, it turns out, were built in a natural cut in the hillside. The sand expands away in both directions, and Lake Michigan is a rippling blue field of sparkling diamonds in the sun. Faye shuffles through the sand straight ahead and plops her bag down a few feet from the water's edge. I spread out my sand blanket and we arrange our things. Faye stares at her bag as if it has offended her. "Forgot a chair."

I frown. "Well shit, so did I." I cast an eye at the stairs, which seem rather far and steep from this end. "I have a couple beach chairs in my van. I'll go get them."

Faye snorts, waving off the suggestion. "Horseshit, missy," she snaps. "By the time you get back up that hill and down with the chairs, it'll be time to go. You'll just have help me lay down and then help my fat ass back up again when I wanna go swimming."

"Faye, you do *not* have a fat ass. You ought to be nicer to yourself."

She turns away from me, grabs a double handful of her buttocks, and jiggles them at me. "This ain't nothin', sweetie." She wriggles out of the coverup, shoves it into her bag, and then faces me again. "Listen to me, now. I'm a billion years old. I've earned the right to call myself a fat ass if I want. When I was your age, I had curves like you wouldn't believe. I had to sleep with a stick next to me so I could fend off my husband long enough to get any sleep, and not a word of that is a lie. The man had an absolutely insatiable sex drive. He'd chase me around the house penis first. Course, I always gave the man what he wanted because he'd get so damned whiny if I didn't." She winks at me. "I'd be lyin' if I didn't say I let him catch me for my own purposes, too."

I laugh, shaking my head. "I love that."

Her eyes scan me as I peel my dress off, revealing my sapphire blue bikini—growing up the way I did, among Mom's free love hippy friends, I've always been comfortable with my body and with nudity. My bikini is…small. And let's be honest, I am not. I mean, I'm short, so I'm small in that sense. But the rest of me is decidedly…juicy. Big tits, a bit of a tummy, wide hips, big ass, big thighs. I keep in shape, despite living out of my van—I do a lot of yoga and Pilates, and a little bit of resistance work with Dutchie's adjustable dumbbells and my handful of kettlebells, and I walk a lot. So, I'm curvy, but I like to think it's a fit curvy.

Faye snorts and shakes her head. "Well now you're just showing off."

I frown at her. "Showing off?"

She gestures at me with a vague flip of a hand. "You. That ridiculous body of yours. That bikini that could fit in a cupholder."

I blush. "Oh, c'mon, Faye. You're being silly."

"*And* she blushes? My my." Faye reaches out and gives the underside of one of my boobs a playful tap. "With knockers like these, girlie? You better carry a big damn stick if you go to a public beach. What was it you said? The boys'll be swarming around you like flies on shit."

"I think I said flies on honey, actually," I say, laughing.

"I think you're mixing up your metaphors with that one, missy. It's bees to honey and flies to shit."

I frown. "Oh." I burst into laughter. "You're right."

"Course I am." She waves both hands at me. "Help me sit my fat ass down. I wanna get some sun before I go for a dip."

I bite down on a comment about her self-denigration and hold her hands, helping her lower herself to the blanket. Once there, she fishes in her bag and comes up with a tube of sunscreen, which she applies liberally to her exposed skin. That done, she lays back, covers her eyes with her visor, and lets out a happy sigh.

I go through the same process, spraying sunscreen on myself and then arranging myself comfortably on the blanket, ereader in hand, a sweating can of sparkling water nearby.

Doesn't get much better, I'd say.

At some point, my eyes droop, and my ereader sags to my belly, and then my eyes close.

3

Felix

T READING WATER, I REALIZE I MAY HAVE SWUM A bit further from shore than was sensible. I'm tired, panting, and still have to swim back…and the shore looks a *lot* farther away than I feel comfortable with.

But I mean, what are you supposed to do at the beach by yourself? I tried my damndest to relax, really I did. I even read a few chapters of *The Sackett Brand* before I got too hot and restless, at which point I waded in and splashed around the shallows for a few minutes. Eventually, however, the drive to *accomplish things*—that ceaseless, nagging, driving, frustrating engine inside me that rules my every waking moment—pushed me to swim away from shore. At first, it had been simply about moving my body, enjoying the cool, clear water, and the sunshine. But then, inevitably, it became a competition with myself.

And now here I am, a good half mile from shore, and I'm a bit concerned about my ability to make it back.

Like an idiot.

I roll to my back with my head facing shore and backstroke leisurely toward land. When I crane my head and twist to check my progress, however, not only have I not made forward progress, I've managed to travel sideways. I alternate between breaststroke and sidestroke. I try a regular crawl, but that's fuckin' exhausting, so I go back to alternating between breaststroke and sidestroke.

Eventually, the shore seems closer, and the vague burn of panic in my gut recedes to a nagging ache of embarrassment. I mean, shit, I'm a Three Rivers boy, born and raised. I grew up swimming in the big water, so you'd think I'd know better—and I do, intellectually. Distances are deceiving once you're in the water: what seems like a short swim from shore or the deck of a boat is suddenly a *lot* fucking farther once you're in the water with no one around to pick you up.

Every limb burning and weighing a thousand pounds, I finally feel lake bottom drag against my toes, and I gratefully slog the rest of the way to shore.

I'm so exhausted that I'm dizzy, panting like I…well, swam a mile. I rub my face and scrap my wet hair back as I drag my stupid ass ashore and to my towel, which I promptly collapse upon.

"Fuckin' dumbass," I growl at myself, out loud, and then adopt a mocking tone of voice. "Oh yeah, let's go to the beach, it'll be fun, they said. Let's swim halfway to fucking Wisconsin and *almost die*, they said."

I hear a snort from my right. Startled, I glance in that direction and see the goddess with the silver eyes and white hair. Amber? No. Cooler than that. Ember. The one with the vintage orange VW and the most amazing tits I've ever seen.

Which are on prominent display at the moment. She's wearing a vivid blue bikini whose color contrasts with her tanned golden skin and white-blond hair. The top is wholly insufficient for the task of containing her monster boobs—it's basically a bit of string wrapped in a complex web around her chest, neck, and shoulders, with two triangles barely the size of a palm covering her nipples and a few inches of skin around them, leaving the rest beautifully exposed. She's laying on her back, so they drape to either side, pulling at the top so the breast nearest me is nearly falling out, showing a hint of areola—a sliver of pale, pretty pink.

The bottoms are just as spectacularly revealing—she has one knee propped up and tilted inward, rolling her hips slightly toward me. The bend at her hip creates a crease into which the string vanishes, hinting at the shape of her pussy, showing off the whole of her bare leg, which I quite vividly remember glimpsing the last time we met—long, despite the fact that she's short, thick and round and smooth, muscular and toned.

"You're staring again, Kayce," she says, smirking at me.

"Name's Felix," I grumble, shutting my eyes to tear them away from her mesmerizing body. "And I can't help it. You in that bikini…fuckin' hypnotizing."

Pink stains her cheeks. "What, this ol' thing?"

I cover my eyes with my hands as if to shield them from the sun, because I'm helpless against the siren song of her nearly nude body. "Yeeeeeahhhhh," I drawl. "that ol' thing."

I hear a cackle from the other side of Ember—the dry, papery laugh of an old woman. "She's somethin', ain't she, son?"

I lift up on an elbow and look, with some difficulty, past Ember. Wrinkled, weathered skin is my reward for trying to see who's talking to me—an old woman on her belly, cheek on her hands, a purple bikini string untied to get sun on her back.

"She is at that, ma'am," I say.

"Ma'am, he says," she cackles, not looking at me. "One of the old breed, with honest-to-goodness *manners*." She twists her head to crack an eye in my direction. "Oh, I know you. You're one of Carson Crowe's boys. Felix, is it?"

"Yes, ma'am," I answer, surprised. I recognize her, but can't put a name to her. "I admit you have the better of me. I know I know you, but I'm not great at remembering names."

"Faye McFarlane. I taught art up at the high school. I retired, ohhhhh, when you were in ninth grade, I think? Over ten years ago, now. Of course, when I say retired, I mean fully retired. After my Thomas retired, I cut back my hours, but that was twenty years ago. I was gonna fully retire, but then Thomas passed and I had to do something with myself, so I only fully retired, what was it…ten years ago, now? Twelve?"

"Well, ma'am, I'm thirty-two. I graduated fourteen years ago."

She lifts a bit further, forgetting she'd untied her bikini top, showing me a dangerous amount of her breasts.

"You sure?" She glances down. "Whoops! Bet you wish that was her, huh?"

Ember rolls her eyes. "Faye, do *not* encourage him. I've met him twice for all of ten minutes, and he's spent most of that time staring at my chest."

Faye holds her top to her chest and laboriously sits up, turning her back to Ember. "Do me up, would you, missy?" While Ember is tying, Faye winks at me over her shoulder. "I mean, I can't say I blame him. Lotta real estate to see, if you know what I mean."

I completely fail to suppress the snicker of laughter.

Ember frowns at Faye, and then at me. "I feel ganged up on. Should I put my dress back on?"

Faye turns to face us both. "No one's ganging up on you, Ember." She tosses her visor aside, rummages in the huge bag at her side, and comes up with an orange life pre-server, the kind that used to be ubiquitous in tin fishing boats for decades.

Ember snickers. "Jesus, Faye, what else you got in there?"

Faye makes a face, shrugging. "Oh, you know, this and that." She works herself to her knees, and then half-kneeling, and then upright. "Whew, that was rough. Gotta do more of those mobility exercises Doc Murthy gave me. The chair yoga ain't cuttin' it. I'll be damned if I'm gonna end up on a Life Alert commercial."

"Going for a dip?" Ember asks.

Faye shakes the big, thick orange flotation device. "Gonna float a bit. If the current takes me and I don't come back, let the lake have me."

Ember blinks at her. "Faye, I can't tell if you're joking or not."

"Me either!" Faye cackles. She gives me a wink. "And don't stare at my ass, Felix Crowe! I'm an old woman."

I choke on laughter as she wades out into the water, settles the life jacket under her shoulders and head while lying on her back, using the chest portion as arm rests, and kicks away to float lazily in the shallows.

"Jesus, Ember," I say, shaking my head. "Where the fuck did you dig up that nutty old fossil?"

Ember rubs her face with both hands. "We met at the Korner Kustard." She smiles as she watches Faye paddle this way and that with her hands only a few feet out from shore. "She reminds me of my grandmother. I dunno…I like her. She's funny as fuck and unpredictable."

"Yeah, no shit she's unpredictable," I mutter. "So, how's the bus running?"

She shrugs. "Fine. She's a fickle old beast, my Pumpkin, but she's home."

I glance at her, searching her face; and look, I know I've spent most of the time I've been around her staring at her tits, but she really is a stunningly beautiful woman. Even, symmetrical features, a graceful jawline, elegant throat, high, sharp cheekbones, deep, wide, bright silver eyes, and that fucking amazing white-blonde hair, currently in a loose braid down her back.

I tear my gaze away before I get gigged for staring again. "Can I ask about that?"

She shoots me a sidelong look. "About what?"

"Living in the van."

"Bus," she corrects.

I chuckle. "Sorry, bus."

She sighs, gazing out at the horizon. "It's a long story."

She meets my eyes. "I thought you weren't gonna ask unless I felt like telling."

"That was about the box in particular. This is more of a general 'what's your deal' sort of question."

The bright fire in her eyes dims a bit, weighed down by the burden of sorrow. "Honestly, Felix, I'm enjoying my first day at the beach in a long time—since…" she cuts off with a shake of her head and an audible gulp. "In a long time. So, I guess if you don't mind, I'd rather not go there."

"I can respect that," I say. "Didn't mean to bring up anything painful. I'm sorry."

She points a sharp, quizzical look at me. "I appreciate the understanding."

My heart pounds in my chest as another, very different question percolates inside me. "How about over dinner?"

She peers at me with a carefully blank expression. "Are you asking me out, Felix Crowe?"

"Yes, I am, Ember…" I trail off, hoping she'll fill in her last name.

"James. My name is Emberly James."

"Emberly, huh?" I say, grinning at her.

She rolls her eyes at me. "Do *not* call me Emberly."

"No?"

"Nope."

"So?" I ask, prompting her to answer my initial question.

She doesn't answer, but the nature of her silence is thoughtful. I couldn't say why it feels that way, but it does, so I let the silence reign until she breaks it.

"Felix, I…" she sighs.

"Forget it," I say. "Don't worry about it."

Rejection stings worse than that time I threw a rock at a hornets' nest. Swallowing the burn in my throat, feeling like a world-class fool, I shoot to my feet, scooping my slides, book, and shirt into the towel I was sitting on. I grab my cooler and head for the stairs.

"Felix, wait, hold on." I hear her feet squeak-crunching in the sand behind me. "It's not like that. I just—I'm not—I don't—"

I pause to let her catch up. Her hair has come loose from the braid, a long tendril sticking to her plump, pink lips. "You don't owe me any explanations, Ember. You're not ready, you don't want to, you're just not into me, whatever. Doesn't matter. It's cool. I get it. Enjoy the beach."

My hand, clearly possessed by some other entity besides my brain, steals out and tucks the flyaway tendril behind her ear.

The action seems to freeze her in place, eyes wide and fraught, the corner of her lower lip caught in her teeth. Fuck, I'd give anything to taste those lips, to tug that lip out of her teeth and kiss it, taste it.

Not gonna happen.

I growl my frustration and hurt, a soft, quiet, sighing rumble. "See ya 'round, Ember James."

I ascend the steps, having to remind myself not to stomp up them like a petulant teenager.

"Felix!"

I'm too hurt to answer, so I ignore her.

I do get it, though. I haven't exactly left the best impression, letting myself stare at her like some fucking creep. It's just been so long since I've felt anything like this that I let myself buy into the notion of hope for a minute. But nah. Not for me.

What the fuck ever.

She'll probably move on soon anyway.

I reach my FJ40, toss my shit onto the front passenger seat, and climb in. The engine catches with a hint of a rattle and a bit of belt squeal. I listen to the engine for a minute, deciding whether I want to carve out my already limited free time to work on it.

Nah. It's good for now.

I pull a U-turn and head south back to town; just as I cruise past the opening of the stairs, I see Ember top the rise, panting. She sees me driving away and looks distraught. She palms her forehead, and I look in the rearview mirror to see her mouthing a series of curse words, most of which, if I'm reading her lips right, are "fuck."

Part of me is yelling at me to turn around and see what she has to say, but I just can't. The instinct to avoid more hurt is too strong. It took a lot of fucking guts for me to ask her out in the first place. I just don't have it in me to try again so soon.

It's hard not to dwell on the past as I cruise south.

Hard not to dwell on Amy.

I know I have no place acting all butthurt about rejection—Amy didn't reject me. She responded—appropriately—to my shitty behavior. There's no excuse for what I did. I mean, sure, you could reasonably argue that there were extenuating circumstances. I don't now and never did blame her for breaking up with me and leaving town to get away from me. I get it—I deserved it.

But tell that to my heart. It doesn't seem capable of understanding that. All my heart knows is that

Amy ran away from me, and I've never really recovered, emotionally.

Asking Ember out was a big step for me. Not that I expect her to understand that, obviously. And look, I can do basic math, okay? A box full of male clothing labelled "donate" plus that deep, fierce sorrow I've seen in her? I know exactly what that points to—she lost someone she loved. I don't need the details to know that much. So I truly do get that she may not be ready. But again, tell that to my heart. All it recognizes is that I took a swing and got rejected.

Sure, maybe it was a shock to her. Maybe she needed more time to process. Maybe I jumped the gun by running. But one thing I know about us humans is that our trauma triggers are not bound by logic or governed by reason.

The drive home flies by in a blip—I pull into my driveway and barely remember the drive here. I put the four beers I didn't drink back in the fridge and hop into the shower.

When I get out, I've got a voicemail from my brother. "Yo, bro. We back. April has plans with her family, so I'm free if you wanna meet at The Cellar for some brewskis. I'll be there in like an hour."

I text him back: *See you at the Cellar in an hour. But do me a favor and never use the term brewksis ever fucking again you toolbox.*

He replies almost immediately: *Looking forward to some BREWSKIS, BROSKI.*

ME: *I hate you.*

His reply is the tongue-sticking-out emoji. I send him a middle finger.

A little over an hour later, we're bellied up to the bar at the Cellar, sipping River Rock Amber—a beer from Three Rivers' only brewery and my personal favorite beer.

"So." Riley takes a sip, swallows with a satisfied sigh, and shoots me a look. "You're in a pissy fuckin' mood."

I nod. "Yup."

"Wanna talk about it?" he asks. "Or just drink our beer in silence and ignore our emotions like real men."

I snort. "Subtle, Rye, real subtle."

"Hey, I'm worse about it than you are."

"True."

"Because you're a pansy." He grins at me, telegraphing the fact that he's teasing.

"You're not helping," I grumble.

"No?" He makes a *huh, weird* face. "I thought some fun brotherly banter would be just the ticket to improving your mood."

"Not this time."

He makes a show of scanning the bar. "Wanna get in a fight? That table of dudes in the corner over there looks like they could throw down."

"Tempting," I say in a dry, sarcastic drawl. "But no. I'm good."

He snorts his irritation. "So, what? You just wanna sit here, drink beer, and brood silently? Then why the fuck am I here? You don't need me for that."

"Because I don't like drinking alone," I say.

He sighs. "Well, Fee, if you want my company, you gotta crack that shell a bit. I'm way too charming to waste my time with your broody ass."

This gets a sniff of amusement from me. "A build on Aspenview sprang a leak and flooded the whole basement."

Riley waits a beat or two. "And?" When I don't fill the space, he snorts. "That's not enough to put you in this kinda mood, Fee. Work setbacks and fuckups are part of the biz. You've always been able to deal with shit like that calmly. That's what makes you so fuckin' good at your job. I'd lose my temper and knock a motherfucker out day one."

This gets a real laugh out of me. "Well, that much is true."

"So?" He elbows me. "Hit me with the real deal, Fee."

I contemplate. For all his devil-may-care attitude toward most things in life, deep down, Riley does have a good heart.

"Fuck. Fine. But Rye, this stays between you and me. I don't want this shit spreading to the crews."

He nods. "I got you. Now spill. Talk to little bro."

"Met a girl a few weeks ago. I was out at my property, clearing some trees, and when I left, she was broken down in the middle of the road. Nearly hit her ass—and I mean literally."

He nods, rolling a hand. "Okay, and…?"

"She's fuckin'…" I shake my head. "A heart-stopper, Rye. Haven't felt that kind of attraction to anyone since… well, in a long fuckin' time."

"How'd you fuck it up?" he asks.

I frown at him. "The fuck does *that* mean? How did I fuck it up? How do you know I did?"

"Because you only get broody and dicky like this when you do something dumb," he answers. "You were fucking impossible to live with back when the whole Amy shitshow went down."

"Fuck you," I say conversationally. "I didn't fuck it up. I fixed her bus and went on my way. She's...she's got baggage. Heavy shit. Don't know what, but I have some ideas."

"Well shit—don't let that stop you. You've got heavy baggage of your own, bro. Everyone does."

"Dude, I know. But after we talked earlier, I decided I'd go to the beach."

"Ooh, nice. Where'd you go?"

"Secret Beach."

"And let me guess...she was there?"

I nod, take a big slug of my beer. "Sure was. Wearing this tiny blue bikini that showed off her..." I cup my hands in front of my chest, blowing out an awed breath with a shake of my head. "Anyway. She looked fucking stunning. I was swimming, and when I got to shore, there she was. And you'll never guess who she was with? And mind you, she's not a local."

He shrugs. "If I'll never guess, then why bother trying? Albert Einstein?"

"He's been dead for like fifty fuckin' years, man. So, no."

Riley frowns. "Fifty? Are you sure? Isn't it more?"

I throw up my hands. "No, fuckstick, I *don't* know when Albert goddamned Einstein died. Jesus, way to focus on the wrong thing."

He laughs at my outburst. "Jesus, whatever happened, it really threw you for a loop. You need to chill, my guy."

I glare at him. "Fuck you."

He just laughs. "Who was she with, Fee? Get on with the story already. God, you suck at storytelling."

"Faye McFarlane."

He frowns, thinking. "*Her*? Good *lord*, she's still alive? She was ancient when we were in school."

"Well, now she has pink and purple hair and a septum piercing. She told me not to stare at her ass."

He boggles at me. "Were you? I mean, no judgment, bro, but I didn't realize the geriatric thing was your scene."

"I'm gonna kill you."

"What? It's a fair question."

"No, Riley, I was not staring at the ass of an old woman."

"Well, at least there's that—and I admit, I am glad to hear you still have *some* standards left, after…what? A decade of celibacy?"

I slowly turn my head to level a death glare at him. "Why did you think it would be a good idea to tell you any of this?" I ask. "I have *not* been celibate."

"Right," he says with a snort. "You shut down after Amy and never came up out of the hole."

"Can you stop talking about motherfucking Amy?" I snap. "And I *have* had sex since then."

"Bullshit."

"Rye, I have."

"Your hand doesn't count. Nor does a sex doll."

I let out a long-suffering sigh. "Jesus, you're a dick." I rub my face with both hands. "With real people—I have had sex with real live women."

"Who?"

"Tourists, mainly."

He frowns at me. "When? You work all day, every day."

"God, I do not, Riley."

"You do too!" He finishes his beer and slides it toward the bartender, tapping the rim. "Name the last time you clocked out from all work, personal and private, before seven at night."

I roll my eyes. "Whatever."

"You can't because you never have."

"Tinder, okay?" I snarl at him. "I have a fucking Tinder account. After work, I'll browse Tinder, find someone, message her, and hookup."

"At home?"

"No, at their hotels, usually."

"How frequently do you do this?" he asks.

I shrug. "Not very. Just to…I dunno. Take the edge off. It's not…" I sigh, finish my beer, and nod when the bartender signals another. "It's not…satisfying. It is fun, and feels good. But…random hookups aren't my thing."

He laughs. "That's why you gotta do what I do."

I blow a raspberry. "Okay, sure."

"I don't like one-night stands either. I like a nice, short-term quasi-relationship. We both know it ain't gonna last, so we let it all hang out, have fun, and when it runs its course, whatever. On to the next. It works."

"Is that why Cole has to put you in the drunk tank every month or two?" I ask.

He chuckles. "I admit, it's not a foolproof system." He gestures at me with the full beer the bartender places in front of him. "On with the story. What did the tourist with the giant bazingas do to piss you off?"

"I don't think she's a tourist, actually." I chew on the painful, embarrassing admission before I let it out. "I asked her out. She hesitated so I freaked out and ran like a bitch."

He stares at me. "You asked her out?"

"Yup."

"As far as I'm aware, you haven't asked anyone out since...you know who."

"She's not fuckin' Voldemort," I say.

"Well, I said her name and you bit my head off."

I scrub my face with both hands, sighing. "Yeah, sorry. I'm out of sorts."

"So, this girl, the not a local but not a tourist. She shot you down?"

I shrug, tip my head to one side. "I took it that way. She seemed to think better of it or regret it or something, but I was too committed to bugging out to find out."

"What does that mean?" he asks.

"She followed me up the stairs."

"And you didn't stop to hear her out?"

"No."

"Dumbass. Maybe she was just...blindsided. If you clocked the fact that she has some sort of baggage, maybe she's like you."

"Like me?"

"Yeah, you know." He leaves it at that.

"No, Riley, I don't know."

"Too fucked up and scared or whatever to let anyone in."

"Like you're any better?"

"No, I'm not. I'm worse. Not the point because we're not talking about me."

I growl, burying my face in my hands. "Yeah," I say, the word muffled behind my palms. "I thought of that...after."

"Dumbass."

"I know. But...it was hard as hell to ask her out. And the way she hesitated. It wasn't, 'ohhhh, I'm thinking about it,' it was a 'yeah, I don't know about that.' Maybe I read it wrong. I don't know. But it sucked, because I…" I sigh, shaking my head. "I can't stop thinking about her."

"So quit being a puss. Hunt her down and try again."

I growl, and then slug back a big swallow of beer. "Yeah, maybe."

Riley claps me on the shoulder. "No, fuckwit, not maybe. Yes. *Definitely*. You haven't so much as looked at another woman since Amy, and hookups to get rid of blue balls don't count."

"Stop saying her goddamn name," I hiss.

"No. You gotta get over her, Fee." He grabs my cheeks and forces me to look at him, squishing my face. "Amy, Amy, Amy. Amy Henderson. Amy Eileen Henderson. Wait, she's married now. I looked her up a couple months ago—what's her married name?"

"Quincy," I mumble.

"Right, right, Amy Quincy. Amy Quincy. Amy Quincy."

I rip myself out of his grip. "Fuck off, Rye."

"No, Fee. You gotta get over her. That was a long time ago. It was a dumb mistake, and, not excusing you, but she wasn't innocent either. You've let it hamstring you. You've spent, like, a third of your fucking life hating yourself for a mistake you made when you were fucking nineteen. Forgive yourself and move the fuck on."

Rage, guilt, shame, confusion, pain…it's all a jumble inside me. I slam the rest of my beer, toss a pair of twenties on the bar, and shove my phone in my back pocket.

"Good talk, Rye. Thanks. See ya."

He shoves the cash into my hip pocket. "I got it, ya fuckin' shithead. Go on—run away and hide like you always do. Keep living your life stuck in the past on a single bullshit mistake."

"Yeah, maybe I will...dick."

By the time I get home, I feel bad, so I text Riley.

ME: *I know you were just trying to help. Sorry.*

He answers a minute later: *You're good. I get it. But for real, find Big Boobs and ask her out again.*

ME: *Her name is Ember.*

Riley: *Cool. I don't care what her name is. Just ask her out again.*

ME: *I'm just pointing out that she has a name, and features other than her boobs.*

Riley: *Well you weren't exactly forthcoming with details other than having large mammary glands but point taken. Ask EMBER out again, and this time sack up and wait for her to answer instead of running away like a pathetic puss-bag.*

ME: *Pro tip, bro, therapy is not a good career choice for you.*

Riley sends a thumbs up, and then a middle finger, and then: *ASK HER OUT. PUSSBAG.*

I put the phone on the charger, pour myself a big whiskey on the rocks, and sit on the couch to look for something to watch.

I end up watching *Yellowstone*.

I don't see the resemblance.

4

Ember

I TRUDGE BACK DOWN THE STEPS, FIGHTING BACK tears. I hate crying, like really, really, really *hate* crying, so that only pisses me off more, which turns into a whole snowball spiral of doom. By the time I get back down to the beach, I'm a total disaster.

Faye is back on the blanket, toweling herself off. She takes one look at me and sighs. "Oh boy. Now what, missy?"

I shake my head, barely keeping the onslaught of emotion at bay. "Nothing."

She snorts derisively. "And I'm Norma Jean Mortenson."

I frown at her. "Who?"

A roll of her eyes. "Kids these days. You might know her as Marilyn Monroe."

I sniff a laugh. "Oh."

Tossing the towel aside, Faye half-sits, half-falls to the blanket, snags her bag, and pulls out the container of brownies. "Well, if you don't wanna talk about it, then at least have a brownie."

I hesitate, but who am I kidding? Of course I'm having a brownie. You don't get an ass like mine eating nothing but salad. I plop down beside her and accept the treat. And good lord, it's a monster of a brownie. Over an inch thick and six inches square, it has a thick, gooey layer of chocolate frosting on top *and* chocolate chips inside it, and it's moist and fluffy yet dense.

"Holy shit, Faye," I say, around a mouthful. "This is amazing."

She grins at me, dabbing away a rogue bit of frosting from her lip with her thumb; the grin is mischievous, which may or may not bode well. "I'm famous in certain circles for my brownies."

"I can see why."

I'm halfway done with the giant brownie when I start paying attention to the actual flavor profile. Chocolate, chocolate, and more chocolate…

And something else. Something subtle but definitive.

I look at the last two or three bites of the thing, and then at Faye. "Faye, my dear…is this a pot brownie?"

She pops the last bite into her mouth. "Sure is, missy."

I finish it, wash it down with sparkling water, and then give Faye a long, droll stare. "You could have warned me."

She cackles. "Where's the fun in that?"

"What if I had to pass a drug test?"

"Do you?"

"No, but—"

'Then don't waste my time with pointless

hypotheticals. You're a hippie's kid. If that's the first special brownie you've ever had, then I really am Norma Jean Mortenson."

"No, it's not. Not by a long shot."

"You need to relax. You're wound up tighter than a nun's cooter."

I splutter. "Faye!"

"I know whereof I speak, young lady. My aunt was a nun. She was a mean, miserable bitch."

"Not all nuns are like that."

"Known a bunch of 'em, have you?" she asks.

I laugh. "Not a ton, no, but I did spend two weeks living with nuns in a convent in Northern California."

She blinks at me. "Wasn't expecting that."

Her expectant silence is heavily leading, so I sigh. "Okay, well, this was before I met Dutchie. Mom had only been dead for like…six months? I was still a mess, emotionally. I had no formal education, no family, no friends, and nowhere to go. I had Mom's bus and like six thousand dollars I found in Mom's stuff. She died in Temecula, so I headed north. I ended up at the convent by accident— the bus ran out of gas and the nuns picked me up, brought me to the convent, and took care of me. They had my bus towed and filled up, gave me a bed, fed me." I shrug. "They were awesome."

Faye harrumphs. "I went to catholic school in the forties and fifties, so my experience with nuns is a bit different."

I laugh. "I bet it is." I glance at her. "Also, are you calling me a mean, miserable bitch?"

She snorts. "No. I was callin' my aunt that." She

softens. "Ember, sweetheart, you gotta let it out. Trust me, I know."

She digs in her bag again and comes up with a bottle of peppermint vodka. She sticks her whole head into the bag, rummaging through it with a muttered grumble, and then comes up with a couple bottles of chocolate Ensure.

She cracks one of the bottles open and takes a healthy slug, gesturing at me. "Go on, take 'er down a notch or two so we can fit the vodka in there."

I stare at her. "Faye, we drove here. And we just ate giant pot brownies."

"So?"

"So...we'll be wasted and we have to drive back at some point."

She stabs the sky with a finger. "At *some* point!" She points down the beach at a stand of trees. "I happen to know there's some good firewood down there. We camp out here. I've got blankets in here."

"You're not supposed to make fires on the beach, I don't think," I argue.

She sighs. "Ember, I was good my whole life. Did everything by the book. Courted my Thomas properly, was a virgin when I married him. Raised our daughter, kept our home like a good wife. When Tina left home, I went to school and got my teaching certificate and taught school. I was on the PTO, and eventually, the school board. I volunteered at church. Never stepped so much as a toe out of line. Never jaywalked, never lusted after a man who wasn't my husband, never drank too much. Nothing. I kept damn near every single one of the Ten commandments faithfully my whole life."

"I sense a but coming," I say.

She nods. "You do. It was a good life. But when Thomas passed away, it broke me. I didn't want to live. Didn't know how. Eventually, Tina convinced me to see a therapist. It took a few months to find one I liked, but when I did, she changed my life. Told me it was time to live for me. I'd lived my life for everyone else. I followed the rules my parents set as a kid, and then the rules society expected me to live by as a dutiful wife and mother. I lived for my husband and child. I wanted to go to school when Tina started school, but Thomas didn't want me to, so I didn't. I waited, like he wanted."

There's a long pause. She sniffles and then pours vodka into the Ensure—spilling it all over her fingers.

"I had to rebuild who I was." She tilts her head, thinking. "No, actually, I had to build myself from scratch. I was a mother and a wife and a schoolteacher…but then Thomas died and I discovered that without him, I didn't know who I was. It was terrifying."

She opens my Ensure bottle and puts it to my lips. "Drink, missy."

So, I drink it down a few inches and hand her the bottle. She tips a long pour into the bottle, caps them both, and then shakes them vigorously.

She hands me one and opens the other. "Better cold, but I wasn't about to haul ice way the hell down here."

I take a sip, coughing at how strong it is. "Jesus, Faye."

"Whooo-wee!" she crows. "That'll scorch the hair right off your cooter."

"Ohmy*god*, Faye. You're a lunatic. What is with you and the word 'cooter'?"

She shrugs, cackling. "I dunno. It's funny to me. I like

it. Vagina is too technical, pussy is...icky, and even now I can't bring myself to say the *other* C-word. So, cooter it is."

"I guess that's reason enough," I say.

"Sure is," she agrees, taking another sip. "So, my point in that whole story is this: you gotta just say 'fuck it' sometimes. I had to learn who I am now that I have no one to please but me. And that person, apparently, likes crazy hair colors, piercings, tattoos, marijuana, alcohol, cursing, and just generally being a loud, obnoxious pain in the ass."

"So you're saying I should just say 'fuck it' and get wasted on the beach with you?"

"Yup!"

"Fine. But if anything happens, I'm blaming you."

She laughs. "Fine by me." She gestured at my drink with hers. "Now drink up. Oh my, what was that phrase my grandson used the other day? Oh! I remember. We have to get litty."

I cackle, and the cackle turns into laughter so hard I snort. "Litty?"

"Ben is a hoot. We were FaceTiming the other day and he was telling me about a party he went to and how all his friends care about is getting litty. I had no clue what that meant. Of course, he had to explain what lit meant first." She taps my bottle with hers. "Here's to saying fuck it and getting litty on the beach with new friends."

"I'll drink to that!" I said, and chugged a bit too much.

Jesus, this shit is strong. I am going to be *so* fucked up.

Faye regales me with stories of the weird, gross, inappropriate, and hysterical things she encountered in her decades of teaching. She's a world-class storyteller with killer comedic timing and delivery, and after a while my sides literally hurt from laughing so much.

Abruptly, Faye slaps her thighs. "Welp. About time to make a fire. C'mon, missy. I'll show you a thing or two."

I follow her down the beach to the stand of trees—a cluster of pines and birches angling over the sand as if reaching for the horizon. We gather sticks and branches by the armful and carry them back to our spot, and then go back for more. Faye has me dig a wide but shallow depression in the sand, and then she carefully constructs a teepee of the smallest twigs. Next, she rummages in her giant bag and produces a small plastic pouch of Kleenex. She twists a few tissues into wads and stuffs them under the teepee and then rummages in her bag again, this time producing a torch lighter.

"What the hell else do you have in that bag, Faye?" I ask.

She gets the fire flickering before answering. "Anything and everything." She digs in and comes up with a package of Chips Ahoy, puts it back, comes up again with a six-pack of yellow Gatorade, puts that back, and comes up with a gallon Ziploc bag full of cannabis flower.

I splutter a laugh. "Jesus, Faye. Why do you have that much with you?"

She shrugs. "Tossed it in, just in case. Let's see, what else…? Oh! I have my knitting." She shows me a ball of baby blue yarn and a knitting needle. "I also have these." She shows me a pair of red-and-black checkered cinch bags. "They're blankets that scrunch up into these nifty little baggies."

"That thing must weigh a ton," I say.

She pats her shoulder. "Been carrying heavy purses my whole life. I could carry you, probably, if you could fit into a purse."

I laugh. "I could probably fit into that bag." I'm starting to feel the cannabis—light-headed, floaty, breezy. "Ohhh, here we go."

Faye cackles. "That's the good shit kickin' in, huh?"

I splutter a laugh., "You sound more like your grandson than an eighty-year-old woman."

She takes a long sip. "I love that boy more than just about anything. He and his mama don't get along right now, so I spend a lot of time talking to him. He thinks it's funny to teach me the lingo of his generation, and I think it's funny to use it with the other uptight fuddy-duddies at Bingo night."

"Bingo night, huh?" I say. "Didn't have you pegged for a bingo kinda gal."

"I'm not. It's stupid and boring and I never win. But I live alone and the hall is walking distance, and what the hell else am I supposed to do on a Tuesday night? I've knitted about a thousand sweaters that no one wants. The other old folks who play may be uptight old fuddy-duddies, but there is a certain...*je ne sais quois*, I guess, about being around people who get it."

"Get what, Faye?"

She feeds the fire some bigger sticks. "Being old. Getting left behind. Friends died, husbands or wives died, kids moved away, grandkids either live far or don't care. The achy joints. Forgetting when you are. I ain't got dementia or nothing, but sometimes I'll be at home and I'll forget and go looking for Thomas. I'll call for him and I'll get mad at him for ignoring me. And then I remember." She gazes at the fire, lost to memory. "I miss him, my Thomas."

"What was he like?" I ask.

"How long do you have?"

"All night, it would seem."

She shakes her head. "Complicated—he was a very complicated man. He could be very tender and sensitive, but he hid it, mostly. His father was a hard, brutal, cruel man, and Thomas learned early to hide his sensitivity behind a mask of toughness. And he *was* tough. He survived Vietnam. He was a police officer, and even up here in this little one stoplight town, which it was back then, he saw his share of unpleasant things. But he never lost that sensitivity, even after the war and the police work. He just...I was the only one he showed it to. He had absolutely no sense of humor. None. It was my mission in life to make him laugh, but it was difficult. We went to see Don Rickles in Las Vegas one summer, and I'm sure you don't know who that is, but he was break a rib funny. The whole audience was in stitches, but not my Thomas. Nope. Arms crossed, grumpy face on, lookin' like he'd rather be back in the P-O-W camp."

I blink. "Wait, what? He was P-O-W?"

She sniffles. "Yeah. For four months, toward the end of the war. He told me a lot about his other experiences during the war, but he never would talk about that. The only thing he'd say was if something bad happened, like a wreck or bad weather or whatever, he'd say 'well, Faye, this may be bad, but it sure beats the shit out of that camp.'" She adopts a deep, surly, gruff voice when she quotes him, and I obviously never met the man, but I get a sense of who he must've been. "When he did refer to it, it was always that phrase—*that camp.*"

"He sounds like a very interesting man."

"Oh, he was. You just...you had to dig a little to get to the good stuff. He kept it buried under a nice, thick, crusty layer of grumpy old codger attitude." Faye glances at me. "You gonna unburden yourself yet or what? Don't think I didn't see you fighting tears after Felix Crowe took off. And the way that boy was lookin' at you? I'd'a sworn you'd have had him eating out of your hand by the time I got in from the water, but instead he took off like his tail was on fire. What the hell'd you say to him, anyhow?"

"Nothing, and that's the problem." I sigh woozily. I'm a lot high *and* a little tipsy, so the truth just sort of tumbles free from the vault, which is normally locked down tighter than Fort Knox. "He asked me out, and I hesitated." It sounds so stupid, said out loud. I groan. "God, I'm an idiot. I'm attracted to him, Faye. Why'd I hesitate?"

She snorts. "Girl, a blind nun would be attracted to that fine hunk of man meat. Even my old Aunt Evelyn, the nun, would've been tempted by Felix Crowe. Did you see the man's abs? You could grate cheese on 'em!"

"Mmmm," I hum. "Cheese. I'd like to try."

She laughs at me. "Got the munchies, do you?"

"Mmmm-hmm."

"Comin' up!" She tosses me the package of Chips Ahoy. "Now, as to why you hesitated…"

I crunch into a cookie, and I swear, nothing has ever tasted so good. "Dutchie."

"Your husband?"

I nod. "Mmmm-hmmm." I wash the cookie down with sparkling water because I've had enough peppermint vodka chocolate shake. "I don't know what to do."

"You wanna talk about him?"

I shake my head. "Nope."

"How long?"

I swallow hard. "Six months, three weeks, two days…"

I glance at my phone and do some math, "eight hours, and five minutes."

She nods knowingly. "Still counting the hours and minutes, are you?"

"Yeah," I say, my voice raspy. I look at her, my eyes blurring. "When does it get easier?"

She grunts, shaking her head. "It doesn't. Time puts layers of scar tissue over it, but if you poke it, it always hurts."

"Oh."

"I ain't got any old lady wisdom that'll suddenly make it all better, Ember. Wish I did. All I got is cold, hard facts. Which is this: you lost him; he's gone and you're not, but you're not allowed to just give up."

"I don't want to keep going. Literally. He and I were on a van life tour of the country. We were gonna see all fifty states together and vlog the whole thing. We have thirty-one. Michigan was thirty-two. I'm stuck here. He—he died in a hospital in Grayling. I...I tried to keep going, for him. We were gonna go up into the U-P and into Wisconsin, but I...I stopped here and..." I shake my head, swallowing hard. "And I can't go any further. Not without him."

The tears blur my eyes again and I fight them off, shaking my head and breathing through it.

I feel a soft, wiry, papery arm circle my shoulders. "No, no, no, no," she murmurs. "You can't do that, missy. You gotta get it out. Holding it in is killing you."

"Can't. I'll break."

"Seems like you already are broken."

"I know," I breathe. "But I...I just *can't.*"

"Let me have it."

I shake my head.

She pulls me closer, smoothing my hair away, tutting and hushing.

"It hurts so fucking bad, GramGram." I realized what I said as soon as I said it and sat up to look at her. "Faye, I'm sorry. I—"

She touches my lips, her dark eyes warm with compassion and understanding. "A grandma's a grandma, missy. I'd be honored to fill in." She pulls me back into her arms and holds me. "Course it hurts. But you gotta let yourself feel it. It's a powerful thing, that kind of grief. Feels like it'll suck you under if you let it—and it will. But only if you fight it. You can't fight it. You gotta give it its due and then keep on living."

"I don't know how."

"You'll figure it out. Got no choice. But it takes courage."

"I'm afraid, Faye."

"Course you are." She pats my shoulder. "A good place to start is a date with a tall stack of sexy like Felix Crowe."

This gets me spluttering tearful laughter. "Ohmygod, Faye. You're incorrigible."

"If I was even thirty years younger, I'd take a swing at him myself." She giggles. "I wouldn't mind being a cougar, but fortunately for all the younger men out there, Faye's Love Canal is closed for business."

"*Un*fortunately, you mean," I say. "You're a catch."

She rasps a laugh. "You're a nut. Sweet, but nutty."

"I feel like there's a dirty joke in there somewhere," I say, "But I'm too high to find it." I point at Faye. "And you leave Felix out of it."

We both laugh at that, and then lapse into a long, comfortable silence.

"Faye?" I ask. She harrumphs an interrogatory sound. "Were you ever with anyone else after Thomas passed?"

"No. He was it for me." She grabs my hand and squeezes hard. "But there's a difference, Ember. I had a lifetime with him. I was seventy...four? Seventy-six?— when he died. I was old already. I met Thomas when I was a young girl in grade school. We were together for over fifty years. When he died, I just...there was no possibility of anyone else. Who could ever know me the way Thomas did? I miss sex sometimes, sure, but I was only ever with Thomas in that way, and it is purely unfathomable to me to be intimate with another man." She wraps both of her hands around mine and shakes. "You're young, missy. I know you miss him—I know it hurts. But you got too much life to live to give up and be a spinster like me."

I nod. "I hear you. I'm just not sure I know how to get over him. How to let anyone else in."

I expect a dirty joke or something, but she just sighs and pats my cheek. "I'm not saying it'll be easy, Ember, only that it's necessary."

"Necessary?" I ask. "How is it necessary? What if I just want to be alone the rest of my life?"

"That'd be a big damn shame," she says. "I ain't known you long, but I can tell you've got a whole lot of love to give, and for once I'm not being dirty. You shine bright, Ember, and the world needs more lights like yours. You can't keep yours hidden."

"It's not hidden, Faye. It's...dimmed. Broken."

"Dimmed, yes. Broken, no. And if this is you dimmed,

missy, when you finally learn how to be happy again, you'll be brighter than the damn sun."

For some stupid reason, I think of Felix. The hurt in his eyes when I hesitated. The way he bolted...he's known sorrow. He's dimmed and broken, too.

I should have said yes. One innocent date couldn't hurt. Right? I admit I'm attracted to him, but as Faye said, who wouldn't be? Attraction isn't the problem, although I haven't felt an attraction to anyone since Dutchie's death.

I just don't know where to start. Especially if he's as fucked up as I am. How do two hurt, closed off people learn how to let each other in?

Someone has to take the first step, take a risk.

Oh.

Oh...*fuck*.

He did.

He asked me out.

I guess that explains his reaction when I hesitated—it would have felt like a rejection. I wasn't—I was taken aback, surprised. But to him, it had to have felt like I was shooting him down.

I think I'm gonna have to find Felix and hope he gives me a second chance. I'm not sure it'll go anywhere, because I'm not sure I'm brave enough or strong enough to open myself up to him, but I know I'll regret it if I don't at least try.

5

Felix

I T'S BEEN A HELL OF A WEEK.

Holden's new hire fuckup left a shitload of problems in his wake. Holden fired him and blacklisted him with everyone he knows in the industry, which is just about everyone in a thousand-mile radius. But the asshole was so clueless and incompetent that we have to carefully test everything he went near in the three weeks he was on the job. We caught a dozen issues that would have meant a dozen catastrophes like the Aspenview house. Holden's insurance covers the cost of the repairs, but that doesn't put my guys back on schedule. It's gonna take a full crew damn near a month to properly repair the basement, which means my whole fucking schedule is now off by a month.

I barely have time to breathe, let alone do anything

else—I'm in that soggy basement with the crew, ripping out flooring and drywall, going over plumbing and electrical, setting up fans and dehumidifiers to get everything dry, and putting everything back in fresh. And when I'm not there, I'm at all my other builds watching every nail and screw go in, every plumbing junction, every foot of wiring, every floorboard, every sheet of drywall. Or at least, that's the intent, impossible though it is.

Despite the sixteen- and twenty-hour days, I collapse in bed and promptly fail to fall asleep. Why?

A certain siren with white-blond hair, silver eyes, and a body I literally have embarrassingly wet dreams about keeps splashing through my mind. I just can't stop thinking about her. I want to know what put the sorrow in her eyes. I want to heal it. Take it away. Put joy in those bright eyes, put a laugh on that beautiful face.

The wet dreams are less altruistic.

I wake up hard as rock, visions of Ember in that damned teeny bikini dancing through my mind...but in the dreams I'm kissing her and my hand is stealing up to her back and tugging on the string, and the blue scraps of fabric are tumbling away to bare the most glorious tits I've ever seen...

I always wake up right before I see them, leaving me aching and frustrated and restless.

Night after night, I have the same stupid, maddening dream. Yet I can't bring myself to allow any relief. It would feel like a violation, or...or taking advantage of her somehow to jerk off to thoughts of Ember James. She wouldn't even go on a date with me, much less let me put my dirty hands anywhere near her perfect, golden skin.

Which means I've gotten intimately acquainted with

the hellish normality of ice-cold showers. Not that it helps, mind you. I still have the dreams, still wake up with an erection so hard I could drive nails with it, and I still can't allow myself to do anything about it. I even tried porn, something I'm not usually a big fan of, but I kept seeing Ember's face when I closed my eyes, and imagined Ember's hand on me when I gripped myself. I just can't do it.

A week turns into two, and the dreams continue, and I'm growing increasingly desperate. I swipe through Tinder and find a handful of good matches that would without a doubt lead to a fun weekend tumble with a horny fudgie, but I can't even bring myself to hit send on the flirty messages I drafted.

Because I don't want some random tourist.

I want Ember.

Fuck.

I don't know what to do.

Find her? Ask her out again? To what end? She's not interested. She'd have said yes if she was.

A quiet, niggling voice in the back of my head suggests that the way she ran after me means she may have had a change of heart. I mean, I'd swear she was crying when I drove away. Why would she be crying?

I just can't find the courage to go looking for more rejection.

It makes me surly at work. Well, more so than usual. I'm not typically a jokey sort of boss. I get shit done and expect my guys to work hard. I'm not their friend, I'm their boss. Bear is an exception to that rule, which is how he gets away with calling me out.

We're sitting on my tailgate at the yard—Crowe Construction and Demolition HQ—sipping from sweating water bottles while the crews clean and put away tools, sweep out equipment trailers, and clock out for the day.

"You know I got respect for you, Felix," Bear says in his bone-rattlingly deep voice, "but you need to figure your shit out."

I press the cold bottle to my forehead—it's a hot day. "What shit?"

He gestures at me vaguely with his bottle. "You've been kind of a dick the last couple weeks, boss."

I glance at him. "I'm always kind of a dick."

He shakes his head. "Nah. You're firm but fair. You work hard, lead by example, and don't tolerate bullshit or laziness. Whatever's going on with you, it's different."

"Different how?" I know he's right, but I need details.

Bear huffs. "Snappin' at people, man. Like earlier this mornin', Larsen and Martinez were fucking around and you ripped 'em a new asshole."

"They were fucking around."

"They were moving shingles up to the roof, and the guys on the roof weren't ready for more yet. They were just fuckin' with each other. You know damn well Larsen and Martinez are solid, Felix. They get their shit done, and they don't' fuck around unless they know they're good to kill a minute or two."

I growl, realizing that he's right. "Fuck."

"And yesterday, you almost made Trent quit on the spot."

I pinch the bridge of my nose, remembering with brutal clarity what he's referring to. "Yeah, I guess I owe him an apology, huh?"

Bear slugs back the last of his water, crumples the thin

plastic bottle into a tiny wad, and screws the top on to keep it compressed. "Larsen and Martinez have been with you for long enough to know that wasn't you, so they're good. But Trent is new, and this is his first real full-time job."

I tip my head back and hiss. "Fuck."

He pats me on the shoulder, which feels sort of like being hit with a jackhammer, albeit gently. "I smoothed it over with him. But you oughta talk to him. And more than anything, figure your shit out."

I wait, but no questions are forthcoming. "Figured you'd ask."

He shrugs a massive shoulder. "Ain't my business, Boss. I'm your friend, I hope you know that. You wanna talk about it, I'm here. But I ain't the type to push."

"It's just…personal shit. And I don't know what to do."

He just eyes me sidelong, allowing a long, leading silence. Naturally, I fill it.

"Girl troubles."

He snorts. "Ain't it always?"

"I can't get her out of my head."

"But?"

"She doesn't wanna give me the time of day, man. She's…she's hurting, somehow. I can tell. And I'm…I ain't the one to fix her, Bear. I got my own shit."

"Speaking from experience, Boss, a lot of the time, women don't want you to actually fix anything." He runs his long, braided red beard through his fist.

"What do you mean?" I ask.

He tips his head to one side. "Well, like the other day. Noelle was all in a tizzy about something that happened at work. She got into some stupid tiff with one of the other stylists and she came home all bent out of shape and pissed off and ranting about it."

I laugh. "Sorry, but I have a hard time seeing her pissed off."

He rumbles a laugh. "It was a shock. But man, she was *hot*, like pissed all the way the fuck off. And I was offering her suggestions for how to handle it. Thought I was helping."

"But you weren't?" I surmise.

"Nope. She yelled at me, which she's never done. She was like, Bear, stop trying to help and just *listen*. I don't need your damn help. I don't want you to fix anything. I can handle it myself. Just fucking listen to me."

I scrape my ball cap off my head and muss my sweaty hair. "She doesn't want to talk about it."

"She doesn't know you."

"I asked her out and she…well, she didn't say no, but she hesitated a long fuckin time, like, well, I dunno…"

He shakes his head. "You're an idiot."

I frown at him. "What?"

"She hesitated, and you took it as a no? What if she needed a minute to figure out how she felt about it?"

I groan. "That has crossed my mind afterward."

"So what are you doing about it?" He correctly interprets my lack of an answer. "Felix, you know better. Shit ain't gonna fix itself."

"Yeah, yeah, I know."

"So when you say you don't know what to do," he says, "what you really mean is you *do* know, you just don't wanna do it."

"I've got hangups, okay?"

"I spent a decade in prison for something I didn't do.

I'm a huge, scary ex-con with more than a little literal blood on my hands. I know a thing or two about hangups." He eases off the tailgate. "In my experience, limited as it is, the idea is usually scarier than the reality."

"I'm not fuckin' afraid," I snap.

Bear just laughs. "Okay, buddy. Pull the other one— it's got bells on it."

"What?"

He laughs again. "Somethin' Noelle's dad says when her brothers spout some bullshit, which is all the time."

I groan a laugh. "Fine, I'm scared outta my fucking mind. I want her, man. Bad."

"Why?"

I frown. "Why? Why what?"

"Why do you want her? What is it you want? And if it's about what she's got going on between her shoulders and her knees and nothin' else, don't waste your time or hers."

"When did you become the voice of wisdom, Bear?" I say, shaking my head in bemusement.

"Noelle is gorgeous, that ain't a secret. Her body makes me crazy. And I love that about her. But that's not what our relationship is about. I'm saying you gotta figure out if you're just hot for her, or if it's somethin' more than that." He holds his arms out and lets them slap against his thighs. "That's about all the wisdom I've got, Boss. But please, for the sake of the guys, do something about it."

I nod. "I hear you, Bear. I will."

"A'ight. Noelle and I have plans, so I gotta get home and grab a shower."

"Well then, what are you still here for, you big lunk? Go!"

I watch him climb into his pickup and drive off. A few minutes later, the yard is quiet and still, and the dust from the gravel is swirling and settling under the hot sun.

Maybe I should find Ember. Shouldn't be that hard, right? That bright orange bus with all those stickers sorta stands out.

I cruise aimlessly through downtown Three Rivers and find no sign of her or her bus. I prowl north of town as far as the beach where I last saw her and then cut through the neighborhoods north of town on my way back south. She's not at any of the restaurants, cafes, or stores in town or around it.

Finally, on a whim, I decide to check the YMCA—the only chain gym in town. There are plenty of independently owned gyms, but my thinking is that if she lives in her van, she needs a place to shower, and having a membership to the Y means she'd have access all over the country.

And…bingo. Her bus is parked at the back of the lot, and she's walking out to it with a gym bag over her shoulder and her hair pulled back in a wet braid. She seems upset though—she yanks the sliding door open rather aggressively, hurls her bag in, and then slumps to her butt in the open doorway, shoulders hunched.

I park a few spots away, and she doesn't look up at me until my boots are in her line of sight.

She looks up at me with red-rimmed eyes. "Felix!"

I hesitate and then point at the open space beside her. "May I?"

She slides over with a nod. "Sure."

She's trying to act like she wasn't just crying, or that her eyes aren't still red and watery.

"Um." I clear my throat. "What's going on? Anything I can do? Or…or just…listen?"

She swallows hard. "My bus died. Like, dead-dead."

"Dead how?"

"I don't know for sure. But there was a loud grinding noise, a thunk, and then the engine just conked out. I barely made it to this parking spot. It won't turn over, just makes this godawful noise like she's sick."

I wince. "Oof. That's not good."

She sniffles. "No, it's fucking not. Pumpkin is my home. She's all I have. Everything I own is in here. I can't even get myself to a short-term rental or a motel. I don't know what to do." She shakes her head. "I'm sorry. It's not your problem. I shouldn't vent to you, of all people."

I frown at this. "Why me of all people?"

She takes a long, shuddering inhale, holds it, and lets it out slowly while wiping at her eyes. "I feel bad about that day at the beach. I just…you took me by surprise, and I—"

"Hey, no, that's okay, Ember. It's fine. I was stupid and overly sensitive. I ran off without giving you a chance to even think. I know you've got…things…that you don't want to talk about which might make me asking you out a tricky situation. I should have been more considerate."

She shoots me a lopsided smile. "You *did* take off. I called after you, and I even chased you all the way up those stupid stairs, all one million of them."

"Yeah, I'm sorry. I…I don't have an excuse. I have explanations, but no excuses."

"I'm sorry, too, Felix. I…I have a feeling it wasn't easy for you to ask, and I know I should have given you a better answer, even if it was just 'I need a minute to think about it.' I know when a guy asks you out, 'let me think about it' isn't what they want to hear, but…."

"It wasn't easy, no. But I…I mean, I don't get it, because I don't know from personal experience what you've been through exactly, but I get it." I hesitate, licking my lips as nerves sing through me. "I, uh, I have a flatbed back at the yard, and my buddy Nyx is the best mechanic in town. I also happen to know he specializes in vintage auto repair."

She tries to smile, but it's wobbly. "That's very sweet, Felix, but then what? Where do I go while it's being repaired? What if it needs a whole new engine?"

"What about Faye?" I ask.

She shakes her head. "I'd ask, and I've thought about it, believe me, but she's been under the weather lately. She says she's fine, but I worry. She's even talking about finally finding somewhere in California near her daughter and grandkids." Another shake of her head. "She should go to California. I love her weird, crazy ass, and I'd miss her, but I think she…" she swallows hard. "I don't even want to say it."

"She doesn't have a lot of time left," I say.

"No," she whispers. "I think she senses it, too."

"Look, let's just get your van out of this parking lot and have Nyx look at it, and go from there."

She nods. "Okay. I…I don't want to impose." She shrugs. "It's not like I have a lot of other choices."

"Come on," I say, and without thinking, I clap my hand on her thigh, a familiar gesture of comfort—except I barely know her and it's way too intimate, especially since she's wearing super short denim Daisy Dukes, so her thigh is bare and warm and smooth under my palm. I yank my hand away. "Sorry. I—sorry."

She doesn't answer right away, her strange, silver eyes searching mine, expressive and intense but unreadable. "It's...fine. It's fine."

I lurch to my feet before my hands do anything else idiotic. "You, um, need anything from in there? We're coming back in a few minutes, obviously, but if there's anything valuable you don't want to leave..."

She shakes her head, shrugging. "I mean, everything is valuable to me—it's my stuff. But nothing of much monetary value." She frowns. "Except..."

She rolls to her hands and knees and crawls into the bus, sliding aside a secret panel under the bench seat to reveal a hidden safe.

My god, her ass is absolutely ridiculous. I can't look away. Perfectly round, delectably plump, and on mouthwatering display in those micro shorts and in that position, facing away from me.

"You're staring at my ass, Felix," she says, over the sound of digital keys beeping as she enters her code.

"Yep," I say.

She snorts. "Not even gonna deny it?"

"Nope." I clench my hands into fists, but that's not good enough so I shove them into my pockets to prevent them from going rogue and petting her perfect, pretty ass. "Art is meant to be appreciated."

I hear the safe door open, and a moment later she sinks backward to sit on her heels, a fireproof, waterproof, zippered cash bag in one hand and a wooden box in the other. She sets them down, turns back to shut and lock the safe, and returns the secret panel back in place.

She returns to sitting on the edge of the open

doorway. "Okay, number one, that was a fucking stellar line, Felix Crowe."

I grin at her. "Wasn't a line, Ember James, it was plain facts. What's number two?"

She shrugs. "Isn't one." She lifts the items she retrieved from the safe. "All the money I have in the world, and my mother's jewelry. Well, my family heirloom jewelry. Belonged to my three-greats grandmother. She brought it over when she left Germany in the twenties."

"They got out early, huh?"

She nods. "Family lore, at least, claims my three-greats grandfather saw what was coming when Hitler first started in politics after World War One and got them out. How true that is, I have no idea, but that's what GramGram told me."

"I mean, sounds believable to me," I say. "They wouldn't be the only ones, if I'm remembering my high school history correctly."

She opens the box, which is about the size of a quart of strawberries. Within is a jumble of silver necklaces with small precious gem pendants—a ruby, a sapphire, an emerald, and a diamond. I'm not a jeweler, obviously, but they look like they're high quality although small. There are a few rings, also with a variety of stones, and also small but of high quality, some silver and some gold. A brooch with a large, oval, opaque reddish stone set in delicately filigreed silver, and a stunning pair of diamond earrings.

"Damn," I say. "No wonder you're not leaving those here."

She closes the lid, nodding. "I mean, monetary value aside, it's all I have connecting me to my family."

I frown. "Really?"

She nods. "I'm sort of alone in the world, Felix." She doesn't look at me, tracing idle patterns on the lid of the box with a fingertip. "All my grandparents are dead, I never knew my father, Mom is dead, and I'm an only child." She waves a hand, giving me a breezy smile that doesn't quite reach her eyes. "But hey, that's life, huh?"

"That all you wanna grab for now?"

She nods. "I'll pack a bag when we come back for Pumpkin."

I hold out my hand, and she accepts it—her hand is small and warm in mine, and I gently pull her to her feet. I make a point of meeting her eyes for a long, intense moment.

"See?" I say. "I can make eye contact."

She snorts. "Lovely. You get a gold star."

I keep hold of her hand, drawing her toward my truck. I open the passenger door and toss the detritus of my job into the back seat—a clipboard and pen, a pneumatic nail gun and its hose, a partial case of bottled water, and a few cardboard tubes containing blueprints.

"Sorry about the mess," I say. "I have a house, but I spend most of my time in here."

Her laugh is bell-like, musical, and infectious—just the sound of it puts a smile on my face. "I am the last person on the planet to judge you for having a messy vehicle you live in, I promise." Once I have the seat cleared off, she leans in, sets her box and cash bag on the seat, and then climbs up and in.

I shut the door after her and round the hood to slide behind the wheel. I start the engine, put it in gear, and glance at Ember.

And for a moment, I have the most bizarre, unsettling, out-of-body experience of my life.

I see her beside me, platinum hair sunlit and gleaming, silky smooth skin sun-bronzed, denim cutoffs bunched up around her thigh-hip creases with the white flags of her pockets sticking out under the fraying hems, a white V-neck clinging to her curves…and I see the future.

I see her there beside me, smiling, laughing, teasing me, a ring on her finger. I see her there beside me with a belly burgeoning with child.

For a split second, I see it all.

And I fucking want it.

6

Ember

I CATCH AN ODD LOOK ON FELIX'S FACE. IT'S A SPLIT-second thing, there and gone so fast I could have imagined it, but I know I saw it. It was…longing.

Raw, potent, fierce, and wild.

And it was leveled at me.

My heart pitter-patters in my chest at the fragmentary glimpse at his deepest emotions, at the knowledge that he was looking at *me* like that.

It's almost too much to handle, for so many reasons. Most of them are to do with Dutchie, and I shy away from even examining them in my own mind.

He jerks the shifter into gear, and the big diesel motor chugs and groans. Moments later, we're out of the YMCA parking lot and heading back toward town. Instead of downtown, though, he takes us into the industrial sector east of downtown. Crowe Construction and Demolition's headquarters is a half-acre lot, with three long, low equipment garages in a U-shape, the opening facing the road, with a small building front and center that used to be a vacation cottage some seventy years ago. The lot is all gravel, and there are vehicles and equipment of varying kinds and ages in the lot—a huge dump truck that has to be nearly fifty years old, a tiny backhoe-thing but with wheels instead of tracks, a massive yellow bulldozer, and several pickups with attached flatbed trailers.

I gesture at the cluster of vehicles. "Why is that stuff not parked in the garages?" I ask. "Wouldn't it be more secure?"

"That's overflow. My grandpa actually started the family business, Crowe Demolitions, more'n fifty years ago. He passed before I was born, and Dad transitioned the company to construction and renamed it Crowe Construction. Later on, Riley reopened Crowe Demolitions. Point is, a lot of that equipment there is old stuff we don't use much. The dump truck is toast—needs a new tranny which would cost more than the thing is worth, the little backhoe I don't fuckin' know what's wrong with but it's fucked—something with the hydraulics, I think—and the dozer is legitimately from World War Two. It does run and work, but it's fiddly and difficult and requires constant maintenance. And those pickup trucks were the first company trucks Dad bought, so they all have like a half million miles on them."

"Oh. So the equipment and such that you actually use regularly does live in the garages."

He nods. "Yup."

He parks his big gold pickup in front of the little house

and shuts it off. "C'mon, gotta grab the keys and sign out the flatbed."

The little house is the actual HQ office—a tiny space in desperate need of renovation. The gray carpet is dingy, thin, and worn to fraying threads in the high-traffic spots, the walls are cheap wainscoting beneath dirty, cigarette smoke-yellowed plaster, and all the furniture is construction site specials—battered metal desks and filing cabinets, with buzzing, flickering fluorescent bulbs overhead. A thin-bladed fan stirs the air half-heartedly.. The smell of old, burned coffee and decades-old cigarette smoke is nearly overpowering.

A woman sits at one of the gigantic, olive-drab metal battleship-desks, three computer screens in front of her, a phone clamped between her ear and shoulder while a waist-height industrial printer noisily spits out pages rapid-fire. She's tall and slender with glossy, wavy brown hair laced with expensive blond highlights; she's remarkably beautiful, in a Skipper Barbie way. She has cat's eye blue-blocker glasses perched on her nose and she's *ummm-humm*ing and scribbling notes frantically. A moment after we enter, she thanks the person on the other end and hangs up, her eyes going to Felix.

"Fee! Just the man I needed to see." Her voice is sing-songy and chipper, her eyes drinking in Felix with obvious thirst.

"Hey, Jess," Felix says, his voice carefully neutral. "What's up?"

"The lumber order got all goofed up, somehow. They caught it before they shipped it, but it's gonna take a week or two before they can rectify it and send the correct order."

"Well fuck," Felix growls. "I need that lumber last fuckin' week. Who do I need to fire?"

"Not me!" She chirps, tapping her notepad with her pen. "They're sending us some pre-built framing at cost, and they're discounting the order by ten percent. I got it *up* to ten, actually—they were originally only offering five."

Felix shakes his head. "That's the third time they've fucked up an order in the last quarter, Jess. I'm losing patience with them." He scratches his jaw. "Get some other quotes for me, will ya? I'm thinking it's time to get a new lumber supplier."

She jots a note, nodding. "Will do. But Mason won't be happy. They've been our supplier since your dad's time."

"I don't care about Mason Carter's feelings, Jess," Felix growls. "We've stuck with them because they've had good prices and they've been reliable up until recently. But they've jacked up their prices several times over the last couple years, and now they're fucking up orders. Find me a new supplier ASAP, please."

She tosses a snappy little two-finger salute. "Yes sir, will do." She shoots me a friendly smile. 'Hey, I'm Jess!"

"Ember," I say. "Nice to meet you."

Felix goes to a metal box on the wall by the side door, unlocks it with a key from his keyring, and finds the set he needs. There's a clipboard hanging on a nail beside the lockbox, and he scribbles some info on it—the vehicle, today's date, and his name, I would assume.

He comes back to me and takes my hand—it's a casual, familiar gesture, a clasp of palms rather than the more intimate entwined fingers, but it's still an unexpected gesture. "Let's go."

Jess's eyes zero in on our joined hands, and the friendly smile melts faster than an ice cube in boiling water.

Uh-oh. I sense jealousy.

I let Felix lead me through the side door and out to the yard, but I can't resist a backward glance at Jess. I know it's petty and probably a dumb move, but I shoot her a smirk. Her eyes narrow, and for a moment, I see the unrequited longing on her face clear as day. Then the side door slams closed on its hydraulic arm, and Felix is dragging me across the gravel yard.

"Hey," I say, tugging at his hand. "Slow down, would ya? Not all of us are six feet tall and all leg."

He glances at me, frowning. "Oh, sorry." He immediately slows his pace to something I can match without trotting.

We cross the yard to one of the garages, and he enters a door around the side. The interior is pitch black and smells of grease and rust and age. He flicks a switch just inside the door, and massive fluorescent lights click on with a noisy buzz, illuminating a small fleet of large trucks. There are newer dump trucks, a wrecker, a big flatbed with stake-sides that has shovels, rakes, sledgehammers, and pickaxes strapped to the sides and several wheelbarrows strapped handles-up to the side-stakes.

He leads the way to a truck in the back, a big brown cab with a long, low flatbed, the kind of thing used for hauling bulldozers and backhoes. Felix hops up onto the bed and rattles a heavy chain the size of my arm, checking that it's secured, and then opens a big metal box at the front of the bed at the base of the cab's rear wall, sorting through rolled-up yellow straps and metal hooks with handles. Once he's satisfied, he steps from the bed to the cab's step, opens the door, and starts the motor. It catches with a deafening rattle and then sets to a low, grumbling idle.

He jerks his head at the cab. "Climb on in."

I go around the passenger side and climb awkwardly up, open the door, toss my things in, and then scramble up onto the brown, plasticky leather bench seat. He stabs a garage door clicker clipped to the sun visor and the massive rolling door squeals open, emitting bright sunlight in a widening crack.

He carefully navigates out of the garage, closes the garage door with another stab of his finger, and then we're out on the road, bouncing and jouncing at each bump and shift of the manual gears. The ride is so jouncy my tits are threatening to smack me in the face and knock me out.

I catch Felix watching the show out of the corner of his eye more than once, and eventually, I have to just laugh. "You picked this one on purpose, didn't you?"

"I have no idea what you mean," he mumbles.

"You picked the truck with the bounciest ride," I explain, gesturing at my chest as a divot in the road sends me flying to the ceiling, my boobs going momentarily weightless before crashing painfully back down. "Because of that."

"I picked the truck that's rated to haul other vehicles that has the necessary equipment to keep it strapped down so your home doesn't go flying off into a ditch." A brief pause. "The show is just an incidental bonus."

I cross my arms over my chest. "Well, show's over. Sorry."

He grins at me. "I'm teasin' Ember. I didn't even consider that aspect."

I roll my eyes. "Sure you didn't."

"It's true! It's not something I go around thinking

about, you know. Like, hmm, how can I get Ember's boobs to bounce the most?"

"You know, we talk about my boobs a lot. Have you noticed that?"

He glances at me. "You brought it up. I'm just driving."

"I mean in general."

"In general, they're fucking spectacular, and worth talking about." He shakes his head, huffing a laugh. "You haven't exactly gotten the best impression of me, I'm afraid. I'm usually more of a gentleman. There's just something about you. I dunno."

"Something about me turns you into a caveman?" I say, snickering. "Not sure whether to be insulted or flattered."

"Go with flattered?" he says, his tone making it a question.

"That would be convenient for you, wouldn't it?"

His answer is a shit-eating grin. "I mean, it'd let me off the hook, yeah." The grin, and the humor in general, fade. "Listen, Ember, I am sorry if—"

I cut him off. "Stop. Please, it's fine. Really."

"I'm not that guy, though. I'm really not."

I arch an eyebrow at him. "It really is just something about me in particular?" I suppress a laugh. "Or maybe two things in particular?"

"Now you're just being mean," he mutters. "I'm not that shallow, I swear."

"Uh-huh," I tease. "Su-u-u-ure." I draw the word out into several syllables.

"I'm not!"

I burst into laughter. "Omygod, Relax. I'm just fucking with you. You're good. It's totally fine. I'm not that easily offended. And if I'm being honest, the attention doesn't suck. I haven't felt attractive in a long time." I slap my hand over my mouth. "I did *not* mean to say that out loud."

Felix is quiet for a while, and I catch him shooting pondering looks at me. Finally, as we roll up to a stoplight, he allows himself a long, lingering look into my eyes. "I'd like to know what that means, but I don't want to push you to talk about something if you're not ready."

"I…" I sigh, shaking my head. "It's all tangled up, Felix. All the shit that's wrong with me is one big jumbled up mess of baggage."

"You can talk to me, you know. I won't judge. I won't push. I know I can't fix anything. But I can listen." The light turns green, and he returns his focus to the road, but I feel his attention on me even when he's not looking at me.

"That's very sweet, Felix. I appreciate the sentiment, I really do. I'm just…I don't know if I'm ready to talk about it. Not just with you, but anyone. Even Faye, I've only sort of touched on some things. She's a wise old bird, though, so she sorta gets the stuff I'm not saying."

He nods. "I get it. It's fine. But just consider it a standing, open-ended offer. Any time day or night, if you wanna talk, I wanna listen."

My heart melts a little more, because it's obvious he means it. And part of me wants to open up to him. Part of me wants to let him in, to share my painful history with him. But something still stops me. Fear? A reticence to open up those wounds that haven't even really scabbed over yet?

"What about you?" I ask. "What's your story, morning glory?"

He shrugs. "Not much of one."

"Oh, come on. Give me something."

He tips his head to one side. "I have a brother, Riley. He runs the demo side of the company."

"Are you close with him?" I ask.

He nods. "Yeah, we are close. We weren't always, though. We fought a lot as boys, especially in high school. He's younger by a couple years, so he was always tagging along and annoying the shit outta me and my friends. And then he sorta got into some trouble and did some time. When he was released, he struggled to find his place again—not just in society but the community as a whole, and our family. He struggled to find a job...it was a rough time for him. That's when we bonded. I had a demo crew that was short-staffed at the time so I put him with them, and he just...took off. He loved it. Eventually, he developed a program to help other convicts with the things he struggled with."

"What's the program?" I ask.

"Oh, it's a work-release thing. He works directly with Holbrook Correctional facility. They put him in touch with inmates that have clean inmate records—meaning, model prisoners, no fights, no demerits, none of that shit. He interviews them and if he accepts them into his program, they work for him on one of his demo crews. They get bussed here to the yard, put in a full day's paid work, and then get bussed back to the prison. There's a deputy from the prison on site at all times. They put in five years on the crew, and if they're well reviewed by Riley, they're eligible for early parole. Once paroled, they keep working for him, which sort of functions as an additional aspect of their parole. They still have to check in with their parole officer, but not as frequently as long as Riley delivers good regular reports of their behavior."

"That's pretty cool, actually," I say.

"Well, that's not the cool part. There are work release programs everywhere. What sets his apart is that their wages, instead of just being paid directly to them, go into an escrow account, part of which goes to pay off their financial obligation to the prison, and the rest goes into savings so they have money to live off of when they get out."

"Wait, what? Financial obligation to the prison?"

He nods. "Jail ain't free, sweetheart. Prisons are privately owned. It's a multi-billion-dollar industry. So yeah, a lot of guys come out of prison heavily in debt, can't get a job, and often have nowhere to go and no car. It's punishment on top of punishment. Riley will be the first to say that he fucked up, and he deserved the sentence he got. But the rest of what he went through was wholly unnecessary and unjust, so he set out trying to fix it, at least as far as he could. When his guys get released, he personally picks them up from Holbrook, sets them up with a debit card so they have access to their money, and he has a deal with one of the apartment complexes in town—they always have a unit open so when his guys get out, they have a place to stay and enough money saved up to afford it. He picks them up and drives them to and from work until they can get their own car."

"That's really, really, amazing," I say. "He sounds like a great guy."

He grins. "I dunno about that. He's still a hothead and a hound dog, but yeah, he's got a great heart under all that. I'm proud of him. He's made some good out of his experiences."

I smile at him. "It has not escaped my notice, you know."

"What hasn't?" he asks, sounding perplexed.

"Your little redirection," I say. "I asked you about you, and you talked about your brother."

He shrugs. "He's my brother. He's a big feature in my life." He grins at me. "I said I won't push, and I won't, but I ain't gonna be the only one to get into my deep shit."

I nod. "That's fair."

We arrive at the Y right then, and I let him focus on getting the huge flatbed positioned where he wants it.

"Grab whatever you need right now and I'll get 'er hooked up," he says.

I shove my clothes into my suitcases, my toiletries, my everyday jewelry, my phone charger, laptop, chargers, and my small white Yeti cooler of perishable items. The cab isn't very big, however, so Felix straps it all down on the flatbed, and then hooks the big chain up to the front of my bus and goes through the technical process of securing my bus onto the flatbed.

"Alright," he announces, after triple checking all the chains and straps until he's satisfied. "We're good. Off to see Mr. Nyx."

"So his name is Nicks, like N-I-C-K-S?"

"No," he says, chuckling. "N-Y-X. It's his last name. Cody Nyx. But literally no one but his mother calls him Cody, and only then when she's pissed at him."

"I don't know how to thank you, Felix," I say, my voice soft.

"Nah," he grunts. "All good."

I reach out and put my hand on his. "No, Felix. It's not nothing. Thank you."

He looks at me for a long moment, his gaze serious. "You're welcome."

I leave my hand on his, although I'm not sure why. It just…feels nice, I guess. I haven't had contact like this with another human since Dutchie died. It's innocent. It's not even handholding, it's just…contact. Human touch.

I don't want him to say anything about it. Don't make a big deal. I'm not ready.

He doesn't. He doesn't even look at our hands. But he does flip his hand palm up; for a moment, then, my little hand is nestled in his much larger one. His hand is fascinating—I feel every point of contact. His hand is as rough as sandpaper and thick with strength. He curls his hand around mine, like a nut within a shell. He squeezes ever so gently, and I get an immediate sense of the massive power in his hands. His hand engulfs mine, swallows it.

Instead of instilling a sense of smallness or vulnerability, I feel…a little safer. A little more secure. As if, because he's holding my hand, everything will be okay.

This freaks me the fuck out.

Panic sears through me, a boa constrictor coiling around my chest, preventing me from drawing breath, making my heart pound and my head throb. I fight it tooth and nail, trying desperately to draw a full breath, to slow my ragged, gasping, panting sense of all-pervading guilt and fear.

I have tunnel vision, barely able to see the road ahead of me; a roaring fills my ears as if a 777 is howling five hundred miles per hour past my head.

Can't think. Can't see. Can't breathe. Can't move.

Trapped.

It's wrong—all wrong.

The world halts. I hear a muffled sound—a thunk. Another. A voice—distorted as if we're underwater.

Movement. Sunlight. Warmth.

A face fills my narrowed field of vision—Felix. He's worried, scared, speaking, but all I can hear is the roaring in my ears, the fury of my all-consuming panic.

He crouches in front of me, slips my baby blue Tieks off my feet, sets them aside. Cool green grass tickles my soles. He guides my hands into the grass, cool verdant blades bending, pricking, tickling, fingers digging into the soil, earth caking under my nails.

He tips my head up, chin pointing at the sun—its rays bathe my face in warmth and light. The sky is blue—the color of my Tieks.

His hand splays on my chest above my cleavage, on the V of skin exposed by the neckline of my T-shirt—his hand is warm and callused, hard and heavy.

"...In, Ember. Breathe in." The roaring dulls a touch, so I can sort of make out his words—most of them. "Feel the grass...sky. Feel my hand..."

I squeeze my eyes shut and focus on his words. His voice. His hand pressing against my skin, fingers dimpling flesh over my heartbeat.

"Focus on what's real." He's behind me, now, big, hard, powerful body framing and surrounding me. Arms around my shaking body, sheltering, protecting. Voice a whisper in my ear. "Take a breath, Ember. One big breath. Focus on the grass. Focus on the sky and the sun."

I focus on him. His voice. His arms. His hands.

"What do you see, Ember? Tell me three things you see."

"B-b-bl—blue s-s-ky," I stammer, barely able to even whisper.

"Great, honey. What else? Two more things you see."

"Grass. Green."

"Yes, perfect. One more thing you see."

"H-h-hands. Your hands." I grab one of his hands and put it in my line of sight. Trace a thin white line creasing the webbing on the back between finger and thumb. "Scars." I flip his hand, touch the hard knot of callus at the base of his middle finger. "Calluses."

"Good, honey, very good." He lets me hold his hand, touch his calluses, count his scars. "Four things you hear."

"Your—your voice." The shaking is less violent, now. "Cars. A—a bird singing. A man laughing."

"Good job, Ember. Good. Now take five deep breaths. I'll count with you, okay? Ready?" I nod. "One."

The first breath is more of a shudder, but my lungs fill.

"Hold it—one…two…three…four…five. Now let it out. One…two…three…four…five."

Without any sense of hurry, he guides me through four more repetitions—inhale as fully as I can, hold it for five and exhale for five.

By the time I've done it five times, I can see, hear, and breathe. But I also feel a full-on ugly cry breakdown building within me, and I know I can't hold it off for long.

I grip his thick forearm, nails digging in. "Take me somewhere, please." My voice is a hiss. "I can't—I can't do it here, Felix. I can't. I can't."

"Can't do what here?"

I swallow hard. "Cry."

"Okay, I got you. I got you." He stands up, effort-lessly lifting me with him. His chest is a broad, firm expanse against my cheek, and I feel his heartbeat under my ear—*thudthud—thudthud—thudthud.*

Up, and plasticky fake leather greets the backs of my thighs. A seatbelt clicks into place across my chest. He goes to step down, and the thought of not having physical contact with him makes me panic all over again.

"Don't!" I squeak, shrill and wild. "Don't let go. Don't let go. Please don't let go, Felix."

"Okay, no problem. I've got you. I won't let go, I promise." His voice is calm and soothing. He slides and twists past me to sit on the bench beside me without letting go of my hand, takes his seat behind the wheel; transfers his grip on my hand to his right hand and buckles up and starts the engine with his left. "I've got you, Ember. I won't let go."

He shifts with his left hand and braces the wheel with his knee.

"Close your eyes and count your breaths. Just count them. See how high you can go before you lose count."

Once again, my hand is cradled in his, nestled like a baby bird. I open my hand, thread my fingers through his. Close my eyes and count my breaths. One…two…three…I get to fifty, and then sixty. The brakes squeal and hiss, and I have to start over.

I lose track of how many times I have to start over, but holding his hand and counting my breaths keeps me grounded, helps me fend off the impending breakdown.

The one I've been denying and avoiding for six fucking months.

It's happening, and I can't stop it, and Felix Crowe, a man I just met and barely know, to whom I am attracted to a silly degree, is about to witness it.

Brakes squeal again, and the truck halts. The motor goes silent. Felix slides toward me, scoops me onto his lap. Shimmies sideways and shoves open the door, descends with me in his arms. I catch the corner of the truck's door as we go down and slam it closed.

Tears are welling, eyes burning, salt haze blurring my vision. I cling to his neck, bury my face in his thick, hard shoulder.

"Felix Crowe, you can't park that big thing on this little street," an old, shaky female voice says.

"With all due respect, Mrs. McCready," Felix growls, "fuck off and mind your own goddamn business."

There's an indignant huff and a slammed door.

I catch glimpses of grass, blue shutters against white vertical board-and-batten. A storm door creaks open—I hold it with my elbow while he wrenches at the door.

"Locked," he snarls. "Goddammit."

He rears back and plants a boot into the door beside the knob—there's a sickening crack of wood and the door shudders open.

"Y-you c-could have…uh-uh-unl-l-locked it," I stammer.

"Keys are in the truck. I can fix it. Don't fuckin' care."

White walls. Black and white photographs—beaches, dunes, trees, snowy fields, a horned owl staring down the camera lens. Dark wood floors. A door toed open. Bright sunlight bathing a bedroom—sheer curtains billow in the gentle breeze. A king-sized bed, white duvet, and a colorful handmade quilt folded across the lower third.

Felix kicks the door shut, shoves the duvet aside. Lowers himself to the bed with me in his arms, on his lap.

"Tell me what you need, Ember. You want to be alone? A cup of tea? Shot of whiskey?"

"J-just h-hold m-me."

"Okay. I got you."

His hard, mammoth arms wrap around me, tightening, and his chest is a cliff-face against my cheek, and he's a cocoon surrounding me with safety.

The stinging blur of tears wells, surges, and then a tear trickles down my cheek. Another.

A sob wrenches through me, a keening cough of agony.

I turn my face into the soft cotton of his shirt, which absorbs my tears. They're flowing now, and I'm shaking, my shoulders heaving as sobs so violent they're soundless wrack me as if I'm being shaken by giant hands.

There are no thoughts, no emotions, just the savage catharsis of weeping. Felix doesn't shush me, doesn't tell me it's gonna be okay, doesn't ask questions. He just holds me silently, tightly, his lips against the crown of my head, breath hot on my scalp.

It's a brutal breakdown. Ugly crying isn't anywhere close to accurate. My lungs ache and scream as sobs clutch my chest and prevent breathing—and then I manage to suck in a wailing, shuddering breath, and now I'm screaming, screaming.

"Let it out," he whispers. "Gimme all you got, Ember. Hit me. Scream. Kick. Whatever you got, I can take it."

I can't help but take him at his word. A wave of fury at the unfairness of life overwhelms me and my scream becomes one of rage, and I let it rip out of me and my hands curl into fists and I bash at his chest with all my might, and yet all he does is smooth back my hair and rub soft slow circles on my back.

Rage becomes sorrow so profound it cuts through my soul like a razor blade, and I see my precious Dutchie across the years I was privileged to spend with him.

Surfing in San Diego. Disneyland with ice cream cones. Smoking pot in Portland with the whacko kind of people my mother would have loved. Over-roasted coffee from the original Starbucks in Seattle. Hiking the mountains in Idaho. Trail rides on a thousand acre ranch in Montana. Yelling incoherently at the Grand Canyon and laughing about the wonder of a good barbaric yawp. Making love in the bus with the sliding door open, the breathtaking wonder of the Rockies spread out before us.

The camera—always the camera going, recording everything. Dutchie driving. Me sleeping. Gas stations on Route 66. Ruler-straight highways across the Nevada desert. The iconic red rock plateaus and the sweeping vistas of New Mexico through my passenger window. Dutchie laughing, drunk, as he dances around the campfire. A riverboat paddling down the mighty Mississippi past Mark Twain's hometown.

Reading comments together. Laughing at the haters. Arguments at highway junctions about which way to go, and miles of angry silence that slowly fade as we forget what we were even fighting about, and then pulling over to have quick but passionate makeup sex. The excitement of our first sponsor. Disbelief as our audience passes a hundred thousand, and then half a million. Our first million-like vlog post. Our first five-figure sponsorship.

Dutchie waking up in the middle of the night, coughing blood so dark it's nearly black. The fear in his eyes. A cold, sterile hospital room in Lima, Ohio. X-rays on a light board. A nameless doctor giving the worst possible news: weeks to live at most.

Dutchie, thin and frail, eyes sunken, cheeks hollow, in the back of the bus as I drive us north, passing through Kalamazoo, Pentwater, Ludington, Manistee, Frankfort, Glen Arbor, Traverse City...

Dutchie asking me to help him to the overlook so he can see the Sleeping Bear Dunes.

His last breath at sunrise, sitting with me on a bench, his head on my shoulder, the Mackinac Bridge soaring over our heads—the bridge we'll never cross together.

He was so emaciated at the end that I could easily carry him back to the bus. Surrendering him to a hospital. Receiving a jar of his ashes a few days later.

Scattering them on a long, dry wind across Lake Michigan as the sun rises—Dutchie loved sunrises best of all.

All of this ravages me, a flash flood of memories that gut me, savage me, shred me.

Felix just holds me through it.

How long it lasts, I couldn't say—hours? Minutes? An eternity?

The sobs slow not because I run out of tears, but because sheer exhaustion pulls me under.

I fall asleep with my head on his lap, his hands trailing through my hair.

7

Felix

I HAVE TO PISS LIKE CRAZY.

Ember is passed out—understandable given the intensity of the panic attack she suffered, followed by a solid hour of the most agonized sobbing I've ever witnessed.

She's asleep on my lap, one hand curled over my thigh with her cheek on her hand, her other resting directly across my bladder. And…elsewhere.

Thank god I had my phone accessible so I could catch up on emails to distract myself from both my bladder and the unintentional intimacy of Ember's positioning. But now I'm out of emails to answer, I've scrolled through my various social media feeds until my eyes are crossing, and my bladder is screaming to the point that I can't ignore it much longer.

When I reach the point, after another fifteen minutes, that I know I have to go right the fuck now, I start worming my way out from beneath Ember, carefully replacing my lap with a throw pillow. Either I'm sneakier than I thought or she's out for the count, because she doesn't stir beyond nuzzling into the pillow and wrapping both arms around it.

I damn near sprint to my bathroom and take the longest piss of my life, groaning a sigh of relief. Wash my hands, check on Ember—still asleep.

I tiptoe out of my room, gingerly close the door, and head out to my back deck to call Nyx.

He answers on the third ring. "Yo, Fee, what's up?"

"No one says yo any more, Nyxie."

"Yeah? Well, I do, so fuck off." I hear a torque wrench zapping in the background. "What's goin' on, buddy?"

"My…uhhh…friend, I guess, has a vintage VW bus that took a shit. She said there was a grinding, a thunk, and then it conked out and won't turn over. She sorta lives out of it, too, so getting it fixed ASAP is a priority. Can you help?"

"Fuck yeah, I can. I actually have a bus in the back lot with a totally shot body and a low-mileage engine. Bring 'er by and I'll hook her up."

"Make it as cheap as possible, yeah? I'll cover your expenses."

A pause. "She means somethin' to you, huh? This girl?"

I hesitate. "I mean…yeah. Maybe? Starting to? I dunno, man, it's complicated."

"No, it fuckin' ain't, brother. You got hung up on Amy,

convinced yourself that you're the worst person in the world, and never so much as dipped a fuckin' baby toe in the dating world again. If I didn't know you had a hookup on Tinder, I'd think you were celibate."

"It's not a hookup Tinder, man, fuck."

"No? Then what is it? How many girls from there've you been on more than one date with?" He laughs. "Wait, wait, wait, I'll go you one better—how many of them have you even taken on a date? Because my sources say you usually skip the date and go right for the hookup."

"You callin' me a manwhore?"

"No. That's Riley. You're…I dunno what you are. A sad strange little man, and you have my pity."

"Fuck you and your *Toy Story* quotes, Nyx."

"Great! Now I have *guilt*!"

I groan. "Fuck off with it, seriously. It's weird."

"Fuck you. Real men watch cartoons, and *Toy Story* is the greatest animated film of all time. Fight me."

"You're a grown man, Nyx."

"The word I'm searching for I can't say because there are preschool toys present." Then, muttered: "Dick."

I laugh, rubbing my face. "If you weren't my best friend since kindergarten, I'd never talk to you again."

"Until you need me to unfuck your pathetic attempts at automobile restoration."

"ONE TIME!" I snap. "I needed your help *one* fucking time."

"JESUS, CONNOR! YOU WANNA KILL SOMEONE? THE FUCK IS *WRONG* WITH YOU?" He shouts away from the phone and then groans a laugh. "New guy, man. I swear, he's dumber than a bag o' hammers, but I've never met anyone who can rebuild engines better or faster. I mean, good god, he's dense. Yesterday, I caught him photocopying his phone so he could show his grandmother a meme."

"Bullshit."

DING. My phone chimes with an incoming message. I put the phone on speaker and open the thread with Nyx—he's sent me a video. In it, Nyx, recording, approaches a short, muscular young man with a shaved head and a long rattail chin-beard standing at a photocopier. And yes, he is photocopying his phone.

"Jesus," I mutter.

"Every day it's something like that. Last Monday, Gibby convinced him that the shop computer was water-cooled and that it had run out of water."

I splutter. "No."

"Yes. I found him with a hose, squirting water into the CD drive."

"You have got to be shitting me."

"Nope. Once I got over my shock and then came down from the fucking roof, it was funny as fuck. That thing was older than Moses, so we needed a new one, but fuck, man. A water-cooled computer?"

I chuckle. "They exist, but they don't work like that."

"No fuckin' shit, Fee." He sighs. "Hey, I gotta bounce, man. Bring that bus over and I'll get it goin' for your girl. And no, you won't cover my expenses. I just got one condition."

"That being what?" I ask, warily.

"Give this girl a shot. Like, all in, balls to the wall, heart on the line."

I groan, rubbing my face with my palm. "Nyx—"

"No, dude. I *know* you. You're already looking for ways

to self-sabotage this because you think you don't deserve it."

"When did you go to therapist school, Nyx?"

"Oh fuck you. I know you. I've watched you self-isolate for the last decade and a half over a silly fuckin' childish mistake. You're so goddamn earnest you took that shit to heart and can't see your way to forgiving yourself. So you self-destruct anytime a woman shows you interest."

"I do not."

"So when Lia Fascinelli—"

"I am not discussing that."

"Because you know what I'm gonna say."

"She was batshit crazy."

"But hot as fuck and she wanted you bad."

"The phrase 'don't stick your dick in crazy' comes to mind when it comes to that woman."

"Sure, but look at her now—she's mellowed out."

"Nyx."

"Fine. What about Dina Calloway?"

"Holden scares the shit out of me. And didn't Dina come out recently or something?"

"As bi, yeah. But I have it on good authority that she'd still be D-T-F if you said the word."

"Again, Holden Calloway. Don't you remember the story Tommy Rooney told about picking her up for prom?"

"No."

"He brought Dina back an hour late and Holden shot him in the ass with rock salt from his sawed off twelve-gauge."

"You're a grown man. Tommy Rooney was seventeen and a doofus."

"Tommy Rooney is still a doofus."

"Exactly," Nyx says. "Okay, what about Kelly Krapowski?"

"Now you're just being cruel."

He laughs. "Fine. We won't go there. But we *will* talk about Maria Hernandez."

I sigh. "That one, yeah. I self-destructed on that one. I wasn't ready. She wanted the whole deal, Nyx. She was talking about wedding dates and picking kid names on the fourth date."

"Listen, Fee, all joking aside, my point is that you owe it to yourself to fuckin' move on. Maybe this girl with the bus is it, maybe she's not. I dunno. Neither do you, neither does she—not yet. And you won't unless you give her a shot without going out of your way to fuck things up on purpose."

"I think if I could get there with anyone, it'd be her," I murmur.

"Love that for you, bro. So just don't fuck it up."

I snort bitterly. "Easier said than done, Nyxie."

"What isn't?" he says. "A'ight. For real, I gotta go."

"See you later. I'll bring the bus over later."

"Cool. Be good, buddy."

"*Me* be good? You're the Three Rivers wild child."

He laughs. "I've outgrown my party animal ways, I'll have you know."

"Cole had to drive you home from The Cellar last weekend."

"A blip." He barks a laugh. "Why is it so fucking hard to hang up on you? Jesus. Fuck off, loser."

Click—silence.

Cody Nyx, ladies and gentlemen—my best friend.

I hear the sliding door and turn to see Ember shuffling out onto the deck, rubbing her eyes.

"Hey you," I say, extending a hand to her.

She takes it and lets me pull her to me, settling on my lap as if we've done it a million times. She leans her ear on my chest and just breathes for a while. "Thank you, Felix," she whispers.

"I'm just glad I was able to be there for you," I say.

She swallows hard. "It just...it hit me out of nowhere." She looks at me, her silver eyes searching, intent, wide. "I'm sorry for putting you through all that drama."

"Don't you dare apologize, Ember. I don't know what you went through, but it was obviously traumatic." I pause, tucking a stray tendril of hair behind the curve of her ear. "I'm honored to have been there for you. And if you want to talk about it, I'd love to listen for as long as you want to talk."

"You're sweet." She inhales deeply, holds it, lets it out. "Is it okay if I'm not quite ready yet?"

"Absolutely."

She licks her lips, bites the corner of her lower lip, searching my face. Lifts a hand and hesitantly rests it on my cheek. "I'll tell you everything, Felix, I promise. It's just hard. It's still pretty fresh, and—and I'm trying to convince myself that this is okay."

"That what's okay?" I ask.

"This." She rests her other arm on my shoulder, her fingers toying with the shaggy hair at my nape. "You. Me. This thing, whatever it is."

It hurts to put these words out there because they're the opposite of what I want, but it feels like the right thing to say. "There doesn't have to be a thing, Ember. If you're not ready, you're not ready."

She sniffs a laugh and gives me a lopsided smile. "Fee, I'm sitting on your lap. There's a thing. I just...I want you to know I'm trying."

"And I just want you to know that there's no pressure, no expectations, nothing. I'm here for you. I'll help you with your van and you can stay with me—there are no strings."

She gazes at me, palm on my cheek, thumb brushing back and forth beneath my eye. "Felix, I..."

Her pink lips are plump and close, damp from her tongue sliding across them, parted, begging to be kissed. Moving slowly, I cradle the back of her head and lean in.

"Tell me not to kiss you, Ember," I breathe.

Her eyes are wide and bright and restless, her breath on my lips. "I can't," she whispers.

"You can't kiss me, or you can't tell me not to?" I ask.

"The second one."

"Fuck," I hiss.

She peers at me. "What?"

"You should have said no."

"Why? I thought you wanted to."

"I do."

"Then what?"

"I'll never be able to fucking stop."

I close the distance between us, and her lips are wet and warm and soft, and her mouth immediately opens for me. She whimpers quietly at this first kiss, and the sound is a live wire sending a hundred thousand volts through my body. She's so fucking soft in my arms, and her mouth is pliant and eager, her tongue dancing with mine. She leans into me, crushing the firm weight of her tits against my chest, and suddenly I'm hyperaware of the fact that she's sitting on my lap, and the curved spread of her ass is nestled over my groin.

I growl hungrily, pulling her closer and tilting my head to take the kiss deeper yet, and she responds in kind, bringing both hands to the back of my head, fingers diving into my hair at my nape and pulling me to her mouth. She's been sitting sideways on my lap, legs pointing perpendicular to the rest of me; now, she sweeps her leg over me to straddle me, humming an aroused groan as she feels my erection wedge against her ass.

I can't stop myself from grinding against her, can't keep my hands from carving down her back, from cupping the taut weight of her ass. She lifts to her knees, allowing me full access—I take advantage greedily, growling with aroused appreciation as I fill my hands with her ass. And my good god, what an ass. So full, so round—big, plump, firm, and fucking perfect. I claw into the soft swell of muscle over the denim, smooth my hands down to the tender silk of her thighs just below the rough denim and fraying hem, curling my hands inside between her thighs and up, and then grip the weight of it again.

She presses against me, clutching my hair and bending over me, kissing me at a downward angle, now framing my jaw to tip my head up. She sits down on me, grinding on my cock—making me ache and throb; I'm bent inside my jeans at a painful, awkward angle. I grunt in pain as she grinds against me desperately, and I'm forced to tilt my hips up to push her up and then sink back down and shove my hand in to adjust myself.

She moans, sliding down to sit lower on my thighs,

digging her hands under my shirt to rake her fingertips down my chest and abs. Huffing into my mouth, nipping my lip between her teeth, Ember rips my fly open and yanks the zipper apart, cupping me where I spring into the opening.

"Fuck," I snarl. "Ember—Jesus."

My words break the spell.

She shoves away and lurches to her feet, staggering across the deck to slump over the railing, shoulders heaving as she pants raggedly. "Holy shit," she whispers. "What the fuck just happened?"

I'm shaking, aching, on fire all over, my raging erection so hard it hurts, leaking and throbbing. I close my eyes and breathe, trying to will it to go away.

"Felix?" Her voice is quiet, hesitant.

I try to zip my jeans, but they won't close over my erection. I hear her steps approach. I turn away from her, feeling guilty that I pushed her into something so fast, so intense when she had literally just finished saying she needed time.

"Sorry, I—" I shoot to my feet and stagger on unsteady feet for the sliding door. Pause partway through, turn to look back at her over my shoulder. "Ember, I'm sorry. I shouldn't have let things go there." I squeeze my eyes shut, furious at myself. "I just—fuck. I'm sorry."

I don't give her a chance to respond, bolting for my bathroom and shutting the door. My arousal hurts like a motherfucker, straining against the confines of my underwear, but I can't bring myself to so much as touch it, because I know the only thing I'd think of is Ember, the soft weight of her incredible ass in my hands, her mouth on mine so hungry and wet and willing and eager, her hands cupping me over my underwear, the quiet whimper as we kissed…

Fuck, fuck, fuck.

I brace my hands on the sink and close my eyes, breathing hard, trying to clear my mind.

The door opens and Ember is there, her hair free of the braid, loose around her shoulders and kinked from being braided while wet—her hair is fantastically long, hanging to mid-back, if not closer to her tailbone. Her lips are swollen from our kiss.

"Felix," she whispers, inching closer to me, warily, as if I were a skittish stray dog. "What are you sorry for? Why did you apologize? Why'd you leave?"

I grip the edge of the sink, not looking at her. "You just said you needed time. After what you just went through, the last fucking thing you needed was my dumb, horny ass making a move on you. You're mourning. I recognize that, at least. I shouldn't have kissed you. Shouldn't have let it go as far as it did, at the very least."

"Oh, Fee," she whispers. "You're taking an awful lot of credit for what happened just now, buddy."

I shake my head. "Ember, I—"

She's right there beside me, now, leaning back against the sink with her hip touching mine. She looks up at me, touches my lips to silence me. "I kissed you back, Felix. Did you miss that?"

"No," I admit.

"What about the fact that I encouraged you at every step of the way? Did you miss that? How about when I sat up because I fucking *loved* the way you grabbed my ass? You miss that part, too?"

I have to look at her. "No."

She looks a little pissed. "Then stop acting like it's all on you. It's *not*. I'm a grown-ass woman, Felix. *I* got carried away just as much as you did." She leans closer, puts a hand on my chest and gazes at me, her voice softening, now. "And I loved every second of it. I was just... shocked. It took me by surprise, how intense it was, how fast it accelerated."

"It was crazy. I just...I couldn't not kiss you. And then..." I shrug, shake my head. "It was like someone lit a match in a roomful of dynamite."

Ember huffs a laugh. "Exactly." She searches my face. "So, why'd you come in here?"

"I needed a minute," I mutter. "Needed to get control."

Her searching gaze flicks down to my crotch, which has stubbornly decided to stay monstrously, painfully erect. Her eyes widen. "Oh. Ohhhh. I—I see."

"And clearly, I have not been successful."

She's unsuccessfully trying to hide a grin, or perhaps smirk is a better word. "You, uh, you need a minute to take care of that?"

The look I give her isn't a glare, exactly, but it's pretty damn close. "No, Ember, I'm not gonna jack off."

"No?"

I shake my head. "I mean, sure as fuck not while you're here."

"But if I wasn't here..." she says, trailing off.

"Still probably not."

This gets me a puzzled frown. "No?"

I sigh, because for some reason I can't lie to her, even by omission. "I mean, I do...obviously. Or, I have, in the past."

"But?" She picked up on what I didn't say, clearly.

"But…" I trail off, embarrassed to the point of nausea. "Never mind."

"No, not never mind," she says, inching closer yet, wedging herself between me and the sink, looking up at me with wide, curious eyes. "Tell me."

"I can't," I say, my voice a rough, low rasp.

"You can't?"

"All I see is you," I whisper. "And it feels wrong to… fuck, I dunno…use you like that."

"Oh, Felix," she sighs, resting her forehead against my chest. "That's so sweet. And *so* fucking stupid."

I frown, caught off guard by her statement. "Stupid?"

"How would I know? Unless you told me, I mean. And I can't imagine why you would tell me. That's none of my business." She reaches up and caresses my jaw, smiling at me sweetly.

"I know, I know," I say, shrugging. "I know it's irrational. I just…can't."

"So you just…suffer?" she says, with another glance down at my raging erection.

I shrug. "It goes away. Usually. Eventually."

"I wouldn't mind," she whispers. "In fact, I might even be flattered."

"Ember, I…" I gaze down at her. "I don't know. I'm all over the place, right now. I want you so fucking bad. I wanna kiss you and never stop. Kiss you until you fucking—" I cut off with a harsh sigh. "I want you naked. I want you coming all over me. I want your hands on my cock. I want to fuck your pretty little mouth. I want to make love to you in every position there is and maybe make up a few new ones."

Her mouth falls open and pink stains her cheeks and

her eyes go wide and wild. "Fee," she breathes. "Jesus. Careful what you say to a girl."

I'm not done, though. "I want to know everything about you. I want to know what happened to you. Why you're so fucking sad. I want to erase that sorrow. I want to be the one to put a smile on your face every goddamn morning. I want to make you forget the sadness."

Her eyes water, and she blinks hard, twin tear tracks slipping down her cheek. "Felix. Fuck. FUCK!"

She turns away, shaking her head violently, hair slapping her shoulders, and then scrubs at her face with both hands.

"Ember, I—"

She shakes her head again, and I go silent. "Fee, I..."

"And I don't think I can have one without the other," I whisper. "I need both. And I don't know if you're ready for the second part."

"I'm not," she breathes, her voice so soft I can barely make out her words. "I'm not sure I'm ready for either part, Fee. I want to be." She looks up at me, quicksilver gaze fraught with a whirling hurricane of emotions. "I fucking *want* to be ready for all of that. But I'm not and I don't even know where the fuck to start."

"That's why I stopped, Ember. And that's why I can't seem to let myself find any relief, no matter how blue my balls are." I wrap my arms around her, turning into her, pressing my lips to her crown and inhaling her scent.

"I don't want you to be in pain because of me," she murmurs.

"I'll be fine. I don't think anyone's ever suffered any long-term effects from blue balls." I kiss her head softly. "I won't push, Ember. Not for you to share anything, and certainly not for you to be ready when you're not. If you're looking for a guy who's gonna push you out of your shell or whatever, I'm not him."

She barks a laugh. "No, trying to force me to do anything will always backfire on you in the most spectacular fashion you could imagine. I have a very serious case of oppositional defiant disorder. Undiagnosed, but I'm pretty damn sure I have it."

I laugh. "Noted. I'll never tell you what to do."

"Safe choice." She leaves my arms and paces a step away, raking her hands through her hair. "I don't know what to do, Felix."

"About what?

A bitter laugh. "Everything? My feelings for you. Whatever the girl version of blue balls is called. My fucked up, shattered heart. My bus. Where to live." She looks at me, her eyes touching on mine, and then raking down to my open fly, my still furiously erect cock. "Everything I want is so mixed up."

"You don't have to do anything about me, or for me. I'm not asking. I'm not waiting. I'm fine, Ember. I promise."

She takes a stalking step toward me. "I'm not."

I go utterly still. "Ember..."

She holds my eyes. Stops in front of me, breath coming in slow, deep, breast-swelling heaves. "I fucking want you, Felix. It's been...a long time—" she blinks, shakes her head. "A long fucking time since I...since I've felt anything but sad and angry and confused and lost."

I slide a thumb across her cheek, beneath her eye, smearing a teardrop away. "Ember."

"I want to beg you to make me feel literally anything else." She licks her lips, dropping her gaze to my crotch again, to the bulge straining against the cotton of my underwear. "Even for five fucking minutes, I want to feel anything—fucking *any*thing, Felix. All I've felt is broken for months."

This is dangerous. For me, but more for her.

"I know the feeling," I whisper. "My shit is different. I know that. I haven't lost anyone like you have."

"But fucked up is fucked up," she murmurs. "It's not a competition, and there aren't any prizes for first place."

"How long has it been for you?" she asks.

"Since what, exactly?"

A shrug. "Anything. Last sexual partner? Last time you got off, regardless of how?"

"Last sexual partner was…" I have to think. "Several months."

"Tell me about it."

"Um…

"I mean, was it a girlfriend? A hookup? Was it good?"

"No, not a girlfriend. A one-time thing. And…" I shake my head and shrug. "It wasn't great. It wasn't bad—and it wasn't her fault. It was just…unfulfilling. Flat. The physical enjoyment was so quick, and once that was over, it was just awkward. I didn't know her. Didn't have any real connection to her or even a real meaningful attraction. She was pretty, sure, but…" I shrug. "I dunno."

She searches me, and I can't fathom what she's looking for, much less what she sees. "You want meaning."

"Guess so."

She rests her hands on my chest. "Ask me."

"Your last time." It comes out as a statement, rather than a question.

"With Dutchie, obviously. My…" she swallows hard.

"My husband." A long pause, her eyes closing, tears leaking down her cheeks. "Seven and a half months ago. At a campground in Illinois, near Lake Michigan, not far from the Michigan border. Early morning. We found out—he, um." Her eyes squeeze shut even tighter. "We found out he was sick three days later. And he, um. He—he—he died less than a month later."

"Ember," I breathe. "I'm so sorry."

She curls her hands into fists in my shirt. "That's the last truly good, pure, and happy memory I have of him."

"I can't imagine."

"Good. I hope you never can." Her fists shake, squeezing so hard her knuckles turn white. "I don't want to forget. Not him, not us, not that memory."

"Of course not," I whisper. "How could you?"

"But holding on to every memory, good or bad, it just hurts. I feel trapped in my grief." She opens her eyes and meets mine. "I...I want to forget. Just for a minute. I want to be free of the grief, Felix, just—just for...for a minute."

"Ember," I breathe.

She holds my eyes, her silver gaze unwavering, wet with tears and turbulent with desperation. "Please, Felix. I...I can't give you everything you're asking for. Not yet. But I...I need to forget. Please, Felix. Help me forget."

How am I supposed to say no?

I fucking can't.

I don't try.

I step into her space, towering over her; she cranes her neck to look up at me, hope in her eyes and desire written in every feature, every shift of her expression. I frame her face in my hands, hesitate—her lips part, and she tilts her face to mine, granting the permission I silently seek in that hesitation.

Kiss her.

Soft, wet lips smear over mine, and her quick, clever tongue sweeps through my mouth, dancing with mine. She whimpers as I kiss her, and fuck, the whimper is my undoing. Dipping at the knees, I scoop her up by her ass, and her sweet silky thighs wrap around my waist, and her hands clutch at my nape to keep me pinned into the kiss, as if I was about to stop.

I walk with her out of the bathroom, set her on the edge of my bed. Stand between her legs and keep kissing her. Run my fingers through the cool, endless locks of her hair.

I break the kiss, pull her hair aside, and kiss the side of her neck. With a shocked gasp, she tilts her head to expose more of her throat, clutching at my face and neck as I kiss her neck, her throat, the hollow at the base. Breastbone. The tender little nook where her cleavage begins.

Drop to my knees, rest my hands on her thighs. Meet her gaze. "More?"

She puts her hands and mine and guides them up her thighs. "More."

"If you need to stop—"

She interrupts. "I won't." She shows my hands the way under the hem of her shirt to the impossibly soft skin of her belly. "Don't stop. No matter what, okay? I might—I dunno. But unless I say the word 'stop,' you keep going." Her hands dive under my shirt and find my abs. "I need to feel something, Fee. I have to."

I run my hands up her sides, taking the shirt up with it—she lifts her arms overhead, and I ease her tee up and off. She's wearing a white bra, the cups fully covering her breasts. Moving as slowly as I can, I set her shirt aside on the bed, smoothing my hands across her back, exploring her shoulders, her back, her sides in slow sliding circuits, coming back each time to the bra strap. Hungry for her now that I'm kissing her, now that she's letting me strip her naked piece by piece, I find it harder with every passing second to go slow, to take my time, to give her every chance to make me stop.

She doesn't.

When I touch my lips to the swell of her breast just above the edge of her bra cup, she flexes her spine to press her chest forward while cupping my head and holding me to her.

I tease one strap off her shoulder. The other. I tug the cup lower on one side, desperate to get her tits bared, to see them in all their glory, to feel them, kiss them, hold them—yet in equal measure I want to draw the moment out, enjoy the anticipation a bit longer.

"Felix," she breathes. "Take it off."

Fuck the anticipation. When she demands like that, who am I to say no?

I take her face in my hands and find her mouth, kiss her until we're both breathless, until my cock hardens all over again and she whimpers and I growl. One hook and eyelet at a time, I unlatch the bra. When it's unhooked, I ease the straps down her arms with my fingertips, and then at the last second, she whips it away and tosses it aside.

I sink back to sit on my heels and just take her in. "Jesus fucking Christ, Ember," I breathe. "Fucking perfect. So goddamn gorgeous I don't even…" I trail off, at a loss for words.

Her tits are everything I'd hoped and fantasized and wet-dreamed they would be, and more. Huge, full teardrops swaying subtly, they're as sun-bronzed as the rest of her. Sitting high and proud despite their improbable size, they swell even bigger at the tips, plump, round and natural, with wide pale pink areolae and thick, rigid nipples, they make her trim waist seem tiny—how an otherwise rather petite frame can support the weight of them, I don't know.

"Gonna just stare at them, Felix?" she teases, her words and tone light. "You are allowed to touch them, you know."

I can't rip my eyes away. "I just….I need a minute to fully appreciate them."

She laughs. "Okay, then." Her hands go to mine again, once more guiding them upward. "Maybe appreciate them this way."

I groan as I fill my hands with their soft weight; she lets out a soft sigh, her eyes shuttering as I caress her breasts. I lift them to test their weight—heavy. Brush my thumbs over her nipples, and she gasps, head tipping back in ecstasy at my touch. As my thumbs trip over them, her nipples visibly harden further. Clearly, I have no choice but to kiss them, now.

I cup a heavy breast in my hand, offering it up to my mouth, suckling her nipple until she groans low and ragged, arching into my kiss while leaning backward.

I help her lay down and brace her tits with my hands, squishing them together so I can lap and lick and suckle both nipples together, and then one and then the other, back and forth, back and forth, and then both again until she's panting.

"Pinch," she gasps. "Pinch my nipples, Fee. Please."

Fuck.

At her words, my cock, impossibly, hardens more, until it feels like it could explode like an overblown balloon.

Greedily, I oblige. Caress them in both hands, lifting from beneath and letting them bounce to sway and jiggle, and then roll her nipples between my thumb and forefinger. Even though I'm barely squeezing, Ember gasps, flinching.

My god, she's so responsive, so sensitive.

I lean over her, half-kneeling on the edge of the bed, and claim her mouth while kneading her tits—squeezing, caressing, squeezing. She moans into my mouth and drives her eager tongue against mine, tasting me, probing, teasing—when I twist my tongue against hers, she retreats; when I deepen the kiss, she pulls back, only to surge up to deepen it when I accept her pulling back, swiping her tongue into my mouth when mine retreats.

I pinch one nipple, exploring her sensitivity. The first pinch is gentle, a slight squeeze; she gasps into the kiss, mouth quivering. I pinch again, harder; she gasps.

"Harder, Fee," she breathes. "Pinch my nipples hard."

I growl, letting them go and then scrubbing my hands up her belly to gather her tits into my hands once more, now pinching both nipples at the same time, and now I pinch as hard as I dare, which feels too hard, in my own mind.

She bucks up with a shrill cry, hips leaving the bed. "FUCK!" she rasps, her voice hoarse from crying. "Yes, god yes. Again, Fee. Please. Harder."

My god—is she even real? Is this happening? This

has to be a wet dream, a fantasy from which I'm about to wake up.

Caressing gently, I let my hands soar the expanse of her breasts, circling them at their base against her chest, down their length to the plump, fat, round ends, rubbing my thumbs over the pale circles of her areolae, and then raking my thumbnails over her nipples. She whimpers, shuddering, her hands diving into her hair to grasp and pull as she arches into my touch, seeking more.

Growling eagerly, I suckle a nipple into my mouth, flattening it between tongue and the roof of my mouth, sucking hard. At the same time, I roll the other one between thumb and forefinger, squeezing harder by increments.

Ember snarls, a low ravenous growl in the back of her throat, a sound of raw female arousal, predatory need. Her hips flex, driving and sinking as I suckle and pinch her nipples, alternating now, sucking on one and pinching the other and then switching.

The harder I pinch and suckle, the more frantic the questing drive of her hips.

Could she come just from this?

God, that would be amazing. I've heard it's possible, but I've never witnessed it.

"Fee, please," she breathes, her voice shrill and breathy. "Don't stop. Feels too fucking good."

So I keep going—pinching, twisting, and sucking, licking, kissing, and compressing with my lips. And with each touch, she pants and whimpers more loudly, more eagerly. Her hands go to my head as I lick and then suck on a nipple, and when I seize its plump pink thickness in my teeth, she sucks in a breath and holds it.

When I apply a bit of pressure while pinching the

other so hard it seems like it should hurt her, she wails loudly, arching off the bed and then sinking down, hips quivering, belly spasming.

"Oh fuck, Fee. Fuck, fuck!" Her voice is rough with arousal, low and hoarse and wild. "Yes, fuck, yes."

"Gonna come for me, Ember?" I whisper.

"Uh-huh," she whimpers. "Just—just don't stop."

"Fuck no."

She rakes her hands down my back, hunting for the hem of my shirt—she finds it and rips it off of me with mad aggression, and then her fingernails dig into my shoulders as I bite her nipple with gentle but increasing force, until she shrieks in a mix of pain and pleasure and pushes at me in a subtle gesture. I let her nipple pop free and soothe it with licks and kisses that make her moan, caressing her tit with my hands, strumming her nipple with my fingers, faster and faster.

Her hips buck and dip, and she whimpers; fingernails raking down my spine, she leaves trails of fire on my back. Down, down, and then her hands dive under my underwear to clutch at my ass, pulling at me, clawing, digging nails in as I move my mouth to the nipple I was just strumming, tweaking and twiddling the one I was just biting.

She's panting now, quick short gasps in time with the flexing of her hips.

"Fee!" she whimpers. "Oh fuck, oh god. You're—oh, oh, ohhh, Fee!"

She yanks me down against her, grinding her denim-covered sex against the hard ridge of my cock that is still sheathed behind my boxer briefs.

"Ember!" I breathe, "Come for me, sweetheart. I know you're close."

"Hard!" she pants, breathless. "Pinch them both as hard as you can, Fee. Now—right now. Fuck, please, please, please."

I slash my mouth onto hers and demand her tongue, balancing above her as I caress her breasts gently, exploring the weight and length and softness of them yet again, finally squeezing her hardened nipples. Harder, and harder, while kissing her. She thrusts her tongue into my mouth in mimicry of fucking, to the same rhythm of her hips' thrusting against me. She shoves my jeans down further, pressing the hard ridge of my aching cock against the rough line of denim that is the crotch seam of her shorts, and I pinch harder yet, until I'm squeezing almost as hard as I can.

With a hoarse scream, her hips buck up against mine and stay there, shaking and shuddering as she arches off the bed, mouth open wide as the voiced scream dissolves with the emptying of her lungs, giving way to a silent scream. I pinch her nipples in a pulsing pattern, and she catches her breath, sucking in a whimper.

"Ohfuckohfuckohfuck," she sobs. "Fee, fuck—Felix, yes, fuck, fuck, fuck!"

She comes for an eternity, sobbing and shaking.

For a moment, she goes still, limp on the bed, panting.

And then her eyes snap open, and they're full of quicksilver fire and erotic hunger.

I have a feeling I've just roused a beast within her.

8

Ember

I'M BOILING OVER WITH A CRAZED CONFUSION OF emotions and sensations. Chief among them at this exact moment is utter relief—I haven't had an orgasm in nearly eight months, and I don't think I really allowed myself to feel the need. I have a tendency to dissociate from my body in times of stress or feeling emotionally or physically overwhelmed. When I'm concentrating on something, I can forget that I have to pee for so long I've gotten UTIs. I'll forget hunger, thirst, pain, anything.

So the last eight months I've dissociated from my body entirely. I had to make myself eat after Dutchie died. Had to force myself through the motions of caring for myself physically, telling myself it's what he would have wanted. And then it went back to being habit—eating because that's what you do, you eat in the morning, afternoon, and evening. You take showers. You use the bathroom. I never felt any of it, I just…forced myself to do it.

But physical pleasure? What a joke. Until I met Felix, I'd legitimately forgotten what that was. I'd shut that part of myself off, divorced my psyche from my innate needs as a biological, human female. I haven't been a sexual being since the moment that doctor said the word "cancer."

And then Felix happened.

Maybe when I whacked my head on the engine compartment, I knocked something loose, I don't know. I just know the moment I saw him, physical sensation came flooding back into my body. It was truly bizarre.

I was no longer just a Gordian knot of sorrow floating through the world.

I was a woman.

I had a body.

I had toes and fingers. Legs and arms. Feet and hands. Hair, nails, teeth. Organs.

Skin.

Breasts and buttocks.

I was a woman, and I needed sex.

At first, it had felt sort of…divorced from emotional need, which is weird for me. I'm on the demisexual spectrum, normally. I don't feel sexual attraction unless I feel an emotional one first. It's connected to my comfortability with nudity, perhaps. My mother's commune was one of open sexuality and nudity. It wasn't at all unusual to enter an RV or bus or van and find a couple in the throes of sex. People would walk around the camp naked. I've never tried to sort out the psychology of it, but I know that there is a connection between how I grew up and my demisexuality.

I spent almost three months getting to know Dutchie and falling in love with him emotionally before I felt even the slightest glimmers of physical arousal. And then, it developed slowly. He was so patient, so kind, so understanding, even though he was a normal guy with a normal sex drive. But he never rushed me, never pressured me. It was over a year after we met before we slept together.

Then he died.

I shut down.

And Felix…quite literally turned me back on. Why and how, I have no fucking clue. I just know that I saw him standing there on the dirt road, all muscle and masculinity and sexiness, and I felt an instant and overpowering attraction to him. An arousal that I couldn't even begin to fathom, because it was so intense, so sudden, and so fucking strange. So unexpected. I barely knew him, but I *wanted* him. I was barely able to hide it. I wanted to rip his clothes off right there in the middle of the road and climb on his dick.

It had shocked me stupid, and I'd been so confused that I'd had to meditate until it passed, and even then, if I let my mind go to him, that attraction would crop back up.

I've tried everything—pot, meditation, mantras… everything but leaving town.

That was not an option.

And then he'd appeared again. At that beach. Shirtless. Dripping wet. Ripped, jacked, and fucking gorgeous. A rippling six pack dusted with fine golden hair that was thicker on his chest and in a line down his belly, darkening and thickening as it delved under those tight, short swim trunks. Brawny arms. Hard, round, massive shoulders. Thick, hard thighs. A bulge that swayed with every step, promising a cock that could show me a sinfully good time.

My arousal had been so complete and so disorienting that I hadn't known how to handle it. It was beyond my experience—my desire for Dutchie had grown as I got to know him. He hadn't been my first, but because it had taken so long to open up to him that by the time we made love, my emotional connection with him had been immense and soul-deep, and so my physical connection to him had been as equally intense.

Felix...

He's cipher to me. A totally alien and unknowable thing. My feelings for him are confusing. I barely know him and yet suddenly I'm wildly horny for him? It makes no sense. I crave him to the point of lunacy. I dreamed of him every night after I first met him, and they were not innocent dreams. They were filthy, sinful, depraved dreams. I'm embarrassed—and turned on—even thinking about it.

Through force of will, I kept myself from acting on those feelings, and hopefully hid them from him while I tried to sort out what the hell was going on inside me.

He took care of me, the bastard. Rescued me from my dead bus. Towed it. Brought me here. Says he's going to help me get it fixed. Held me without a word as I had the emotional breakdown I'd been denying myself since my husband died. Asked for nothing. He just wanted to help. Showed me kindness after kindness, and when his own desires and attraction to me cropped up, he left the situation rather than let it affect me.

And when I saw him outside on his deck, I was... god, I don't know.

Half asleep and emotionally depleted. Maybe, for the

first time since Dutchie's death, I was free of the weight of my long-pent grief. I don't know. I just that I saw him there lounging in dark blue Adirondack chair in the shape of Michigan's lower peninsula, and I was totally fucking gone for him.

Need was a savage mistress within me, raging and pounding on the bars of the cage I'd kept her in for so long.

And when he kissed me?

Fuck.

The man can *kiss*.

And again, rather than allow his needs to take over, Felix had fled. The instinct was both sweet and frustrating. Because my needs are complex. I don't just want to be touched. I don't just want to be kissed, held, caressed, and given orgasms. I want all that—need it. But just as much as I want to receive them, I want to *give* those things. I want to touch. I want to kiss. I want to lick. I want to taste. I want to give him an orgasm that makes him forget his own name.

Which is where I am right now: laying sideways on his bed, naked from the waist up, shaking with orgasm aftershocks—from an orgasm he gave me exclusively through nipple-play.

I came close to it a few times with Dutchie, but never truly got there.

I don't dare examine that particular thought too closely—my emotions are still locked up at the moment, rampaging behind a very thin shield. My guilt over enjoying this will burst through sooner or later—probably sooner. I'll be a fucking disaster, and it'll likely happen pretty explosively.

But for now, I'm determined to force myself to enjoy

this moment of quasi-normality. Feeling pretty. Feeling female. Feeling wanted.

Being touched.

Held.

Kissed.

It's fucking amazing. Like droplets of water dripped onto a cracked, parched tongue. But like someone dying of thirst, I dare not drink too deeply all at once.

That's the idea, at least.

Desire has other plans.

Felix is half-kneeling on the bed above me, one foot on the floor, the other knee bent and braced into the mattress while I lay with my torso and ass on the bed, feet dangling just above the floor...since I'm too damn short to touch.

His eyes are ice chips, palest blue and glittering, shockingly intense, piercing and heated. His eyes are on mine, searching me—for signs of upset, probably. He must know I'm on the verge, and he's being so careful not to push me.

It only makes me want him all the more.

It makes my belly burn, my core heat. My nipples harden and my skin tingles.

I crave his touch. His skin. His muscles. His hands.

"Kiss me," I breathe. "Kiss me and don't stop."

The words are not mine. They didn't come from my mind or my heart, but somewhere else. My soul? From my very core—from my pussy. My aching nipples. My pulsing sex.

"Fucking *kiss* me, Felix."

His tongue darts out and slides along his lower lip,

and I lift swiftly, knot my fingers in the shaggy hair at the back of his head and kiss him.

And oh, oh god, the man can fucking kiss. Have I mentioned that, yet? His lips are pillowy soft in contrast to the masculine hardness of his body everywhere else. Wet and warm and soft, they scour mine with relentless verve, and his tongue is nimble and slippery and insistent.

I groan into the kiss, and I feel him tense at the sound, feel his hands twitch on my tits, squeezing involuntarily—drawing a gasp from me.

Need more. Need him. Need to touch.

Need to escape the maelstrom of emotions inside—all the things I haven't dealt with. I can't deal with them right now, and the only way to avoid doing so is physical sensation.

Some part of me niggles with guilt, knowing I'm using him to escape my feelings.

Knowing he wants more—he wants my feelings. He wants my story. My truth—the fullness of me.

Most women would sell an ovary to have Felix Crowe in this position—craving not just their bodies but their hearts.

I'm not ready.

He knows this, yet here he is, letting me take advantage of him.

And I can't stop myself.

I need his skin and muscle—pulling at his shirt, I work it up his body. He breaks the kiss long enough to let me tear it off and throw it aside, and then his mouth is savaging mine, kissing me with starving intensity, all tongue and lips and breath and growls.

I clasp his shoulders, dimpling my fingers into the

hard give of muscle, and then explore his shoulders, his back, my fingernails carving lines down his lats and obliques until I get to his jeans.

I delve under, find skin, find muscle. His ass is a work of art, hard and taut, a big round firm pair of perfectly formed bubbles, smooth and warm and soft to the touch yet harder than iron. I clutch and play, squeezing, digging my nails in until he grunts and then petting it and smoothing away the sting.

God, I need more—this need is all-consuming and relentless.

I push his jeans down, and he lifts without breaking the kiss, and we work together to remove them. I shove them past his butt and down to his knees, and then he balances on his knee in the bed and yanks them off his extended leg, and then switches his weight to kick them off the rest of the way.

I take claim of his abs and pecs, raking them with my nails and exploring them with my palms and fingertips, tracing the outline of his pecs, running my fingertips in the grooves of his shredded abs, tracing the thick line of hair down his belly to the band of his underwear. I slide my hands under the elastic again and explore his magnificent ass some more, because holy fuck, it's amazing.

But then Felix plays a mean, dirty trick on me.

He breaks the kiss, panting, and stutter-trips his mouth down my throat, over my breastbone, down between my tits to my belly, tickling my navel with his tongue until I shriek a giggle, feet kicking. He pins my legs with his body and yanks open the fly of my jean shorts, and oh, oh fuck, He's going for it. And I'm going to let him—my need to touch him takes a backseat to the promise of another orgasm.

I play with his hair as he kisses my belly while his hand cups my tits. My fly is unbuttoned but the zipper is up; he tweaks my nipples until I shriek, bucking off the bed as a lightning bolt of arousal sears through me, and then he tugs down the zipper. I lift my ass and he takes the cue, yanking them off inside out—the only way to remove shorts as tight as those.

"Fuck me," he growls, his voice farther away now.

I snap my eyes open to see him staring down at me, pure awe in his eyes, his expression painted with peak male appreciation. I forget which panties I put on, and glance down—oh.

They're the only ones I had clean…a red lacy thong, the triangle just barely wide enough to cover my seam, the strings sitting low.

He seizes my hips and before I know it, I'm on my belly and looking back at him over my shoulder as he gazes with reverence and adoration at my ass.

"Fuck me," he growls again, reaching for my ass.

Restless, eager, delirious, I hold still, resting my cheek on my forearm as I watch him cradle the outside of my ass in both hands.

I don't think I've ever been looked at the way he looks at me.

Again, I have to file that feeling away to examine later. Because I *know* I haven't. No one has *ever* looked at me the way Felix is right now—not with possession or jealousy or love, but raw need.

Unfiltered, savage, primal lust.

It's fucking intoxicating.

"Felix," I whisper.

He grips a double handful of my bare ass, making a rough sound of aggressive appreciation in his chest. "What?"

I try to roll over, but he prevents me.

"Not yet." He hooks fingers in the string sitting low on my waist. "Wanna rip this thing off."

"Don't," I whisper. "I haven't done laundry in a while. I don't have any more clean underwear." His growl is so frustrated that I can't help but laugh. "What if I promise to let you rip my thong off me another time?"

"Fine," he mutters.

His hands are busy, petting, caressing, kneading, squeezing—worshipping. He spends as much time just appreciating and exploring my ass as he did my tits, and all the while, my core is boiling with need, desire pooling low in my belly, heat building more with every minute I'm denied the release I need.

Because I'm starting to understand that the orgasm he gave me was just the beginning—for as much as it provided relief, it also only served to underline the true depths of my need.

Which is...borderline rabid.

I don't know myself.

This is so utterly unlike me that I don't know what to do, how to behave, and I have no control over myself, over my words, my hands, my thoughts—all I can do is hold the shield around my emotions in place and let my body take over.

"Felix," I murmur, wriggling impatiently. "Please."

He rumbles wordlessly. "Tell me what you want,

Ember." He kisses the small of my back. "Tell me what you need."

The kiss slips down, hopping the line of my thong to touch the upper swell of my ass. Lower, lower. Everywhere. His hands scratch my back in soothing circles, at odds with the fiery kisses he presses to my bottom. He rakes his fingers, splayed out, down my back, and this time he doesn't stop, but keeps them sliding down, taking my thong with them. I tip my hips up, and the thong pulls free, slipping out from the catch-point of my touching thighs with a snap. He drags it down to my knees, and I lift my feet to let him pull it off; I'm naked with a man for the first time in nearly a year.

His palms rake up my thighs, burn over the backs of them to sear against my ass cheeks, and then up my back to my shoulders, and now his weight is above me, hovering over me, and he's nuzzling my ear. "What do you need, Ember?"

"I need to come again, Fee," I whisper, the truth tumbling out of me, bold as you please.

He flips me to my back as if I'm no more than a porcelain doll, and I land with a bounce that has my tits rolling side to side; his gaze follows their movement hungrily, and he bends to kiss one, lick the other. I gasp, catch at his hair.

He suckles at my nipple, and a line of lightning sizzles from nipple to clit, forcing a whimper from me. That sound I make, the helpless whimper—it makes him crazy. He snarls like a lion, teeth nipping my aching, rigid nipple until I whimper again, and now his hand skates down the outside of my hip to my knee and slides back up between my thighs. Willingly, greedily, wantonly, I part my legs for his touch.

But he doesn't give it to me right away.

Anticipating it, needing it, I pant, waiting, wanting. When it doesn't come, when his hand carves up my hipbone to my belly, I growl in frustration. Tip my hips, indicating what I need.

His finger trails down my belly, over my mons pubis— My lungs seize, my eyes shut. He trails his touch over my seam, a delicate, tender quest of his index fingertip, barely touching. I gasp.

"Fee!" I whimper. "More. Please."

"Look at me, Ember." His voice holds a note of command.

In another extraordinarily unlikely turn of events, I find myself obeying. "What?" I whisper.

"I want you to look at me when I make you come." He fits his hand between my thighs, an inch or so down from my sex.

"Felix," I whisper, my riot of emotions noisy and demanding behind the shield. "Please." I can't put any of it into words.

I can only shut my eyes, shake my head.

He slips his finger down my seam again. "Ember."

I shake my head. "Don't make me."

Once more, his finger teases down my seam, trails down my lips, leaving a burning line on my skin. "Ember…"

I shake my head, swallowing hard. Build up the shield, push the emotions away. "Don't make me, Fee, please. I fucking *can't.*" I put my hand over his. "Please, Fee. Please. Just…touch me, please. Make me feel. Make my body feel." I whimper as his finger ghosts down again, this time delving in between my plump lips a tiny bit. "I can't bring my heart into it, Fee. Not yet. Don't make me. Please."

"Okay," he whispers. "I get you. I hear you."

Tears burn behind my eyes, guilt at feeling like I'm using him searing through me. "Fee, I...I want to. But I can't."

His weight shifts. His lips nuzzle mine. "Hey, it's okay. It's fine. I understand."

I shake my head. "You don't. You can't." I force my eyes open, knowing they shimmer wetly. "I'm using you, Fee. I need to—I need this. I can't explain it. But I *need* it. And I can't give you what you want. I'm sorry, Fee, I'm—I'm fucking—"

His mouth slams painfully into mine, shutting me up instantly as he kisses me—a hard, greedy, bruising kiss. I groan into his mouth at the sweep of his tongue, desperately lose myself in the kiss, throw myself into it. Heat builds behind my chest, swells behind my navel, spreads to my core, throbs in my sex, pulses in my clit.

He teases my slit with his finger, swiping up and down in short strokes against the lips with his fingernail, and I twitch at each slide, shiver at each touch. I whimper again as he sucks my tongue into his mouth and then opens his for me, offering himself to me, growling as I take his mouth, taste his tongue, his lips, his teeth.

He adjusts his weight to free his other hand, and now he's kissing me and teasing my pussy and caressing my tits, and my whimper becomes a gasp, and the gasp becomes a moan. When I moan, he growls, biting my lower lip, and then kisses his way down to my breasts. His mouth seizes my nipple while his fingers roll and tweak the other one, and now I'm gone, hips bucking as that searing shaft of heat and electricity crashes through me, lancing straight to my clit as if there's a live wire connecting my nipples to my clit.

When he nips one and pinches the other, I nearly come right then, crying out in a shrill voice—that's when his finger slips inside me, one thick digit penetrating my slick flesh.

His finger hooks and curls, expertly finding my sensitive, sacred place and massaging it with his fingertip, while his mouth and other hand lick and twist, suckle and pinch.

I scream through gritted teeth as an orgasm rips open inside me, and then Felix is sliding his lips down my belly and his mouth fuses to my pussy and his tongue slithers against my clit, and my scream goes hoarse and then silent as my climax detonates into fiery fury.

I arch off the bed, grinding my pussy against his ravenous, relentless mouth, and my hands bury in his soft cool hair and I clutch him to me and scream and gasp and whimper and moan and flex and fuck and thrust, lost in the enthralling mayhem of an orgasm unlike any I've ever felt in my life.

He adds a finger, and then a third, and now he's fucking me with his fingers, slicking them in and out and in and out, curling them in against my G-spot with each thrust, and his tongue is thrashing my clit side to side and up and down and circles in a patternless assault, and my pussy clamps around his sliding, plunging fingers and my screams are wild and loud and hoarse. He finds my nipple with his unoccupied hand and pinches it with sharp, rough pressure in a pulsing pattern timed to my clamping, clenching inner walls, and the orgasm shatters once more inside me, and I can't breathe for the intensity of it, can't scream, can't move—I'm bowed up off the bed, only my shoulders and heels pressed against the mattress.

I fall, crunch inward, sucking in a sobbing,

overwhelmed, shuddering gasp of oxygen, but his tongue swipes against me and his fingers fuck into me. I'm shaking all over, shuddering and spasming and curling inward and arching upward as wave after wave after crash through me.

Weeping uncontrollably, I none too gently shove Felix away from my pussy and clamp my legs closed, curling into a tiny ball as the waves wrack me like the aftershocks of an earthquake. He scoops me up in his arms and settles on the bed with me on his lap, sheltered in his arms, and he cradles my face on his bare, hard chest and his heart thuds steadily and comfortingly under my ear, and I cannot stop crying.

He just holds me through it—yet again.

When I come back to myself and my eyes are dry, I realize I must have passed out.

I blink up at him. "Did—did I pass out?"

He strokes my hair out of my face, smiling down at me with what can only be described as self-satisfied pride. "For a few minutes."

"How long is a few?" I ask.

A shrug. "Five minutes, maybe. Not long."

"Oh." I lick my lips, a different kind of desire flaming to life within me. "Felix, that was…hot as fuck."

"Yes, it certainly was." His lips brush my ear as he murmurs. "Getting to touch you, getting to see your gorgeous, perfect naked body, getting to make you come? Fucking privilege, honey."

"Fee," I whisper. "Don't be sweet. I can't handle it."

"I should be an asshole?"

I hold my forefinger and thumb apart an inch. "Maybe a tiny bit of asshole. For the sake of my heart."

He rumbles a laugh. "Not sure I can do that. You deserve all the sweetness in the fuckin' world, Ember."

I cannot answer that. I don't even examine it. Instead, I focus on the sensations in my body.

Limp, boneless, jellied legs. Still-twitching belly and core. Aching, throbbing nipples. Flushed, tingling skin. Heavy breasts.

What else?

Desire.

To touch. To give. To take.

I slide off of his body so my head is on his chest but my body is on the bed, and I look at him, taking in the hard planes of his face, the set of his jaw, the haze in his eyes. Soak in the glory of his muscled, shredded body, the anvil slabs of his pecs, the grooved wonderland of his abs. His boxer-briefs stretch around narrow hips, bulging with the hard-on he's been rocking for at least half an hour now, without letting me so much as touch it. Thick, hairy thighs, densely muscled and as defined as the rest of him.

My eyes slide back to the bulge of his cock. I lick my lips, swallow hard. His eyes are on me, but I can't read him.

I rest my hand on his belly. Watch him closely—his eyes narrow, his jaw sets, and his belly pulls in. He wants me to touch him, but he's fighting himself on it again.

Something tells me he has a hangup about something—letting me touch him seems to be a sticking point for him.

My greed for him only grows hotter the more I look at him. I let my hand drift south to the waistband of his underwear, holding his eyes.

"Ember," He breathes. "I…"

"Let me, Fee," I whisper. "Please."

He squeezes his eyes closed, drapes an arm over his face, the other hooked around my shoulders. A non-answer is as much as I'm going to get, I think, and I'll take it as permission.

I pull the elastic away from his belly and pull down, exposing his cock—and holy fuck, what an instrument the man is blessed with.

Getting the waistband past the bulbous head of his long, thick cock, I slide my hand to the other hip, pulling them lower. He lifts his ass and I strip them off—he toes them away from his feet and drops them off the side of the bed, and now he's naked for me.

I look again at his cock.

"Holy shit, Felix," I whisper.

He doesn't answer, except a loud gulp.

His cock is, to put it succinctly, a work of art. I don't know measurements because it doesn't matter, I just know it's long and thick and straight. A slightly lighter shade than the rest of his skin, it's pinkish and tan and studded with rippling purple veins and wreathed at the base with a thatch of dark, closely trimmed fuzz. The base of him is thicker than the top and the head is broad, fat, and round, glistening with his smeared pre-cum.

I slide my hand down his belly beneath his cock, so the soft weight of it rests on the back of my hand, watching his face, his expression.

His jaw tightens, and his breath comes short. "Fuck. Ember, I—"

"Hush," I say. "Just let me. I want to."

He shakes his head, but when I slide my hand out from under his cock and wrap my fingers around his thick hard shaft, he groans in raw, ragged relief. "Fuck, Ember. Jesus, I…"

I stroke him, then, down to his root, twist my fingers

around him a few times, and then slide my grip back up around his plump pink head. He jerks, curling forward, groaning—

And then he's gone, ripping himself out of my grip, rolling off the bed, and staggering toward the bathroom. He slams the door closed, but I hear him growling wordlessly, uneven, ragged groaning, panting.

Goddammit. Again?

I don't think so.

I roll off the bed and get to my feet, but I stumble and stagger the first few steps—I'm still jellied from the orgasm. Righting myself, I stalk to the bathroom and let myself in.

"Ember," he snarls. "Don't."

"Fuck that, Fee," I snap. "What's your deal? Why won't you let me touch you? You can touch me and make me come harder than I've ever come in my fucking life—I still can't walk properly, thank you very fucking much. But you won't let me return the favor? Who's this about? You or me?"

"Both." He's hunched over the sink, gripping the edge of it so hard his knuckles are white, shoulders bunched, spine bowed, cock jutting proudly upward and outward, begging for my touch.

"Well, let me update you on where I'm at right now, okay?" I duck under his arm and insinuate myself between him and the sink, and his cock nudges my belly. "I don't just need to receive, Felix. What I need is a full experience. You gave me half of it, and now I need the other half."

"I fucking *can't*, Ember," he growls.

"Why not? Why can you let yourself make me come, but you can't make yourself let me touch you?"

"I know. I'm sorry, I—"

"Don't be sorry. Explain it so we can get past it."

"We're not doing deep shit, I didn't think. I've got my own hangups, Ember."

"Clearly," I answer. "And that's okay. But, Fee, this has to go both ways. I'm not ready to get into deep shit. But this...I fucking need this—I *need* it. Okay? I..."

"Why?" he demands. "*Why* do you need it?"

"Because I was fucking *dead* inside, Felix!" I yell. "My husband died and I died with him. Okay? I was going through the motions of life, but I wasn't alive. I was...a zombie. And then I met you, and suddenly, I felt alive again. I saw you standing there in the road, and for the first time in almost a year, I *felt* something. And every second I spend with you, I feel more alive."

He opens his mouth to speak, but I touch his lips with my fingers.

"Let me talk, Fee."

He nods. "Okay, then."

"I'm not okay. I'm gonna have another breakdown at some point. That one earlier was just..." I shake my head and shrug. "The tip of the iceberg. My heart is fucked up. *I'm* fucked up. But I want to be alive again. I want to feel again. And I don't—I don't know how to explain it, but I need this. I need to feel like a woman again. I need to feel beautiful, wanted, and desired—and you give that to me. You make me *feel*. I can't deal with my emotions yet, but you let me feel other things. When you touch me, it reminds me that I'm not dead. I'm alive, and I'll be okay someday, and—and—" I cut off, shaking my head. "But it's not enough, Fee. I need *more*. I need *you*. I need to know I can..." I swallow hard. "I can still enjoy life. I can give pleasure."

"Ember, I just—"

"No, shut up and hear me, please. Sex, for me, is just as much about giving as receiving, and I need to do this. I want to. I want to make you feel good. We don't have to get into the deep shit—we will, soon, I promise. But I need this right now."

"And I don't know if I can," he whispers. "I...I did something a long time ago, and it messed me up. I did something wrong, and I'm...I don't deserve—" he shakes his head. "I can't."

"Did you hurt someone?" I ask.

"Not physically."

"You made a mistake."

He nods. "A big one. A bad one."

"And you're still punishing yourself for it." I rest my hand on his chest.

"Yeah, I guess so."

"So forgive yourself. You made a mistake. So what? It happens. You're human. We all fuck up. That doesn't mean you're not allowed to receive good things in your life ever again."

"I'm just...stuck. In my own mind. In my heart. I'm stuck."

I push against him, trapping his hard cock between our bodies—between my soft stomach and his hard abs. "Felix, maybe...maybe this is the start of the way forward. Letting yourself have something good. Something innocent."

He arches his eyebrows. "Innocent?"

"Yes, Fee, innocent! We're two consenting adults. I'm single, you're single—right?"

"Right."

"So, this is okay. This is good. This is just...two adults having fun together." I reach up and take his face in my hands. "I'm not ready to have sex with you, Felix. But I *do* want this much for right now. If you won't do it for yourself, do it for me? Let me use you. It's shitty of me—I'm hiding behind sex. I'm deflecting my emotional baggage by using you for physical pleasure."

"Is it still using me if I fully understand what you're doing and continue to allow it?" he asks.

"I dunno. I just want to be clear about what's happening, because this is..." I shake my head. "I don't know who I am right now. This is...it almost feels like an out-of-body experience—I'm not like this. It takes me a long time to open up to men, and I usually need a strong emotional connection with someone before I can even feel attraction, much less feel comfortable with sex. But you, Felix..." I shake my head. "It's totally different with you, and it's freaking me out, because I want this, I fucking need it, and I want it and need it so desperately it scares me, but I'm not looking at how I feel at all, I'm just...I'm letting my body take what it wants, and it wants you." I rub my face. "It makes no sense, I know."

"It doesn't have to make sense," he says. He licks his lips, sighing, thinking. "Ember, I...I want to let you. Believe me."

"You've had an erection for a long time. It has to be uncomfortable."

He closes his eyes, nodding. "It hurts."

I gyrate against him sinuously. "So let me help." I kiss his jaw, beside his ear, then whisper to him. "Whatever happened, Felix, it's in the past. I promise you, you're the only one holding it against you."

"I was young and dumb."

"Don't tell me anything else, Fee. For now, this is just...bodies. Physical need." I kiss his cheek beside his nose, his lips, his jawline. Whisper in his ear again. "We'll share everything. I promise. Later. For now, we just feel. Can you do that with me, Fee?"

He nods jerkily. "I'll...I'll try."

"Good." I take him by the hand and lead him out of the bathroom to the bed, turn us to push him backward until the bed hits his knees and he sits, falling backward to lean on his hands. "All you have to do is let me make you feel good and we'll figure the rest out later."

His eyes lock on mine as I stand between his knees. "Ember, you're so fucking beautiful."

I trail my fingertips up his thighs. "So are you, Felix."

Heart palpitating, pulse thundering in my ears, I grasp his cock, stroking him from tip to root—I sigh in anticipation and pure female appreciation as his thick hard shaft slides slowly through my loosely curled fingers, and I relish each stutter of his veins, the smear of his essence on my palm and fingers, the delicate give of his fat round head as I squeeze.

Felix throws his head back, groaning. "Jesus."

I grin at the raw wonder in his voice. "I'm just getting started, Fee." I lean into him, kiss him as I caress his length again, a long, slow slide of my fist down his shaft. "You have an absolutely gorgeous cock, by the way."

All he can do in response is groan, and I'm okay with that.

I sink to my knees between his powerful thighs, kiss his chest, his belly, lick the grooves of his abs, plunging my hand around his cock in slow sensual strokes. He moans, eyes closing, hips tipping up. I clutch his cock in both hands and carve them down, but I don't stop when I reach his root—I keep my hands caressing down to cup his balls, squeezing delicately, massaging gently. His groan goes guttural at this, and my smile of enjoyment makes my cheeks hurt.

"You like that?" I ask.

"Fuck yes," he snarls. "So fucking amazing, Ember."

"This?" I breathe, twisting one hand around his glans, smearing his leaking essence while I stroke down his throbbing shaft with the other. When I reach his root, I cup his balls again, kneading and squeezing and playing with them while I caress his length with my other hand, down, down, down. I trade hands, bringing the first back up to his plump, straining head while massaging his balls with the other.

"Oh, fuck—fuck, Ember. Jesus, that feels so fucking good, I—*fuck*." His voice is raw and ragged.

"Watch me, Fee," I whisper.

HIs head snaps up and his eyes fly open, and he watches me repeat the process, massaging his balls with one hand and stroking his cock with the other, and then trading, and then caressing his hard length with both hands and playing with his balls with both—and then one hand and the other again, repeating the process until he's growling nonstop and his hips are flexing.

When I sense he's close, I focus on his balls, and now I lean close to him, kissing his hipbone, his belly, his other hip, his thigh, his belly again, everywhere but where I know he wants it most.

He falls backward to the bed and his hands clench into fists, press into his eyes, and he groans, bucking upward and sinking back to the bed as I continue to massage his taut, heavy sack with both hands.

"Ember," he whispers. "Fuck. Fuck, I—"

"What?" I whisper. "Say it. Tell me what you want. Tell me what you need."

"Fucking hurts. So hard it hurts."

"What do you need, Fee?" I ask again.

"I need to come," he hisses, voice hoarse and rough.

I laugh. "Oh, you're gonna come, trust that, baby." Baby? Fuck me. Where did that come from? My heart twists in my chest, but I shut it down, push it aside, shove it all behind the shield and focus every shred of my attention on him, on his big, beautiful cock.

As I continue to play with his balls, ignoring his cock, Felix starts to thrust, needing more. "Ember, fuck. I—please."

"Please, what, Fee? Say it. Ask me for anything."

"Put your hands on me."

I grasp him with both hands, give him a soft, slow, lingering caress. "Like that?"

"Fuck yes."

"What else?"

His eyes open and his fists smack into the bed at his sides, and he bucks into my hands as I plunge them down his cock in a slow hand-over-hand movement. "More."

"More what?"

His glacier-blue eyes fix on mine, warring, fraught, conflicted. "I…"

I lick his salty flesh from the crease of his thigh to his navel. "I want to hear you ask for what you want, Felix." I lick the same line again, and then inward an inch, closer to his cock—my cheek nuzzles along his shaft. "Ask me. Tell me. Tell me what you want."

"Your mouth," he growls, "I need your mouth, Ember."

I lick him on the other side, and then grin up at him. "Ask…and you shall receive."

Eyes locked on his, I pull his shaft away from his belly, cupping it so I can lick the underside of it from balls to tip. His belly curls in and his balls tug up against his shaft as he tenses, anticipating…

There's no teasing, now. I give him what he asked for—my mouth, rolling over his fat, leaking head, tasting his smoky, salty, tangy pre-cum on my tongue.

"Oh, fuck," he snarls. "Ember, fuck—*fuck*!"

I let him pop free, grinning at him as he stares down his body at me in awe. "How's that feel?"

"Too fucking good."

"I can make it even better."

His groan is disbelieving. "Feels like heaven already."

I laugh. "It can get better."

"How?"

"Like this."

I take him in my mouth again and cup his balls in both hands, massaging them as I slide my lips down his shaft, taking as much of him as I can—which isn't much; I have a quick gag reflex. I make up for not being able to throat much of his impressively long cock by eagerly suctioning around his head, slopping as far down as I dare and back up.

He bucks up suddenly, groaning, and I know he's building toward that orgasm I'm so greedy for. I keep cradling and caressing and squeezing his tender soft heavy balls in one hand while grasping his thick, pulsing root in the other, my mouth busily and messily glomming around his glans, my tongue swiping and smearing and licking with each bob of my head.

He grunts raggedly and his hands settle on my shoulders; I reach up and guide them into my hair. He gathers my long, loose hair, wraps the thick mass of it around one fist and rests the other on the back of my neck.

"Mmmmmm," I hum, smiling up at him as I let him pop free of my mouth. "Show me how you want it, Fee. Take it from me."

"God, Ember, you're so fucking sexy, Jesus. I don't deserve this—don't deserve you."

"Shut the fuck up with that," I snap. "You do. You deserve this. You know why? Because I'm choosing to give it to you. The only words I wanna hear are encouragement. Tell me how good it feels. Tell me when you're coming."

"Yes ma'am," he says, grinning at me for the first time since we started this.

"Good boy," I tease. "Now show me how you want it."

"Open your mouth for me," he mutters.

I part my lips, gazing up at him from beneath my eyebrows. "Like this?"

"Yeah," he murmurs, "Just like that."

"I need your cock, Fee," I whisper. "Fucking give it to me right now."

He growls, guiding me down to his cock. I stick out my tongue so it's the first thing he feels, and I keep my eyes locked on his, barely daring to even blink. His silky soft, hard-as-iron cock slides over my tongue, and I taste his flesh and then I taste his pre-cum as he starts to fill my mouth.

"Oh god, fuck yeah, Ember. Take it."

"Mmmm," I say, whispering into his leaking tip as if it's a microphone. "You like that? Is it good?"

"So fucking good. Do it again, Ember. Please."

"Oooh," I say with a laugh. "I like it when you beg."

"Fucking take it, Ember," he growls. "Please. Take it all. Suck my cock and don't stop till I come."

"I could make it take an hour," I tell him, in between licks of his tip and glans. "Draw it out until you lose your fucking mind."

"I already am. I've been so hard it hurts for so fucking long, I can't take it any longer. I need to come." He cups my jaw, brushes a thumb over my lips. "Wrap this pretty little mouth around my cock and don't stop until you've taken my cum."

"Ahhh fuck," I groan. "Keep talking to me, Fee."

I circle his cock with my lips and take him to the edge of my gag reflex, back away, licking and swirling with my tongue, using both hands on his balls as I start to work his pulsing shaft with my mouth.

"Ember, fuck. So fucking good." His voice is rough and feral, his grip on my hair tight, even though he's not pressuring me to take any more than I'm comfortable with. "Your sweet, sexy mouth is fucking heaven. Oh fuck, yeah, just like that. Keep going, please. Please, don't stop."

"Mmmm-mmmm," I hum the negative, squeezing his balls as hard as I dare while softly, slowly, gently bobbing my mouth around his glans, taking no more than an inch or two, but taking those few inches with my tongue and lips, all suction and saliva. "You gonna come for me, Fee?" I whisper.

"So hard," he answers, now pushing down on my head a little. "Is it okay if I do that?"

"Mmmmm-hmmm!" I hum, the agreement eager.

"Fuck, you feel so good. So fucking hot watching you suck my cock, Ember."

"Mmmmm," I groan. "Come for me, baby."

There's that damn word again.

Ignore.

I pull away, sinking back to sit on my heels, and pull him to his feet. Gaze up at him. Pull his cock toward me and slide him into my mouth and to the back of my throat, keeping my gaze up on his.

Focus on the feel of his cock in my mouth—jaw stretched wide, salty flesh against my tongue and lips, pre-cum dripping into my mouth, his balls squishing in my hands, pulsing and twitching as he nears his climax. I tongue his sliding shaft, taste veins and skin. I keep one hand on his taut balls while clawing the other into his ass, pulling at him—the muscle is hard and the skin warm and fuzzy with hair. I clutch one cheek, dig my nails in, and then the other. Cover the crack and claw at both sides, pulling him into me to encourage him to move, to fuck.

I want his orgasm more than I want my next breath— it's a manic desperation I don't dare look at, I just go with it. Let it take over my whole being. I'm wild with need, greedy for his cum, his pleasure, eager to know how he sounds when he comes, mad to feel his body tense and his muscles harden, desperate to hear him curse and growl, call my name, beg me to not stop.

He starts to move. He grips my hair tight enough that my scalp pulls, and he pushes me down while thrusting. "Mmm!" I moan. "Yes! Take me. Show me, Fee. Give me everything." The words are whispered swiftly, my mouth wrapping around him again as fast as possible.

Faster now, I move on his cock, mouth sliding and stuttering—I pull him free and produce saliva, let it fill my mouth, drop it onto his tip and then cover him with my mouth again, and now my lips glide easily down his spit-slick length.

"Ohhhh fuck, honey, god that's incredible. I'm so fucking close."

"Mmmmmm!" I groan, gripping his ass in both hands now, palms on his hard muscle, fingers digging in, pulling hard at him, pulling him deeper, faster. He pops out of my mouth for a moment. "Fuck my mouth, Fee. Come for me. I want you. I fucking want it. I want your cum, Fee. Give it to me."

I'm an alien inside my own body, a wild creature of pure sexual frenzy, a desperation I never knew existed, never knew I was capable of. I don't recognize myself at all, and yet I like this new self. She's free, she's wild, she's a little crazy and a lot filthy.

New chapter of life, new me, I guess.

Felix unlocked something in me, brought me to life and now I'm half-feral with an all-consuming need that will not be denied, cannot be quenched.

He's about to try, though.

"Ah, god, oh fuck—Ember, fuck." He uses his grip on my hair to push me onto his cock, but it's careful, gentle, almost sweet. "Oh god, I'm gonna come, Ember."

I feel it. I cup his balls and claw at his ass and suction around his glans, pull away to lick his frenulum until he jerks, hissing, and then I swallow his hard hot length all over again, and I'm rewarded with a long low growl and the wild pulse of his balls in my hand as they prepare to unleash his orgasm. His cock pulses, pounds in my mouth, and I let my saliva pool and coat his length and drip down his shaft and leak out of my mouth as I sloppily swallow around the broad salty head of his surging cock.

"Oh fuck oh fuck oh fuck, Ember!"

"Mmm-hmmm!"

He grips my head in both hands now, and hunches over me, hips pumping hard, thrusting himself between my lips. I pull at his ass and let him move, meet him thrust for thrust, humming my enjoyment of this act.

"Oh f-f-f-fuck!" He shouts. "Ember!"

I whimper a shrill, eager sound of encouragement, jerking his taut, flexing ass toward me, fingernails digging into marble-hard muscle. And then he arches backward, thrusting into my mouth, into my throat, fingers clawing into my scalp, head thrown back, and I taste his release, a salty flood of cum.

I gulp it down, open my mouth to pant for breath, and then take him to the back of my throat and bob there, feeling the next rush spurt directly down my throat—I swallow frantically, desperately, gulping and panting, backing away to move around his head again. I capture his balls in my hands and squeeze them, massaging—fit my middle finger along his taint and press, and he shouts wordlessly, a guttural roar as he shoots another hot wet load of cum into my mouth. The next release is right on the heels of the last one, and I can't swallow it all. He surges into my mouth with his spasm of release, and the movement forces cum to leak out of the corners of my mouth and dribble down his shaft. I let him out and lick it away, pump his length with both hands, jacking him hard and fast, relentlessly, until my hands blur. He staggers, legs giving out, and falls to his ass on the bed—I follow him, sucking around his tip with my tongue twiddling his frenulum, and he grunts, thrusts helplessly. He spurts one more time, a little trickle leaking out of him onto my tongue, but I'm not done.

Even after he's done coming, I swallow around his shaft and caress his slick, sticky length, bobbing on him until he grunts helplessly, breathlessly, spasming again, even though nothing comes out.

I go down on him until he's softening in my mouth, and only then do I let him go and sit back on my heels, raking my fingers down his hard, flexed abs as they ripple with his panting breath.

"Holy fuck," he gasps.

"Was it okay?" I ask coyly.

"*Okay?* Jesus. I didn't know a blowjob could feel that way."

I tap the tip of his cock as it dangles. "That was fucking hot, Felix. I loved doing that to you."

He gazes down at me, jaw clenching, eyes primal with arousal. He cups my jaw, thumb wiping at the corner of my mouth. He presses his thumb against my lips, and I open for him, tasting a faint tang of his cum.

"Good girl," he praises. "Taking every last drop."

My thighs press together at his praise. "Mmmmm... fuck, Felix." I gaze up at him, and I know my expression must be damn near reverent—every bit as much as his is as he looks at me. "Love how you talk to me like that."

"Never been one for dirty talk," he mutters, "but you—fuck, Gorgeous, you do something to me."

"Same. I don't know who I am with you, Felix, but I admit I like it."

He takes my hands and helps me stand up—my knees hurt from being on them for so long. He seems to anticipate this, because he bends to grab my ass and lift me off my feet.

He claims my mouth with a savage kiss. "You're fucking incredible, Ember James."

I feel it again—the surge of overwhelmed emotion.

His praise undoes me. Turns me on, thrashes my heart.

I'm about to start bawling again, even as I feel so turned on I could...god, what wouldn't I do?

He cups my face. "You gonna cry again?"

I can only nod, the tears starting despite my efforts to hold them back. "I—I'm sorry. I'm sorry, I—fuck, fuck, I—"

He sinks onto the bed and takes me with him to his back, cradling me to his chest, strong arms pinioning me, securing me.

"No apologies between us, Ember. Give me all you got. I can take it."

Those words are the last straw—I can take it.

I give it to him. All the sorrow, all the turmoil, all the conflict.

I break apart in his arms all over again.

9

Felix

THIS IS A CONFUSING SET OF SENSATIONS.

On one hand, she's naked in my arms, soft skin silk smooth and warm, her big lush tits pressed against my chest and draped on my arm, knees drawn up to present her ass in a broad, intoxicating curve that my hand naturally rests upon as I hold her; yet, on the other hand, she's bawling raggedly, her whole body wrenched with sob after sob.

There's nothing I can do or say, so I just hold her. Rub her arms, caress her thigh and ass, nuzzle the top of her head and inhale her scent.

I lose track of time again, and this time she doesn't fall asleep. She slowly calms down, the wracking sobs subsiding to hiccuping whimpers. Her hand rests on my pec, curled up like a sleeping sparrow. Her breath washes warm on my skin.

"His name was Richard Declan James," she whispers. "But everyone, his parents included, called him Dutchie. The story, as he told it to me, is that his grandmother, who was from the Netherlands, made Dutch Apple turnovers one day when he was four or five. He loved them so much he ate six or seven of them and got sick, but even after that, whenever his grandmother came to visit he demanded she make dutchies, as he called them. It became a whole joke in the family, and they all started calling him Dutchie, and it stuck."

"His name was Rick James?" I ask.

She sniffs a tiny laugh. "Yes. The other reason he went by Dutchie." She shivers. "I'm cold."

I shimmy and tug the blanket out from beneath us and drape it over us, settling it on her shoulders. She grips the edge, tucks it under her chin, and then settles her curled-up hand on my chest once more.

"I met him when I was twenty. A year after Mom died."

"How'd she die?" I ask.

She shakes her head. "Forgot I didn't tell you—I told Faye. Um. She was a Phishhead. Like, as a lifestyle. I grew up nomadic, living in that same van out there, following Phish around the country. I was homeschooled by Mom's friends—by her commune. She was a real deal hippy, smoked pot, sold drugs and merch to make ends meet. When they weren't touring, we'd stay in a long-term rental hotel and Mom would get a real job and save up for the next leg of the tour, or we'd head to Florida to spend time with GramGram. But mostly, we were on the road."

"Jesus—for real?"

She nods. "For real."

"That's...kinda crazy."

She sighs. "I know. But it was my life. I've never stayed in a real actual house for more than a few weeks. I've never owned a TV."

"So living in your van is just...normal for you."

"Exactly." A long sigh. "So, when I was nineteen, Mom cut her leg somehow at a show. It got infected, like a staph infection or necrotizing whatever it's called. Fasciitis... something like that. I don't know. The show was in the country, way out in the middle of nowhere, far as fuck from a hospital, which she wouldn't have gone to anyway, since she hated the government, hospitals, doctors, all of it. It happened *so* fast, Fee. She got cut, didn't think anything of it, started feeling sick, and then by the time we realized how serious it was, it was too damn late. She died not even a week after it happened."

"Fuck me, that's awful," I murmur. "I'm so sorry."

"It was awful. I was so lost. She was my life. I went where she went. Did what she did. Her commune was my family. And then she was just fucking gone in the blink of an eye and I was alone in the world. For most of a year, I just wandered around the west coast from San Diego to Seattle, doing nothing, going nowhere, just...lost." A pause, rife with the weight of her memories. "I ran out of money outside Portland, so I lived in the bus and found work at a farm. Dutchie's family's farm. They grew hops for a local brewery and raised goats and pigs. I was sad and lonely, and Dutchie was an only child. So we...clicked. It became a romance. He was patient with me, and god, I needed patience. I was angry and shut down and *so* sad, and I liked him but I didn't know how to—" she shrugs. "How to express it. He drew it out of me. I lived on their farm for a year and a half, and in that time Dutchie and I...became a couple, I guess. His family accepted it, accepted me, took me in. Showed me kindness. But I got restless, and when I told Dutchie I wanted to leave he decided to come with me. He'd been talking about leaving home for a while, and I gave him the excuse. So we left together."

"What was he like?" I ask.

I feel her mouth curve with a private smile. "Sweet. Endlessly sweet. He was kinda short, only five-eight. Slender, but strong—he was a farm boy. Sandy blond hair, brown eyes. Real puppy dog eyes. The boy had a smolder for the ages—he could convince me to do just about anything with this look he'd give me. He knew it, too, and definitely took advantage of it."

I chuckle. "I bet he did."

She tilts her head to look up at me. "Does it upset you? Hearing about him?"

I shake my head. "Not at all."

"Sure?"

"Absolutely. You can tell me anything."

Another thoughtful sigh. "He was a virgin when we met, and because of how I was, we didn't sleep together until after we left his farm."

"How you were? What does that mean?" I ask.

"I've identified as a demisexual for a long time."

"Don't know what that is."

"Someone who has to establish a strong emotional connection before any kind of sexual contact is possible." She must feel me thinking, because she huffs a laugh. "Thus why I said that what we just did is so unusual for me. We

just met. I barely know you. Maybe I never was demisexual, maybe I was just...a heartbroken kid who fell very
slowly in love. I dunno."

"I couldn't say. Not sure a label is necessary, if you ask
me, but that's up to you."

A shrug. "I dunno—I have a lot of reflection to do, I
guess." A pause. "Things developed very slowly, like I said.
It was a full year before I even kissed him, and then almost
two months before I was comfortable going any further,
and he never rushed me, never expressed any kind of im-
patience. He was just...so damn sweet all the time."

"Sounds like it. That's a lot of patience for a
twenty-year-old kid."

"That's Dutchie for you. Wise beyond his years. He
was the definition of an old soul. Patient. Kind. Not an aggressive bone in his body." Pause. Her voice goes soft, hesitant. "Sex with him was...soft and sweet. Passionate, but
always sweet. And that's what I needed. My, um...my first
time wasn't great, and it sorta messed me up, but that's a
story for another time."

"Doesn't have to be," I say. "Up to what you feel ready
to share."

She sighs. "Okay, well, here you go, then. A quick aside
to tell the awful story of how Ember lost her virginity and
regretted it forever." A lip-fluttering sigh. "I was sixteen, and
I'd lived my whole life, as previously established, with Mom
and her commune. Being hippies, they were all about free
love and were totally okay with nudity. That's why I'm fine
showing a lot of skin—I grew up seeing people naked and
being naked around people from a very young age. It was
never a big deal—it's just bodies. But they were also very
free with sex. It was common to walk into a trailer or RV

or whatever and see people having sex, or having just had sex. But I hadn't been with anyone, and I was ready. But I was also looking for love. I was a romantic sixteen-year-old, you know? I wanted a big, crazy love, and I didn't want my first time to be with the person I loved. I knew it would be awkward and probably not great. So I..." she sighs, but it's more of a growl. "We were living in Atlanta between tours, and there was a guy who lived in the unit a few doors down from ours in the motel. We started flirting, and I made it clear I wanted to sleep with him. I told him I was a virgin."

Another long pause. I can sense that this isn't going to go well.

"At first, he was cool about it. Kissed me. Touched me. All that first base, second base, third base stuff. But then, once he was ready to have sex, he...he just went for it. Turned into ramjet the rookie. He wasn't gentle about it. He just—" a shudder, a shake of her head. "He fucked me, *hard.*"

"Jesus," I snarl. "What an asshole."

"Yeah," she whispers. "I asked for it, so I can't say it was rape, and I do mean that literally. I gave him my verbal consent before we started. I just...I didn't think he'd do *that*. He was—it was *painful*. Excruciating. And he wouldn't stop. Kept moving me around like it was a porn shoot."

This makes my blood boil. "How old was he?"

A long pause. "Twenty."

I go still, fighting my fury. I only realize how unsuccessful I am when she squeaks in protest. "Fee, you're squeezing too hard. It hurts."

"Fuck," I snap, immediately loosening my grip. "I'm sorry, Ember. I just...that was assault, you know. Consent is one thing, so is it technically rape? Maybe not. That's not for me to decide. But it *absolutely* categorically *was* sexual assault. *And* statutory rape."

"I was sixteen, and the age of consent in Georgia is sixteen."

"Fuck that." I growl, fury boiling my blood. "What's his name?"

"Felix, stop." She twists to gaze up at me, tugging my chin down. "It was over ten years ago."

"Doesn't matter. He oughta have his fucking skull caved in with a framing hammer."

"Felix!" she snaps, angry now. "*Stop* it!"

I growl again, a long rumble of fury. "You were sexually assaulted by a grown man. Makes me fucking furious." I try to calm myself with some deep breaths, but it doesn't do dick. "The phrase 'murderous rage' comes to mind."

She rolls to her belly on me, tits draped onto my chest like heavy warm silk weights. She cups my jaw in her hands, nuzzling my chin with her lips. "I'm okay, Fee. Really, I am." She shimmies higher, snaking her arms around my neck and burying her nose and mouth in the side of my neck. "No violence, okay?"

I let out a sigh. "As long as I never see that motherfucker."

I feel calmer; it has more to do with Ember's embrace, the warmth and softness of her skin against mine and the press of her curves than any deep breathing I might do, and certainly not because she doesn't like violence. If I came face-to-face with that fuckstain, he wouldn't be walking away. I don't tell him that, though.

"You're still stewing," she murmurs. "You gotta let it go. I'm over it."

"How'd you know?" I ask.

She snickers. "You're tensed up harder than a brick wall." She nips my earlobe. "Do I need to relax you again?"

I can't help but laugh. "Yeah, maybe." I palm her ass. "Keep telling your story. Please."

"Okay, but no more murder talk."

"Is there any more sexual assault?"

"No."

"Then we're good."

She stays like she is, arms around my neck, fingers laced at my nape, cheek on my clavicle. "So okay—the point in telling you that was that Dutchie was the healing I needed. I didn't trust anyone after that. But he...he had the patience of a saint. I watched him sit in a meadow once with a handful of birdseed. He sat there and waited without moving for so long that a bird landed on his hand and ate the seed."

I snort. "Bullshit."

She raspberries my neck. "You calling me a liar?"

"Yes."

"I took a picture. It's on my phone. Remind me to show you later—I'm comfortable and I'm not getting up right now."

"I wouldn't let you get up."

She giggles, which does delicious things to her curves. The giggle vanishes, replaced by a sigh. "For a while, we just traveled. I let him pick where we went because by then I'd already seen pretty much all of the contiguous US. I don't remember which one of us had the idea, but we decided to try being van life vloggers."

"What now?"

"Hashtag van-life. It's a whole thing on social media.

We were one of the first accounts. We bought some equipment and started recording our travels, our lives living out of my bus. Eventually, we got a sponsor, and then another, and after a couple years we were able to stop taking random work and live off our sponsorships."

"So you were, like, professionally nomadic."

"Yup."

"Wow." I nuzzle her temple. "Pretty fuckin' cool."

She grins against my cheek. "You really think so?"

"Hell yeah, I do."

She's quiet for a while, and then sighs. "It was a good life we had. Way outside the norm, but it was ours. Dutchie loved it. He'd lived his whole life on that farm, and I mean he never once left even the county he lived in until we left. So traveling the country, seeing so much of it? He fucking loved every second of it. He had a passion for life, Fee. Everything was an adventure, even when things went wrong. He was never cranky, never yelled at me. We almost never argued. And if we did, it was about stupid shit and we made up fast."

She shudders, shakes her head.

"We got married in a little white chapel in Roanoke, Virginia, two years after we left Portland. It was a justice of the peace and three people we'd met in town." Ember swallows hard. "My wedding dress was a little white sundress. I loved it because it had pockets, and he loved it because my boobs looked great in it. He bought a suit off the rack that fit like shit, but I still thought he looked super handsome."

"Mmm," I growl. "You in a little white sundress."

She giggles. "I don't have that one anymore—our luggage got stolen out of the van in Red Hook, New Jersey a couple years later. But I do have other sundresses. I'll wear one for you."

"Who the hell steals someone's luggage?" I grumble.

"Assholes," she murmurs, "that's who. Dutchie used it as an excuse to spend a week nude. That was fun. He only put on clothes when we had to go into a town. Eventually we got tired of it and bought new clothing."

"He sounds amazing."

"He was. I loved him with my whole heart. We were together for almost eight years." A long silence. "And then he got pancreatic cancer. It started as pancreatic and metastasized before we knew he had it. By the time we knew he was sick, it was everywhere. He didn't live a month past the diagnosis." Her voice drops to a whisper I have to strain to hear, even with her mouth inches from my ear. "His death was fast and agonizing. Just…just like Mom. It was so fucking fast, I barely had time to process that he was sick, that he was gonna die, and then he was gone."

"What…" I clear my throat, emotion thick in my throat. "What about his family?"

She doesn't answer for a long time. "His father passed of a heart attack while plowing a field a few months before we got married. We drove back for the funeral. His mom died of a broken heart, essentially, just a few months later."

"The man buried both parents within months of each other?"

She nods. "Yeah, he did."

"Fuck, man."

"It's part of what bonded us. We were both alone in the world." She pats my chest. "There. Now you know."

"Thank you for sharing that with me, Ember."

She wriggles and then goes still. "Where are you, with us?"

I sigh. "I…I don't know. That was…fucking magical. But I…there's so much beneath it, you know?"

"You're not talking about my story."

"No."

She nods, sighs. "I'm struggling with it, if I'm being honest." She lifts up to meet my eyes. "Not you. And I don't regret it. Not at all. Just the opposite, and that's the problem."

"I guess I'm not following," I admit.

Sighing, Ember rolls off me and scootches up to a sitting position, tucking the quilt under her arms. "It's hard to explain, and I'm not sure how much you really want to hear."

"Why wouldn't I?" I ask.

"Because in order for it to make any sense, I'd have to talk in some detail about my relationship with Dutchie. Sexually, I mean."

"I mean…" I stare into space, taking the time to truly consider what she's saying and how it'd feel. "I'd really like to understand, Ember. I know it might be a little awkward or uncomfortable, but it's important. It's not my call, though. It's your story to tell, and only if it's not too painful to talk about."

She rakes stiffened fingers through her hair, nodding absently. "It's going to be painful. But there's nothing about this that isn't." She glances at me. "I just…I'm confused."

"Did…" I wince, not wanting to ask the question for fear that the answer will be yes. "Did this—you and me, just now…did it confuse you even more?"

She barks a laugh. "Fuck yes it did, Fee. It didn't confuse me *more*—it's the entire reason I'm confused."

I sigh, thunking my head against the headboard. "Oh."

She looks at me, smiling. "Don't take that personally, Felix. It's not about you, it's about…everything. Me losing Dutchie. How I came into my sexuality with him after what happened with Rob." She points at me. "I'm not telling you his last name. Murdering him won't do anything for me."

I hold up my hands palms out. "Fine. No murders."

"I was…both innocent and jaded by the time I met Dutchie. Like I said, I grew up seeing sex and nudity regularly, so it wasn't some weird foreign concept to me. And I'd had sex. Which, up until he actually got inside me, was actually pretty enjoyable. The initial exploration, I mean. Kissing, touching, all that. I liked it. He was a good-looking guy, an older guy, a bad boy, tattoos, rode a motorcycle, all that."

"Everyone likes a bad boy until he does something bad," I say.

She snorts. "No shit. Learned that one the hard way. Anyway, after what happened with Rob—after he sexually assaulted me—" she trails off, staring at nothing, and I see her eyes go hazy.

"Ember?" I ask, turning toward her. "Hey. What is it?"

A shake of her head. "Just—I…I never framed it in those terms, in my mind. I guess I knew it wasn't *right*, but I've never, like, identified as a survivor of sexual assault. It sort of skews my whole perspective on it. On everything." She sniffles, swipes her middle fingers under her eyes. "It was traumatic. I was scarred by it. It went from being something I'd been enjoying to terrifying and painful like that—" she snaps her fingers. "And he wouldn't stop.

I told him I didn't like it. I asked him to stop, to be gentle. He—" She shakes her head. "It doesn't matter."

"Have you ever spoken about it? Like, told the whole story to anyone?"

A small shake of her head. "I told Dutchie pretty much what I told you. There are details I've never...never been brave or strong enough to talk about."

"You can tell me." I face her sitting cross-legged, the quilt across my lap.

"I don't know if I can, Fee," she whispers.

"And you don't have to. But..." I rub my jaw. "When Riley got out of prison, there were things that he saw, things he had to do on the inside that really fucked him up. And until he told someone about it, like got it out of him and into the world, he was a fucking mess. He had panic attacks all the time. That's how I knew how to help you when you had yours. Maybe a professional therapist is a better option for you. God knows I'm not one. I'm just saying, I'm here. I'll listen."

"Part of me is like, I've cried enough today. I fucking *hate* crying, and it feels like all I've done with you is fucking cry and be all emotional and shit." She shakes her head, running her hair through her fists. "But then, I also feel like if I don't get it out now, I never will."

"Up to you. I'm here for whatever you need."

She gives me a smile—grateful, sweet, tender. "I can't with you, Fee. You're too fucking sweet."

"Sorry. I'll try to be more of an asshole."

She looks at me with wide, bugging out eye. "I was kidding, I hope you realize that. Please don't change, Fee."

I laugh. "I know. I couldn't intentionally be a dick to

you if I tried. Which is not to say I'm not gonna do something stupid and asshole-ish on accident."

She lets out a sharp, short sigh. "I can't do it here, like this." She slips out of bed and traipses naked to my closet. "Can I borrow a shirt?"

"Of course."

She pulls open the tri-fold door, flips through my limited selection of button-downs, and selects a plain white one. She slips it on, buttons it, and rolls the sleeves to her elbows. The hem falls to just below her butt, and with the top three buttons left undone, her goddamned magnificent cleavage is on mouthwatering display.

She opens my bedroom door, pausing in the doorway. "Coming?"

"Yep." I hop out of bed and grab a pair of workout shorts from my bureau, following her out of my room.

I'd expected her to sit on the couch, or at the island in the kitchen, or on the deck. Instead, she goes out the front door, clambers up onto the flatbed—incidentally flashing her bare ass, which she doesn't seem to notice or care about—and tugs open the sliding door of her VW. She rummages in an upper cabinet and comes back with a small leather zipper bag, a toiletries case kind of thing. She hops down, shuts the door, and breezes back into the house and out onto the back deck.

"What's in there?" I ask.

"The only way I'll get through this." She sits in one of my Adirondacks with her legs crossed and opens the case.

Inside is cannabis paraphernalia—several glass jars with dried flower, a glass pipe, rolling papers, a grinder, and several glass tubes containing pre-rolled joints.

She glances at me. "You okay with this?"

I shrug. "Sure. It's recreationally legal in Michigan."

"But you don't use it?"

I shake my head. "No. Never got into it."

"It was obviously a common thing in my life, and Dutchie grew up outside Portland where it's been recreationally legal since like 2014, I think." She opens one of the pre-rolled joints, finds a lighter in the case, and sets the open case aside. Lights the joint, takes a long inhale. Hands it to me.

I hesitate, and then sit in the other Adirondack next to her, and take the joint. "Can't hurt, I guess."

She laughs. "Just take a hit or two. I don't want to be responsible for you greening out."

"Greening out?"

"Get so high you can't function."

"Oh, yeah, don't want that."

"So just take a little puff, inhale it, and blow it out right away. No need to hold it—that doesn't do anything." She watches me take a small puff, laughing when I dissolve into hacking. "Now wait a bit and see how that feels."

She takes a much longer hit, closing her eyes and exhaling the smoke in a thick, rolling cloud. She scoots down in the chair and kicks her legs out ankle over ankle, rests her head against the chair back, and takes another long hit. Passes it to me. I take another puff, and now I'm starting to feel...

Loose. A little floaty, as if my head is a balloon. Mellow.

I grin. "Not bad."

She smiles at me. "I rarely drink. This is my vice." The smile fades, the distance of memory occluding her expression. "Hard not to think of him, though."

There's nothing to say to that, so I say nothing.

She smokes in silence for a while. I wave off another hit. She puts it out about halfway through it, and puts it back in the tube, then closes her eyes and just sits in silence for a few minutes.

"It was...it was horrific." She's speaking barely above a whisper. "We kissed. Got each other naked. He fingered me—that felt good. I'd done that for myself, so I knew what that felt like. I touched him—the first time I'd touched a penis. I liked it a lot. He..." she sighs, voice shaking. Starts over. "We messed around for a few minutes. But then he... he put on a condom. I was on my back, sort of just...expecting that to be the position. But he—he flipped me onto my stomach, yanked me up by my hips, and...just—just... boom. Went for it. Right inside. No warning, no build up, just...wham. *Hard.* And he...he wasn't small." Her eyes go to me. Away. Close, hiding the pain of the memory. "He fucked me. Hard and fast, like I knew what I was doing, like I was used to it. It hurt. I could feel that I was bleeding. You know, from being a virgin."

"Jesus," I mutter.

She reaches out and takes my hand. "Don't interrupt, please. I have to just get it out."

I squeeze her hand in response, and she continues. "He, um...did it like that for a while. I don't know how long—It felt like hours. It hurt. I was crying. He knew, but he didn't fucking give a shit. He pulled out after a while, dragged me to the edge of the bed, bent me over it, and went at it again, standing up behind me. Even harder."

I have to grip the arm of the chair so hard my hand aches, but the fury I feel is overwhelming. I'm seeing red— murderous fury.

She squeezes my hand. "Breathe, Fee. Just...breathe with me." She inhales deeply, and I follow suit. After we exhale, she resumes. "That lasted for a while, too. Again, I couldn't track the time. I tried to...to go away in my head. And then he pulled out again, and...um." A pause, her voice shaking. "He shoved me to my knees facing him, took off the condom, and fucked my face. Like, down my throat, like I was some porn star who knew how to deep-throat. I couldn't breathe, and I kept almost barfing, but I couldn't, and...he wouldn't stop. I was sobbing, gagging, snotting, pushing at him, hitting him, but he had my hair and he was so strong, and he...he wouldn't stop. Until he finished, which was...*awful*. He just tasted gross. His cum, I mean. It was nasty. And there was so much of it. When he finished, he shoved me to the floor, laughing." She wipes at her eyes. "He stood over me, buckling his jeans. And he—he said...'now you ain't a virgin anymore, are you, cunt?'"

Silence.

She looks at me, wiping at her eyes again. "There. That's the story I've never told anyone."

"Forget what I said before," I growl, my voice shaking with rage. "That was rape. In so many ways, that was rape. It may have started out consensual, but the minute you said *anything* that even hinted that you wanted to stop or slow down, it should have been over." I close my eyes and lean forward, elbows on knees, fists gripped so tight they shake—my whole body is trembling with hate, with fury, with rage. "I'm so, so, so fucking sorry you went through that, Ember."

She rests a hand on my shoulder. "Hey, it's okay now. It was hard to talk through, but I really am okay. It's just..." her voice shakes. "I never wanted to apply that word to me.

Sexual Assault. Rape. Survivor. Victim. I always framed it as he went too far, that I just got more than I bargained for."

I shake my head. "Fuckers like that oughta be castrated with a dull butter knife." I hiss. "Sorry—sorry, I know the violent talk bothers you."

"Don't be angry for me, Felix. Please."

"Yeah, well, I am." I look at her, trying to swallow the hot lump in my throat. "I'm more than angry."

"Should we talk more another day?"

I shake my head. "Not unless you want to."

She shrugs. "No, I'd like to get past this." She rubs my back. "Just...try to let it go. Okay? I'm okay. I forgave him."

"How?" I ask. "How *the fuck* do you forgive someone who does something that evil?"

"I had to. It was eating me alive. I couldn't...I couldn't function. I couldn't let Dutchie even kiss me. Not until I told him what happened. And he...Dutchie told me that forgiveness was the only possible path to healing."

"Fuck that."

"No. It worked. I wrote Rob this big, long letter. I dumped everything I was feeling into it. How much I hated him. All the ways I'd fantasized about hurting him for what he did—and believe me, I can be *really* motherfucking creative. I wrote about how it had screwed me up. Made me distrustful not just of men, but everyone. I mean, I knew Rob was a quote-unquote bad boy, but he didn't seem...all that bad. He was flirty, funny, easy to talk to. Bought me beer, and we'd smoke down together. Treated me like an adult. But then it was like a switch flipped inside him, and he just...he was someone else. A monster. And I told him about that. It must have been ten or eleven pages both sides. And I tracked him down, and I mailed

him the letter. The last three words of which were 'I forgive you.' I don't know if he read it, if it found him, but it
didn't matter. Telling him how I felt and writing the words
that I forgave him…it sort of set me free. It wasn't magic.
I wasn't okay all at once. It took Dutchie another two or
three months of patient exploration before we went past
second base. I kept having flashbacks when he touched
me, but I…I had to work through that. I'd have Dutchie
do something that gave me flashbacks, and we'd just let
me go through it, and he'd hold me and the next time it
wasn't as bad. Eventually, doing things with Dutchie felt
good, physically and emotionally."

She lights the other half of the joint and smokes it
while talking.

"But it progressed by degrees. Kissing, making out,
heavy petting. Letting him see me naked—I wore baggy
clothes for a long time after what happened. Letting him
touch my body. Touching him—that part was easier. Rob
hadn't ruined that for me. I liked making Dutchie feel good.
With my hands, at least." She laughs. "I must've given him
dozens of hand jobs because it was all I could handle, and
I liked how he reacted. I liked seeing him lose his mind.
Making him feel good made me forget. I couldn't go down
on him for a long time, though, even after I was okay with
sex. The way he did that—Rob, I mean. It…that really
messed me up."

"I can't fucking imagine. It's kinda incredible to me
that you can do that at all." I frown. "Jesus, Ember. If I'd
known—"

She lunges across the space between us and claps a
hand over my mouth. "Nope, nope, nope, nope. You are
not doing that, Felix Crowe. You absolutely, categorically

are *not* allowed to treat me any different because I told you that. " She keeps her hand on my mouth, eyes blazing and intense. "I...am...*healed*. It still hurts to remember, but it doesn't haunt me. I don't think about it almost ever. And I *never* think about it during sex. Never. You wanna know what I was thinking when I was sucking your big, beautiful cock, Fee?"

I nod. "Mmmm-hmmm."

"I was thinking, 'god, his cock is amazing.'"

I snort. "Mmm-hmmm." It's a sarcastic sound, this time.

"It's true!" She protests. "Do I need to prove it?" Her smirk is teasing, but I suspect if I said yes, she would.

"Ember," I say, pulling her hand away from my mouth. "You don't have to prove anything."

"I just mean I need you to believe me. I *loved* every second of what we just shared, Fee. I said I'm confused and conflicted—and I am. But not because of you, or because I still have hangups about sex. I don't. My hangups are emotional—it's about grief, not that."

"I believe you," I say.

"Now, back then, when I first got together with Dutchie? Yeah, that's a different story. For two, almost three years after we started, having sex was sorta like walking through a minefield. Poor Dutchie—I don't know how many times we had to stop because something he did triggered something. Never a complaint. Just love and patience and understanding. But I was sick of it. I was sick of having sex ruined. So I set about trying to move past it. Oral sex was the hardest. Dutchie would have been fine had I decided to just not do it, but I didn't like that. I refused to let that shithead take anything from me, from Dutchie, or from us."

"Brave girl," I murmur.

She smiles in acknowledgment of my words. "It took a long time. Months of…practice."

I grin. "Poor Dutchie, having to endure all that practice."

"You jest, I know, but at first it was…rough. I'd get triggered and be crying and have to stop and he'd be left halfway to orgasm with a sobbing wife. He kept asking me to stop trying, but I can be stubborn. He enjoyed it—I could tell how much he liked it when I did it for him… before I got triggered. And I was determined to stop being triggered by it. And…I won."

"Clearly," I say.

"The fun part for Dutchie was when I was finally able to perform the whole act without being triggered, because that's when I started to practice different techniques on him. I'd pay attention to how he reacted when I did different things." She closes her eyes, smiling at the sky as she remembers, taking a long, leisurely hit of the joint. "That was a very, very fun period for us. When I was past all my sexual dysfunction and could just enjoy everything. We had *so* much sex, Fee. Dutchie must've gotten a blowjob every day for a fucking month, sometimes more, just because I wanted to prove to myself that I could. And also because it made me so fucking hot watching him when I did it for him."

I grab her hand and squeeze. "His love and patience were amply rewarded, I'd say."

She laughs, nodding. "Yes, I like to think so." The

humor fades almost instantly. "This brings me to the reason for my emotional conflict."

"Okay."

"I fucking…" a sigh. "I don't even know where to start." She rubs her face, the joint now a roach pinched between her finger and thumb, trailing a thin plume of smoke with every gesture. "What we just did, Fee, it was… *so* fucking hot."

"It was, no lie, the hottest thing I've ever experienced," I say. "I mean it."

"For me, too." I can barely hear her. "That's the conflict."

"Ember," I murmur. "I—"

A shake of her head. "No, I'm being honest. What I shared with Dutchie was…it was what I needed. He healed me. Took care of me. Showed me love. Taught me how to trust again. He was my home, every bit as much if not more than the bus. I loved our sex life together. I craved him all the time." A pause. "But…"

"But?"

"This is so hard to put into words, Fee."

"So don't."

"I have to." She puts the roach out and drops it into the tube. "Sometimes, I felt like I…like I wanted…more. I don't know how else to put it. I wanted…god, how to say it? Dutchie was good and sweet and gentle down to his fucking atoms. I'm not. I was raised mostly without rules. I lived among adults. I did what I wanted, said what I wanted, and answered to no one. Mom was more of a friend than a mother, especially once I was out of the young child phase. After nine or so, I was considered able to take care of myself, and I did. Mom provided for me. We had food. I had clothes. She maintained the bus. Drove us. Made sure I knew who was safe to be around and who wasn't. But I'm a wild child, Fee. And Dutchie was..."

"Too good? Too sweet?"

She nods. "Sometimes, yes." Her eyes squeeze shut, and tears trickle down. "It feels like a betrayal to say that. I loved him. I fucking loved him so much. But sometimes, I wanted more. I wanted him to..." She bares her teeth and shakes her head and growls like a she-wolf. "Fuck! I wanted him to be rough with me sometimes. To take the stigma off of that for me. That was the last piece, and he just couldn't go there."

"That's a big ask, Ember. For a naturally sweet kid who knew what you went through? Or suspected, I have to imagine, despite what you may not have told him."

"I know!" she says. "I stopped asking. I knew he couldn't. It just wasn't him. Never would be." She looks at me. "Deep down, I've always wanted to be...to have a partner who could go there with me. Lose control totally, but safely and respectfully. I...I always felt like there was more that I wanted, I just didn't know how to say it. My sex drive was...maybe too much for Dutchie. I wanted things he wasn't comfortable with. And I wasn't about to pressure him into anything, obviously, so I let it go. Put those desires in a box and forgot about them."

"And then Dutchie passed away."

She nods. "And then Dutchie passed away. I shut down. Couldn't cry. I was a ghost. A zombie. For months. Till I met you." She looks at me, her gaze intense, emotional, tearful. "I don't know what it is about you. I mean, I guess I do. You're hot as fuck. My attraction to you is just... fucking *wild*, Fee. It's on a molecular level. But that doesn't totally explain it. I trust you implicitly. Even though I don't know you. Or barely. It took me *years* to fully trust Dutchie with my body, and yet I trust you that way within...what, days? Hours? Why? I don't fucking get it. And not only that, I'm fucking hot for you. I dreamed about you. After we first met, before we ran into each other again, I couldn't stop thinking about you. Having dirty dreams about you that I'd wake up from and have to masturbate."

My cheeks burn. "Jesus, Ember."

"That embarrasses you?" she asks, grinning despite the watery gleam of unshed tears.

"I dunno how to respond." I roll my shoulders, not quite able to look at her.

She laughs. "Oh, Fee. You're ridiculous."

"What?"

"You wouldn't jerk off to me. You ran away from me rather than let me touch you, not once but twice. And you blush when I talk about having wet dreams about you." She gives me a hot, smoldering look. "And yet, you gave me orgasms so fucking good my legs are still shaky. You gave me a nipple orgasm, Fee. That's fucking rare."

"That's all you, Ember. Sensitive. Responsive." I shift, feeling myself growing aroused.

She notices. Grins. "Let's call it a team effort."

"Deal."

She looks away, then. "It's hard to not think about Dutchie. It's hard to do things with you, to you, for you—things that I did with him. Things that were *ours*—his and mine." When I open my mouth, she silences me with a raised hand. "Let me finish, please." A tense silence. "The way I touched you, the way I went down on you—that was all stuff I learned with him. Developed or figured out or whatever—ways of making it feel as good as possible. For him. And now I'm using it with you, and…I don't want to think about someone else when I'm with you. That's not fair to you. But I can't forget Dutchie. So…what do I do?"

I can sense she's not done, so I stay quiet.

"And to compound the whole situation…with you it was…." She closes her eyes as if to hide from the truth she's about to speak. "It was fucking hot. You gave me exactly what I've always craved. It was…so good." She covers her face with both hands, her words muffled. "It was better."

"Fuck, Ember. No wonder you're confused."

"How can it be better? I loved my husband. I'll always love him. I loved our sexual relationship. But with you— that wasn't even really sex, just…messing around. Foreplay. Whatever you wanna call it. And it was so fucking amazing I almost—I *did* forget…him." She looks at me with tears tracking down her cheeks, her words shaky and fraught. "I forgot about him, Felix. And—and—it was a relief." That last sentence is barely audible.

My eyes sting. "Ember, I—fuck, honey. I don't know what to say."

She shoots to her feet, shaking her head. "I can't—I can't. I…I need a minute." She pauses in the open sliding doorway to the living room. "Felix, I—"

I go to her, clasp her face in my hands and kiss her softly, sweetly, gently. "Take whatever time you need. Whatever it looks like."

"I need to get out of here. I need to be alone."

"Go get dressed," I tell her. "Meet me out front."

10

Ember

I PULL ON A PAIR OF BLACK LEGGINGS AND THAT'S it—still wearing Felix's button-down, no bra, no panties. Fuck it, I don't give a shit. My favorite pair of Tieks, scrape my hair into a ponytail, grab my purse, and head out the front door.

Felix has pulled around the vintage SUV he was driving that day at the beach. The engine is idling with a bit of a squeal, and it has a white top on now, whereas it was topless that day at the beach—it looks like it could rain at some point, so a top is probably a good idea.

Barely containing my maelstrom of emotions, I can't look at Felix as I stop in front of him, twisting the strap of my purse in my hands. "Felix, I…"

He takes my hands in his, pressing a business card

into my palm. "That has my cell on it. You call me if you need fucking *anything*, Ember."

"Felix, I just need—"

"I'll handle your bus repair. Take all the time you need." He holds my gaze, and I see a very complicated world of emotions hidden in the depths of his pale blue eyes—I only see it now that I know him better.

"I'm sorry, Fee."

He puts a finger over my lips. "No apologies. You've been through hell. I don't expect you to just jump into something with me."

"But we—"

"Shared something enjoyable," he cuts in. "It was fun. It doesn't have to be anything more than that, Ember."

I have to blink hard yet again, and my fucking god, am I sick of crying. "I don't know what it was, and I don't know what I want."

"And you don't have to."

"I don't do casual sex, Felix." I crush-grip his hand with mine. "Whatever it may have been, it wasn't casual."

"It's okay if it is."

I frown. "I'm not sure—I'm not sure I want you to be okay with it being casual, Fee."

He chuckles. "I'm just saying, no expectations. I know I have no claim on your heart because we…" he shrugs. "Hooked up, sort of."

"I feel like you're maybe not being totally truthful with me, Fee."

His expression shutters. "You don't need to worry about my feelings."

"But I do," I whisper. "I'm not running away from you. I just…I need to be alone to process things."

"Ember. I get it."

"We only talked about me," I say. "I never even asked you about you. About why you keep running away from letting me touch you."

"When you come back, ask me anything. Okay? I'll tell you the whole unvarnished truth."

I bite my lip, glancing at the idling vehicle. "I'm nervous about borrowing that. It looks old and valuable."

He twists to look at it, patting the hood. "Old, yes. Valuable? To a degree. As is, it's worth twenty, maybe twenty-five grand. I haven't done anything to it, so it's pretty much all original. If I do a thorough restoration, it could be worth more like fifty." He rolls a shoulder. "It's in good working order, but it's still a fifty-year-old vehicle, so it is possible something might break down on it. I don't anticipate it happening, but you should be aware that it's possible."

I roll my eyes. "Felix, I drive a 1967 Volkswagen Type 2. I grew up driving that same exact vehicle. Mom's father, my grandfather, who died well before I was born, taught my mom a lot about cars and engines, so she did all the maintenance, repairs, and replacements herself, and taught me. I know my way around cars."

"Well, good. There's a toolkit in the back, in case, and a box of the more common parts that may need to be replaced."

"I'll be fine," I say. "I don't think I'm going anywhere. I just need to think. Process. Figure a few things out in my head. Or, more accurately, get my head, heart, and body in alignment."

The next thing I know, his mouth is covering mine and I'm whimpering at the desperate soft sweetness of his kiss, losing myself in the warmth of his mouth, the strength of his hand framing my cheek and jaw, and I could just live here in this moment, in this kiss, drowning in him, vanishing into his strength and sweetness and depth.

And then he's gone, backing away from me, his gaze haunted for a split second before his expression shutters again.

"Fee," I whisper. "Goddammit, you can't kiss me like that. It's not fucking fair."

"Sorry. I keep forgetting to be more of an asshole."

I knot my fist in the front of his shirt, yank him to me, and kiss him hard and fast. "You can't be *more* of an asshole because you're not an asshole at all."

He snorts derisively. "You don't know the half of it."

I shake my head. "Somehow, I doubt whatever you have to tell me is half as bad as you're making it out to be. Unless you're a totally different person now or something."

He shrugs. "I don't even know anymore." He grabs me by the shoulders and guides me to the driver's side, opens the door, and when I climb in and sit down, he reaches across me and buckles me in. "Your box of antique jewelry and your cash bag are in the safe in my garage, and I'm the only one with the code. Your suitcase is in the back, there."

I twist, seeing my suitcase. "Fee, I'm not leaving."

His answering expression is…complicated. "Not forever, no. I have your bus. But you're a nomad."

"Fee, I—"

He kisses me again, this time soft, hesitant. "Go. Just…go. I think you and I could talk forever."

"That's what scares me, Fee," I whisper.

"I know. Same." He backs away, shuts the door, and shoves his hands in his hip pockets.

Gives me a very male upward jerk of his chin as a goodbye, and then turns on his heel and heads for the house, as if it's too hard to watch me drive away.

I twist again to back out of his driveway, and I notice not only has he made sure I have my suitcase but also my toiletries bag, my laptop case, and my box of everyday jewelry. Pretty much all of my most important worldly possessions, except the stuff in his safe and the bus.

My stupid eyes sting at the thoughtfulness of the gesture—at the courage and selflessness he's demonstrating by releasing me rather than trying to hold on to me.

No, no, nope. Can't go there.

Not yet.

God, I'm a sissy. I can't face my shit. It's too hard.

I shake my head, turning around to face the front and put the shifter into first, let out the clutch, and set the SUV into motion.

For a while, I just drive. Get used to driving something other than the bus—that's weird. Eventually I find myself parking in Faye's driveway and then ringing her doorbell.

It takes a while but eventually she appears in the doorway—my heart sinks. She's lost a ton of weight, looking haggard and frail. Not at all the vibrant, active, vivacious old bird I'd known just a few weeks ago.

"Why, it's my girl Ember!" she exclaims, her eyes lighting up. "You came to see me!"

She opens the door and I throw myself into her arms. "Faye, I missed you. I couldn't stay away any longer. I just had to come see you."

"Well, I'm mighty glad you did, missy." She kisses my

cheek and then pulls me inside. "Come on in. You want some coffee?"

"It's seven in the evening, Faye," I point out.

"So?" She waves a dismissive hand. "YOLO, bitches."

I cackle. "God, I love you. Yeah, sure, let's have coffee."

I follow her into a postage stamp foyer—a four-by-four square of tile a few inches lower than the rest of the room, with a waist-height half-wall on the right and a bi-fold coat closet on the left. The living room features a big picture window facing the street, a long, low, battered green velour couch facing the picture window. A fireplace occupies the wall between the couch and the picture window, with a wide, deep mantle across the top. The mantle is cluttered with photographs ranging from black-and-white photos of Faye and her family when she was a little girl, what I assume are Thomas and his family when he was young, Faye and Thomas as a young couple, and then graduating to faded color photographs from the early sixties and seventies, through the eighties, and into polaroids and digital photographs leading up to the present day—including a printed and framed photo I took on my phone of Faye and me at the beach together. I'd emailed it to Faye upon her request when I took her home that day. In it, we're sitting on the blanket, it's late evening, the fire is just out of the frame, and we're both laughing...and visibly stoned out of our minds.

My throat closes up and goes hot and thick. I hear Faye approaching. "You put us up on the mantle?"

She puts a mug in my hands. "That was the best day I've had in twenty goddamned years, missy. Of course you're on my mantle."

"Gah," I hiss. "Can *one* person just be mean to me for

two fucking seconds so I can stop crying? Jesus." I rub my eyes with my empty hand.

She laughs. "Sorry, darling, no can do. Sit down, drink that, and talk to Grammy." She nuzzles my cheek with her prickly lips and soft nose. "That's what Ben and Alaina call me."

I let her guide me to the couch, and once I've sat down, I rub my hands on the lime-green velour. "This couch is amazing."

She snorts. "I love it. Tommy hated it. I think he sat on it a total of six times, ever. I bought it just because of how much he hated it." She points at the decapitated head of a deer on the wall. "That was his revenge."

I gag. "Ugh. Deer heads as decoration."

She laughs. "Oh, I know. But he shot that with a bow. He was *very* proud. We had venison with every meal for months." She eyes me. "Why, Ember James, are you stoned?"

I hold my thumb and forefinger an inch apart. "A little. I was with Felix, and I needed some...courage."

"Still dancing around that boy, are you?"

I nod. "I told him everything. I told him things I never even told Dutchie. I told him things about Dutchie and me that should have been private. But then..." I sip coffee and discover that she's spiked it with Kahlua. I cough in surprise. "My god, that's strong. You're a party animal, Faye."

"I know. Making up for lost time, you might say." She pats my thigh, squeezes it, and then jiggles it. "My god, these legs, girl. Solid muscle!"

I roll my eyes. "I'm out of shape. I stopped working out after Dutchie died. I've actually gained a good bit of weight."

"Oh, hush your mouth," she snaps, and then smirks at me. "What did our delicious Mr. Crowe have to say when he saw you naked?"

I frown at her. "How do you know he saw me naked?"

She plucks at my shirt. "Still smells like him."

I put my nose to the shoulder and inhale—she's right, it does smell like Felix. I have to stop myself from sniffing it again. "Oh."

"Well?" she demands.

I can't quite suppress a grin. "I think his exact words were 'Jesus fucking christ, Ember.' Followed by 'Fucking perfect.'"

"So then shut the hell up with that 'ewww, I gained a few pounds' bullshit." She adopts a simpering, whining, mocking tone.

I roll my eyes. "Not what I said or how I said it, but point taken."

"So why are you here instead of there, with him, naked, getting plowed six ways to Sunday?"

I choke and nearly splutter Kahlua and coffee all over Felix's white shirt; I spend several moments hacking my lungs out while trying not to spew it everywhere.

When I can breathe again, I swallow and wipe my mouth on my arm. "Jesus, Faye," I rasp. "Getting plowed?"

She cackles. "I'm a bored, lonely old woman. Got nothin' to do but watch TV all day. You pick things up." She takes a sip of her coffee, flicking a finger at me. "So? Why are you here instead of there?"

"I need to think. I need to process. I…" I shake my head, huffing. "I'm confused. Scared. Lost. And he just confuses me worse."

Faye shakes her head. "Ohhhhh, girly." She points at

the hallway leading to the bedrooms—moving boxes are stacked along both walls, some closed, taped, and labeled, others open. "You can help me pack, if you're gonna insist on being a daft bimbo and hang out with my fat old ass instead of letting that fine hunk of man mean diddle your bean."

"Faye—"I start, but she waves me off.

"Nah, nah. Don't start, missy. I know, I look like hell. Don't worry about it." At my expectant stare, she sighs. "I'm almost out of time, Ember. I can feel it in my bones."

"Faye," I whisper. "Don't say that."

"I'm ready, honey," she whispers back. "I miss my Tommy too much to live without him any longer. But I need to spend some time with Tina, Ben, and Alaina before I let the good lord take me home."

I tip my head back and blink hard. "Then you have to let me take you there."

She grins, resting her head on my shoulder. "Nothing on this earth could make me happier than to go on one last road trip, missy. You and me. No bras, lots of pot, and lots of snacks."

"Fuck yeah," I say. "Sounds perfect. When do we leave?"

"Well, if you help me pack up all this stuff...next year?" She laughs. "I have a lifetime of stuff to go through."

"Do you *need* to go through it?"

She frowns. "Who else would?" When I shrug, unable to verbalize what I mean, she pokes me in the boob. "Out with it, missy. What do you mean?"

"I mean, bring the few most essential things you need, your most sentimental stuff. Everything else, put it in storage. Hire a moving company to do it."

"And then it just sits in storage?"

"And then whenever Tina is ready, she can go through it, keep what's important to her. Don't waste your precious time on stuff, Faye."

She lets out a harsh sigh. "Oh. I see what you mean." A pause. "Let her sort through it after I'm gone."

"I mean…" I shrug. "Yeah, I guess. I don't mean it like—"

"No, you're absolutely right. It was making me sick, the thought of having to sort through my entire life. All of Tommy's things I never got rid of. Tina's things from when she was young and living with us." A laugh, a shake of her head. "I never got rid of anything. The attic is full, the basement is full. It'd take me forever. Even if you helped me, it'd take weeks to go through it all, and it would be heartbreaking for me to try to decide what to keep and what to throw away."

"I just mean maybe that shouldn't be your job."

She lets out a sigh of relief. "You just took a huge burden off of me, Ember." She reaches into the pocket of her pink crushed velvet track suit bottoms and pulls out a chunky Nokia flip phone from the early 2000s, opens it, finds a number, and calls it. "Hello, Roger? It's Faye. You have a minute? Good. So, I've decided I'm not going to sort through my things before I leave—I want you to handle it. Hire a company to pack everything up and put it into storage. Have the house cleaned and staged, and sell it. Add the proceeds to my will. Okay? Good." She eyes me thoughtfully. "Actually, wait. Do everything but sell it. I have to think about that. I'm not sure I want to sell it to random strangers. But put the stuff in storage, and once I kick the bucket, send the key and information to Tina.

Have the old place cleaned up in the meantime. I'll email you with further instructions regarding what to do with the house after I'm gone." She pauses, listening. "Thank you, Roger. You as well. Goodbye."

She hangs up, clicking the phone closed and tossing it aside.

"You're a genius, Ember." She kisses my cheek. "Now I just need my clothes and a few odds and ends. We can leave tomorrow." She frowns at me. "You should go back to Felix, though. I can take the Greyhound."

"Fuck that, number one. You're not taking the fucking bus." I wrap my arm around her, take a sip of spiked coffee so strong my eyes water. "Number two, I need time to think about Felix. And talk to you. You're not getting out of this road trip, Faye, so stop trying. I'm the queen of road trips, I'll have you know."

She sighs, shrugging and nodding. "Okay, okay. But if you let that man go, I swear to the Almighty, missy, I will haunt you 'til the day you die."

"We can talk about him later. For now, let's plan."

C⌒੭

Apparently, when I said "plan" Faye thought I meant "get hammered and watch The Notebook," because that's what happens.

What do you want? *WHAT DO YOU WANT*?

I don't fucking know, Noah. Jesus. Lay off.

C⌒੭

When I wake up, I'm disoriented. Someone is snoring loudly next to me.

Faye.

I have vague memories of us helping each other down the hallway, tripping over boxes as we laugh like drunk hyenas, and toppling into her bed. I'm still fully clothed, and so is she. God, she's a bad influence on me, but I love her to pieces.

I slip out of bed and tiptoe out of her bedroom, pausing in the doorway to actually see the room for the first time.

Pale blue walls, and a very old, heavy, ornate oak bedroom set—a giant king bed you damn near need a ladder to get into, a matching nightstand set, and a six-drawer bureau. The bureau is littered with life-detritus from a bygone age: a wobbly, handmade-by-a-child ceramic dish containing loose change, a gold Rolex of the type police departments give to cops when they retire, and a worn wooden-handled folding pocketknife. Beside the dish, a fat brown leather tri-fold wallet stuffed to overflowing with photos, receipts, credit cards, business cards, cash, and who knows what else. The wallet is decades old, curved concave from the shape of Tommy's butt.

My heart breaks for Faye, seeing that stuff. Her closet is open, and it looks like she tried to start going through his clothes but only got a few hangers in and gave up—there are a handful of flannel shirts crumpled on the floor, still on the hangers…dropped when the pain became too great.

I can't just leave them there.

I pick them up, re-hang them with the others, and close the closet door as quietly as I can.

I get a pot of coffee brewing and then rummage in the fridge, find ingredients, and set about making French toast—a favorite of Dutchie's that I haven't made since he died.

Faye shuffles out a few slices in, her white-pink-purple-blue-green (she added a few streaks) hair sticking up in every direction.

She shuffles straight to me and slams into me, arms snaking around my waist. "Thank you, girly."

I frown, hugging her back. "For what? It's just French toast. " It's not, but she doesn't need to know that—at least until after coffee.

"Putting his shirts away," she whispers. "I couldn't—after I dropped them, I couldn't make myself touch them again. They still smell like him after two decades in that closet. I know it's not possible, but I swear they do."

"I've got you, Faye."

She pulls away, patting my hips. "French toast—haven't had homemade French toast in I don't even know how long. Smells good."

"Mom used to make it for me. It was her rainy day special." I swallow hard, blink harder. "I kept the tradition going—I used to make it for Dutchie on sad, boring, rainy days. He—he loved it." I shake my head. "Sorry, sorry."

Faye wipes at my cheeks. "Ain't gotta apologize to me, missy. We widows know how it goes."

I frown at her. "Widow."

She shrugs, turning away to pour herself a mug of coffee in a gigantic black mug with "world's greatest grandma" hand-painted on the side in big, blocky, wobbly, backward, third-grade handwriting. "Didn't think I'd need to explain that one."

I snort. "No, I just...I never really thought to apply that word to myself." I snort again, shaking my head as I flip the bread in the frying pan. "Learning a lot of new words to apply to myself lately."

She stirs a nauseating amount of sugar and cream into her coffee and sits at the little round table—as time-worn and love-smoothed as everything else in this time capsule of a house; the walls in the kitchen are a pale yellow, the appliances from the late nineties, and the flooring and counters are laminate. A backdoor beside the battered white four-burner electric range leads to a small fenced-in backyard, overgrown now, the grass knee-high. If I squint, I can see what it must have once looked like—a play structure, a sandbox, a little girl running around as her parents watch from the kitchen. Maybe a puppy bounding after the little girl.

"Like what?" Faye asks, shaking me out of reverie.

"Oh. Um." I sigh. "Nothing."

"Don't start that 'nothing' bullshit with me, missy," she grumbles. "Ain't been any secrets between us yet, no sense starting now."

So, over French toast and half a dozen cups of coffee, I relate the story I told to Felix, and this time it's easier to get through. Getting it out once loosened its grip on me, I guess. It hurts less. I feel…lighter. Freer.

Faye doesn't say much—she doesn't have to. She just rests her hand on mine and stares into space, and the brief, haunted expression on her face tells me she knows first-hand that there isn't much to say, one woman to another.

I glance at her, after a while. "You tell Tommy?" I ask.

She shakes her head. "Goodness, no. That's one secret I kept from him—the only one. It'd have killed him. Or put him in prison, which would have been worse. He knew something happened, but I told him I would be okay. And

I was. Wasn't the first woman to go through that, and won't be the last. Knowing about it wouldn't have helped him, and he couldn't have done anything about it—the man who did it was killed in a robbery gone wrong a few months later anyway. Tommy had just made detective and his caseload was just unbelievable. He'd have torn the planet apart trying to find the man, and if he had?" She shakes her head. "No. I think he suspected. He was…he knew what to do. Hold me. Give me time. Just love me, and be patient. I got through it and moved on, the way we women always have and always will. God knows men aren't strong enough for some things."

"You're my hero, Faye," I whisper, holding her hand and holding back tears. "I mean that."

She dashes a wrist under her eyes and shakes her head. "Enough of this maudlin bullshit. Let's pack up and get this show on the road." She points at me. "You wearin' a bra?"

I lift up the shirt, flashing her. "No ma'am, I am not."

She unzips her track suit top, yanks it open, and shows me her boobs, too. "Me either! Let's fuckin' go!"

I whoop and dissolve into laughter as Faye shakes her wrinkly, saggy tits at me, and I do the same to her.

☙

It turns out Faye only needs one big suitcase and one small one, and one box of her most sentimental objects—a handful of photos, a few mugs and other tchotchkes, and the precious items of Tommy's I'd seen on the dresser.

I stock the vintage SUV with the requisite road trip snacks and a cooler of sparkling water and soda. After inputting her daughter's Los Angeles address into my phone's GPS, we're on the way, California bound, just two crazy widows on a cross-country road trip.

In the back of my mind though, I know I'm only delaying my introspection.

But come on. How could I not go with her?

11

Felix

MY HOUSE FEELS EMPTY, NOW. WHICH IS ODD, because Ember was only in it for a few hours, but in that time she filled it with life and personality. It's always felt empty because it is...but now, without her in it anymore? Feels like a tomb.

She has my FJ40, so I can't even busy myself with that. I consider heading out to my build site, but for once, I just...don't want to.

I putz around for a while, doing a few odds and ends I've been putting off—fixing the guest bathroom sink so it doesn't drip, replacing a handful of screens that have been ripped and patched a billion times, replacing the loose, creaky boards on the steps to the back deck, putting WD40 on the squeaky hinges of the door into the garage...

It's bullshit busy work, but it keeps my mind occupied…ish.

Okay, no, it doesn't.

More than once, I find myself standing around with a tool in my hand, staring into space, thinking about Ember. Mostly, I'm daydreaming about her body and the borderline miraculous things she did to me.

Thinking about that stuff is a hell of a lot easier than thinking about what she told me. Or about my own shit. Yeah, no. Fuck that.

Daydreaming about those big, fat, juicy tits is way better than thinking about Amy Quincy, or Ember's tragic history.

Problem is, thinking about those big, fat, juicy tits makes me horny, and as has been established, Ember is gone.

Eventually, I run out of busy work projects, leaving me at loose ends again. I could bust into the materials I have stored in the basement and start putting down that luxury vinyl plank like I've been putting off for months, but it's already almost nine o'clock at night and I'm in no mood for that.

My phone rings as I'm contemplating what the hell I'm going to do until I'm tired enough to fall asleep—it's Riley.

"Hey, Rye. What's up, bro?" I sound pathetically glad to hear from him—because I am.

"Whoa, you sound chipper. You on coke or something?" Riley says.

"Fuck you, no, I'm not on coke."

"There's the grumpy Felix I know and love."

"I'm not grumpy."

"He said, grumpily."

I groan. "I was glad to hear from you, but now I'm rethinking that position. Did you call for a reason or just to annoy me?"

"What are you doing right now?"

"Not a goddamn thing. Why?"

He sighs. "If you were smart, you'd be balls deep in Ember right now."

"Hey, don't talk about her like that," I snap. "It's not like that. *She's* not like that."

He chuckles. "Wait, hold up—you get shot down?"

"Rye, do me a favor and fuck all the way off with the questions."

"Mmmmm…probably not. Come outside."

I peer through my front window—his big silver truck is at the curb behind the flatbed with Ember's van on it. "You're here."

"Excellent powers of observation, Sherlock. I'm kidnapping you. Let's go."

"Go where?"

"I dunno. Get into some trouble."

"You broke up with April already?"

"I'll tell you in the car. Fuckin' come on."

I sigh. "Alright, alright. Be right out."

I grab my wallet, keys, and phone, slap a ball cap on my head, and stomp into my Redwings. When I slide into the passenger seat of Riley's truck, I'm immediately greeted by the fact that his truck is immaculate, despite being older than mine and despite the fact that he lives in his every bit as much as I do mine.

"Who cleans out your truck, man?" I ask. "Fuckin' Snow White and her forest critters?"

He yanks it into gear and pulls away from my curb. "Um, me, bro. Unlike you, I'm not a fuckin' slob. Every time I get gas, I clean it out, and every Saturday morning I vacuum it and wipe it down. Which is why *my* truck looks like an adult human drives it and yours looks like a rabid racoon on meth drives it."

"Rabid racoon on meth, " I mutter. "Fucking dick."

"So. You and Ember."

"No."

"Oh, c'mon, brother. You gotta gimme *some*thing. Her van is on our flatbed outside your house and she's not with you. And your FJ40 is gone."

I frown at him. "How do you know that?"

A shrug. "You left the garage door open."

"Well? Turn around so I can close it."

He waves a hand. "Nah. Mrs. McCready will keep an eye out. That nosy old bat never sleeps."

I snort a laugh. "You're not wrong. Fine. Whatever."

He pokes me in the arm. "Something happened. Tell me."

"We…messed around."

He grins at me. "Are her tits as fucking magnificent as I want to believe they are?"

"However magnificent you're imagining they are, they're a billion times better."

"You lucky motherfucker." He glances at me. "So… why'd she leave? Pussy game is weak since you're a fuck-ing monk?"

I growl. "Fuck you, no. My pussy game is not weak, you trashy shitbag." I shake my head. "I'm not a monk. We've talked about this already."

"And you haven't used it in how long?"

"We've talked about this already, too," I say. "Also, I'm not talking about Ember anymore."

"Oh fuck off, Fee. She's got great tits—that's all I get? I coulda told you that."

"She's more than her tits, Rye."

"That ass, though, amiright?"

I give him a glare that promises bodily harm. "Riley Frederick Crowe. Do *not* fuck with me on this. I swear to fucking god I will break your goddamn jaw."

His eyes widen and he turns his head exaggeratedly slowly to stare at me as we come to a red light. "Okaaaaay, then. Message received. You have never once used my middle name." He slaps a hand on my shoulder. "I'm just fuckin' with you, Fee. I'm sure she's got a *great* personality."

"RILEY!" I shout.

He leans against his window, covering his mouth with his hand, cackling like a mentally handicapped hyena. "You *are* serious about this."

"Yes, I fucking am," I snap.

He gives me a long, sober look. "Like for real, for real?"

I close my eyes and stare at the ceiling of the cab. "Yes, for real."

"Like, you *care* about her?"

"I…I don't know. Yes. Maybe. I think?" I shake my head. "It's complicated."

"It's never complicated."

"This is." I look around. "Where the fuck are we going, anyway?"

"We're meeting Cole and Nyx at The Borderline."

I groan. "Fuck me. Really? That skeezy-ass dive?"

The Borderline is a shitty, sticky, smelly dive bar that's

on the county border some twenty-five or thirty minutes east of Three Rivers. It's a popular spot on the weekends because they always have a live band and great specials on domestic pitchers. It's where locals go when they want to get naked-wasted. Part of its draw, band and beer aside, is that they share a lot with the one taxi company in the whole county, and they've developed a deal with the taxi people that keeps drunk people from driving and the taxi company solvent.

Riley chuckles. "Yeah, it's Nyx's idea."

"Of course it is. That toothless hillbilly loves The Borderline."

"I'm gonna tell him you called him that."

"You will not," I say, pointing at him.

"He's sensitive about his teeth."

"It was a joke."

"*You're* a joke."

I sigh. "Very mature, Rye."

Nyx lost most of his front teeth in a bar fight. He has implants, now, but for a while he had to wear denture things that he was super sensitive about. He still gets pissy if you bring up his teeth, even though you can't tell anymore.

Riley elbows me. "Come on. No more jokes, I swear— what's up with you and Ember?"

I shake my head. "I don't know. After we..." I tip my head side to side. "It wasn't a hookup. Whatever. After whatever happened, happened, we talked. She told me some stuff she's been through, and..." I shake my head again. "She needed time alone to process her feelings."

"You tell her about Amy?"

"No. But she knows there's something."

"You're one big ball of issues, bro—of *course* she knows there's something." He glances at me. "You're still hung up, aren't you?"

"No."

"You are! You're hung up on Amy still." He groans. "Bro, for real, you may need a therapist."

"Bro," I mock, "Shut up."

He rolls his eyes. "Oh, very mature, Fee."

"We didn't talk about me. But let's just say that yes, my issues did present themselves."

"What's she like?" he asks. "As a person. I'm not being a jackass this time."

"For once," I mutter. "She's amazing. She's lived a crazy life, been through a lot of seriously hard shit and she's still…just full of light and life. She's funny, interesting, strong, resilient." I sigh. "But she has things in her past that are…holding her back. Which obviously you know I understand more than most."

"Yeah, I do know that. So what are you gonna do?"

"Fuck if I know. What *can* I do? If she's not ready, she's not ready. And honestly, I don't know if I am, either."

Riley stares at me. "You don't know if you're ready… to not be a lonely, grumpy old ogre?"

I glare at him. "I'm not grumpy!"

"Hey Siri," he says in a loud, clear voice. "Call Nyx."

"Calling Nyx—cell phone," a disembodied voice says from the speakers.

It rings twice and Nyx's voice fills the cab. "Motherfuckin' Riley Crowe in the hizz-ouss!"

Riley laughs. "You're already into the whiskey, aren't you?"

"Fuck yeah, man. You on the way?"

"Yeah, me and Fee."

"How'd you convince his cranky ass to crawl out of his cave of solitude?"

Riley hoots uproariously, driving with his knee so he can clap his hands. "What'd I fuckin' say!"

"Oh for fuck's sake," I grumble. "I'm not cranky *or* grumpy and you're both assholes. What I get for thinking I could go out with my friends and not take a bunch of shit."

Nyx laughs. "I'm on speaker, huh?"

"Yeah, you are," Riley says. "I was calling to ask you for one word that describes my brother."

"Crank-o-saurus rex!" Nyx yells. "That's you, Fee! Crank-o-Saurus rex. You know what you need, my man? A blowjob and at least six shots of whiskey. I can provide the whiskey, but you're on your own for the first part."

"Got that handled," I mutter, not quite suppressing a grin at the memory.

Riley hoots and claps even more raucously, clapping me on the arm. "And you're *still* cranky? Jesus. Stubborn motherfucker, you are. That girl is a fuckin' smokeshow, Fee. You got head from her, and you're *still* pining after Amy?"

"You're fucked in the head if that's true," Nyx adds.

"Fuck you both. I'm not pining after fucking Amy." I snatch Riley's phone out of the cupholder. "See you in a minute, Nyx. Gotta kill my brother." I end the call and toss the phone back into the cupholder, giving my brother a death stare so vicious he taps the brakes and pulls over onto the shoulder.

"Fee, I was just—" He starts.

I slug him in the jaw—hard enough to prove a point, but not hard enough to cause any real damage. "I fucking told you, Rye. It wasn't like that—*she's* not like that. She's not some Tinder bunny that I hooked up with while she was on vacation. I don't mind sharing details in those situations, and I don't mind the crude fuckin' jokes, either. But Ember is different. So *fuck off* with the crass bullshit or the next time you'll be scheduling a visit with Dr. Pritchard." That being Three Rivers' orthodontic surgeon.

Riley jacks the shifter into neutral, working his jaw with a speculative expression. "Wow, okay."

"I fuckin' warned you."

He nods, a hardness in his gaze. "You did."

I rub my face with both hands, knowing my temper got the best of me. "Rye, I'm sorry. I shouldn't've hit you."

The hardness evaporates. He rubs his jaw while shaking his head. "Nah, you warned me. I have a hard time knowing when to quit, especially when making people laugh."

"Fuck knows Nyx's laugh is hard to resist," I say.

He snorts, nodding. "Yeah, it is." He eyes me. "You're for real about this chick, huh? Like, real feelings and shit."

I sigh and then groan. "I don't fucking know, Rye. I told you, it's complicated. Usually, it's not actually all that complicated—usually, it's more of a matter of a decision you don't wanna make. This is…" I shrug. "It's *actually* complicated. For her *and* for me. And for us, assuming there can be an us. Assuming she *wants* there to be *and* assuming I'm fucking even *capable* of that."

"Don't be a dipshit, of course you are."

I roll my neck, twist it to the side to pop the joint. "Rye…listen, this isn't me sharing details. This is me confiding in my brother and best friend here, okay?"

He twists in his seat to face me, still rubbing his jaw

with the back of his hand. "Dude, you got me good." He hikes his left foot up against the console, knee resting against the steering wheel. "I'm listening, Fee, and this stays between us, I swear."

"We didn't even have sex, like actual sex, and it was still the most fucking…" I shake my head, at a loss for words. "I felt…*connected* to her, man. Like deep, and real. And all we did was mess around. And to make matters—I dunno about worse, but just more intense, I guess, she outright admitted she was using me to avoid dealing with her feelings. For me? About the situation? I don't know. But that's what she said. And after she told me her story, she freaked out and bolted. She was…she couldn't avoid her feelings anymore, so she fuckin' ran. I mean, she's coming back since I'm having Nyx fix her van, but still."

Riley stares at nothing for a moment. "Some of the most intense sex I've ever had has just been messing around and not, like, penetrative sex. It's something about the intimacy of…I dunno how to put it. There's something about holding back from sex that creates a strange kind of…yeah, intimacy is the right word. Just your hands, just your mouth—I don't know, Fee. I get it. But I gotta warn you, in my experience, when you share something like that with someone, that kind of intimacy, when you do have actual sex with her, it's gonna fuckin' rock your whole goddamn universe."

I sigh, tipping my head back. "Yeah, that's what I'm afraid of. And I think that's what she's afraid of." I frown at my brother. "And hey, man, look at you talking about intimacy and shit."

He grins and laughs, flipping me off. "Ohhh fuck you.

I know I have a reputation as being a himbo, and I admit it's well-deserved, but there's more to me than that."

"There is?" I say, playfully shoving his shoulder. "Since when?"

He turns back front and pulls the shifter into gear, pulling away from the shoulder. "Wouldn't you like to know?"

"Actually, yeah, I would. For real."

He shrugs. "I dunno. Seeing Bear turn his life around. It's had an effect on me. Watching him fall in love with Noelle and putting a real life together with her, I guess it…" he rubs the back of his neck, shaking his head with another shrug. "Suddenly, a different chick every weekend was losing its appeal."

"Every weekend?" I say, laughing. "Every night, more like it."

"Not any more. Not for a long time, actually," he says. "My last few relationships have lasted a few months each. I was with April for almost three months." He points a finger at me. "Not a word—that's a long time for me."

"And what happened with her?" I ask.

"Nyx was asking too, so I'mma hold off on that until we're all together."

"Wait, three months?" I ask. "Really?"

He nods. "We kept it quiet for a while. I…" he swallows. "I liked her. I was hoping…ahhh, fuck. Never mind."

"You were hoping what, Rye? C'mon, bro, I opened up to you."

He sighs. "I was hoping it'd be different. I want something different. I want what Bear has." He grabs the giant wrench that is his shifter and pushes it into the next gear.

I nod. "Yeah, I know what you mean, actually. Seeing the way they are together…"

He clears his throat. "Sex is fuckin' awesome, don't get me wrong, but…what they have that I want is the non-sexual stuff."

"What do you mean?" I ask.

He shrugs. "It's stupid. You'll make fun of me."

I grab his forearm. "Rye, brother. We like to fuck with each other, but you know I'm on your side. I wouldn't mock you about something you're for real about."

"It's the little stuff. Couple weeks back, April and I met them for drinks at the Cellar. We parked together and walked in, right? Well, Bear and Noelle were ahead of April and me, and they were holding hands." He pauses, sighs. "It's such a stupid little thing, but it's stuck in my fucking head. She was holding his hand with one hand, and she had her other hand around his arm, and she was all up against his side like she couldn't get close enough to him. And every time he was talking to her, she was looking up at him with this look on her face. It's fucking *haunting* me, Fee." His voice drops to a murmur. "She looked at Bear like…fuck, I don't know how to put it."

"I know exactly the look you mean," I say. "Like he's the most important thing there has ever been. Complete and total adoration."

He nods. "Yeah, exactly. Complete and total adoration. No one's ever looked at me like that, man. I mean, look what we came from, huh? The way Mom and Dad treated each other? The fucking divorce? How ugly shit was for years afterward? The shit they both pulled, the shit they put on us?"

I thunk my head against the headrest. "Jesus *fucking*

Christ, Riley. Why the hell'd you have to go and bring up all *that* shit?"

"Because it's fucking relevant, Fee. Why do you think we're both so commitment-phobic? Don't tell me you haven't put that shit together."

I stare at him. "The hell are you talking about?"

He rolls his head on his neck in a gesture of disbelief. "Dude, I'm talking about Mom and Dad. Their toxic-as-fuck relationship was *the* defining feature of our lives growing up. Dad getting drunk and slapping Mom around. Mom throwing fuckin'...*everything* at him? Plates, mugs, bowls, fuckin' silverware. The screaming matches at three in the morning. Mom cheating on Dad with the literal UPS guy and making sure he caught 'em—"

"If you use the phrase 'balls deep' in reference to our mother, Riley, I swear to fucking god..."

He cackles. "I wasn't going to, as a matter of fact. I was gonna say in flagrante delicious or whatever that fuckin' phrase is."

I laugh. "I think it's 'delicto' or 'delecto' or something like that. Sure as fuck isn't 'delicious.'"

He waves me off. "Whatever. You know what I mean."

"What does that shit have to do with us being commitment-phobic? Which I am *not*, by the way."

We pull into the parking lot of The Borderline—the lot is packed, and the only spot is in the far back. He parks and shuts off the engine, but doesn't get out.

"You are, too, and so am I. We don't trust people. We don't trust women in particular, Fee, and why do you think that is?"

I think back, and I realize with a nauseated horror that he's right. My distrust is compounded by my distrust of myself because of what went down back in the day, but it goes deeper than that. I've never even *tried* to let anyone get close to me—I troll Tinder for easy, no-mess hookups with random chicks on vacation. It's cheap, meaningless, and strings-free. We both know the score, which means it's risk free. No chance of the girl wanting to get close, wanting to put her hooks into my heart.

Why didn't I want that?

Because I watched what Mom's infidelity did to Dad. It wasn't some accidental drunken hookup—it was intentional, calculated. Our UPS route driver was an acquaintance of Dad's, someone he'd known most of his life.

When Dad walked in on them, it was…bad. He nearly killed the guy, for one. Spent two months in jail for aggravated assault and battery, and his already problematic drinking habit only worsened to apocalyptic levels after he got out. He was the one to file, and Mom fought him every step of the way, just to fuck with him, just to spite him, even though she wanted out worse than he did. And no, Dad was far from innocent. He didn't beat her but he did get wasted regularly and started shit with her, and more than once he slapped her. She slugged him back, of course, because our dear old Mom didn't take any shit from anyone, least of all Dad. The divorce was long, nasty, messy, and chaotic. They talked shit about each other to us boys constantly. Pitted us against the other. Used us for leverage. Dad especially was bitter and angry—after jail and the divorce, he never again referred to Mom as anything other than "the whore" or "that fucking whore." He never dated again, and every female he ever encountered thereafter until the day he died, he treated with disgust and disdain.

Hard not to absorb all that, I guess. And clearly, it left scars on Riley and me both.

He's watching me. "Yeah, now you get it."

I frown at him. "When did you become so introspective?"

He rolls his eyes. "When every woman you seriously date says the same damn thing, you start paying attention."

"And what do they say?" I ask.

He doesn't answer right away. "That I'm fun, great in bed, and nice to look at, but not real boyfriend material. That I'm…shallow. A hound dog. Man-whore. Himbo."

"Rye, you're not—"

He cuts me off with a raised hand. "You know what really fuckin' sucks, bro? Realizing that they're all right." He blows out a blustery breath, shaking his head. "Fuck all that mess. Let's get bombed."

12

Ember

I CAN'T SLEEP.

Every time I close my stupid eyes, I see Felix.

Naked.

Standing there by his bed, panting, eyes glazed over and staring down at me with an expression that...I don't have the words to capture the way he looked at me after I finished blowing him. Reverent. In awe. Stunned speechless. Those are all close, but not good enough.

Good girl. Taking every last drop.

Apparently I have a praise kink, suddenly? That's new, and unexpected, and fucking weird.

I also can't sleep because this couch is all springs and no cushion. I tried the floor a few hours ago, but that was worse. Sort of like when it's torrentially downpouring so hard it seems like the wipers aren't doing a damn thing, so you turn them off and it does, in fact, get much worse.

The trip out here to LA with Faye was one for the ages. It took us just shy of three days, and those days were some of the most memorable of my life. Faye is endlessly hysterical. Turns out she brought her stash of pot and decided to get stoned and stay that way, and god, is she funny when she's high. Full of wild stories, twisted and crude jokes, and the occasional nugget of wisdom.

We actually got busted once, on I-80 somewhere, late at night. We got pulled over, and the state we were in—I forget which—wasn't a legal state. But I guess Faye has a medical card and a magical ability to talk even the most hard-ass of cops into letting us go with a warning. She actually, legitimately asked the cop, "You're not really going to arrest a little old lady on her way to see her grandkids one last time before she dies, are you?"

No, he was not.

We laughed our asses off, ate a toxic amount of shitty fast food, smoked a *ton* of pot, listened to great music, slept in shitty motels, and talked about everything and nothing. We stayed away from touchy and painful subjects like our dead husbands, and I stayed away from talking about Felix, even though he was on my mind constantly.

Tina lives in a decent but not great part of LA in a three-bedroom apartment on the fourth floor, no elevator. When we got there, Faye stood at the bottom of those stairs with dread in her eyes.

"Guess I'll be staying home more, huh?" she'd said to me.

Tina is a darling—sharp-tongued like Faye and dryly funny. She works as a hospice care nurse; and in the two days I've been here, I've never seen her out of scrubs. Ben is an adorable kid who developed an immediate crush on me—I don't play into it or encourage him to think anything inappropriate is gonna happen, but I do pay him attention because growing boys need attention. Alaina is a precocious little thing with a truly *wild* vocabulary and a penchant for sass that does her grandmother proud.

Faye and I spend the days with Ben and Alaina while Tina works—we take them out for lunch and ice cream, to the nearby park where Ben at first pretends to be too old and cool to play, but when his sister begs him to push her on the merry-go-round, he can't help but end up having fun. We watch TV and movies, and Ben makes me play Mario Kart with him—I suck horribly, but he thinks it's hysterical.

The only less-than-stellar part is Faye's health. It's like now that we've made it to California, her grip on life is just…slipping. She hides it behind a facade of bravado, hilarity, and orneriness, but I see it and Tina does, too. Faye just seems thinner and paler every day, has to take longer and more frequent breaks from walking, and eats very little.

Eventually, I decided to just get up. The small apartment is quiet and still in the pre-dawn gray. I set a pot of coffee to brewing and once there's enough, I sneak a cup and take it out onto the landing outside the door, where Tina has set up a folding camp chair for smoking her cigarettes—a habit which she and Faye have already fought about twice since we arrived.

I sip black coffee and watch the horizon above the LA skyline ombre from gray to pink to orange as the sun rises, and I cautiously pick apart the shield behind which I've hidden my feelings.

Mom always said I'm a freak of nature for my ability to compartmentalize like that—I can put my feelings aside and focus on something else entirely, pretending whatever bad thing I don't want to feel doesn't exist. It's not healthy, I'm aware of that. But it's just what I do. I like to process my feelings in my own time, when I'm ready.

With this, I'll never be entirely ready. But I have to go back to Michigan soon, and I need to face the mess that is my life.

Dutchie.

His face fills my mind's eye—his sandy blond hair that was always messy and sticking up in every direction, no matter how much he tried to comb it. His puppy dog brown eyes. His lips.

I remember his kisses. The softness of them—sweet and tender, as if I was the most precious thing in the world, delicate and fragile and priceless. He'd frame my face in his hands and move in slowly, eyes open and searching me as if my face somehow held the answers to everything. His lips would touch mine and he'd breathe out as if in relief, as if he'd been longing to kiss me.

He was subtle about wanting sex. He'd kiss me like that and his hands would slowly wander to my waist, find the hem of my shirt and hesitantly wander to my chest. I thought his hesitancy was sweet, although it also frustrated me at times, especially later in our marriage. Even though I literally never turned him down unless I was on my period or legitimately sick, he was always a little shy about it. I didn't know how to talk to him about it, though, and never really did. I wanted him to initiate it more—I was almost always the one to start things. Which I didn't mind, most of the time.

There were just times when I wanted to be…taken. Dominated a little. Treated like I wasn't a delicate flower. I was hesitant to show him the true depths of my need— the real intensity of my desires. I tempered my responses to things because it seemed like it made him uncomfortable when I went too crazy.

I was holding back.

Fuck.

Our whole marriage, I was holding back. I never gave Dutchie *all* of me. I didn't think he could handle it. There were times when I wanted sex and he was…I don't know. Not indifferent, just…not as eager for it as I was. Not as excited. I learned to recognize when he wasn't in the mood and I'd keep it to myself. Sometimes I'd wake up in the middle of the night and masturbate as silently as possible. And let me tell you, that's tough. You know how much it sucks having to tamp down your orgasm?

But how could I be mad at him about it? I couldn't. He was just so fucking loving. He lived to take care of me. He cooked for me all the time. Opened doors. Held my hand everywhere we went. Constantly asked me what he could do for me and never so much as blinked at my requests, even when they were odd or inconvenient for him.

Snuggling with Dutchie was the greatest. He loved to snuggle more than just about anything—I think that was his real love language. Laying in bed in Pumpkin, watching a show on our laptop, my head on his chest, his arm around my shoulders—that's when Dutchie was the happiest.

He never raised his voice to me, even in our worst argument.

He had the most incredible sense of direction of

anyone I've ever met, as if he had an internal compass as accurate as a Canadian goose's.

He could be uproariously funny, especially stoned. He would do these crazy impressions of famous actors—they weren't necessarily *accurate* impressions, but they were funny as hell and you knew who it was.

My thoughts turn dark, then.

To that night.

He'd been feeling under the weather for a while. Weird back pain. Loss of appetite that meant he was dropping weight when he was already a pretty slender guy. He was tired all the time all of a sudden. Stomach issues.

And then, that day, I noticed a yellowish tinge to his skin, and that *really* worried me. And then he started vomiting.

I drove us to the nearest ER. We waited. And waited. He got examined, got blood drawn, poked, prodded, x-rayed, MRI'd…the works.

Then came the results. A nurse guiding us to a different part of the hospital. A placard outside an office with the doctor's name and that awful word: oncologist. All I really remember is the scan results on a computer screen turned to face us. A mass over his pancreas. A big one. But not just the one—lots of them, as if the big mass had spawned a horde of little ones.

It was everywhere—stomach, lungs, bones, brain.

I remember the phrase "weeks at most" being uttered.

Palliative care. Make him comfortable. Get your affairs in order. Do you want to speak with a social worker? We have clergy available.

Dutchie fought it like a warrior—he was calm. Talked

about what we'd do after he beat it…even though we both knew there was no fucking hope.

And then, at some point, there was no more fight. There was a skeleton in the hospital bed, wrapped in jaundiced skin, all sunken eyes and wheezy breath. There were the endless hours of silence broken only by the beep and hiss and whirr of the support machinery. His eyes cracking open to find mine. That small, cheerful, loving smile would light up his face, no matter how he felt.

I lost time in that hospital room. Hours, days, and weeks jumbled together. There was no sun, no clouds, no moon, no stars, no soil, no wind. Just that room with the generic wallpaper and the machines and the bed and man I loved wasting away to nothing before my eyes, in agony even the strongest of drugs couldn't entirely mask.

Then there was the end.

His hand curling around mine with sudden strength. His last words that I've never been able to repeat, in my own head or out loud.

The monitor *beep-beep-beep*ing…then *beep—beep— beep*ing, and then *beep…beep…beep*ing…

And then…*beeeeeeeeeeeeeeeeeeeeeee*.…

The endless beep.

Flatline.

Eyes gone vacant. Staring at me but seeing nothing. The body an empty shell—a husk.

A hand touches my shoulder, shocking me. "Ember, honey? Are you alright?" Faye, her voice thin and shaky.

I nod. "Just…grieving." I realize I'm weeping.

"You want company or you want to be alone?"

"Alone," I whisper. "But I love you, Faye."

She presses a kiss to the crown of my head. "Love you too, missy."

I hear the door close and I'm alone again—alone with Dutchie stuck in that moment of death like an air bubble encased in ice.

I think about his last words to me again, but they skitter away from my mind. I just...I can't go there.

I'm still not ready.

I think about all the good times—which was pretty much all of it. Even the handful of arguments we got into I remember with happiness, because our best sex was after those arguments.

He once accused me of picking a fight just so we could have makeup sex. He was right, but I wasn't about to admit that, which turned into a whole other fight, which led to some seriously hot makeup sex. Oh, the irony of that. We laughed about it later.

The only stain on the joy of my memory of our life together is the reality of his death—the sudden and abrupt nature of it.

"I miss you so fucking much, Dutchie," I whisper out loud.

I feel his hand squeezing mine. The noise of LA waking up fades, and honking horns become the beep of the monitor.

"Em...ber." His voice was a file rasping over a cinder block.

"Dutchie-baby," I whispered—my favorite pet-name for him. "I love you."

He squeezed my hand again, shockingly hard. "Listen...Emmy." That was his nickname for me—Emmy.

No one before or since has or will call me that. That was his and his alone.

"I'm listening." I scooted my chair closer to the bed and put my face as close to his as I could.

"You're a light in the dark." His voice strengthened a little. "You can't hide it. Can't let it go out."

"I won't," I whispered, my voice wet with tears. "I promise."

"*Listen*." Another hard squeeze. "Your love is fire. A big bonfire. The sun itself."

"Dutchie—"

He spoke over me, his voice intense as he strove to get his point across with the last of his life. "When I'm gone, Emmy, you *can't* let your light go out." He squeezed my hand. "Ember. You can't let your light go out."

"I won't."

"Yes, you will." He was crying. "I want you to love again."

I shook my head. "No. No. Dutchie, *no*."

"*Yes*, Ember." He touched his clammy forehead to mine. "Your love is your light. Don't let it go out. You're gonna hide. Run. Bury it. But you gotta…" a wheeze, a cough, a groan of pain. "You *have* to love again. You won't want to, but you have to."

"I can't, Dutch. I can't. I can't do this without you."

"Have to."

"I won't."

He tried to laugh. "Not sure…I have time for a fight… or—or the strength for…for makeup…sex."

My laugh was a sob. "How can you joke, Dutchie?"

"How can I not?" He struggled to pull my hand to his lips. "Promise me."

"No—no."

"Emberly James. I've never asked you for a promise."

I wept bitterly, nodded. "Okay. Okay."

"Don't placate me. I want your vow—" he kissed my wedding band, and then moved his hand to my lips, "on our wedding rings."

"Damn you, Dutchie. I love you. I need you. I can't do this without you."

"No choice. And not…the point."

"Goddammit, Richard."

"Oh…shit. The real…name." He was weakening. Fading. "Vow. On our rings. You'll let yourself love again. You'll give him your light. You have to. The world needs your light. And out there somewhere is a man who will need the love you have to give. Swear it."

I shook my head. "Dutch."

"*Swear it*, goddammit!"

I stared at him, stunned by the ferocity in his gentle voice. "Dutchie—"

"Emberly. Please. I'm begging you." He'd looked at me with such desperation that I'd dissolved into helpless sobs.

"Okay, okay." I kissed his ring and then mine. "I swear to you on our rings that I'll…" I couldn't finish it. Swallowed hard. "That I will love again, someday."

He nodded. "The world needs your light. *He* needs it." His eyes closed. "Love you, Emmy."

"I love you, Dutchie-baby."

His grip on my hand weakened. His eyes opened. Saw me. He smiled.

For a moment, then, it seemed like he was seeing something else. His eyes brightened, and he smiled faintly.

And then…he was still, and his body was empty, and Dutchie was gone.

My husband was dead.

And he'd extracted a vow on our rings—which he knew damned well I held more sacred than any other possession—that I would love again.

Except I don't know how to keep that promise.

I fucking miss him.

It hurts.

I'm angry at him for leaving me.

I don't want to love again. I want Dutchie back. I want his soft kisses and tender snuggles. I want his hesitant hand reaching for my breast as he kisses me, as if we're sixteen and it's our first time instead of adults who've had a *lot* of sex together. I want his goofy humor. I want his irrational hatred of celery. His odd fondness for spiders. I want his ability to drive for hours on end without a break. His eyes glittering in the dark of our bus in a rest area somewhere in Kansas, listening to a couple in the RV next to us fucking loudly for hours on end. I want his weird ass taste in music—the most obscure indie folk you can imagine, and the more obscure the better.

He's gone, though.

He's gone.

Our rings are in that jewelry box he made for me—the one in a safe in Felix Crowe's garage back in Three Rivers, Michigan.

And I vowed that I'd love again.

I just never thought it would ever happen. Or if it did, I figured it'd be years from now, when my grief is a scar rather than a crusty, multi-colored scab on a barely healing wound.

How do you love again after loss? Faye never did. I know, I know what she'd say. What she *did* say—she had a whole life with Tommy.

I had not even eight short years.

Felix.

I see him in my mind, too. My heart pitter-patters in my chest at the thought of him, and even that hurts like a punch to the gut. How can I have butterflies for a man when Dutchie hasn't even been dead a year? What's wrong with me?

I sucked his cock.

He made me come—*so* hard, *so* many times.

I want it again. I want that again. I want *him* again.

I want to race back to Three Rivers right now and climb into his bed with him and fuck him until he sees his ancestors.

That's not love—that's lust; I lust for Felix.

He's fucking hot as hell—what red-blooded, straight female wouldn't lust after him? I mean, shit, Faye lusts after him and she's an eighty-year-old widow.

But…there *is* more, isn't there?

Deep down, I know there is.

We didn't fuck, we messed around. Why? Because I knew, instinctually, that if and when I sleep with Felix, it'll be over. I'll not be able to get away. I won't want to.

Because there's something there. Something real and big and deep and absolutely terrifying. I've only caught hints of it—in those few precious moments of emotional intimacy with him afterward, when I told him things I've never told anyone, not even Dutchie. The safety I felt— the ease in his presence when I let my walls down a little bit, the knowledge that he'd protect me, take care of me.

I saw it most of all in the way he let me go.

In some ways, I'm a wild animal. You can never totally domesticate me. I'll always, always have blacktop highway in my blood and the hum of tires in my veins. It's all I've ever known. If he'd tried to keep me there, I'd have left for good, bus be damned. Or, probably, I'd have raised almighty hell until I could leave with Pumpkin.

But he didn't. He understood and he released me. He has collateral, sure, but I know he didn't want me to leave.

Even though he's just as scared and fucked up as I am.

I also know he feels the connection between us. The seed of love.

I don't know what to do about it. About him.

I don't know how to let him in. I don't know how to let myself love him.

The door creaks open behind me and a little hand touches my shoulder. "Ember?"

I dash away tears and offer Alaina a little smile. "Hey there, honey. What's up?"

"Do you know how to make pancakes?"

I poke her ribs, eliciting a giggle. "Why, yes I do. Why do you ask?"

She rolls her eyes at me. "Because I want pancakes, silly lady."

"Ohhhh. I see." I pretend to think really hard. "I can do that. But I have two conditions."

She eyes me warily. "I don't got any money."

I laugh. "No, I don't want money. The first condition is that you have to help me make 'em. Can you do that?"

"YES!" she screams.

I laugh and cover her mouth. "Hey, now, people are still sleeping." I narrow my eyes at her. "The second condition…" I lean close to her and act like I have a secret. "This is the big one. You ready?"

She nods seriously. "Yes."

It's so hard not to laugh. "We have to make enough to share with *everyone*."

She lets out a disgusted sigh. "Well, duh! You can't just make *one* pancake. That's stupid!"

I dissolve into laughter, tickling her. "It is? Weird!"

I carry the howling, kicking Alaina back inside and we make a huge plate of thick, fluffy pancakes.

And we share them.

Even though Faye only nibbles at hers and then claims she needs to lie down, even though it's only eight in the morning.

13

Felix

S HE'S BEEN GONE FOR OVER A WEEK. SHE SENT ME a text yesterday explaining that Faye isn't doing well and she needs to stay in LA for a bit longer. I tell her I understand and to do what she needs to do. I'm not going anywhere.

The boys—Riley, Cole, and Nyx—have decided to break me out of my funk by taking me out every night. I haven't drank this heavily since Amy left. I wake up with a sour stomach and woozy head, slug back some coffee and Tylenol, and get to work, stopping for a breakfast burrito from Larry's taco truck. A greasy lunch cures the stomach, and by the end of the day, I'm feeling back to normal…ish.

But then one of the guys shows up and I end up in

some dive bar somewhere, throwing back shots of Jameson and pints of Labatt like I'm twenty-one all over again.

They categorically disallow any mention of Amy *or* Ember. No pining, they tell me. Just dick and fart jokes, stories of our high school antics, and discussions of good lays from days gone by...

Dude stuff.

They're distracting me, and it works. Mostly.

Thirteen days after Ember took my FJ40 and headed for LA with an old lady she wasn't related to, I found myself colossally wasted with the guys. Cole was the DD for the night and we'd all driven here in his sheriff's department SUV—we got a kick out of being locked in the back. Well, Nyx and I did. Riley sat in front with Cole, because being in the back would've given him nasty flashbacks, he said. Which is fair.

We're at a dive bar in the next county over, a place Nyx knows about. Dive is a nice term for the place. Shithole is closer. The floors are wood planks so old, sticky, and creaky, I'm worried my foot is gonna stick to one and then go through it. The ceiling is drop tile barely seven feet high—I can touch it if I go on my tiptoes and hop. The walls are covered in the requisite neon beer company paraphernalia, spotted, filmy whiskey brand mirrors, and holes from bar fights past. A band plays in the corner—good ol' boys with long gray beards playing rollicking bluegrass except the lead singer is rapping...about possums? I don't know. The bartender is a woman in her late thirties wearing ripped black jeans shorts so short her entire ass hangs out beneath the frayed hems and a black tank top that leaves her improbably gargantuan tits almost totally bare. For some reason, mixed drinks are popular. You know, the kind that require a lot of shaking of those silver cups.

Nyx is at the bar, ordering shot after shot and working his magic on the bartender. She's eating it up in a way that says they've probably gotten it on a few times.

Riley watches, snickering behind his hand. "Now I know why he wanted to come here."

Cole leans back in his chair, drinking beer straight from a pitcher. "Those two have been on and off for years. They go through a whole circus. He shows up, flirts with her, flashes that stupid grin of his, they hook up for a coupl'a months, and then he does or says somethin' stupid and she kicks his ass to the curb. He ignores her for a few months, but then he gets a hankering for those giant bazingas of hers, and off they go again."

I glance at him. "Thought you were the DD?"

He juts his chin at a uniformed deputy sitting by the door, sipping a bottle of water and reading a paperback thriller. "Called in a favor. Brian'll drive us. He's a teetotaler and he owes me."

"For what?" Riley asks.

Cole snickers into the pitcher. "Let's just say he fucked up big time, I found out and saved his ass—and his career. He'll be doing me favors for a decade."

"Aw, c'mon," Riley says, throwing a shelled peanut at Cole. "Details, bitch!"

"What is this, real housewives?" Cole asks, flipping the peanut back at Riley. "It was official police business. I ain't tellin' you shit."

Riley hucks the peanut clear across the bar, nailing Brian in the face—a reminder that before he went to prison, he had full-ride offers from no fewer than eight

Big Ten universities. His QB records still stand at Three Rivers High. "Yo, B!"

Brian frowns, stuffs a slip of paper in his book to hold the place, sets it on the chair, and ambles this way. "Crowe boys. Sheriff. What's up?"

Riley cracks a peanut open and tosses the halves in his mouth. "What'd you do that you owe Manny-boy a decade's worth of favors? His ass has clammed up."

Brian—all six-six and three hundred pounds of him—frowns at Riley. "You'd have to get me drunk to tell that story, and I don't drink."

"That's what Cole said," Riley says. "Never?"

"Let's just say the last time I got drunk, I decided to have an impromptu rodeo with my Uncle Roy's prize bull."

Riley snickers. "How'd that go?"

"Stayed on." He shrugs. "Had to rebuild half the barn, though."

"I..." Riley frowns, trying to picture what happened. "Um. What?"

Brian shakes his head. "Problem with an impromptu rodeo is that there wasn't no arena and there wasn't no clowns. If I'd'a let go, he'd've killed me. So I stayed my ass on while he tore up the fence, the chicken coop, flipped over the Gator, and wrecked most of the barn."

Riley blinks at him. "Jesus. And you survived?"

Brian just shrugs. "Got a hard head, I guess." He nods at Cole. "Ready when you are, boss, but no hurry. Lisa's at a girl's night with her cousins, so I got nothin' better to do."

Cole just nods back. "Thanks, Brian."

When Brian goes back to his post, Riley bursts into laughter. "What the hell?"

Cole grins. "Brian's one of a kind. Was on a domestic

call with him once, year or two back. Some ol' boy was whalin' on his woman, neighbors called it in, we show up thinkin' it'll go how most domestic calls go. Well, no, not exactly, it turns out. Motherfucker came at Brian with a Louisville Slugger. Cracked him clean across the back of the head. Brian didn't so much as flinch. I'm dead-ass for real. Bleeding like a stuck pig, that big motherfucker didn't so much as twitch. Clocked the bastard in the nose, dropped him, and hauled him off to jail for assaulting an officer. Sixteen stitches and a concussion. Woulda killed most people." He glances at Riley. "Reminds me of your boy Bear, actually. Just...less scary."

I grin, laughing. "No one is as scary as Bear." I shrug. "When he's pissed, at least."

Cole widens his eyes. "I'll never forget that call, man. I thought for sure I was rollin' up to a murder scene."

"If it wasn't for Noelle literally climbing him like a tree and making him stop, it would've been," I say. "That girl has some serious cajones."

Cole nods. "No shit. I was tryin' to figure out how I was gonna stop Bear without hurting him. I doubt a taser would do much."

Riley pulls out his phone. Dials. Puts it on speaker— Bear answers. "Yo, Rye. What's good?"

"Hey, Bear. You ever been tased by cops?" Rye asks.

Bear chuckles. "Hell yeah. Few times."

"Did it drop you?"

He barks a laugh. "Hardly. Not gonna go so far as to say it tickled, but no, it definitely didn't drop me."

"Guess I'm gladder than ever that your girl was there that day, then," Cole says.

"That the Sheriff?" Bear asks.

"Yep," Riley answers. "That was it, buddy, thanks."

Bear is quiet for a second or two. "You'd'a had to shoot me, Sheriff. Trust me when I tell you nonlethal stuff don't work on me when I get like that."

"And trust me when I tell you I pray you never get like that again, Bear," Cole says, his voice earnest. "And I ain't a prayin' man."

"You and me both, Sheriff," Bear rumbles. "And it won't, if Noelle's got anything to say about it."

After a bit more chitchat between Riley, Cole, and Bear, they end the call and we get back to crude jokes, increasingly ridiculous stories, and drinking way too much shitty domestic beer.

At some point in the night, Nyx vanishes with the bartender. Maybe an hour before close, Riley leaves the table and goes to mingle with the crowd on the dance floor, and Cole and I watch him flirt with and charm an absurdly hot girl in her early twenties. By the time the bartender hollers last call, those two are all but fucking on the dance floor, and when the lights come on, they bolt out the front door—Riley turning back in the doorway to shoot us a grin and double finger guns.

Cole and I trade glances.

"Your brother sure does have a way with the ladies," Cole says.

I laugh, shaking my head. "Yeah, he does. Always has."

"Think he'll ever settle down?" Cole asks.

I shrug, hesitate, and then nod. "I think so, someday. It'd take a hell of a woman to tame him, though. He may be reformed somewhat, but he's still got a wild streak a mile wide and a mile deep."

Cole claps me on the shoulder, standing up unsteadily. "Well, buddy, time to get on."

I wobble to my feet, closing one eye as the world splits into two and three whirling versions of itself. "Oh, shit. I'm drunker than I thought."

"You and me both, Fee," Cole says. "C'mon. Bry! Help us get outta here, rookie."

Brian shoves his book in his back pocket and ambles over to us, hooking a big arm around each of us and helping us to the squad SUV.

I peer at Brian—or at the three of him. "How'd you get here?"

He snorts a laugh. "Wife dropped me off. Her cousin lives in the area."

"Well, I'm thankful, sir." I give him a salute that almost pulls me off balance.

"Yeah, yeah," Brian says. "Just get home without barfing in the car and we'll be good."

"Imma do my best, but keep them window buttons handy," I say. I squint at Cole as we settle in the backseat, leaning against each other. "I know why I'm drunk. I know why Riley's drunk. Nyx is just a fuckin' animal. But you, Cole, my guy. I don't know about you." I clap him on the chest. "Whazzup with you, Shurrrrif Mannix?"

Cole groans, shakes his head. "Ah, fuck. Don't ask me that."

"Too late. Already did."

Cole rests his head backward, letting it loll and roll with the movement of the vehicle. "I'm drinkin' about the one who got away, Felix."

I blink at him. "Whoozzat?"

His head moves side to side—it could be him shaking

it, or it could be a loll as we go over a bump. "Nope. Not goin' there, man. Why d'you drink I'm thinkin' about her? Wait, no. That's not right. Why do you *think* I'm *drinking* about her?" he says, over-enunciating the last sentence.

"Alright, fine," I slur. "What the fuck ever, man. Keep your secrets."

"Don' be mad, Fee. I just...I can't go there. Fuckin' hurts, you know?"

I look at my friend, and for a split second there's only one of him—golden-blond hair cut short and swept to one side, buzzed to the scalp on the sides, with a short neat beard and brown eyes. I happen to know quite a few of Three Rivers' female residents, married or otherwise, would sell an ovary to get Cole's attention, because the fucker is just that damn pretty. I mean, picture a Midwestern, all-American, down-home boy next door. Picture the swoony hero from a Hallmark romance movie. That's Cole Mannix. Clean cut, jacked, handsome, easy-going but with a firm grasp of his authority as county sheriff.

Back in high school, it was always Riley, Nyx, Cole, and me—Riley and Nyx were the black-haired bad boys, and Cole and I were the golden-haired good boys. Riley was the quarterback who slept with all of the attractive girls in our year and several from the years below us and most of the one older than us; Cole was the star running back with the captain of the cheer squad girlfriend; Nyx was the tight end party animal, and I was the wide receiver who was somewhere between Riley's cocky bad boy and Cole's white knight.

It's the four of us again, and it feels good to be among my guys again. Nyx is always just himself. Back in high school, Nyx was then as he is now—a party animal, the class clown, the one who'd jump off a roof into a pool for laughs and to get the attention of the girls, the one who rode a chopper he built himself to school; he's the one who, unless you really know him well, you'd never suspect the hidden depths he hides behind the lunatic adrenaline-junkie facade.

God, I'm maudlin.

Thinking about high school sucks. Because it always and inevitably leads to thoughts of Amy.

Fuck.

No, no, no.

I've done so good tonight. Haven't thought about Ember *or* Amy even once.

But now I'm remembering the good old days, when it was Riley and whoever he was banging at the time, Cole and Lacey, me and Amy, and Nyx usually by himself. We'd take Cole's beat-up old GMC Savannah to Secret Beach, light a bonfire, and get wasted on beer purchased with Riley's fake ID from the corner store in the next town north. We'd all go skinny dipping, skin flashing in the moonlight, laughing as the firelight flickered on the night-still waters of Lake Michigan.

Amy, an all-state swimmer, would be way ahead of everyone, and I'd be gamely trying to reach her. She'd let me, eventually, and we'd tread water and whisper to each other. Swim back to where we can touch bottom and make out. Find a spot on the beach away from the others and have sex.

Find our way back to the fire and keep drinking.

God, those were fun days.

"'Member the bonfires at Secret Beach, Cole?" I ask.

He groans. "Ah fuck, Fee. Don't talk about that shit." He covers his face. "I can still see Lacey stripping out of her shorts. That was the hottest thing I could imagine, back then. The hottest girl in Three Rivers shimmying her fine ass outta them tight little shorts, peeling off that shirt and lookin' at me like I'm dessert. Fuck." He rubs his face. "Goddammit, Fee. I hate you for bringing that up."

"I know. I hate myself."

"Still the hottest thing I can imagine," he mutters.

"Think we'll ever get over 'em?" I ask.

"Fuck if I know," he growls.

"This is you, Felix," I hear Brian say. "C'mon, I'll walk you in."

I paw at the door, forgetting I'm in the back of a police car. The door opens and I tumble out into Bryan's hands. He hauls me upright, sets me on my feet, and walks me with his hands on my shoulders to my front door. I wobble, topple forward against the storm door, and fumble my keys out of my pocket. Drop them. Brian retrieves them and unlocks my door.

I hold on to the door for balance and salute Brian. "I'm good. Thanks, buddy ol' pal."

Brian pats me on the shoulder. "Drink water. Take Tylenol. Sleep on your side."

"Not m'first rodeo," I mutter. "But I appreciate the advice."

When he's gone, I stagger into my kitchen and pour myself a big glass of water from the tap and spend a long time drinking. Throw back a few Tylenol and then take a few more and a full glass of water to my bedside table.

Even hammered, I can't sleep in clothes, so I struggle

out of them. Collapse on my left side in my bed with the bathroom trashcan on the floor beside me, just in case.

The last thing I remember is my phone dinging with a text message, but I'm too close to passing out to read it.

I'm pretty sure it's from Ember.

Then, nothing.

⌒꙳

I wake up dying of thirst. Groan as I try to sit up—my head is pounding and my mouth is a desert. I'm disoriented, still drunk.

"Here, let me help you," a soft, familiar female voice says.

Soft hands touch mine, help me put the glass to my lips, tip it. Fingers put a pill in my mouth and help me chase it down.

The world is spinning.

It's fun *getting* drunk, but it's not fun *being* drunk. Or maybe I'm getting too fucking old for this shit.

Wait…who's helping me?

I peer around my room and see a female figure perched on the edge of my bed. A familiar one.

A figure I couldn't forget no matter how drunk I am.

Long black hair glinting in the moonlight from my window. Olive skin from her Italian heritage. Long, slender legs bare beneath khaki shorts. A sleeveless V-neck top showing off her cleavage. Bare feet. Those damned eyes that I used to love staring into, brown and heated.

I stare, blinking. Surely I'm dreaming. "The fuck?"

"Hi, Fee." Her voice is different—a little lower, a little more grown-up.

"No. Uh-uh. I don't want this dream." I rub my face, grind my knuckles into my eyes. "Wake up, goddammit."

She touches my arm. "Hey, relax. You're not dreaming." Her laugh is low and amused. "You are hammered, though."

"Not hammered enough." I cover my face, take a few deep breaths, and lower my hands—she's still here, in Three Rivers, in my house, on my bed.

Amy.

"Is it that bad to see me?" she asks with a little laugh. "Thought you'd be happier."

"Shit." I just look at her—I'm sober enough that I'm only seeing one of everything, at least. "You sure this is real?"

She's as beautiful as ever—maybe even more. She's still tall and svelte, but she's put on some curve in her hips and thighs. Her hair is expensively and expertly cut. Pin straight, jet black. Perfect makeup. Bright red lips—she always did like bold red lipstick. I used to have to wipe that shit off me all damn day 'cause she was always kissing on me.

Fuck, fuck.

I stare at her, blinking—she's real. "Amy."

She smiles. "Hi."

"What—um. What are you—how?" I take another long drink of water. "I'm confused."

"My husband had one too many affairs, so I left him. My girls are with their grandparents in Florida for the summer while Greg and I figure things out."

"Oh." I have no idea what to say, what to think, what to feel—other than confused and drunk.

"I kept tabs on you over the years," she says, tracing a

fingertip across my knuckles, from knuckle to dip, knuckle to dip. "No wife, no girlfriend, huh?"

I shake my head. "Nope."

"Is that my fault?"

I frown at her—god, she's gorgeous. Age has refined her beauty. Age, and clean, expensive living. "Fuck, Amy, are we really going there right now?"

"It's been over a decade. We never talked about it. " She shrugs. "May as well, right?"

"Well then, yeah, it is your fault." I close my eyes and sigh. "But then...no it's not. It's mine."

"I should've given you a chance."

"Yeah."

"But, Fee..." She moves her hand from my hand to my thigh. "I was just so shocked and hurt. I never thought you'd do that."

"I'm too drunk for this," I mutter. "Or not drunk enough."

"I drove almost four hours to be here. To see you." She pushes her fingers into my hair. "I thought about you a lot over the years."

"You're all I thought about." I stare at her, because it's so surreal that she's here like this, so suddenly, so un-expectedly. "I was so young, Amy. So dumb. So drunk. She...I—"I shake my head. "Sounds stupid to even say it, but I thought it was you. That's how wasted I was. Fucking Cassie Miller."

Amy groans. "Cassie Miller. She always did want you, and she hated me for having you." She frowns at me. "She came on to you?"

I shake my head. "No. She...I was almost passed out. All I really remember is..." I close my eyes and for the first time in years I go back to that night in my mind. "Dark hair, hands, being kissed. Being touched. Jacked off. It felt good, and I was drunk. Couldn't see straight—could barely fuckin' move. It's honestly shocking that my dick even worked. But she was like, 'c'mon Fee, it's me. Don't you want me?'"

She closes her eyes, wincing. "She really said that? It's me?"

I nod. "Yeah. Black hair, similar skin color." I cover my face. "She…she did everything. I couldn't even sit up. When she finished, she got off and leaned down to kiss me. And then I…" I scrub my face, wishing to hell I was sober for this. "I realized who it was. Who I'd just fucked. That it wasn't you."

"*Everyone* saw, Fee." She says it in a whisper. "I saw. I watched it all happen."

"You did?" I shake my head. "I didn't know that. Why didn't you say anything? Do anything?"

"I was across the field with Becky, Rachel, and Fiona. I didn't understand what was happening at first, and then when I did I was so stunned I couldn't move. And you… you went with it. That's what I saw—you laying there letting another girl put her hands all over you, letting her fuck you. That's what I saw."

I nod, guilt and regret burning in my belly. "I…Amy, I…I'm sorry. It was dark and I was so goddamn drunk, and I thought she was you."

"I never let you get two words in," she whispers. "I've regretted that every single day since. I should've let you explain. I knew how drunk you were. I knew how Cassie felt about you, and how much she hated me. I knew she'd do anything to get you. I just…I was so shocked and hurt that I never…I couldn't think straight."

"I've hated myself ever since," I whisper. "That I did that to you. That I let that happen." I fight nausea at the memory. "I haven't been that drunk until now." I laugh. "Except for the year after you left. I was a colossal mess for a while."

She laughs bitterly. "Me too. I went boy crazy in college. Slept with every guy I could, trying to erase you from my system."

"Did it work?" I ask. "I mean, I guess it did. You got married and had kids."

Her laugh is not just bitter, now, it's…whatever is uglier and angrier than mere bitterness. "That was more of the same, babe. Greg was…everything you're not, in both good ways and bad. He was the right choice, on paper. Smart. Successful. Rich. Stable. Attractive. Sensible."

I bark a wry, sarcastic laugh. "All the things I'm not, huh?"

She shrugs a slender shoulder. "He was also egotistical, narcissistic, chauvinistic, self-centered, vain, and a totally elitist snob."

"More things I'm not, eh?" I say, snickering.

She nods. "It was a horrible marriage. I gave up my career to have his kids and raise them. And once he had the two kids to show off at the country club and the church and bring your kids to work days, he wasn't interested in me at all. He left me at home to raise the girls and take care of the house like a good little wifey while he went golfing and fucked every secretary and assistant and temp he could get his hands on while if I so much as looked in the direction of another male, he'd lose his shit."

"He hit you?" I ask.

She shakes her head. "No, just mental and emotional abuse, abandonment, neglect, entrapment…you know, the standard stuff."

"That shit ain't standard, Amy."

She snorts. "You'd be surprised, Felix."

"Why are you here?" I ask.

"Here in Three Rivers or here in your house?"

"Well, let's start with in my house at…" I check the clock on my bedside table, "three-forty-five in the morning."

"I had a nasty argument with Greg about custody. He thinks he's getting full custody, but I have all sorts of evidence of his infidelity, as well as recordings of him screaming obscenities at me, threatening to hurt me, talking about framing me for drug possession…I lost my shit, got in the car, and drove away. I ended up here."

"But…how'd you find my house?" I ask.

She grins. "Well, when I finally realized that I had to leave Greg, I had to start getting money of my own, since in usual abuser fashion, he controlled the finances. So I reached out to a friend of mine who's a private investigator, and she hired me to be an online investigator. I'd dig up everything I could find on social media and the internet about her targets. I got good at it. Which meant it was pretty damned easy to find your address."

I nod. "Okay, but…you just sorta came in?"

She grins sheepishly, shrugging. "Your door was wide open and the lights were on."

I frown. "My door was open?"

She nods. "Front door was wide open."

I groan, laughing. "Wow, thanks for looking out for me, Brian. Jesus."

"Brian?"

I shrug. "Friend of a friend who drove me home and helped me inside."

She pats my legs. "I was worried, so I called out but you didn't answer. I came in to make sure everything was okay and found you passed out. I wasn't here more than two minutes before you woke up to get a drink."

I shake my head. "It's so surreal that you're here."

"It's surreal to be here with you, to be honest."

"But...at four in the morning?"

She shrugs. "I was just gonna drive by so I knew where it was, but then I saw your door open."

Silence.

"I missed you, Fee."

"Amy," I whisper. "You have the worst fucking timing."

"Why?" She asks. "You're with someone?"

"Um, sort of."

Her grin is actually sort of cocky. "Well, sort of isn't yes, is it?" The cocky grin fades. "I am sorry, Felix. I'm sorry for...not letting you explain. For derailing both of our lives over something that wasn't even your fault."

"It was, though. I should've known."

She's somehow closer, smelling of expensive perfume and radiating warmth. Her hand slides higher on my thigh—the blankets are around my knees, and I'm wearing nothing but a pair of black boxer briefs. "It's not your fault, Fee. It's Cassie's. She took advantage of you. You were drunk and couldn't consent."

My heart lurches—I've fantasized about almost exactly this situation happening countless times over the years. Amy appearing like a ghost from the past but real, apologizing, taking the guilt away, wanting me again, making everything okay.

I'm woozy. Disoriented, confused. It hurts—she hurts to be near. Her hand on my thigh is like fire...and I'm not sure it's the good kind of fire.

"Amy, I—"

She's leaning in. "Fee, c'mon. You *have* to have thought about this. Wanted this. I'm here. I want to...I want you." Her hand is centimeters from my junk. Her lips are ghosting across mine as she whispers. "I've never stopped wanting you. I...I imagined you every time Greg and I had sex. It was always you."

I hear something, somewhere in the house.

My stomach twists, and my heart protests; my body tingles, aches. "Amy..."I grab her wrist. "Hold on."

Her lips halt, her hand freezes. "Fee, I thought—"

"Now not, Amy. Not like this. I...fuck." It's like a nightmare flashback. My heart hammers in my chest, my breath coming short. I'm back in that field, a teenager again, so stupidly drunk I barely know my own name, about to make the biggest mistake of my life. "I can't. Not—not now. Not like this."

"Fee," Another voice says from the hallway outside my room. "I'm back. I hope you don't mind I let myself... in." Ember—her voice pierces my very soul. The hurt. The shock. The confusion. "I see."

I hear feet on the floor, the door slam.

14

Ember

M Y HEART IS CRUSHED. I'M SHAKING ALL OVER, hyperventilating too hard to even sob.

I can't think. Can't even feel—it's not numbness, it's…shock.

I drove here like a bat out of hell, ready to throw myself at Felix, ready to beg him to comfort me, to hold me, to make me feel safe again.

To soothe my grief-riddled heart.

Instead, I find a gorgeous woman in his bed. Tall, skinny, with perfect black hair and a twenty-thousand dollar Birkin bag on the foot of Felix's bed, her French manicured fingernails flirting with his cock, her mouth on his, kissing him.

His lips that are supposed to be mine.

His cock that's supposed to be for me.

I was ready.

I wanted it.

His heart.

His love.

Rage at the unfairness of life smashes through me like a hurricane, and I feel my lungs freezing solid in my chest, and my head vises in on itself until it's three sizes too small, and my heart is pounding against my ribcage with such rabid ferocity that it's physically painful and medically worrying.

Gears grind as I try to get the shifter into first. I know I shouldn't be driving in this state, but I have to get away. I know he'll have an excuse or an explanation, and I just don't care.

"*FUCK!*" I scream, and then smash the steering wheel with my fists, screaming my throat raw.

I take a deep breath and hold it—finesse the shifter into first and messily lurch away from the curb.

Past the sleek black Mercedes convertible which must belong to that woman.

His ex. The one who fucked up his heart.

Well, let her repair it, then.

Fuck him.

I can't even really run away—he still has my bus.

My cell phone rings—I ignore it until it stops, only for it to start ringing again immediately. He calls six times in a row and leaves six voicemails. And then the barrage of text message alerts, coming so fast that the alert tones overlap.

I can't see through my tears. I have no idea where I'm going. I'm not even sure I'm on a road. I shouldn't be driving, but I can't risk letting Felix catch me. I'll be weak and let him explain. I don't want an explanation. I don't want to know why his ex was in his bedroom at four in the morning.

A little voice niggles at me, deep down, whispering questions.

Why was she dressed and sitting on the edge of his bed as if she'd just arrived, while he was in bed and half-naked?

(*They just finished fucking and she was about to leave*) answers the hurt in my soul.

Why did he look so upset, so confused, so hurt?

(*Because he knew he was guilty, guilty, guilty*) answers the hurt in my heart.

Why was there a glass of water and a bottle of Tylenol on his side table and an empty garbage can beside his bed?

(*Drunk ex sex, obviously*) answers the hurt in my mind.

Streetlights pass overhead, glowing orange-amber. On my left, the lake is a dark void. Headlights approach. Flash at me. A horn honks.

I realize I'm on the wrong side of the road. Swerve to put the white line on my right.

My phone rings again.

And again.

And again.

More texts.

I'm tempted to throw my phone out the window—and I'm just as tempted to see what he has to say for himself.

No.

Don't go there.

Don't open yourself up to bullshit. Because you just know it's gonna be bullshit.

Men are just naturally cheaters, Mom used to tell me. Especially once I got to dating age. It was a refrain for her— *men are just naturally cheaters; have fun with 'em but don't trust 'em...not a one.*

I always dismissed it as the bitterness of a woman cheated on. Mom was a hurt, bitter woman—something I only really came to understand after she was gone, as I entered adulthood myself. I've never known my father's identity, and I now suspect it's because he hurt her. I always assumed it was because he was just some rando she hooked up with at a show, and that's possible, but it seems more likely that he meant something to her. She wouldn't have erased all evidence of his existence if he hadn't hurt her. If he was just some hump-and-dump from a show, she'd have told me something about him. His name. Where in the country I was conceived—a*nything* about him.

But no. For all the information she ever gave up on the subject, I may as well have been an immaculate conception.

I've thought about looking for him but I've always decided not to—it's not like he's going to suddenly want a relationship with a daughter he doesn't know exists, or worse yet, knows about and abandoned anyway.

It's fucked up that it's easier to think about my long-lost father than Felix.

I'm alone on the road again, and now the streetlights are gone, leaving me in darkness with only the moon for light.

I think I'm heading north. Not like it matters. Not like I care.

Maybe I'll just leave the bus. I have the rest of my things. Clothes and toiletries, at least. I could come back for the rest later, once I've had some emotional distance.

Yeah, that's the only answer. I can't deal with him.

I can't deal with any more heartache, any more loss, any more grief…any more anything.

It's too hard.

I've lost too much. I've lost everyone I've ever cared about.

GramGram.

Mom.

Dutchie.

Faye.

Now Felix before I even really had him.

It's just so fucking unfair. I fought with myself all the way here from California—about Felix, about my heart: I'm ready…I'm not ready.

By the time I reached Michigan, I was fully on board. Despite my hurting heart, despite my fear, I realized that Felix is important. I just feel safe with him—or, I did. I instinctively trust him. I was willing, almost immediately, to offer my body to him. My heart is a different topic, but that wasn't far behind.

Now?

I'm so mixed up I don't know what to do, how to feel, what to think, where to go.

I wonder how long you can endure a panic attack before it becomes a medical problem? I can't breathe properly; it feels like an elephant is sitting on my chest. My hands are shaking and I'm crying so hard it's almost like a seizure.

Yet, my brain is going a million miles an hour.

Hating Felix.

Loving him.

Wanting to find him and slap him and curse him out for fucking with my heart like that.

Wanting to let him explain, hoping there's an explanation that lets us be together.

I have flashbacks of that magical moment I shared with him. Kissing him. Touching. The pleasure was almost secondary to the emotional intimacy—as if it was more than mere foreplay.

He touched me and kissed me like…god, I don't even know. Like I was…precious. But not fragile. He didn't treat me like a porcelain doll. But he was still respectful, considerate.

And my god, how hard he made me come…multiple times.

FUCK!

Why did he have to go and fuck his ex? We could have had something real.

Tears flow faster as hurt and anger boil over and turn acidic in my gut—nausea bubbles in my belly, threatening to spew my chaotic emotions past my clenched teeth.

Maybe he didn't fuck her. Maybe it was a misunderstanding. I want so desperately to believe that.

I wish Faye were here. She'd have something saucy, sassy, sarcastic, and insightful to say.

God, I miss that woman already.

My phone jangles again, and I'm more tempted than ever to either pick it up and talk to him or pick it up and throw into the fucking lake.

The temptation is too powerful—I let my gaze steal down to the passenger seat, to my purse, to the blue-white-glowing rectangle inside.

No.

I rip my gaze back up the road, but it's too late. A fat raccoon crouches in the middle of the road, eyes glowing in my headlights.

I know better, but instinct takes over. My foot smashes the brake pedal and the back end fishtails, tires squealing, and I feel them stutter and skip on the blacktop. I wrench foolishly, stupidly, recklessly at the wheel to get the nose under control, but the SUV bobbles, swerves too far the other direction.

Time becomes elastic, stretching like taffy.

I feel gravity twisting and grabbing at me as the vehicle hurtles airborne, and then my purse is above my head and everything is tumbling out of it—phone, wallet, lip gloss, wrapped tampons, pens, hand sanitizer, the box of condoms I bought on the way to Michigan, a transparent yellow plastic lighter, a pre-rolled joint in a glass tube…

The stretch of time lasts for a singular eternity as the SUV rotates midair; the tires smack blacktop with a sickening crunching squeal, and time snaps back and speeds up, everything happening all at once, too fast. I'm rolling, and glass is shattering and metal is screaming and agony is crashing through me and I'm seeing stars and feeling lances of pain in a delocalized rain of razors.

The rolling lasts for an hour.

Stopping abruptly, the SUV teetering on two tires and then topples to its side, driver's side facing the sky. I'm suspended in the air sideways. Hot blood trickles into my eyes, tangs in my mouth. Smoke swirls. Silence, but for the faint creak of a still-spinning wheel.

My eyes scan, search—find a glowing blue-white rectangle below my face, just out of reach.

I stretch, gritting my teeth around a scream. Tap the

screen—it tries to recognize my face but I'm out of range or it's too dark. The keypad pops up, prompting me to input my code. Dizzy, woozy, agony radiating from a dozen places, darkness enveloping me, I struggle to remember my passcode and then struggle to input it correctly. I succeed after a failed attempt. The home screen appears, and I tap the green messages squircle with its red icon telling me I have twenty-one unread messages.

Blood trickles down my arm, over my wrist, onto my finger, smearing the screen with dark red streaks. Tap the bar at the bottom, bringing up the keyboard.

I'm faint, fading. It's hard to think.

Fucking raccoon. Next time, I'm plowing over the fat little bitch.

H—

E—

L—

P—

I have to type each letter carefully—everything is dark and twisty. I think I sent the message—I squint at the screen as if I'm drunk and see each letter in blue on the screen, but the blue bar is stuck a quarter inch from the right side of the screen, indicating the message hasn't gone through yet.

Please, please, please.

Fucking raccoon.

Also, fuck that stupid tall skinny rich bitch for poaching my man.

Bloop.

The letters arrange themselves higher on the screen, and the word "delivered" appears beneath the P.

Read it.

Read it, goddammit.

I can't make my arm work, can't move my fingers, can't stop my eyes from closing.

Stay awake.

Stay the fuck awake, Ember.

The last thing I see is "Delivered" switch to "read" and a gray bubble with three dots appears, the dots rippling.

I hear the reverse *bloop* of incoming messages, but my eyes won't focus, and the narrowing dark surrounds me with swirling hungry shadows.

F-E-E—

I manage to get them all together, smearing blood on the blue send arrow.

The last thing I see is a gray box appear: ***I'm coming. I'll find you. I love you.***

Fucking *what*?

This is when he says it? When I'm fucking dying?

That's my final thought before the ravenous dark swallows me.

15

Felix

AMY IS HOVERING AS I SCRAMBLE OUT OF BED, ignoring her barrage of questions. I topple to the floor as I try to work my legs into my jeans, but I'm too frantic and still half-drunk.

Fuck pants.

I snag a pair of shorts from a drawer and pull them on while still on the floor, then stagger to my feet.

"FELIX!" Amy shouts, grabbing my shoulders. "What the fuck is happening?"

I wrench out of her grip, stumbling unsteadily away from her. "She needs help! I don't fucking know. I don't fucking know."

She shoves past me and pushes on my bare chest. "Stop! You can*not* drive like this, Fee."

"Fuck, fuck—*FUCK*!" I stab at my phone's screen until Riley's name appears and the burble of the ringing line emits from the speaker.

"'Lo? Fee? Whazzit? Whazzwrong?"

"Ember—Ember," I choke out. "Texted help. I'm too drunk to drive. Please fucking tell me you can drive."

He's instantly awake and alert. 'Yeah, I'm good, I'm good. You're at home?"

"Yes."

"Be there in less than five, brother. I'm coming."

Amy vanished while I was talking to Riley, and now she reappears with a T-shirt which she shoves unceremoniously over my head and guides my arms through the sleeves. She vanishes again and reappears with my running shoes, a ratty pair of black New Balance sneakers that I've had for years—they're green from being worn while cutting grass, and they're knotted and sagging open from shoving my feet into them without untying them.

I slam my feet into them, and then peer at Amy. "Thanks," I mutter.

"Fee, I—" her eyes are scared, worried.

My gut tells me something is terribly, terribly wrong, and I'm panicking and terrified and angry.

"A couple months ago, I'd have…" I shake my head. "I'd have thought I still loved you."

"Fee—"

I hear tires screech in the distance, and I make for the front door, phone gripped in my hand in case she texts again or calls.

"Guilt and regret aren't love." I scrub at my face with one hand, trying to push sobriety into my brain. "I don't love you. I did, back then. But I fucked up. Maybe it was my fault, maybe it wasn't. Dunno. But we can't get that back, Amy. We can't get back there."

"Fee, we can. Not back there, maybe, but somewhere new."

I shake my head. "No. Because you're not her."

Riley's headlights stab the darkness out front of my house, and he skids to a stop. I jog out the front door, leave it open, leave Amy standing alone in my living room, staring after me with tears in her eyes.

Riley leans across his cab and shoves the passenger door open. I hop in and slam it closed.

"Where is she?" he asks.

"I don't know. I don't know. She's not sharing her location with me."

He's pulling away from the curb with a bark of tires, and within seconds we're out of the neighborhood and onto Main Street heading north.

"I already called Cole," Riley says. "Brian is picking him up and they've got units looking for her. What happened?" He glances at me. "Was that—?"

"Amy."

"No fucking way," he breathes. "What in the actual unholy motherfuck is *she* doing in your house at four in the goddamn morning?"

Nauseous, I roll my window down, inhaling the fresh air.

Nope.

Bile stains my teeth, presses against them—I lean out the window and let it rip, spewing backward until my stomach is empty.

"Ah, Jesus, bro," Riley grumbles. "At least you did it out the window." When I pull my head back in, wiping my lips with the back of my wrist, he grips my shoulder. "What the *fuck* is Amy doing in your house?"

I shake my head. "She was just...there. I thought it was a dream at first. She split from her husband and came up here to find me. Drove by, according to her, and saw my door wide open and came in to check that I was okay." Another wave of vomiting hits, and I barely get it out the window in time. "Fuck, I'm never drinking with you assholes again. This shit was fun when we were nineteen or twenty, but it's not fucking fun anymore."

"Hear that," he mutters. "So...what? What happened?"

"She—" I shake my head. "Find Ember. I can't think about Amy right now."

"Okay, but we have no idea where she went."

"North, at a guess." I scrub my face again—vomiting helps a little. I feel less woozy and not as intoxicated. "Ember came home and saw Amy sitting on my bed, trying to—I stopped her. Before I knew Ember was there, I told her no. It didn't—it wasn't right. I didn't want her. But Ember saw and—"

"Made an assumption and bolted."

"Right." I check my phone—my last message to her is unread. "And then a few minutes later I got a text from her—the word 'help' spelled out in individual texts."

I show him and he glances at it. "That's weird."

"Something is wrong, Rye," I whisper. "She's hurt. We have to find her."

"We'll find her, bro."

"She has to be alive," I breathe. "She *has* to. I fucking love her."

Riley's gaze cuts to me. "No shit?"

"Her thinking I was doing something with Amy, and

then this fucking terror that she's gone, or hurt, or—or—"
I shake my head, fighting hyperventilation. "It was Cassie's
fault. Not mine. I was drunk. Amy watched the whole but
didn't realize how fucking gone I was. She thought I was
just hooking up with Cassie fucking Miller. She took off
and never gave me a chance to explain. Blocked my number, told her parents not to let me in, refused to see me,
refused to speak to me, refused to hear a single fucking
goddamn syllable of explanation."

I smash my fist into Riley's dash, denting the airbag
cover and most definitely breaking something in my hand.

Riley grabs my wrist. "Hey, whoa, fucking Jesus, bro,
cut that shit out!"

"Cassie just...took what she wanted. I guarantee
she knew how fucking wasted I was. I couldn't sit up. I'm
pretty sure I was lying in a puddle of my own goddamn
vomit." I tip my head back, face covered with my palms,
and groan. "She jerked me off till I was hard, climbed on,
and fucked me. I was too hammered to say anything—yes,
no, or otherwise."

Riley claps a hand on my arm, frowning at me. "You
never said much about what actually happened. We all
heard the rumors, you know? People talking about seeing you and Cassie fucking. But you never confirmed or
denied anything, you just..."

"I was focused first on Amy, on trying to get her to
hear me out, and when she wouldn't, I..." I shrug. "I tried
to move on. But I always harbored this...guilt. I felt like I'd
fucked up. Like I'd..." Words won't come. "Like I should
have been able to stop her. To say no. Or not get so drunk
I couldn't. I dunno. She just—Amy left without a single

fucking word to me, and I…I took on the guilt. I've lived with that guilt for almost fifteen fucking years."

"Fee, brother," Riley grabs my hand. "What happened? What Cassie did? That's called rape, man."

I shake my head. "I don't know how to apply that word to myself."

"Start with telling yourself that it wasn't your fault. You didn't do anything wrong." He squeezes my hand. "Try to—I dunno, man, I'm not a fuckin' therapist. Just…it's *not* your fault."

"She apologized," I mutter. "Amy. For leaving. For not hearing me out. She told me…she told me she thought about me every time she and her husband had sex."

Fee makes a face. "I dunno how I'd feel about that."

"Me either," I say.

We're well out of downtown Three Rivers by now, past the streetlamps and into the dark ribbon of highway running parallel to the lake. Mile after mile, my stomach tightens and my sense of impending doom ratchets to higher and more panicky levels. I can't breathe. My stomach is in knots.

"Ohhhh…*fuck*," Riley breathes.

My gaze snaps forward—red and blue lights wash the night sky in orbiting flashes. Flares burn red, shedding ghostly, nightmarish light on the scene.

Squad cars. A fire engine. An ambulance.

Riley skids to a stop a few feet away from the uniformed deputy assigned to deal with traffic. I leap out of the truck before it's stopped, lurching, hitting blacktop and rolling, staggering to my feet. The deputy tries to stop me, but I shove him aside.

"FELIX!" I hear a voice in my ear, hands pulling me backward. "We've got her, brother, we've got her."

"LET ME FUCKING GO!" I scream, fighting the many strong hands holding me back from getting to Ember.

Cole's voice is in my ear, quiet, stern, compassionate. "She's alive, Fee. Stand down and let them do their job."

"I have to see her. I have to—I have to—"

He walks me backward, his hands bruisingly powerful on my arms, his forehead against mine. Riley is behind me, both arms around my midsection. Together, they haul me away.

"She's alive, Felix. They're extricating her right now." His tone is the calm stolidity of a professional law enforcement officer—this is not my best buddy, this is the sheriff. "She's hurt pretty bad, but she's alive."

I hear the buzzing screech of a saw on metal, voices chattering and snapping orders. I can't breathe—it's my fault.

It's my fault. Everything is my fault.

"No, it's fucking not, Fee," Riley growls in my ear. "It was an accident. It's not your fault. Don't take this on yourself."

"I should've stopped her. Should've—I should've sent Amy away. This shouldn't've happened."

Cole reappears in front of me, ducking to make sure I meet his gaze. "They've got her out. You're gonna ride in the bus with her but only if you can keep your shit under control."

"Okay, okay, I—"

He grabs my head. "Felix. Fucking listen to me."

I'm dazed. Trying to breathe and failing. "What."

"Sit next to her and hold her hand. Talk to her. But *do not* interfere. They have to work on her."

"Work…work on her?" I blink, trying to make sense of what's happening.

"She's in pretty bad shape," Cole says. "Unconscious, broken bones, I don't know. Critical condition. So prepare yourself, okay? If you can't keep calm, they're gonna sedate you and you'll miss shit. So *stay fucking calm*, Felix. You hear me? She's alive—focus on that."

For the first time since arriving on scene, I look at Cole—notice him. He's wearing his sheriff department button-down open over a plain white tee with ratty, torn blue jeans and knee-high rubber boots, no equipment belt. His eyes are bloodshot, and he has circles under his eyes.

"How are you functioning, Cole?" I ask.

"Wasn't as drunk as you, for one. Years of practice going from asleep to dealing with an emergency for another."

Swallowing hard, I wrap him in a hug. "Grateful for you, brother."

Cole slaps me on the back. "Had your back since pre-K, motherfucker." He pulls back, shakes me. "I've fuckin' *got* you, Fee. Always."

Fucking fuck—my eyes burn. I pull away, growling. "Cole, I—"

He spins me in place and pushes me toward the ambulance, where two medics are lifting the stretcher into the back of the vehicle. "Shut up and go be with your girl, Fee. I'll see you at the hospital."

I spot Riley hovering at the edge of everything, staying out of the way and watching. "RYE!"

I'm an emotional wreck. As he jogs over, my throat is

closing, and my eyes are burning. I shove it all back down savagely, shaking my head.

The medics are busy inside the ambulance, securing, hooking up lines.

Riley pushes me toward the bus, forcing me to climb up and in. "Shut the fuck up and go, dude, Jesus. I'll see you there."

He slams the doors closed behind me, slapping the glass with his palm. I press mine to his, and then the ambulance pulls away. His palm leaves a clear handprint on the glass.

The medic in back with me is a microscopic woman with jet black hair bound back in a tight braid, the long part of the braid coiled at the back of her head and fixed in place by some sort of girl magic. I recognize her—she's the same medic who patched up Bear after that shitshow with Duane. She's stunningly beautiful, with angular features, big, bright blue eyes contrasting with her dark hair, and a Julia Roberts-esque mouth.

She's injecting something into the IV, and then prodding gently at Ember's ribcage—they've cut her clothes off completely, the scraps laying open to either side. I can see that she's got at least one broken leg, but the medic doesn't seem concerned with that. She's focusing on Ember's ribs, prodding here and there on both sides, listening to her breathing with a stethoscope that she hangs around her neck when done.

The ambulance is howling, racing south toward town. I sit at the back edge on the right side, shaking all over, barely breathing. Ember is covered in blood—the whole left side of her face is a crimson mask, and it's all down her arms, neck, and chest. She's covered in a myriad of tiny cuts.

The medic glances at me. "You can hold her hand, Mr. Crowe."

I slide down the bench until I'm within reach of Ember, and gently, gingerly fit my hand under hers. "Em, honey. I'm here." I look at the medic. "Can—can she hear me?"

Without looking away from what she's doing—swabbing something orange-ish over the side of Ember's ribcage on her left side—she shrugs. "Dunno for sure, but I've always thought so. Can't hurt to talk to her." She glances over her shoulder at the driver. "Hold it steady, Mike. She's got a punctured lung. Need to aspirate it."

"We're five minutes from the hospital, Chels," Mike says, "better to wait."

"I don't know if she *has* five minutes. She was there for several minutes with an untreated pneumothorax. She can't breathe."

"Fuck. Fine." Mike glances back at me. "Stay cool, man. It's gonna be scary, but Chelsea is the fucking best."

"O-okay. Just—just save her."

"That's the plan, my man," Chelsea says, not looking at me as she readies a giant needle. "Beginning needle aspiration."

She presses her fingertips along Ember's ribs, finding a specific location and marking it with a gloved fingertip—she slides the needle between Ember's ribs and removes part of the syringe or whatever the hell the thing is. There's an immediate hiss of escaping air, and Ember's chest noticeably deflates—she unconsciously sucks in a desperate, gasping breath, and her breathing normalizes to a degree. Chelsea then secures the needle-thing in place.

"There, done," she says.

"Is she okay now?" I ask.

She glances at me. "She's not out of the woods, no. She's got a fractured skull, but her pupils are equal and reactive, so I'm hopeful she's avoided major TBI."

I shake my head. "I—I'm sorry, I don't—"

"She hit her head really hard," Chelsea says, rephrasing, "but I'm pretty optimistic that she won't have any lasting brain issues. She's got the collapsed lung and a tibia fracture. Lots of minor cuts and bruises, but the skull fracture and collapsed lungs are the major concerns."

"Just hang on for me, Ember," I whisper. "I'm here."

A few minutes later, we're pulling up to the ER of Three Rivers Medical Center, where a renewed flurry of activity takes over. Hospital nurses yank open the ambulance doors, and Chelsea immediately starts barking out medical jargon that I don't follow—she's covered Ember from the neck down with a white sheet that sticks to her skin where she's bloody. The nurses hurry the stretcher into the hospital while listening to Chelsea's report—I follow them, walking beside the stretcher with Ember's hand in mine. They bring her to the curtained-off section of a room—the ER is bustling and noisy—children are crying, someone is moaning, someone else is shouting, things are beeping and hissing, doors open and close, shoes squeak on tile.

As soon as she's in place, a cluster of nurses and a white-coated doctor surround Ember, pushing me out of the way.

The doctor, examining Chelsea's needle insertion, glances at me. "You're her husband?"

"Um—n-no. I—I'm her...boyfriend, I guess," I answer.

"Then you need to wait in the waiting room. Family only."

"She doesn't *have* family," I snap. "I'm all she's got."

"No parents, siblings, aunts—no one?"

"No, no one. Just me."

He points to the corner of the curtained room. "Stand there and stay out of the way."

I move to the indicated corner and stay out of the way, watching as they work on her. I don't follow most of what they do, but they work on her for what seems like a long time. They tend to her head, set her leg, replace the needle in her ribs with a large clear tube, and then go over her whole body thoroughly, checking her pupils, listening to her breathing, connecting wires and patches and a heart monitor on her finger.

Eventually, the chaotic flurry of attention stops and the nurses scatter to tend to other emergencies. The doctor, a good-looking man in his late forties with salt and pepper hair, strips off his bloody rubber gloves and washes his hands, addressing me while drying them.

"Mr. Crowe, your girlfriend is stable."

I exhale a sigh of relief. "What about her head?"

"Well, her pupils are equal and reactive, but she's still unconscious, so it's hard to say. We've got her scheduled for an MRI. Ortho will be here at some point soon to put a cast on her leg."

"Her lungs?"

"They'll re-inflate on their own. The puncture was small enough that it'll resolve without surgical intervention. We'll leave the tube in for a few days, but for right now, the biggest question mark is her brain. Once we get the MRI results back, we'll know more." He glances at a cell phone, and then at me. "I have to go. For now, just sit tight. They should be here within an hour or two to take her back for the scan."

"Thank you, Doctor," I say, moving for the hard plastic chair in the corner.

He nods, offers me a brief professional smile and then bustles out, yanking the curtain across the opening to provide us with some measure of privacy.

I move the chair closer to the bed and take her hand. Kiss the back of it, not caring about the dried blood. "I'm here, Ember. You're gonna be okay."

I'm hoping for a hand squeeze or something, but there's nothing. Just the beep and hiss of machines and the chaos on the other side of the curtain.

I rest my cheek on her hand, and I'm lulled into sleep by the steady beep of the heart monitor.

C⁄ଚ

Groggily, I follow the gray scrub-wearing orderly or nurse or whatever as he pushes Ember's bed through the maze of hospital corridors, into an elevator and up several floors—confusingly, when we emerge from the elevator, we're only a floor two above ground level despite having gone up several levels.

I wait on the other side of a wall of windows as Ember is moved to a machine that retracts her inside it. There's a lot of clanking and banging for a long time. The nurse moves her back to the bed and then it's back to the room.

More waiting.

⌒⊘

"Mr. Crowe?"

I blink awake—my first instinct is to look at Ember. She's still asleep—or comatose.

I peer at the nurse. "Mmm?"

"We're here to put a cast on Ms. James."

"Okay."

It's a strange, complicated procedure. When they're done, she has a cast up to her hip on her left leg. As this is finishing up, the doctor returns with an iPad in one hand and a small paper cup of coffee in the other. "MRI results are back," he says, setting his coffee down beside the sink.

My heart palpitates. "Okay, and? Is she okay?"

He shows me the iPad screen and I recognize the shape of the brain, but the images otherwise mean nothing to me. "There are no signs of damage to the brain tissue. She's very, very lucky."

"But she's still unconscious."

He nods, sighing. "Yes. It's her body's way of helping her heal. She suffered what we call a moderate TBI—-a moderate traumatic brain injury. With these kinds of injuries, it's not uncommon for the individual to remain unconscious for up to twenty-four hours. But from what we can see here, there's every reason she should wake up without any deficiencies."

I frown. "Deficiencies?"

"Well, it's her brain, Mr. Crowe." He takes a sip of coffee, lifting it afterward. "My apologies for this, but I'm at the end of a thirty-hour shift."

I pull a shocked face. "Damn, that's a long shift."

He shrugs. "Emergency medicine." He sets the cup

down. "Deficiencies can mean any number of things and come with more severe injuries. Mood swings, personality changes, sensitivity to noise and lights, cognitive difficulties, memory loss, the list is long. But as I said, I don't foresee Ms. James experiencing too much of this. That said, however, the human brain is the most mysterious and complicated organs in the human body, so until she wakes up there's just no way to know."

"More wait and see, then," I say with a sigh.

He gives me a sympathetic look. "Unfortunately, yes. I know you've been here for a while, and I know those chairs suck. We are going to admit her to keep her under observation for a few days at very least, so we'll get you sent up to a room, at which point you can bring your visitors in."

"Visitors?"

He blinks at me. "Uh, yeah. There's a good half-dozen people out there asking for updates."

"Fuck, I—I forgot. I've been focused on her and then I fell asleep."

He smiles. "A nurse informed them about—" he checks a wristwatch worn against the underside of his wrist, "thirty minutes or so ago that there should be news soon. We'll get her admitted and moved in the next few minutes and you can go talk to your people."

My people.

"Thank you, Doc."

He nods, whacks my knee gently with the iPad. "There are better options for sleeping up there, so hang in there, alright, bud? Your girl will be okay. I mean, she's got a pretty long recovery ahead of her, but with the right support, she'll come through it just fine." He stands up.

"Alright. Well, on that note, I'm out of here. I'll be back on in a couple days. I'll try to come check on her. Take care."

"You too."

"The next few minutes" turns out to be forty-five minutes. I make sure to memorize the route from the ER to her room, and once she's settled, I head back down to the ER waiting room.

I find Riley, Nyx, Cole, Bear, Noelle, Amy, and—oddly enough—Layla and Lainey Cartwright, owners of The Alt Cafe all clustered in chairs together. Cole and Nyx are huddled together watching something on Nyx's phone, Riley is asleep with his head on Bear's mammoth shoulder—Noelle is asleep on his other shoulder, and Bear is reading a dog-eared paperback.

Amy is the first to spot me coming. "Felix!"

She shoots to her feet and scurries over to me, reaching for me—she stops herself at the last second. "Is—is she okay? They wouldn't tell us anything."

I don't know how to handle Amy. For a minute, I just stare at her, trying to form words, or even coherent thoughts. Behind her, I see Riley jerk awake and sit up, wipe at his mouth with his sleeve, and stare at Bear's shoulder as if it offended him somehow. Bear's lips twitch in a smirk, but he doesn't otherwise react—saving Riley's dignity. In moments, I'm surrounded and being peppered with questions.

Bear's voice pierces the barrage with a low but powerful snap. "Yo! Let the man speak."

"Um. Sorry I didn't come out earlier, I—" I sigh, shake my head. "She's okay. I mean, relatively speaking. She has a moderate TBI and she's still unconscious. They don't think there will be any lasting brain issues, though. She also had a collapsed lung and a broken leg."

Amy turns away, shuddering as she tries to contain some powerful emotion.

I have no space in my brain to deal with her right now.

Riley moves beside me and wraps an arm around my shoulders. "What can we do?"

I swallow, shake my head, shrug. "Dunno. She's still unconscious and she's been admitted upstairs. If you wanna visit her, you can, but we've got no way of knowing when she'll wake up." I look at the Cartwright sisters. "I didn't know you two know Ember."

Layla, the older sister with shoulder-length black hair, smiles sweetly. "She's been coming into The Alt to study for months. She's a darling and we just adore her."

I blink. "Studying? For what? She hasn't mentioned that to me."

The other sister, Lainey—the younger one, her hair cut razor-straight at her chin—smirks at me. "She's taking online courses to become a vet."

I scrub my face, wondering how I possibly could have missed this about her. "Oh."

"Yeah, she took her final not long before she went to LA," Layla adds.

"Haven't spent a lot of time talking, huh?" Lainey says, grinning and wiggling her eyebrows suggestively.

I roll my eyes at her—the Cartwright sisters are sandwiched around me in age—Layla is older by a year and graduated before me, and Lainey is a year younger and graduated a year after me; I know them, but not well enough that I'd expect this kind of teasing, especially in

this situation. "We've talked plenty, Lainey. She just...
never mentioned it."

She claps a hand over her chest, feigning shock. "Felix
Crowe knows my name? Holy shit."

Layla elbows her. "Lane. Not the time, not the place."

Lainey rolls her eyes. "Whatever. I'm just lightening
the mood."

I send Layla an appreciative smile—I've got no problem with Lainey's humor, I'm just not in a place to laugh.
Sighing, I address the group. "I appreciate you all being
here. I'm not sure there's much point in hanging around
right now, though. The doc said she could be unconscious
for up to twenty-four hours. Hopefully less. I guess for
now just head home and I'll let everyone know when she's
awake and ready to see people."

Nyx claps me on the back. "I never met the girl,
man—I'm just here for you." He squeezes my shoulder.
"I popped by the salvage yard on my way here and checked
out your FJ, by the way. They had to cut the roof away to
get her out, and it's mangled to hell and gone."

I wave a hand. "Least of my concerns, Nyxie."

He grins at me. "Wasn't finished, bro. I can totally fix
it. It'll just be...permanently topless."

"Like your bartender girlfriend?" Riley teases.

Nyx gives him a no-look middle finger. "Fuck off.
Barbie is not my girlfriend. We're just friends with benefits. And she's not permanently topless."

"Those tops she wears barely count, man."

Nyx smirks at him. "You're just jealous that I get to
play with those F-cups and you don't."

Riley splutters. "F? Jesus."

Noelle cups her own breasts, looking down at them in

shock. "And here I thought I was well-endowed. My god, does she wear a back brace?"

Lainey snickers, glancing at Layla. "Each one has to be bigger than both of ours combined."

"Her name is Barbie?" Cole says. "For real?"

"Barbara Yanetti," Nyx says. "She's talked about a reduction, but she never does because she's worried she'll get tipped less."

"That's fucked up," Layla says.

"Like for real," Lainey adds. "That's the most sexist bullshit I've heard in a long time. I need to have a chat with the poor woman."

Nyx chuckles. "Go for it."

"You'd be okay with her getting a reduction?" Lainey asks.

Nyx shrugs. "Not my body, first of all. Second, she's not even my girlfriend so it's not like I get a vote anyway. And third, even if she was my girlfriend or whatever, yes, I would be. If it would make her life easier, she should do it." He arches an eyebrow at her. "What, you think the only reason I hook up with her is her tits? She's a great girl. Funny as fuck, laid back, easy to talk to."

Lainey shrugs. "Not a wild leap of logic, Nyx." She arches an eyebrow. "If she's so great, why is she just a friend with benefits and not a girlfriend?"

He rolls a shoulder. "We've talked about it, but neither of us is looking for a relationship right now, and we agreed we wouldn't make a good couple anyway. We fight a lot. If we lived together, it'd get volatile."

"You gonna keep seeing her if you ever do date anyone?" Lainey asks.

Nyx gives her a puzzled look. "What is this, Lainey?

An inquisition? No, I would not. We both agreed a long fuckin' time ago that if and when one of us starts seeing someone seriously, we'd cut off all contact. We've both been cheated on."

I shake my head, throwing up my hands. "As interesting as all this is, I need to get back to Ember's room."

"Mind if I tag along?" Riley asks.

"Nah, 'course not," I answer. I turn to Cole. "I just wanna—"

He stops me with an uplifted hand. "Nope. Just doing my job. I'm here as your best friend. You'd be here if the situation was reversed."

Nyx shoves Cole playfully. "Hey now, asshole, *I'm* his best friend."

"You're *both* my best friends," I say, cutting off a thirty-year-old argument before it can start. "Jesus. When will you two let that shit go?"

Cole shoves Nyx. "Who are you callin' an asshole, asshole?"

I shake my head and sigh, leaning in to give Bear a quick hug. "Appreciate you guys being here." I hug Noelle next. "For real. Means a lot."

Noelle pulls back from the hug and rubs her hands up and down my arms, offering me a supportive smile. "We're here for you, Felix."

Bear nods his agreement. "I got things handled at work, Boss. Take time."

Riley leans in, stage-whispering. "*We* have things handled."

"Call me if you need anything," I tell Bear. "Yeah?"

"Course I will," he rumbles. "Go be with your girl."

Everyone but Riley and Amy file out of the ER, then.

I hesitate, glancing at Amy. She swallows hard, looking physically ill.

"Fee," she whispers. "I'm so sorry."

My throat goes tight. "Amy, I…" I sigh, rub my face. "I don't know what to say, to be honest. I'm a fuckin' mess right now."

She licks her lips. "It's obvious you and me are…we're not—"

"Maybe we can talk another time," I suggest. "After things have settled. I dunno what's the future for either of us, but I do know we got some shit to talk through. At the very least, so we both get closure."

She nods, eyes watering. "Not why I came up here, I'll admit, but…" She attempts a brave smile, lower lip trembling. "We'll talk later. By Fee. Good to see you again, Rye."

Riley nods. "Yeah, you too, Aim." When she's gone, he shakes his head. "Haven't seen her in almost fifteen years and we're Rye and Aim again? Like she didn't fuckin' ghost you and ruin your fuckin' life over somethin' you were a fuckin' victim in?"

"Rye," I say, letting out a groan. "I can't hold onto that shit anymore. I've been angry and guilty for a decade and a half. I wanna be over it."

He hooks his arm around my shoulders and shakes me gently. "About goddamn time." He guides me toward the elevator. "Let's go see your girl. You can tell me what the fuck happened with you and Amy."

16

Ember

THE DARKNESS IS NOISY ALL OF A SUDDEN.

For a long time, there was just darkness. Soundless, warm, and infinite.

And then, slowly, there were sounds: beeps, whooshes, murmurs, coughs, laughs, squeaks. The sounds came and went. Became louder and quieter, interspersed with long stretches of thick silence.

At first, the noise is unwelcome; the warm, dense silence is luxurious, enveloping, restful. But then, when the sounds grow loud and the murmurs become voices and the voices become not just word-sounds but meaningful and real, the return to silence takes on a frightening quality.

One voice is a constant. A male voice. Deep and rough and familiar. That voice is always near. Comforting.

Sometimes he whispers. Sometimes he's silent, but even in his silence, he's near.

The first major shift is the transition of the word-sounds and the voices into language, into speech patterns with context and meaning.

"…more severe than we anticipated, but she's showing signs of improvement."

"…Wake up, doc?"

"—To know for sure, as I've said, but I think soon."

"Can she hear me?"

"Again, there's no way to know for sure, but the coma patients I've worked with have told me that they do hear and understand sometimes. Not all of them, and not all the time, but those who say they heard their loved ones speaking to them all agree that they were comforted by the voices of their family. So yeah, I'd encourage you to keep talking to her."

I wonder who they're talking about.

Someone's in a coma? Poor thing.

I hear other sounds—a scrape, soles squeaking on tile, a door latching.

The Voice is close, now. "Wish I knew whether you're hearing me, Ember."

Ember? Who's Ember?

"The Cartwright sisters told me you're studying to be a vet? Why didn't you say anything? I guess maybe it didn't matter. I dunno. I just…I wanna know everything about you, Em."

Em. Ember.

Emberly.

Is…is that…me?

He sounds sad. Scared. I just want him to know it's okay. I don't want him to be sad.

"Those weeks you were in California sucked, Ember. I know we didn't spend much time together, but...fuck, how do I put it? It meant a lot to me. I feel things with you that I've never felt. A connection that—it's just different, Em. And the longer you were gone, the more I...the more I missed you. The more I realized how stupid I was being for letting that bullshit with Amy hold me back."

California. The word feels heavy. Laden with sorrow.

Amy brings anger. Jealousy.

"I just want you to wake up so we can talk. I don't—I don't know if you read that message, but...I meant it, okay? I did. I know, I know, it's fuckin' nuts. But I fuckin' meant it." He clears his throat as if to swallow a lump. "I won't say it. Not until I'm looking into those big silver eyes, not until I know you hear me."

What did he say? What's the message? I need to know. For the first time since the sounds resolved into speech, I can understand, I feel impatient. Frustrated.

Now, the darkness feels more like prison than comfort. The silence becomes oppressive. I want out of the silence. I want out of the dark.

How do I get out?

Something implacable pulls me deeper into the darkness where the sounds are far away.

C᠎

"...not a medically induced coma, so I can't just bring her out of it. She has to wake up on her own."

"You said twenty-four hours. It's been almost three days."

"I wish it was an exact science, Felix, but it's not. As I've said before, the human brain is, in many ways, still largely a mystery to us. We've learned a lot in the last few decades of medical research, but there are still a ton of question marks, things we just don't understand. Consciousness is one of them."

"The longer she's unconscious, the higher the chances of deficiencies...is that how it works?"

"It's not that cut and dried, I'm afraid. I've gone over her scans. I've compared her first scans to the results from this morning, and she's showing signs of improvement. She's breathing on her own. Her nervous system is responsive. Steady heart rate. Reactive pupils. Her body just isn't ready to wake up yet."

The Voice sighs. "I know I've asked you the same questions a billion times. I'm sorry, doc, I just..."

The Doctor Voice is understanding and patient. "I get it, Felix, believe me. The waiting and not knowing is the worst. Just keep talking to her. I truly believe she will come out of it soon, and we'll be able to assess better once she does."

Felix.

The name inspires complicated feelings. Blue eyes—paler than the sky, sharp and deep and piercing. Blond hair. Scruffy jawline. Hands like cinder blocks, nonetheless gentle. Lips that kiss.

There's anger, though. Confusion. Hurt.

Need.

Felix.

He's the Voice.

I want out of the darkness. I want to see him. Talk to him. I want to remember.

But something in the darkness isn't ready.

I go back under, but this time it feels more like drowning.

C⌒⊘

The silence is not totally silent this time.

There are faint sounds—the beeps, the hisses, the squeaks of shoes, the murmur of voices.

The darkness isn't totally dark anymore, either. It's... filtered. Not absolute black but a fluttering haze.

A word pops into my head: *Eigengrau*. Intrinsic gray. The specific darkness perceived when eyes are closed.

Beep—beep—beep—beep.

A latch clicking—hinges creaking quietly—the latch clicking again.

A faint sound—hard to identify; a chair settling as it adjusts to weight.

"Hey, Em." Felix. He sounds tired. "I've sorta run outta things to say, so I, um, I sorta went through some of your things and found a book that it seems like you really like. Thought I'd read it to you."

Felix clears his throat.

"Uh, okay. I'm not great at reading out loud, so just... y'know, bear with me." Another nervous throat clearing. "'I first met Dean not long after my wife and I split up. I had just gotten over a serious illness that I won't bother to talk about, except that it had something to do with the miserably weary split-up and my feeling that everything was dead...'"

Heartache blazes through me—sickening and vicious and boiling and acidic.

Dean.

Marylou.

That prose, that voice, the sense of adventure and the joy of traveling.

Reading it out loud. Back and forth—me and him. I'd read a page or two or ten, and then he'd read.

Him—not Felix.

Someone else.

Who?

The darkness disgorges a name: Dutchie.

Dutchie and I read this book to each other. Not just once, but…so many times. It's like an old friend. One you've been through so much shit with, you've argued with them, fought bitterly even, but always find a way to mend the breaks, forget the nasty words and sharp retorts. Because that friend just *knows* you.

Felix keeps reading, and I could almost recite the next words for him.

The hurt is massive and magnificent—deep and sharp and potent. But…it's a beautiful kind of pain. I don't shy away from it as Felix reads Dutchie's and my book to me. I embrace it. I can almost feel Dutchie somewhere within the dense, star-bright center of the pain.

I can almost hear him. His voice is the silent brief pauses between Felix's words, the swift intake of breath.

The dark thins. The hazy flutter shades from eigen-grau to a less intrinsic gray, to a low shadowy yellowish wash over my eyelids.

He reads well, despite his word of warning. Slow but fluent, carefully handling each word, cautiously

enunciating each sentence. Felix reads and reads, pausing to drink something, to turn pages with a flapping rus-
tle of paper.

I want him to stop.

Read something else. Something less fraught.

Another hazy flutter—light; dim and warm and in-
viting. Shapes. White wall. A blank TV screen.

Flutter of eyelashes obscuring the scene.

The light returns.

Felix sitting a couple feet away, ankle on knee, my
battered, dog-eared, highlighted and underlined and
written-in-the-margins library sale copy of *On The Road*
by Jack Kerouac in his big hard hands, a ratty, faded gray
Detroit Tigers hat on his head, pushed up a touch so a few
stray dark blond curls sweep his forehead beneath the brim.
His jaw is shadowed by stubble so thick it's more beard
than stubble, and he has dark purple bags under his eyes.

I try to say his name, but I feel as if I'm filled with
lead—my tongue, my lips, my hands, every part of me
feels so heavy. Even blinking requires effort—if I'm not
careful, a blink could plunge me back into the darkness,
and I don't want to go back down there.

The attempt at "Fee" ends up in a nearly silent breath
between slightly pursed lips. He doesn't hear it.

My throat hurts. Breathing hurts.

Everything hurts.

I need to get his attention. Only, I can't even wiggle
my toes. I feel them, but it's like when you first wake up
after a long, deep nap in the sunshine, when you're heavy
and drowsy and sun-warmed and lazy, and you could just
lay there forever, because even opening your eyes just

seems too hard and so pointless. It's like that, but times a thousand.

I try a sound in my throat, just a soft hum of air past my vocal cords. "Mmmm."

He doesn't hear it—it barely registered in my own ears.

C'mon, Ember. Try again.

Louder.

"Mmmm."

He hears it this time. He lets the book drop to his lap, his piercing blue eyes flicking to me. Shock sears through him as he realizes I'm awake.

"Em!" He lunges forward and takes my hand in his, kisses my knuckles. "You're awake!"

I try to smile at him, but I'm not sure it reaches my lips. I think maybe my eyes communicate it, though. "Mmmm."

His eyes shimmer. "Hi." He lets out a breath, a long, ragged sigh as if he's releasing a half-held breath pent up in his lungs for days. "Shit, the doctors. I gotta—I gotta—"

I manage to apply the slightest amount of pressure on his hand with mine—*not yet. Don't go yet.*

"Em, I—" he closes his eyes, and I think for a moment he's about to shed tears, but he shakes his head and gruffly clears his throat. "You're okay. You're okay."

It sounds like he's trying to convince both of us.

He presses the back of my hand to his lips, staring into my eyes with such intensity I wonder if he intends to look away ever again.

"F—" That much saps my energy. I try again anyway. "Fee."

"I'm here, honey. I'm here."

"W—" it's a twitch of the lips more than a sound. "Wha—-"

"What happened?" he guesses. I blink hard, once, hoping he interprets that as a yes. "Once for yes, twice for no, huh?"

I blink once again.

"You got into a wreck. Broke some ribs, punctured a lung and collapsed it, broke your leg. Hit your head really hard, too, so you've been in a coma for three days. Well, two and a half. Almost three."

I can't remember. I wrack my brain, but I can only remember driving back from California, being so excited to get to Felix. It all goes gray, then.

They're there, the memories, but I can't reach them. They're just out of reach, hidden behind a swirling curtain of fog.

"Hey, don't worry about it. You're gonna be okay. We can…we can talk once you're up to it. For now just rest."

I blink twice—I don't want to rest. I don't want to go back into the drowsing dark.

I shift my gaze to the wired remote thing connected to the hospital bed, focusing on the call button.

He follows my gaze. "Want me to call them?"

I blink once.

He presses the call button, and a minute or so later the door opens to admit a young woman wearing maroon scrubs and white sneakers, auburn hair pulled up into a messy bun.

"Oh! She's awake!" Her smile is bright and eager. "Welcome back, Ms. James! How are we feeling?"

"She can't really talk, I don't think," Felix answers for me.

"Oh, that's perfectly normal. Her body was shut down for quite a long time. It'll take time for her to get it all back." She peeks at the monitor, checks a chart on her iPad, flashes a penlight into my eyes, one and then the other, pokes the bottom of my foot with the clicker of her pen. "Seems like she's doing pretty well, all things considered. I'm gonna go get Dr. Richardson, okay? He'll check you out and go over a few things with you guys. Think you can stay awake a bit longer?"

"Mmm…hmmmm." I blink once.

The nurse grins at me. "We've got a fighter on our hands, huh?" She pats my foot over the scratchy white blanket. "Be right back."

Despite my assurance to the nurse, it's harder with every passing minute to stay awake, but I'm scared of falling asleep.

My mouth is dry. I look at Felix, squeeze his hand— squeeze is a generous term, though. "W—wah…" the rest won't come out. I manage to get my tongue across my lower lip. "Wah—"

"Water?" Felix guess. "Thirsty, huh?"

I blink my eyes once, wait, blink once again.

"Alright, I'll get you some water. I'll have to ask the nurse, though—all I have is old coffee." He kisses my hand again. "I'm not going anywhere, okay? Just popping out."

He pulls away and stands up, and the terror I feel at his distance is shocking. My heart pounds and the monitor beeps faster.

Don't go—don't leave me. Not you, too.

He doesn't even leave the room, just pokes his head out—his words are muffled, and then he comes back to me.

He notices the speed of my heart, sees fear in my eyes.

"Hey, hey, I'm here. I'm here." He takes my hand, and immediately my heart rate slows. "There you go. You're okay. I'm here, Ember."

The same nurse swishes into the room with a Styrofoam cup with a plastic lid and straw. She rolls a tray over to the bed, lowers it, and puts the cup on it. "Let's get you sitting up a bit, huh?"

She presses a button, and the upper half of the bed hums quietly as it elevates me to a reclined sitting position. She removes the bottom half of the straw wrapper, stuffs the straw into the cup, and whips off the top half. Places the straw between my lips.

"Just little sips at first, okay?"

I suck a tiny bit of cold water into my mouth—it's shocking, like a blast of cold air. My mouth seems to absorb some of the liquid before I can even swallow. I hold the water in my mouth for a moment, swirl it a bit with my tongue, move my jaw around—eventually, I swallow it. And god, that feels good.

"Ready for more?" she asks.

"Mmmm-hmmm," I say, the affirmative not much more than a hum. Still, it's communication, right? It counts.

"Here we go—another tiny sip. Not too much." The nurse touches my lips with the straw, and I pinch them around the plastic O, pull in another tiny mouthful. My throat is so dry it hurts, scratchy and sandy-feeling. Once again, I swish the water around my mouth, swallowing even the tiny amount in fractional portions.

"Good, good." The nurse waits patiently until I'm ready for more.

Swallow by swallow, she helps me quench my thirst— or at least drink enough that I no longer feel genuinely parched. I only stop when it feels like my stomach can't handle any more.

"All done?" She asks, when I close my mouth to refuse the straw.

"Mmmm-hmmm."

"Good, it's important to listen to your body. You've been getting your liquids and nutrients intravenously for the last few days, so your stomach might have a hard time at first." She sets the cup on the tray and glances at Felix. "You'll have to help her until she has her mobility back. Just take things slow, okay? Dr. Richardson should be in soon."

We're alone again. My gaze goes to the book—he set it on the edge of my bed when he got up.

"Want me to read more until the doctor comes?"

"Mmmm...mmm," I grunt, the negative somehow slightly more difficult to form than the positive.

"No?"

I don't know how to communicate my extremely complicated feelings toward that book, especially without the ability to speak. My left hand rests on my thigh above the blanket. I look at it and wiggle my ring finger—tap my thigh a few times. "D—Duh..."

His gaze follows mine, and he frowns. "Dutchie?"

My heart pangs, and I blink once. I try to form the R sound, meaning to say "read" but all I manage is a garbled grunt. I look at the book again. "Duh...sh...ee."

God, this is difficult. Frustrating and infuriating to have the words in my head yet unable to get them out.

Understanding dawns on Felix's face—understanding that morphs into horror. "Dutchie? That was Dutchie's book?"

I blink twice, and then once.

"No and yes. I...I'm not following." He flips through pages, opens the front cover to look at my name written in my best calligraphy on the inside of the cover. "It's your book—your name, your writing in the margins."

"W—we..."

The horror on his face deepens. "We?" He scrubs his face. "We, meaning you read it together?"

I blink once. "Mmm-hmm."

"It hurts," he whispers. "It reminds you of him."

Another blink.

He hangs his head. "Fuck, Ember. I'm so sorry." He sweeps his hat off and tugs at his hair. "God, I'm an idiot. I just...I saw your name in it, all the markings and...it just...it looked like a book you loved."

I squeeze his hand, having no other way of communicating with him. "L—Luh...love."

"You do love it."

Blink.

"But it's hard to..." he trails off. "I'm sorry, Ember. I'm sorry." He leans toward the floor, stuffing the book into a faded black Jansport backpack.

The door opens, admitting a handsome doctor in his forties—actually, he looks kinda like Dr. McDreamy from Grey's Anatomy. His smile is warm and professional and kind as he sweeps toward the bed, white lab coat fluttering behind him.

"Well, if it isn't Ms. Ember James." He consults his iPad, and then closes it with a snap of the lid and tosses it onto the rolling tray as he rounds the bed to my left side. "Wow, you have the most stunning eyes I've ever seen, you know that? Can you follow my pen with your eyes?"

Up, down, side to side, up, down...

"Good, very good. Quick look with the light." A penlight flashes into my eyes, forcing me to squint. "Excellent. Now, it's not unusual for you to have to work at your motor skills, so don't panic, okay?" He goes to the foot of the bed, tugs the blanket up to expose my feet, and puts his palm against the sole of my left foot. "Can you push against my hand?"

I try, but I'm not sure how much progress I make.

"Hey, that's great! Now the other one." I do it again, and he praises the effort the same way. All that done, he hooks a rolling stool with a foot and drags it over to the side of the bed and sits, leaning on the railing. "I'm sure you've got a lot of questions, Ms. James. I also know you're probably frustrated with how hard it is to talk at the moment. I promise that will fade quickly. We'll have a lot of tests and assessments to do—you know, cognitive stuff, just to see where you are. You suffered a pretty decent traumatic brain injury. But you seem lucid and coherent, and your scans are all pretty good. I feel confident you'll make a full recovery, in time. But..." he pauses to think. "You're going to have to be patient with yourself. Brains are funny things. You might have balance issues. Random bouts of irritability—like, something totally innocuous will send you into a fit. Lethargy. Confusion, brain fog. All this is normal and it should clear up, but it might take a while to do so."

I have a thousand questions, and can't verbalize any of them.

He puts his hand on mine. "I know, I know—you have questions and you can't ask them. We'll get to it all. But you do have other injuries. You broke several ribs and one of them punctured your lung. That's coming along nicely, but you've got some work ahead of you to get your lung back where it needs to be. You also have a compound fracture of your tibia." He indicates my left leg, which is in a cast and elevated. "You were in a hell of a wreck, Ms. James. You're truly lucky to be alive—if EMS had gotten to you any later, that punctured lung could've been…well, no sense dwelling on that. Just try to remember to be thankful, okay? You're alive. You'll recover. In time, you'll be back to normal. But for now, just rest, okay? Get some sleep."

I widen my eyes, fear filling me. "C—coh…coma?"

He gives me a reassuring smile. "You won't go back into a coma. You *will* sleep very, very deeply, and there will still be some confusion and disorientation, speech difficulties, everything you're feeling now." He pats my hand. "I know it's all scary and confusing." He indicates Felix. "But lucky for you, you've got this fella here. He hasn't left your side for a second since you came in."

That makes my heart do funny things.

Felix is stoic through all this, just holding my hand and listening—when the doctor mentions him, Felix ducks his head and moves to withdraw his hand—I hold on as tightly as I can, and he allows me to keep holding it.

The doctor slaps his knees. "Well, I think that's enough for now. You need to rest. And don't fight it, okay? If you fall asleep, you *will* wake up. And don't be shy about pain control, okay? If it starts hurting so you can't rest, you hit that call button. You're in good hands, Ms. James. We'll take the best possible care of you."

"Th—thay…"

He winks at me with what is, I assume, his most charming smile; he's a good-looking man and he knows it. "No worries, Ms. James. I'll be by in a while to check on you." He gently taps Felix on the back of the shoulder with the iPad. "Take good care of our girl, huh?"

"Yeah, I will. Thanks, doc."

When he's gone, I meet Felix's eyes. For a long time, we just look at each other. There's so much I want to say, but it's all behind that impenetrable wall of fog.

Eventually, the leaden weightiness in my limbs spreads to my eyelids, and I find myself drifting.

I force them open and squeeze Felix's hand as hard as I can. "F-Fee…"

"I'm here, Ember. Not goin' anywhere." His voice is rough and ragged, as if he's swallowed gravel. "Got you, Ember. I've got you."

I don't want to sleep. I want to remember what happened. I want to know why there's a rattling little hot hard ball of anger in my belly when I look at him. I want to know why the thought of California brings such sorrow. I want to know why I got in a wreck—I'm normally a very careful driver. I've never gotten a ticket, never been in a fender bender, and I've covered literally over a million miles. Dutchie and I did some back-of-a-napkin calculations, using estimates of places I know I've been since I personally started driving—it'd probably be more than double the number if you include the years I was just mom's passenger as a kid.

Felix lifts my hand to his lips and kisses it—I wriggle my fingers, feeling the scratch of his stubble under my fingertips.

"Bee…Beer…beard," I whisper. "L-lie…like."

He gives me a lopsided grin, putting my palm to his cheek and jawline. "You like the beard, huh?"

"Mmm."

"Then I'll leave it." He touches my cheekbone with a fingertip. "Rest, Ember. I'll be right here when you wake up."

I can't fight it anymore.

This time, there is no darkness, no eigengrau…just the nothingness of sleep.

17

Felix

TWO WEEKS LATER

"NO WHEELCHAIR," EMBER SNAPS AT THE NURSE holding the device that is the bane of Ember's existence. "Walk."

The nurse looks at me for help, but I shrug. "Don't look at me. I can't make her do anything."

Willa, the nurse, knuckles her forehead. "It's just hospital policy, Ember. We all know how hard you've worked on using your crutches."

Ember narrows her eyes at the wheelchair. "I hate thing that." She growls at the slip. "That thing."

"It's no different than the crutches, honey," Willa says—Willa is an actual saint, I'm pretty sure, anointed and shit. Or, she has the patience of one, at least. "It's just a tool to help you. And in this case, hospital policy is that every admitted patient must be wheeled to the exit by the nursing staff." She leans forward toward Ember. "Dr. Richardson broke his leg and got a nasty infection a few years ago and had to be admitted. And wouldn't you know, he pitched an almighty fit about being wheeled out like every other patient? But you know what happened? I wheeled his ass out of here. You can't out-stubborn me, sweetheart."

Willa is the day nurse—she's in her sixties, with thin dishwater blond hair, a smoker's rasp to her voice, and a loving and compassionate but firm bedside manner; she's also a real stickler for the rules.

"I did *not* pitch a fit, Nurse Ratched," comes Dr. Richardson's familiar voice. "I calmly expressed my wishes. Which you ignored. As usual."

Willa grins at Ember and then quickly wipes her face clean, adopting a scowl. "You wanna see me go Nurse Ratched on you, Dr. Richardson? Call me that again. And you did not calmly express anything. You whined like a little bih—baby. And I only ignore you when you're being difficult."

"I'm a doctor, Nurse Wright. I'm always difficult. Comes with thinking I'm the smartest person in the room—and usually being right."

Willa snorts. "Oooooooh-kay," she drawls, "keep telling yourself that, buddy."

These two have a gift of banter—it's been the centerpiece of every day for the last two weeks. Neither of them ever lets on that it's all in good fun—they bicker like an old married couple, scowling, needling, teasing.

But underneath it all is a deep respect for each other that somehow shows through despite the constant jabs.

Dr. Richardson stands next to Willa—close enough to communicate a comfort level with each other's personal space. "So, today's the day my star patient goes home."

Ember isn't successful at hiding the wince at the word "home." Her ability to filter her thoughts and words has taken a pretty big hit from this injury, as has her ability to deal with her emotions. She's more mercurial than ever, prone to outbursts of anger, crying, or manic excitement. She's not always aware of what she's doing or saying.

In one memorable incident, she hit on Dr. Richardson, called him Dr. McDreamy—which he found funny for some reason—and she tried to grab his butt. He handled it like a pro, clearly used to situations like that, and never referenced it again. She doesn't remember doing it.

Her memories are pretty fuzzy, still. She remembers some of the accident but not all, and her memories of the first few days after waking up are mostly a fog.

I think she thought recovery would be a lot of sitting around and reading or watching TV, but that's definitely not the case. Every day has been filled with speech therapy, physical therapy, fine and gross motor skills, testing, assessments, scans, talk therapy...lots and lots of all of that, plus nurses and doctors coming and going at all hours, poking, prodding, taking blood...

Today being release day, she's antsy as hell. Has been all day. Practicing with her crutches, going up and down the hallway outside her room, pausing to chat with whoever's at the nurses' station, popping into other patients' rooms to hang out...restless, anxious, and difficult.

I've been assured all this is normal. Or, at least, normal for a fucked up situation.

We haven't talked about that day—her walking in on me and Amy. What she saw, or thought she saw.

It's funny—we barely knew each other before the accident, but out of necessity and desire I stepped in and took care of her. I've helped her to the bathroom. Fed her when her hands decide not to work. Gave her sponge baths when she couldn't stand up long enough to take a shower and helped her wash when she could. I've slept on a thin, hard folding cot for so long I'm not sure my back will ever be the same.

I wouldn't change any of it.

I know her, now.

I know her moods. I can tell when she's about to blow a fuse over something—usually silly shit that's just one thing too much for her frustration level—a tremor in her hand will make her spill her Jell-O and she'll burst into tears, or she can't make her mouth form the right word even though she has it in her brain or it comes out all twisted up and she'll have a fit of anger.

I know when she's exhausted and needs to rest. I'm getting better a understanding what she's trying to say—and still not so good at letting her get it out, right or wrong, instead of guessing to take the work out of it for her.

We talked about her college degree aspirations, her nomadic childhood with her mom. We talked about how she never knew her father and doesn't want to. We talked about how she wants kids someday—in the future. Two or three, she thinks. Boys, girls—doesn't matter. She's not sure about settling into a house, though. Being in the hospital for two weeks is the longest she's been anywhere but her bus in many years—even in California, she, Faye, and Faye's family took trips together, so she wasn't just in LA the whole time.

We talk about Faye a lot. Those weeks in LA with her, watching her fade from a hale, sassy, sprightly old woman to a fragile little thing, tired, eyes dim, often lost in memory. Waking up one morning and finding her gone, having passed in her sleep.

We talked about her actual grandmother—GramGram. She and her mom would spend a week at a time throughout the year in Florida with her GramGram, and according to Ember, those were always her favorite weeks. She told me she dreamed of running away from her mom and going to live with her grandmother. That was never a real possibility, though, as her grandmother lived in an assisted living facility. Not a great place for a kid.

I told her about my parents, although I tried to spend more time listening than talking.

Glaring at the wheelchair like it's her arch enemy, Ember sighs. "Fine. Last ride in that tham ding." A huff. "Motherfucker. Damn thing I mean."

That's her most stubborn speech issue—flipping words around or mixing them up like that. It annoys her to fits of rage.

Willa moves for her, but Ember glares at her until she holds her hands out in surrender. Wedging the crutches in her armpits, Ember levers upright on her good leg, wobbles, and catches herself—glaring at all of us, daring us to help; we don't. Pivoting and hopping backward, Ember lowers herself into the wheelchair and lays her crutches across her knees.

"Ready, missy?" Willa asks.

Ember's head snaps around. "*Do not* call me that. Ever."

Willa rears back in surprise. "I…okay. I'm sorry."

Now tearful, Ember sniffles. "No, *I'm* sorry, Willa." She paws at her face. "I'm sorry. It's just…a very dear friend of mine used to call me that, and she, um…she died right before the accident."

Willa bends to hug Ember from behind. "I had no idea—I'm so sorry. I didn't mean to hit on a sore spot."

Ember pats Willa's forearms where they're wrapped around her shoulders. "Of course you didn't." She sighs. "Okay. Let's go."

Cole and Riley brought my truck to the hospital yesterday, and now it's idling in the pickup-dropoff line of the main entrance. I follow behind Willa and Ember as we make our way from Ember's room to the elevator; Ember makes Willa stop at several rooms on the way so she can say goodbye to her new friends. We reach the automatic sliding doors to find the whole crew waiting with cards, flowers, oversized teddy bears, and, in Nyx's case, a small handbell.

Ember covers her face with her hands, shoulders shaking; she bends at the waist, putting her face to her knees for a moment. Everyone here—Cole, Nyx, Riley, Bear, Noelle, and the Cartwright sisters—have visited her just about every day since the accident, and I know she's gotten particularly close with Noelle and the sisters.

"You guys," Ember whispers, voice shaky and eyes streaming tears. "This is ridiculous. Too much fuss."

Cole is the first to approach her, handing her a bouquet of colorful flowers. He kneels in front of her wheelchair, presses the flowers into her hands, and leans forward to whisper in her ear for a moment. Ember nods, sniffling, and kisses his cheek.

The bastard has the gall to go and blush like a fourteen-year-old virgin.

Riley is the one with the giant teddy bear—it obscures him as he holds it. He peeks his head around the side of the absurd thing, grinning at Ember. Playfully, he sets it on her lap, but it's so huge its arms and legs trail on the ground.

"Riley, you're such a fucking goofball," Ember laughs. "What am I supposed to do with this thing?"

"I dunno, snuggle it when my brother's being an obnoxious bitch-cake?" Riley answers.

"Bitch-cake," Ember echoes, snickering. "I'm stealing that one."

Lainey and Layla give her a gift certificate to their cafe—instead of a dollar amount, however, the certificate only bears a sideways 8...the infinity symbol.

Ember hugs them both at the same time. "You guys—what? I got in a wreck, I didn't, like, cure world hunger. Good grief."

Nyx is next, handing her the handbell, the handle of which he's tied a red ribbon. "So you can summon Felix whenever you need something."

I fake a glare. "Wow, Nyxie, thanks. Super helpful."

He flips me off. "It's not for *you*...bitch-cake."

I glare at my brother next. "Look what you started, asshole."

Bear and Noelle approach next, each bending to hug her.

"We didn't get you anything," Noelle says, "but I'm

gonna be bringing by dinners for you guys, since according to Riley, Felix can't cook for shit."

I tip my head back, sighing. "How did this become a make-fun-of-Felix contest?"

Riley shoots me double finger guns. "I mean, every day is a make-fun-of-Felix contest—you just make it so easy."

Nyx leans in again, stage-whispering. "The bell is just for funsies, by the way. Your real gift is waiting in Felix's driveway."

Ember's eyes widen. "Pumpkin?" Her voice is filled with excited hope.

"Yeah, I fixed 'er up for you," he answers, grinning at her. "You know, I've been wrenching since I was old enough to hold a wrench, and that bus of yours is probably the most incredibly well-maintained vehicle I've ever seen."

Ember grips his hand. "I can't thank you enough, Nyx."

He rolls his eyes and clears his throat. "Yeah, well, it's selfish. I'm hoping you'll stick around once you're healed, mostly because when you're around, my boy Fee is less of a bitch-cake."

"Hear, hear!" Riley says, amid the laughter of everyone else.

"My god," I sigh. "Really? What the fuck even *is* a bitch-cake?"

"You," Nyx, Riley, and Cole all say in perfect unison.

More raucous laughter greets this. But when I glance at Ember, I can tell she's getting overwhelmed and emotional and wants to escape.

I step forward. "I think we oughta get her—" I almost

say home, but stop myself. "Back to the house. I appreciate all of you."

Riley straps the giant teddy bear into the bed of my truck while I help Ember climb up into the cab and buckle her in. A few minutes later, everyone has said their good-byes, and we're heading toward my house.

Once we're off the hospital campus, Ember rests her head against the seatback with a ragged sigh. "Thanks for getting me out of there, Fee. Your friends are amazing. I just—"

"They're your friends now, too," I tell her. "But they can be a lot."

"I've never really had a friend group," she whispers. "I don't know how to..." she shrugs. "I don't know how to be a person who lives in one place and has all these friends."

"They don't expect anything from you, Ember," I tell her. "They like you for you. So just be you."

She glances at me. "Fee, you've been—"

I cover her mouth with my hand. "Nope. We are not doing that. Not now."

She blinks hard. "But there are things we need to talk about."

"Sure. But not now." I take her hand. "Right now, we get you settled. Doc said it'll be a few months of PT and rehab and all that before you're totally clear to go back to life as normal."

She works her jaw, shaking her head and fighting tears. "I don't think my life will ever go back to normal, Fee." She groans. "God, I fucking *hate* being so emotional all the goddamn time."

I just squeeze her hand. She withdraws her hand from

mine and wipes at her face, sniffing a few times and then shaking her head like a dog shaking off water.

"Ugh. Okay." She takes my hand in both of hers, rubbing her thumb over my knuckles. "I have to say this. So just let me, please."

"If you say thank you, we're fighting," I say.

She stares at me for a moment. "Of *course* I'm gonna say thank you, Felix. I...I...I don't know where I'd be without you. You've been there with me at every turn since the wreck, and now you're letting me live with you while I start the real recovery...I just..."

"Ember—"

"No, look—I know you don't wanna talk about what happened. And my memory is still pretty fuzzy. I almost don't care what happened. You've been there for me when I needed someone in my corner the most." She kisses my knuckles. "So yes—thank you. You don't owe me anything. And I...I don't even know what we are, Fee. I just know that...that I care about you deeply and I'm grateful to have met you."

My throat goes tight and hot. "I care about you, too."

"But we're talking about it soon, Fee. Right?"

I shrug. "Sure."

She laughs. "Very convincing response."

"I just think you need to focus on getting better."

"And I think it's equally important that I understand what happened and why. My emotions are all mixed up and complicated and I need to understand." She pauses. "Besides, if we don't talk about it, how are we supposed to move forward together?"

"I..."

"You *do* want to move forward together with me, don't you?" she asks.

"Yeah, but…once we talk about it, things might change. For you."

We pull up to my driveway, and I park behind Pumpkin—mercifully, our arrival puts off the rest of that discussion.

Ember shoves open her door and wiggles to the edge of the seat. "Help me out, Fee, I need to see her."

I shut off the motor and circle the hood to stand in the doorway. She reaches for me, her arms wrapping around my neck as mine go around her waist. I lift her out of the cab but don't immediately set her down; her big silver eyes pierce mine, fraught with a complicated swirl of emotions. Her lips are close, her breath warm.

God, I want to kiss her.

I don't.

I don't know where we are in our relationship. I don't know what she wants. I don't know how she'll feel after she finds out why she wrecked. That it's my fault.

I set her on her feet, hand her the crutches, and step back. I wish the disappointment on her face when I don't kiss her was less obvious.

She searches me for a moment and then closes her eyes, letting out a breath before turning to her bus.

She crutches along the left side, touching a sticker here and there before stopping at the driver's door. She braces against the van's body and holds both crutches in one hand while opening the door, hops forward a few steps, and then climbs up to sit behind the wheel, her cast-encumbered left leg hanging out.

I dig her keys out of my pocket and hand them to her. "Here. Start her up."

She bites her lower lip in anticipation, and then inserts the key and turns over the engine; it catches immediately, settling into a healthy, humming idle. "God, she sounds amazing!"

"Nyx is a miracle worker," I answer. "He and his guys totally rebuilt your original engine and transmission from the top down and the inside out, plus he overhauled your suspension, did the brakes, some underbody rust mitigation, and put in a new radio faceplate."

She covers her mouth, eyes shimmering. "Fee...*what*? Are you *serious*? That's—fuck me, Felix. That's tens of thousands of dollars' worth of work." She touches the radio faceplate. "That original radio looked cool but it didn't work for shit."

"That's Nyxie for you," I say. "Doesn't do anything by halves."

"How much do I owe him? Even just parts is—"

I laugh. "Good luck with that. If you even so much as bring up paying him, he'll get pissy. It's a gift, Ember."

She shakes her head. "No. No. It's too much. And—why? What did I do to deserve...any of this?"

"*Deserve* doesn't have shit to do with it, babe," I answer. "They're just good people. They care. And they've decided to adopt you into the gang, it would seem. And no matter what Nyx said about me, in reality it's got nothing to do with me. They just like you."

She holds the steering wheel, not bothering to hide her tears. "I remember Cole's face. After the accident. I was..." She closes her eyes, rests her forehead between her hands on the wheel. "I was suspended sideways—the car was on its passenger side. I—I couldn't breathe—I remember that. I was bleeding. Everything hurt. I was—I was so scared." I can barely hear her. "I knew I was going to die, and I didn't want to. I didn't want to."

"Em," I whisper.

She doesn't hear me. "I felt myself fading." She rolls her head side to side, groaning. "I told everyone I don't remember this part, but I do. I just…I wish I didn't. Knowing you're dying…it's the scariest thing you can ever imagine. And then I heard a siren. Tires. Feet. And then Cole was there. He laid down on the ground in the broken glass and my blood and held my hand and talked to me until the firefighters got there. He kept me awake. Kept me talking." She's speaking through tears; she sits up, tips her head back, and talks with closed eyes, dripping tears from her chin. "I don't remember what he said, what I said—I just remember him laying there beneath me, holding my hands and… staying with me while they cut me out."

"That's Cole for you," I murmur.

She looks at me finally. "Fee, please. Just fucking tell me what happened."

"Fuck. Now?"

She nods, wiping at her face. "*Please*, Felix. I've compartmentalized and repressed and avoided thinking about it for two weeks. I can't do it anymore. I *have* to know, and no matter how fucking hard I wrack my brain, I can't remember." A pause. "All I've got is that it's got something to do with—shit. I knew her name. Your ex. A-something. I remember feeling angry. Just…not why."

"Amy," I mutter. "Her name is Amy."

"Amy, right."

I go around to the passenger side and climb in beside

Ember. Leave the door open. Trace the outlines of the plethora of stickers covering the dashboard in front of the passenger seat—breweries, distilleries, dispensaries, farmer's markets, sustainable clothing brands, eco-friendly co-op grocery stores, band logos…

I let out a long sigh. "The short version is that you came back from LA in the middle of the night—or, actually, it was early morning. Like four, I think. You walked in like you had something to say to me. But Amy was there. And it—you assumed, based on what you saw, that something either had happened, was happening, or was about to happen between us."

She's silent for a long time—almost a minute. "The way you're phrasing that suggests nothing *did* happen."

"No, Ember, I swear—nothing happened."

"But it looked like it did."

"Yeah, I…yeah. It definitely would've looked like I.."

She nods, looking at me. "I'm gonna need the long version, Fee."

"I know. But how about we go inside and get settled first?" I suggest.

Ember sighs. "Okay." She glances at the ground outside the vehicle near her foot and then at me. "I'm gonna need help getting down."

"Got you."

I help her out of the bus and precede her to the side door and into the kitchen. She swings into the kitchen and then the living room, eying my front door.

"Fixed your door, I see."

I snort. "Yeah, long time ago." I gesture at the couch. "Have a seat—I'll bring everything in."

She sighs. "Felix, I can help."

I give her a droll stare. "I'm sure you could, if you had to, but you don't."

She ducks her head. "I hate feeling useless. I hate... needing help."

"You're not useless—you're injured and in recovery."

She nods, head hanging. "I know, I know. It just sucks."

"When I was...oh, shit—twenty-one, I think, I fell off a roof," I tell her. "Broke an arm, a leg, and several ribs. I was stuck flat on my ass at my dad's house for almost four months before I could go back to work full time. And the hardest part of the recovery was having to ask for help for the simplest shit. Getting dressed, opening a jar, getting into and out of cars. Yeah, it fuckin' sucks—no two ways about it."

"Aren't you supposed to be, like, harnessed or something when you're on a roof?"

I laugh. "Of course—OSHA standard is harnesses on any roof over six feet...which is all of them. I wasn't supposed to be working on the roof that day, though—didn't even have a harness. Two of the roofers were cousins and their family member died unexpectedly, so I had to fill in. Like a dumbass, I figured I didn't need a harness." I laugh again. "Spoiler alert—I needed one."

I bring her stuff in—bags, purse, and the giant stupid bear that takes up most of my living room.

Ember is laying down on the couch, staring at the ceiling. When I finish bringing in her things, I sit at her feet and lift them onto my lap.

"Comfy couch," she says. "I don't mind sleeping here, if..."

"You really think I'd make you sleep on the couch?"

I ask, frowning at her. "What kind of a dick do you take me for?"

She twitches a shoulder. "I dunno. You're not a dick. I just don't want to...y'know. Assume anything."

"Well, funny you should say that," I tell her. "Because I also didn't want to assume, so I redid my spare bedroom."

"Redid it?" she asks. "Meaning what? And when? You never left the hospital."

"It was a home office for doing paperwork and stuff. And Bear did it for me. Well, for you, for me."

"Fee, you shouldn't have given up your home office."

"Nah. I never used it." I point at a small desk in the corner of the living room, on which is my laptop, a printer, a Crowe Contracting mug of pens and pencils and highlighters, and a few other odds and ends. "That's all I really need. A whole room was wasted space, and now I have a guest room."

She doesn't respond for a while, just looking at me. "What do you want? Like, where do you want me to sleep?"

We're dancing around the real issue.

"I just want you to be comfortable," I say. "I know there's a lot of...unfinished stuff between us. But right now the priority is getting you better."

"You didn't answer the question, Felix." She swings her legs off my lap and pivots to sit up beside me, tugging her hair out of the loose, low ponytail and shaking it out.

"I don't know, and that's the truth." I shake my head, glancing at her. "It's all...complicated. I'm no less attracted to you than ever, obviously, and of course I want to be close to you. But I'm worried that if we're in the same bed that things would get complicated and...I dunno. I dunno. I want you. But I don't want you to think that by staying here while you recuperate that you're, like…obligated to be with me. Maybe you feel differently. Maybe you will once I tell you everything."

She slides a hand between her cast and her leg, growling in irritation as she tries to scratch herself. "Fucking itches where I can't reach." She yanks her hand out and sits on it. "So tell me everything."

"Well, you need backstory for it to make sense," I say.

"I'm not going anywhere," Ember says.

"Amy and I were…" I roll my eyes. "The 'it' couple in high school, I guess. Most likely to get married first. Prom king and queen. Y'know, the whole small-town sweethearts thing. I had offers to play football and baseball from U of M."

She looks at me, then. "Wow, really? I mean, I'm not surprised you were a star jock."

I laugh. "Yeah, I guess so. That's how the four of us became such good friends—me, Rye, Cole, and Nyx were Three Rivers sports royalty from the time we hit middle school. Rye was the QB, Cole the running back, Nyx the tight end, and I was the running back. Some people called us the four horsemen, and others the three musketeers, because there were actually four of us."

She chuckles at this. "Some high-brow humor there."

"Actually, only Mrs. Jones, the lit teacher, called us that."

"Now that makes more sense."

"Anyway." I rake my hand through my hair. "A year or so after graduation, Marty and Marcus Gershwin threw a giant-ass party in a field on their parents' property, and I mean that shit was massive. Pretty much the whole school

showed up, as well as quite a few kids who had just graduated or or were home from college."

"Nothing good ever happens at parties like that,"
Ember says. "Been to a few of them."

I eye her. "Really?"

She shrugs. "Sure. I was great at sniffing out parties. By
the time I had my license, I was pretty damn sick of Phish
concerts, so once Mom was occupied I'd take the van and
go looking for trouble. And I never found as much trouble
as those rural small-town field keggers."

I laugh. "Facts."

"So. You and Amy, the golden couple, were at a keg-
ger. What happened?"

"I got obliterated. Like, how did I not end up in the
hospital with alcohol poisoning type of obliterated." I shake
my head. "So fucking stupid. I'd driven, of course. Most
of the party, Amy and I were together. We were always together. Usually at those things we'd camp out by the bonfire and sort of…hold court, I guess. But that party, we
ended up getting separated. One of Amy's friends was having drama with her boyfriend or something, so all the girls
in the crew were huddled together talking about it, which
meant I was left to my own devices."

Ember cringes. "Oh boy."

"Yeah. It's not like Amy was policing my alcohol intake—she could get just as wasted as me. But when I was
with her, I was usually more concerned with when I could
sneak her away from the party so we could mess around."

She grins. "Of course you were."

"I couldn't begin to tell you how much I drank. Only
that the last thing I clearly remember is realizing way too

late that I was *not* in good shape. I realized this when I puked everywhere, fell into it, and couldn't get up."

Ember cringes again, this time in disgust. "Ew."

"Yeah. For a while, I just laid there hoping I'd feel less…whirly."

"That doesn't work," she says.

"No, it does not." I rub my face. "This is where it goes sideways. See, there was this girl, Cassie Miller, who was sort of obsessed with me. I swear I never encouraged it—I tried not to be a dick about it, but I was with Amy. Cassie never got the hint. She'd wait for me at my car after school and try to seduce me, follow me into bathrooms and offer to blow me, show up at my house on the weekends."

Ember looks at me with wide eyes. "Wow. That's…a lot."

"Yeah, it is. I even had Amy try to talk to her—let's just say that didn't go well and leave it at that." I sigh. "I was almost passed out on the ground. In my own vomit, remember. So, y'know, not at my best. All I remember is a dark-haired girl appearing and talking to me. Touching me. How I got hard with as drunk as I was, I don't know. At this age, I'd have whiskey dick, but I guess when you're nineteen, it's different. I dunno. I just know I couldn't see straight—and I don't mean seeing double, I mean I was seeing, like quadruple, and it was all spinning. It felt like I was on an out-of-control merry-go-round."

"Oh god." She looks at me. "It wasn't Amy, was it?"

"Nope, it was Cassie taking her shot. I…" I cover my face and groan. "Right there on the ground, in front of the whole party, when I was hammered."

"Jesus. What a whore."

"Amy watched the whole thing happen. But she didn't

realize how drunk I was. She'd been with her girls most of the night. So all she saw was Cassie and me fucking."

"Did you tell her no?"

I shrug, shake my head. "I was so far gone I couldn't have said anything. And I don't think I realized it wasn't Amy. I don't really remember it, to be honest, just a vague memory of being drunk and some girl with dark hair on top of me."

"Fee," she whispers.

"I guess Nyx and a couple others got me home. No clue. I woke up late the next day, and—"

"Your parents were fine with this?" she cuts in.

"Well, Mom was long gone by then, and Dad was an alcoholic and a workaholic. So no, no one gave a shit what we did."

"God, Fee."

I rub sweaty palms on my jeans. "The first thing I did was call Amy to make sure she got home okay. She wouldn't answer my calls or my texts, or return my voicemails."

"No. She blamed you?"

"I showed up at her house, and her dad ran me off with a shotgun." I close my eyes, the pain of memory sharp and acidic. "I called her friends and they wouldn't answer. I followed her to work the next day and she called the cops, saying I was harassing her."

"Jesus. What? For real?"

I nod. "Yup. I called her a hundred times a day. Sent her fuckin' *thousands* of text messages. Wrote her fuckin' letters and put 'em in her mailbox. Left notes on her car. Everything I could think of. I even did that fuckin' John Cusack thing with the radio outside her house. Her dad nearly shot my ass." I shrug and then slap my thighs. "I

kept at it. Everything I could think of to get her to just...
fuckin' listen to me. Hear me out."

"She wouldn't? She just...cut you off totally?"

I nod. "And then one day, Cole told me she'd left.
Transferred from the community college here to a nursing
program down in Metro Detroit. I never saw her again."

Ember sits in silence. "Holy shit. What a bitch! Even if
you had intentionally hooked up with someone else, you'd
think if you loved someone, you'd at least give them five
fucking seconds to say their side." She tilts her head to the
side. "Wait. You said you had a scholarship for Michigan.
But after graduation, you were still up here?"

"Amy wanted to stay up here together. We had a whole
plan. She was gonna get her nursing degree and I'd work
for Dad, and we'd get married, buy a house, have kids, and
live happily ever after." I sigh. "I'd already passed on the
scholarship by then."

"You gave up U of M for her?"

"Yup. Full ride."

"And then she ghosted you and moved away after convincing you to give up a full ride to a Big Ten school."

"Correct."

"Because you got sexually assaulted and she just assumed it was your fault."

"Pretty much."

She looks at me with sorrow and compassion. "Fee,
that's awful."

"I've lived with that guilt ever since. I just—"

She rocks forward, slicing the air with both hands.
"Wait, wait, wait—*guilt*? What guilt? You were the fucking victim!"

"Not how I saw it. Not how she made me feel. I never

talked to anyone about it—I wouldn't…couldn't. Everyone else was just as hammered as I was, so it's not like too many people had a clear memory of it anyway. I dunno. I just…I should've done something. Said no. Stopped her. I'm stronger than her. I could have." I close my eyes. "I shouldn't have been so drunk. I should've…I dunno. But it never once occurred to me that I was a victim. That I was…" I shake my head. "I can't even say it, even now. Fucked up, sure, but I felt like I'd ruined everything by letting that happen."

She shakes her head, looking away thoughtfully. "You never dated anyone else, did you?"

I shake my head. "No." A shrug. "Tried a few times, but…no. I never felt like…like I deserved to. No one gets it. Cole, Rye, Nyx, they all feel like I should just be over it—it was so long ago and it was not my fault, but…I just can't convince my heart to believe it. Maybe it's…I dunno. The way she treated me, like I'd murdered her dog in front of her or something. Giving up that scholarship—my dream of getting out of Three Rivers and doing something big with my life. Plus all the shit with my fucking parents."

"We gotta get back to your parents," she says, "You touched on it in the hospital, but I need more. For now, though, explain the accident, now that I have the sordid backstory."

"I went out with the boys. I was…missing you. Not in a good place. And I got a little sloppy. Brian—one of Cole's rookies—drove us home. I passed out in bed, and he took Cole home. I woke up thirsty—you know that feeling, I'm sure."

She nods, feigning retching. "Ugh, yes. I don't get

drunk anymore. Not worth it. Cannabis is clearly superior for just that reason."

"Not gonna hear any arguments from me on that score, especially after this." I rub my face. "Well, when I woke up to get a drink, there was a woman in my room with me. She handed me water and helped me drink, gave me Tylenol."

She shakes her head, waving her hands. "Whoa, hold the fuck up. *What*? She was just *in* your house? In your *room*?"

"I thought I was hallucinating. I haven't seen her, spoken to her, messaged her, nothing since that party. And then I wake up hammered and she's sitting on my bed. Acting...sweet. Putting her hand on mine, touching my leg. Telling me she drove four hours after leaving her husband so she could come see me."

"But she just walked into your house like that? Who *does* that?"

"Well, according to her, she drove by not planning on stopping, just to see where my house was so she could come back later, but my front door was wide open. And that does make sense—I don't usually go in that door, and Brian walked me inside and then had to get Cole home, so it does make sense that he'd leave assuming I'd close my door. But, again, I was hammered. So she came in to make sure nothing bad had happened."

Ember frowns. "That makes sense, unfortunately."

I chuckle. "Why, unfortunately?"

"Because I want to hate her and that's perfectly logical." She pinches the bridge of her nose. "So, when I walked in, what I saw was a gorgeous woman leaning over you in your bed with her hand on your dick. But that's…not what happened, is it?"

"No. I moved her hand and told her no before you walked in."

She closes her eyes, wincing as if in pain. "And I ran away without letting you explain. Just like her."

"The, um, parallel did not escape me, no."

"And then I go and almost get myself killed." Her face screws up with intense, conflicted emotion—anger, regret, guilt. "I shouldn't have been driving. I knew it. I was too upset. Crying too hard. And you were calling me and part of me wanted to answer and hear you out but I was scared of what you'd say, because I…" she trails off, shaking her head.

"You what, Em?" I shift closer to her.

She doesn't seem to hear me. "I remember looking down at the seat, at my phone. Looking up. And there was a raccoon in the road. I braked and swerved, even though I knew better. I fucking *know* better, but I hit the brakes and jerked the wheel like a *fucking* moron." She shoves her crutches away and they hit the ground with a clatter. "And now look."

"Hey, easy." The most I've touched her since the accident is holding her hand—aside from whatever was necessary to help her, that is, but that's clinical contact; now I tentatively put my arm across her shoulders. "It's okay."

"It's not!" She shakes her head savagely, scrubbing angrily at her eyes. "Nothing is okay. I'm not—you're not. We aren't."

"Honestly, Ember, I don't know what we are."

"Me either." She looks at me with reddened eyes. "It

feels weird, now, though, doesn't it? Sort of...I dunno... friend-zoned, kind of."

I nod. "I know what you mean, and yeah."

"That's not what I want," she says.

"Me either."

She turns toward me, cast nudging my ankle. "When I left California..." Her voice trembles, but she shakes it off. "I wasn't sure what I wanted. I still...I'm not, like, *over* Dutchie. But I talked to Faye a *lot* and...I promised him."

"Promised him what?" I ask.

"That I'd move on. Find someone else. He made me swear on our wedding bands. But I...I miss him. It feels wrong to enjoy life, to...to fall in love, to enjoy sex with someone new. It feels like I'm betraying him. I know he's gone. I know I have my whole life ahead of me, but...like you said earlier, try convincing my heart of that."

"I understand," I say. "I mean, sort of. I understand feeling something that you know you shouldn't."

She rests her hand on my knee. "By the time I made it here to your house, I was all in, Fee." She tips her head back, sniffing. "I was coming to tell you that I...I wanted to be with you. I wanted to try. And then I saw you and her, and..."

"Worst-case scenario," I say.

She nods. "Exactly. But I should have slowed down and listened. I'm sorry." A thoughtful pause. "What I don't get is why she thought she could waltz back into your life like nothing happened."

"I mean...she did apologize," I say. "I just...I dunno."

Ember frowns at me. "What? Say it, Felix."

"If it wasn't for you being in my life, I would have taken her back. But it wouldn't have lasted."

A brief silence. "No?" she asks, her voice soft. "Why not?"

"Because I don't know her anymore, and she doesn't know me. I'm not the same person I was at nineteen, and neither is she. She's had a whole life—college, a career, a husband, kids, friends, all of it. She's looking at me and seeing nineteen-year-old Felix in a thirty-two-year-old body. But I'm not him anymore. I've had my own life. We…" I shake my head, sighing. "No, forget that part."

Ember touches my hand, looking at me with curiosity. "Don't do that, Fee. Don't hold anything back."

I eye her and then shrug. "Fine. I was gonna say that we would have gotten together, and it probably would have been pretty great at first. She's been neglected, I think. Her husband cheats on her. So she's probably starved for attention. It'd have been hot at first. Reconnecting with an old flame, thinking we're making up for lost time or healing old wounds, that kind of thing."

I don't miss the hurt in her eyes, the hardening of her expression.

"*But…*" I say, emphasizing the word to get her attention.

"But what?"

"What do we have in common aside from the past? Not a goddamn thing. She's rich. She's used to a certain lifestyle. I don't know dick about purses but I'm pretty sure the one she's carrying is pretty expensive."

Ember cackles. "Try abhorrently expensive, Fee. That was a Birkin."

I shrug. "Means nothing to me."

"Twenty grand, give or take a few thousand. And even

if you have the money, they're exclusive and nearly impossible to get. Like, you have to be on a list."

I snort and roll my eyes. "That's more than my truck is worth." I wave a hand. "But that's exactly my point. Look, there's nothing wrong with having money and spending it on things you find valuable. But that just doesn't fit with who I am. I don't know…I guess I just…the more I think about it, the more I realize if I was to get back together with Amy, we'd very quickly realize that our shared history isn't enough to overcome everything else. How she left me, the effect that her leaving and the way she left had on me and on my life, the decade and some years of living two totally different lives. And no amount of sex, no matter how good it may have been, can cover over all that."

Ember nods. "That makes sense."

"There's one other issue I keep coming up against when it comes to Amy."

She looks at me again, curious but cautious. "Hmmm." It's not quite an interrogatory sound, more of an "I'm listening but I'm skeptical" verbal expression.

"She's not you."

This gets her attention, eliciting a small, hopeful smile. "Go on."

I guess I'd thought that would be enough, but it seems she needs elaboration.

"When she was here, apologizing, touching me like she had every right to, acting interested, telling me she fantasized about me during sex with her cheating asshole husband…I felt nothing for her. Zero. If I felt anything, it was…pain. Guilt. Regret. Bitterness. Anger." I hesitate, and then go for broke. "And yeah, listen, she's aged well.

She is, objectively speaking, a very beautiful woman. She's taken great care of herself."

"Great," Ember whispers. "Your ex is tall, skinny, has big tits and a great ass, she's rich, single, and probably does hot yoga and runs marathons."

"How do you know she has big tits and a great ass, Ember?"

"I don't. I'm assuming."

"You may be right. I didn't look all that closely, if I'm being honest."

Again, this statement brings her attention back to me rather than the rug beneath her feet. "No?"

"I told you—I felt nothing. Because she's not you. I saw her again at the hospital—"

She frowns, cutting me off. "Wait, she came to the hospital?"

I nod. "I think she feels partially responsible for what happened. She said she was sorry. I just…I didn't really give her the time of day, to be honest. I didn't know how to feel about her, how to—where to put her in my mind or my heart or whatever. So I more or less ignored her."

"Fee, I…I'm worried you're not thinking clearly about her," Ember says, her voice small, her eyes on the rug again. "About the situation. What if she *is* who you're meant to be with? What if…what if you can bridge the divide of the years and everything that happened and have the happily ever after you should have had?"

"Just one problem, Ember."

She rolls her eyes at me. "She's not me. Right. You said that, Fee."

"I'm not attracted to her. I don't know that I've ever

had a type, per se. The girls I've...well, dated is a strong word for it. Seen? Been with? Whatever. There's no pattern."

Her brow scrunches. "Why are you telling me this?"

"Because it turns out I do have a type. And it's not tall, skinny, rich women with black hair and too much makeup."

She lets the corners of her mouth lift in an almost-smile. "I'm pretty sure I've heard this one, but go on."

"It turns out my type is short girls with white-blond hair."

"Those are a dime a dozen, Fee," she whispers. "Might have to be more specific."

"Oh, hmmm—you're right. She has to have the biggest, juiciest tits I've ever seen."

She looks down at her chest. "Oh." She cups and lifts her breasts. "Like these?"

"Exactly like those," I say. "But that's not all of the requirements."

"There's more?"

"Oh yeah. She has to have an ass that doesn't quit. Her eyes have to be the most unique shade of gray on the planet—the color of quicksilver." I shift closer to her. Stare into the aforementioned silver eyes. "She has to be...undomesticated. Wild. The kind of woman you know you're never, ever gonna tame. She has to drive a 1967 VW Bus covered in stickers, and it has to be pumpkin orange."

"Fee," she whispers, eyes shimmering. "Stop."

"Mmmm, not quite done. Just a few more items on the list."

"Fine," She sighs, her expression complicated—curious, cautious, hopeful, scared. "I'll bite. What else?"

"Well, let's see—she has to be amazingly brave, resilient, strong, and kind. Funny. Weird."

"I'm not weird," she protests in a whisper.

"Yeah, you are," I say. "She also has to be willing to adopt crazy old ladies as surrogate grandmothers. She has to click with my friends. She has to have an easy laugh."

"Easy laugh? What's that?"

"Someone who's easy to make laugh. It makes you feel funny, and that's excellent for your self-esteem."

"Oh," she breathes. "And I'm an easy laugh?"

"Yep."

She swallows hard. "That's a big list to fill, Fee. Is that it?"

"One last thing," I say. "The sex has to be out of this fucking world."

"But we haven't even actually had sex, Fee," she whispers. "We just…messed around a little bit. Once."

"And that was, by far and bar none, the hottest sex of my life."

She squeezes her eyes shut, shaking her head. "Don't lie to me or butter me up, Fee."

"What makes you think I am?"

"I'm not all that."

I laugh. "Ember, I literally described exactly, specifically you."

She just looks at me, uncertain and emotional. "I don't feel like that, Fee. I don't feel…sexy. Or confident. Or… anything. I feel beat up. Not just physically from the accident, but…everything. Life. I've lost everything and everyone. GramGram, Mom, Dutchie, Faye. My life on the road. My sense of purpose. I need help to do everything. I'm living with you because I literally have nowhere else to go and no one to…to take care of me. You're only doing it out of pity."

"Okay, honestly, Ember, that last part pisses me off a little bit." I run my hand through my hair, sighing. "There's no pity involved. And you *have* options. Lainey and Layla would take you in and help you get back on your feet, literally and metaphorically. I know Bear and Noelle have a spare room and they'd help. Shit, Cole's sister lives alone and she's a freaking home care nurse. You're here because I *want* you to be here. I *want* to be the one to help you. It's not fucking *pity*, Ember, it's….if anything it's self-interest. I want to see you every day. I want to…I want to see what could be between us."

Ember drops her gaze. "I'm in a weird place, Fee. The accident changed things for me."

I swallow my hurt. "That's okay. If you'd rather find somewhere else, I get it. I'll take you wherever you want to go. I've got the Cartwright sisters on TikTok—I can DM them."

She shakes her head, tears leaking again. "No, Fee. I don't want to go anywhere else. I just…I don't feel like myself right now. Maybe it's the TBI, I don't know. I just…I think I might need to focus on getting better before I can think about being involved with you. Like that, I mean."

I nod, feeling guilty for the disappointment that burns in my gut. I take a moment to swallow it, bury it. "Of course, Ember. There's no time frame on anything. No pressure. No expectations."

"I do care about you, Felix," she whispers. "So much. I'm attracted to you. I think you're the most amazing man I've met in a long time, maybe ever, and you've done *so* much for me. I just…Dutchie hasn't been dead a year, and now I meet Faye, fall in love with her, and lose her. And then this accident, and I just feel…scrambled up in my head. My emotions are all over the place. Things are foggy. And I…I just…I guess I'm saying I just need time."

"And you've got all the time in the world," I tell her. "I'm not going anywhere and I'm in no hurry."

"I feel like I'm letting you down. Disappointing you," she says.

"Never," I answer. "You're doing what you need to do for yourself. I'm just here to facilitate that. And if…" it hurts to think and hurts more to put out into the world. "If it turns out that things between you and me can't be what I want, that's okay. If you…if you don't feel that way for me anymore, that's okay. I can handle that. I promise."

She lets out a shaky breath. "I'm sorry, Fee. I'm sorry." She levers to her feet. "Can I…can I just have some time alone in my…in your guest room?"

"Hey, don't be sorry." I summon a smile, stand up and help her to her feet. "You can have all the time alone you want in *your* room."

She swings down the hallway to the first door on the right, pauses to open it, and covers her mouth. "Fee?" She turns to look at me. "You…you did this for me?"

"Like I said, Bear and Noelle did the actual work. I didn't want to leave you."

All her stuff is in there—a bureau holds her clothes, a shelf holds her books, and a desk has her laptop. On the bureau is her box of jewelry—miraculously, it survived the accident unscathed. Noelle went out of her way to make it pretty, also—colorful throw pillows, a bright patchwork quilt covering the bottom third of the queen bed, landscape paintings and photographs on the walls, and a vase on the nightstand with flowers. I had Bear bring the safe in, also—it's in the closet, with the code on a sticky note for her to memorize.

I gesture at the safe. "Your cash and antique jewelry are in there. That's the code. I can change it for you, if you want. Or tell you how to." I point at the door beside the bed. "There's a full en suite in there, and all your shower stuff is there."

"Fee..." She leans on her crutches and wipes her eyes. "I don't know what to say. I've never had a room like this. One that's..."

"Yours," I finish for her. "It's yours for as long as you want, even if we're only ever friends and roommates."

I'm at the end of the hallway, keeping my distance so she doesn't sense my hurt and disappointment—I know she needs time, I know she's been through a lot, and I know my feelings are selfish. I won't burden her with them.

"Fee, c'mere." She waves me closer, still leaning on her crutches.

I lick my lips, hesitate.

She laughs. "I'm not gonna bite, Fee, Jesus."

I cross the space, stopping a foot away. Smile for her, even if it feels a little forced. "Hi."

She searches me, and then rolls her eyes and sighs. Sets her crutches against the wall, holds her hands out, forcing me to take them or let her lose her balance. She hops toward me on her good leg, wincing as her ribs protest.

"Ow, ow, ow." She slides her hands from mine and rests them on my shoulders. "Sorry, okay—Felix, listen to me." She gazes up at me with compassion and under-standing. "I don't think you understand what I'm saying.

I don't want to be *just* friends or roommates with you. My feelings for you haven't changed. I care about you deeply. I'm attracted to you in a way I've never felt for anyone before, including my husband, and to be honest, that's one of the things I need time to work through. I just need time. I need to put myself back together. And I really, *really* hope you'll be there waiting for me when I'm ready."

I open my mouth to answer, but she puts her fingers over my lips.

"You deserve *all* of me, Fee. My whole heart, everything I am. And I *want* to give that to you. But I can't—*yet*."

Stupid feelings, making my eyes burn. Fuck.

I shake my head and check the ceiling overhead for cracks, blinking hard. "Sorry, I'm just—shit. I feel like an idiot."

She palms the back of my head and pulls my face down so I have to meet her eyes, and she lifts on her tiptoes, soft lips touching mine briefly. "Felix, you have the biggest, most tender heart. You hide it well, but I see it. Be patient with me, okay?" She wipes her fingers beneath my eyes. "And this? Don't hide it from me. It's okay."

"It's not. It's stupid. You don't need to deal with my shit."

She laughs. "Fee, you've been through a lot, too. You're allowed to have feelings about it. And I *want* you to share them with me." She kisses me again, another soft, damp, quick touch of the lips—a promise of a kiss. "Just be patient with me, okay?"

I nod. "That I can do."

18

Ember

I'M CRANKY, SWEATY, TIRED, SORE, HUNGRY, AND SICK of…well, everything. Connie, my physical therapist, worked me to the bone today—I'm still having balance issues, and now that my cast is off, I have to rehab the atrophied muscles in my leg. Fine motor skills—like holding a pencil, buttoning a shirt, tying shoelaces… they're all harder than they should be.

Fucking racoon.

Fucking Amy whatever the fuck her last name is.

And fuck my dumbass for making the decision to drive when I knew damn well I was in no state to be behind the wheel. PSA, kids: driving while hysterical is just as dangerous as driving while drunk or texting.

I glare at Connie as she wipes the equipment down. "I hate you, you know."

She just grins at me, taking my ire in stride, as usual. "Honey, that's fine. Hate me all you want—my job ain't to make you like me, it's to get you mobile again. And you're almost there."

Connie is fantastic. She's a six-foot-tall Black woman with waist-length micro-braids shot through with pink and purple streaks that remind me of Faye. She has multiple degrees and more certifications than I can list, a wicked sense of humor, and a way of getting that last bit of effort out of me even when I'm at my worst. Which I am, today.

I love Connie.

I also love to hate Connie.

Today is the latter.

"I thought we were friends," I tell her.

"We're friends until your session starts and we're friends when it's over," she says. "During your session, I'm not your friend—I'm the taskmaster who's gonna whip your ass into the best shape of your life."

She's doing exactly that. Apparently, rehabbing my leg, lungs, ribs, and motor skills means working me like I'm training for the Olympics. I lift weights. I cycle on those medieval torture devices where you pull the handles and pump the pedals at the same time. I do burpees—fuck burpees, by the way. I do a lot of single leg work, balancing, lifting while balancing, and standing on one leg while holding a weight overhead. I swim. I jog. I blow into a machine to test my lung capacity. Run while connected to a bunch of shit to test my VO2 Max.

All that is three days a week. I also have speech therapy to help me stop flipping words around or smooshing them together. I have PT focused on my fine motor skills. I have talk therapy to help me past my freight train of emotional baggage—that was my idea, though.

And through it all, Felix has been my rock.

He drives me to all my appointments and picks me up. Takes me to ice cream after and listens to me bitch. He takes me to The Alt so I can hang out with the girls—Lainey and Layla, and sometimes Noelle and Raina—and do homework and study.

MSU, apparently, has a satellite campus in Three Rivers that operates out of the community college; I transferred my handful of credits and now I'm finishing my degree through them. Which means Felix is also taking me to school and picking me up twice a week.

We've established a kind of detente of sorts—we're more very good friends than anything, at the moment. Albeit friends who hold hands and occasionally share a kiss. It's been hard, if I'm being honest. I see him doing so many things for me—he cooks or brings food home most nights, drives me everywhere, and until I got my cast off, carried things for me, opened doors…and he never complains about any of it. Never acts like he's sick of doing it. Never asks for anything in return. He respects my space and privacy, my determination to fix my body, emotions.

But I live with him. I hear him shower. He walks around in nothing but a pair of shorts. We sit together and watch TV at night, and more often than not, my head ends up on his chest and his arm around me.

Basically, he's doing all the work of taking care of me, supporting me, and being there for me in every possible way—like a very needy live-in girlfriend—without the benefit of sex.

Like a friends-with-benefits situation in reverse: all the commitment, none of the fun.

"You're spacin' out over there, honey," Connie says. "Back to earth, now. Your man's gonna be here any minute."

"He's not my man," I argue.

Connie tosses the antibacterial wipe into a trash can and levels me an incredulous head tilt/stare of disbelief. "Not—? Ohhh, lordy, help me. *Not* your *man*?" She turns away, shaking her head in disgust. "Not your man. Child, I thought you were smart."

I frown at her. "Excuse me?"

"Yes, ex*cuse* you. That man has gone so far above and beyond, taking care of you. He brings you to every appointment, and you have to shoo him away or he'd be here holding you up instead of letting you do the work. He packs you a lunch for your classes. He cooks for you. He did your laundry—including folding your unmentionables. Honey, I've been married for fifteen years, and I can't get my man to switch the damn laundry, never mind fold my panties. 'Too slinky,' he says." She pokes the air in front of my face. "That man is head over heels in love with you. If you're tellin' me you've got his fine ass in the friend-zone, I might have to go old school on your ass and smack the stupid right outta you."

Defensiveness seethes through me. "He's *not* in the friend zone. Felix and I talked about this when I first moved in with him. I need time to focus on…" I waved a hand at the PT facility. "All this."

"He's runnin' a company *and* seeing to your every need." She leans closer. "Please tell me you're at least helping the poor man out once in a while. If you know what I mean. Givin' him a little somethin'-somethin.'"

"That would defeat the purpose, Connie," I say, hearing myself snap and hating it, even as I fail to stop it. "I care about him. I'm doing this *for him*. I recognize how much he's doing for me, trust me. I just…I need to feel whole before I can put myself into a serious relationship."

Connie shakes her head. "All that may have been true at one point, but I think now you're keeping him at arm's length for a different reason. I see the way he looks at you—like the sun rises and sets with you. When will you be whole? How will you know? When will you be ready to take that chance? How long is he supposed to wait?"

"It's been eight weeks, Connie, not eight months or eight years."

"When you're living in his house, being driven around, cooked for, provided for, and taken care of like a queen, eight weeks is an eternity to live with unrequited love."

"It's not unrequited!" I snap. "I requite it."

"Oh yeah?" she asks, doing the head tilt again. "Does *he* know that?"

"I thank him all the time."

"That's just manners."

"So I should thank him sexually—is that what you're saying?"

"It's not about sex, Ember. And it sure as hell ain't transactional, so don't gimme that shit, either." She gets close and holds my gaze. "It's about opening up to him. Letting him in. Giving back to him."

I turn away, angry and guilty. "It's not that fucking easy."

"You needed time. I get that, and I'm sure he does, too. I *know* he does, actually—because he's given it to you." She moves around in front of me. "This is me as your friend, honey. There's no good time. It's never gonna get easier or less scary. You gotta just…jump."

"I'm starting my life over, Connie," I whisper. "This is the longest I've ever been *any*where in my whole life. I…I have friends. I'm going to school—in a building, for the first time ever. I'm relearning…it feels like everything. *Everything* is different. It's scary. It's taking everything I've got to not run away. You know how many times I've woken up in the middle of the night wanting to get into Pumpkin and just drive away? Go back to the life I knew? But I haven't. I'm still here. And that *is* me trying."

"Alright, alright, I hear you." She pats my cheek. "I just wonder if maybe *he* needs to hear all that."

She's right. God, she's *so* right.

Someone calls Connie's name. She gives me a quick hug. "I gotta go, boo. I'll see you Friday for our last session. But you think about what I said. Maybe it's time for you to take things to the next step with Felix."

"Wait—last session?"

She grins. "Yeah, baby, you're done!" And with that, she's gone, her track pants zip-zip-zipping as she hustles to greet her next victim—I mean, client.

Great. Now I'm cranky, sweaty, tired, sore, hungry… *and* feeling guilty.

I snag a towel from my bag, top my water bottle off at the filling station, and exit the facility, dabbing at my face as I wait for Fee.

He's as punctual as ever, and this time his truck is dripping wet from the car wash, the gold paint sparkling. When I climb in—on my own, because I told him last week I needed to start doing it on my own—the interior has been vacuumed and detailed.

"Wow," I tell him. "Truck looks great!"

He grins, shrugging. "Gotta clean 'er up once in a while." He pulls away from the building and turns onto the street, heading for The Alt, where I'm meeting Noelle and Raina for lunch. "How was your session?"

I sigh a laugh. "Oh, y'know, brutal as usual. Single leg deadlifts, pistol squats, curtsy lunges."

"Last session on Friday."

"I know! Connie just said that. I'd forgotten. It feels… weird. Like, what do I do with myself without P-T three days a week?"

"Whatever you want?" he suggests. "Sleep in. Get a job. Go on a road trip."

"Felix, do you resent me?" The question pops out before I even realize I was thinking it.

His frown is one of utter perplexity. "What? Resent you? Why the fuck would I resent you?"

"Or…feel taken advantage of is maybe a better way to put it."

He squeezes my knee, smiling at me reassuringly. "No, Ember. I do not resent you or feel taken advantage of. Why do you ask?"

"I…" I have no idea how to answer that.

He searches my face as we sit at a light. "Is this about…us?"

It's the closest we've come to addressing the status of our relationship since I came home from the hospital.

I nod. "Yeah."

He shifts into first and then second. "I don't expect anything. My feelings haven't changed—if anything, they've grown. But until and unless you're ready, I'll keep my distance. Keep the status quo. Ball's in your court, sweetheart."

"But you've done so much for me," I protest. "Too much."

He doesn't answer for a bit, thinking. "Do you think if it was Riley, or Cole, or Nyx that was in your situation, I'd do anything different?"

That stings. "I...I guess not." I duck my head.

"You've become one of my best friends. I'd do anything for you, Ember."

"So...friends, then." I know how petulant I sound, and how stupid it is since I chose this.

He shifts gears, then adjusts the dirty, battered ball cap on his head. "You asked me to wait for you, Em. I am and I will. But I...I have to put you somewhere...In my head, or my heart, or whatever. I have very strong feelings for you and I'm doing my fucking best to keep that shit to myself and just be your friend, because I can't live in a quasi-not-really-but-sort-of state with you. Maybe I'm just not strong enough. I don't know." He glances at me, and his gaze is a little distant. "I don't resent you. I don't feel taken advantage of. Everything I've done for you, I've done because I luh—" his teeth click together. "I care about you as a human being, and as my friend. If there's ever gonna be anything else, it's gonna happen on your time, in your way. You know how I feel, and I'm not gonna push that on you when you made it very clear you're not ready."

"Fee," I whisper.

He shakes his head, tugging the curved brim of his ball cap lower. "Don't do that."

"Do what?"

"That sad, hurt whisper. The way you say my name when you don't know what to say." He pulls into the parking lot of The Alt and into the handicapped spot nearest the door, leaving it in gear, idling. "I'll wait as long as you need. But you can't ask me for emotional vulnerability too. It's too hard. Too complicated. So yeah. Friends. And no, throwing sex into the mix is not the answer. That would just confuse me more, because I can't—I wouldn't be able to separate my feelings from the sex."

I nod, hoping my stupid, irrational, selfish hurt doesn't show. "I understand." I push open the door and slide to the ground, landing easily and without pain or wobbly balance.

He tips his head back, groaning. "Em, wait."

I look at him—he's grown his beard out and it suits him. His hair is longer and shaggier than ever, almost long enough that he could pull it back. The beard, though. Hot, rugged, manly...woof. I bet it would scratch and tickle when he went down on me—

I squash that thought. Or at least bank it for later.

I wait for his reply, and it's a long moment coming.

His glacier-blue eyes are piercing and intense. "I'm just trying to give you what you asked for."

"I know," I whisper. "Haven't you ever gotten what you wanted, only to realize it's not what you thought it'd be?"

He sighs, scraping the hat off to scratch at his scalp before settling the hat back on one-handed. "If you want things to be different, Ember, they can. In a heartbeat. Right the fuck now." He grips the shifter, his gaze intense. "Just...be sure. Okay? I'm hanging on by a thread, and I couldn't go back if we—if you...I just couldn't go back."

"Felix, I..."

His phone rings. "I gotta go. Call if you need anything."

"Okay. I'll see you later, Fee." I step back, but don't close the door yet.

He stares at me for a moment, and then closes his eyes, shakes his head, and then opens them and stabs the answer button. "See you, Em," he says to me, then puts the phone to his ear and shifts into reverse. "Hey, Bear. Brennan show up yet? No? For real? Fuck. Alright, I'll swing by his place and see what's up. He's never even been late, let alone a no-call-no-show."

I shut the door, and he immediately reverses out of the spot and is gone in a cloud of diesel fumes. Heart aching, eyes burning, body, heart, and brain giving me wildly mixed signals, I head inside to find Noelle and Raina waiting for me at a four-top.

"Hey, girl!" Noelle says, all sunshine and eager joy. She shoots to her feet and hugs me as I approach the table. "Did Connie break you?"

"Nearly," I mumble.

Raina—Noelle's friend, and now mine—rises as well and embraces me. Raina is a couple inches taller than me and similarly built, with long, thick black hair and brown skin. She's funny in a dry, reserved way, and far more conservative than I am, having come from a very traditional Iranian family. She moved up here a few years ago to forge her own path, and is now a dental hygienist at Three Rivers' best dental office. I adore her.

She's also very perceptive. "What's wrong?"

Lainey sweeps over, wearing an ankle-length floral skirt and a tight white tank top, her short hair held back by a headband with a big bow. On anyone else, it'd look sorta silly, but she pulls the giant bow off, somehow.

"Here ya go, Sparky." She sets my usual order on the table—chicken pesto sandwich and a small Greek salad. "Last sesh on Friday, right? Bet you're ready to be done with that."

I cock an eyebrow at her. "Sparky?"

She shrugs, giggling. "I dunno. Ember? Sparky? No? Never mind. Enjoy!"

The sisters still won't let me pay. I've tried stuffing twenties into their tip jar, but I always find them returned to me somewhere, somehow.

"Actually, Lane," I say, acting on an idea as it pops into my head. "Do you guys need any help? Once I'm done with the P-T and all that, I'm gonna need a job, now that my vlogging days are over. I've gone through a good bit of my savings."

Layla is at the till, counting ones—she and Lainey trade glances, and then Layla nods. "You're hired."

I grin. "Really? That would be cool. I love this place, and I love you guys."

Layla smiles back. "Absolutely. We've been tossing around the idea of hiring someone, but everyone we've interviewed hasn't been a good fit. And you, my dear, are perfect."

Raina turns me to face her. "That's great. Back to me, though."

I shrug her off. "I'm fine."

She taps my nose. "If you were Pinocchio, your nose would have just grown a foot."

I groan. "I'm hangry, Raina. Let me eat and then we'll talk."

She sighs. "Fine. Be all needy and human, if you must."

I feel eyes on me as I eat, but I ignore them. What

I'm feeling is complex and weird, and I don't know what to do with it.

I let Raina and Noelle's idle, friendly chatter wash over me as we eat, and I occasionally chime in, but mostly, I'm thinking about Felix.

The distance in his eyes. How he said he was 'hanging on by a thread.' The sense of hidden pain.

When we're done eating, Noelle gathers our plates and silverware and brings them into the kitchen—we're all here so much we're not really even regulars anymore—we're more like fixtures. We take our various beverages and go sit outside in the sun under the pergola.

Noelle smacks my knee as she passes me to sit on my left while Raina sits on my right; the cafe is empty, so Layla and Lainey pull an ottoman over and squeeze onto it together, facing me.

"So," Noelle says. "Why are you upset?"

"Who said I was?" I ask.

Lainey traces a line down between my eyebrows. "Your elevens."

"My what?"

She frowns and points at the two vertical lines that appear between her eyebrows. "Your elevens. They show up when you're upset."

"Maybe I'm just tired from Connie's torture session."

Layla snorts. "Okay, biyotch. I wasn't born at night *or* last night. Spill."

Raina leans against my shoulder. "We're your friends. You can talk to us. We may not be able to *do* anything, but we can listen."

"My friends," I say, fighting emotions. "Ugh, god, the

emotions! When will I stop crying at the drop of a hat? Fuck!" I scrub my face.

"Maybe," Noelle says, "you're suppressing your feelings and they're trying to come out."

"I'm not suppressing anything!" I protest.

"Okay," Lainey mocks in a voice indicating a distinct lack of intelligence. "Whatever you say, girlfriend."

"It's the T-B-I," I argue. "Emotional dysregulation is one of the symptoms."

Layla scoots toward me and takes my hands in hers, going so far as to set my plastic cup of iced tea aside. "Sweetie, we love you." She twirls a finger to include all five of us. "This here? This is our girl gang. In this gang, we don't lie to each other or ourselves. We pull up our thongs and face the hard shit like the powerful boss bitches we are."

"How do you know I'm wearing a thong?" I ask.

She snickers. "Well, it was a turn of phrase. But also, leggings that tight with no panty line? Either you're commando or you're wearing a thong."

Raina makes a face. "I don't know how you wear those things. I absolutely *cannot* handle having my butt-crack flossed all day long. It's like the underwear version of toe socks." She shudders. "Ick. No. Nope. No way. I'll go commando before I wear butt floss."

I shrug. "I dunno. You get used to it."

She shakes her head vigorously. "Lies. I desperately wanted to be a sexy girl who wears thongs, so I wore nothing but thongs for a month except during period week and I hated every single second of it. The first thing I did the second I got home was take it off."

Noelle shoulders me. "Raina, you're letting Ember sidetrack the conversation."

I splutter indignantly. "Excuse the fuck out of you! *She* hijacked the conversation talking about butt-floss, not me."

"Actually, it was Layla," Raina says.

Lainey claps her hands. "Ladies. Enough. Ember, just spill already. Is Felix being mean or something?"

"Felix doesn't have a mean bone in his body," I snap. Then, I cover my face. "Yikes."

The girls all laugh.

"Okay, someone is defensive," Layla says, cackling.

I sigh. "No, it's not Felix." I tilt my head to one side. "Well…it *is* Felix. But not…he didn't…ugh!" I shake my head, blinking hard. "See? I cry—all—the—time! I'm sick of it!"

Noelle eyes me. "If I didn't know better, I'd think you were pregnant."

"Oh *hell* no," I say. "No. No way. Not possible, first of all. I haven't had sexual intercourse since before Dutchie got sick and that was nearly a year ago. So unless you can get pregnant orally, it's definitely not that."

"Orally?" Noelle says. "When did this happen? And… with Felix, I hope."

"Yes, with Felix," I answer. "Before the accident. We… we messed around a little bit."

Lainey rubs her hands together. "Deets, bitch, deets. I had the most embarrassingly huge crush on him in high school."

Layla snorts. "Every straight female in Three Rivers between the ages of puberty and death has had a crush on Felix Crowe at some point."

Raina bites her lower lip, grinning. "It was Riley for me when I first moved up here." She looks away, covering her face. "Still sorta do have one, actually. But you can't tell him that."

I mime zipping my lips closed. "Your secret is safe with me, babe."

Layla sighs. "Oh, Rain, you poor thing. You gotta get over that. Riley is a horndog. Yes, he's hot as sin, but he'll only break your heart. Ask me how I know."

"How do you know, Layla?" Raina asks.

"Because I hooked up with him once, a long, long time ago, and he moved on faster than I could get my clothes back on." She rolls her eyes. "He's a good time and that's it."

I frown. "I don't know if that's true anymore, actually. He came over to drink beer and watch football with Fee last week. I was in my room doing homework, and...well, Riley's voice carries."

"And?" Raina demands, when I don't continue.

"And I heard him saying that he's losing his touch because he's not hooking up like he used to. I think he might be starting to think about settling down." I shrug. "I dunno. Just what I heard."

Layla waves her hand. "Don't say that too loudly, Ember. You'll have half of Three Rivers chasing Riley Crowe down Main Street throwing their panties at him."

Raina doesn't say anything, but her gaze is speculative.

Noelle taps my knee. "You're not escaping the question that easily, Ember."

"I'm not avoiding." I sigh. "Fine, I'm avoiding. Connie made it seem like I'm taking advantage of Felix by living with him and letting him do everything he's been doing but not...being with him."

"Do *you* think so?" Raina asks.

I shake my head, pause, and shrug. "I don't know. I didn't until she said something. And now…yeah, I do. I mean, we talked about this, Felix and I, the day I left the hospital. I told him I needed time to sort my life out."

Layla touches my hand. "Honey, of course you'd need time. You went through hell. Your husband dying, and then dear old sweet crazy Faye, and then the accident?"

"I think it's getting to be really hard for him though," I say. "We talked a little on the way here, and I think he's hurting. It's taking a toll on him, and…I'm worried I'm gonna lose him."

Lainey shakes her head. "He wouldn't do all that and then be like, nah, forget it, too much trouble."

"He said that he was just doing what he'd do for any of his friends, like Cole, Nyx, or Riley." I sip my iced tea, grimacing when I discover it's just watery, vaguely tea-flavored ice-melt.

"Well, what you have to understand," Layla says, "is that those four are not just friends. It's more like family. They've been best bros since pre-K. All three of them visited Riley in prison every week, together. So putting you in the circle with his boys?" She shakes her head. "That's a big statement from him."

"You know him pretty well, huh?" I ask.

She shrugs. "It's a small town, babe. We all know each other. I was a year above them in high school and had a lot of the same classes with Felix. We were never friends, exactly, but I know him well."

"But what do I do? I needed the time. I'm still kind of a mess about Dutchie, but I'm doing a lot better. I don't fall apart as much when I talk about him. I just…it feels like there's a gap between us, now. I just…" I sniffle, groaning.

"I don't want to jump into bed with him just because. There are real feelings between us. He…" I hesitate. "When I was upside down in that SUV, I texted him. And he wrote that he loves me. I don't know if he even realizes it. And he almost said it when he dropped me off. But I want…I want it to be real. Not just hot sex."

Lainey grins at me. "But the sex *is* hot as fuck, right? It has to be."

Layla shoves at her sister. "Lane! God, get a grip."

Lainey sticks her tongue out. "Oh fuck off. I haven't gotten laid in months."

"Dan Hibbard last week doesn't count?"

"No, because he went down on me, which was great, but then he had whiskey dick and passed out. So no, I didn't actually sleep with him. Sadly."

"No take two for poor Dan?" Noelle asks.

Lainey shakes her head. "Nah. I can deal with you getting whiskey dick once in a while if I'm, like, *really* into you, but if it's a hookup and you give yourself whiskey dick? Sorry, no. That's the ick, and there's no getting past it."

Noelle takes my hand, clasping it in both of hers. "None of us are here to tell you what to do, honey. No one can. Only you know what's in your heart. If you have real feelings for him and you're worried you're gonna lose him, then what are you waiting for? And I don't mean just sex. But, for what it's worth, sex may be the best way forward—*if* you're sure your feelings for him are more than just physical attraction."

A bell rings somewhere inside, and Lainey pops to her feet—a little too quickly, perhaps. "I got it."

Layla rolls her eyes as she watches her sister head inside to take care of the customer. "Lainey is allergic to feelings. Any discussion of true love makes her run for the hills."

"Commitment-phobic?" Raina asks.

Layla shrugs, shaking her head. "Not commitment-phobic so much as once bitten, twice shy. That's her story to tell, though, not mine."

"I think we've all been there," Raina says, her gaze distant as if remembering something unpleasant.

Noelle ignores this side conversation, focusing on me. "Hey," she says, nudging me with her elbow, her expression warm and understanding and compassionate. "I get it. I mean, my husband didn't die, he just treated me like garbage and cheated on me a bunch. But I get what it's like to be scared to let yourself fall in love again."

"It's not just that," I whisper. "It's everything. Being with Felix represents a whole new way of living for me. I've been a nomad my whole life. I've literally *never* lived in a house this long in my life. Every day and more so as time goes on I have to fight the urge to just fucking leave. I really do care about him. I have very real feelings for him. But I just…I don't know if I'm cut out for the whole…stationary, domestic thing." I shake my head, sighing. "But I gotta ask, what do you mean, sex may be the best way forward if my feelings are real?"

Noelle laughs. "Well, I mean…" she glances at the sky, sighs, and starts over. "Sex is complicated, right? I mean, it seems simple, but it's not. Like, on the surface, it's part A goes into slot B, right? And if you're hooking up with someone casually, I can see how it would seem pretty simple. I wouldn't know, as I've never had casual sex. But… in a long-term relationship, sex changes. It's not static. It's not like…spicy and intense all the time. Sometimes it's more of an emotional connection than a physical release, if that makes any sense."

I nod. "It does. That's what it was for Dutchie and me—it was for more of an emotional connection than a physical one." I cover my face. "That's part of my hangup. I've been avoiding this topic because of how tricky it is."

Noelle frowns. "Can you elaborate? You don't have to, but I guess I don't really understand what you mean."

I shoot to my feet. "Yeah, but I need to walk. Wanna walk and talk?"

Raina and Layla are deep in a conversation together, and barely notice as we exit the outdoor seating area and stroll along Manitou Boulevard next to the Crooked Trout river, away from Main Street.

"I love this part of town," Noelle says, grinning happily at the sun overhead and taking in the admittedly picturesque area.

The river is narrow but deep, a good eight or ten feet below the street—the water is dark with tannins, flowing rapidly enough to churn white around a few huge boulders at the edges. Willow trees line the opposite bank, their long, dangling fronds twisting and swaying just above the river surface. Here, Manitou Boulevard is actually a boulevard, with two lanes in each direction separated by a median planted with a profusion of colorful flowers and low shrubs.

"It's beautiful," I say. "I only had one sexual partner before Dutchie—my first, and it was…well, not to put too fine a point on it, but it was fucking horrific. I didn't have sex again for years after that, and it took Dutchie *months* to get me to trust him enough to go there."

Noelle rubs my back. "Girl, you've been through some stuff, haven't you?"

I sniff a laugh. "Yeah, I guess so." I shake my head. "Dutchie healed me. He…he gave me the time, space, love, and safety I needed in order to learn how to enjoy sex."

"But?" she prompts.

"But in the…oh god…six months to a year before he got sick, I was…I wasn't content. With him. Sexually." I swallow hard, feeling my eyes burn. "Fuck, this is hard."

"You need a minute?" Noelle asks.

I nod. "Yeah, thanks. I…"

She rubs my back again. "Hey, you're okay. Take your time. I can fill the silence, trust me."

I sniff a laugh. "Go for it."

"My ex-husband Brennan barely looked at me. He wanted to control me. Wanted me to be the good, dutiful, obedient little pastor's wife." She laughs bitterly. "He expected me, sooner than later, to stop working and focus on being his wife, pop out a couple kids for him, and submit to his every whim."

I retch, and it's not exactly faked. "Fuck that noise."

"Right? The sad thing is I went along with it until I found out he was having sex with a bunch of women from the church."

I give her a wide-eyed glance. "No shit?"

"Three of them at once. Well…not at once like a foursome, but three different mistresses while with me he acted like forty-five seconds of missionary in the dark with his T-shirt on was all I should ever need or want."

"Oh. Wow. That's…"

"Hypocrisy upon hypocrisy? Yeah. And he made me

feel like a shameless whore if I ever expressed interest in anything more. I left him, and eventually I met Bear."

"Who's the sweetest man I've ever met, by the way," I say. "I admit I was a little scared of him at first, but he's just a giant loveable teddy bear."

She smirks at me. "Oh, he's a teddy bear, all right." She wriggles her eyebrows at me in an expression she probably meant to be suggestive but was really just silly, cute, and funny. "Let's just say he's not *always* a sweet teddy bear, though."

I cackle. "If you could never do that with your eyebrow again, that'd be great."

"Oh, shut up," she teases. "My point is, I was scared to trust Bear. And I know, he's scary at first, and that includes in bed." She leans close, lowering her voice. "The answer to the question everyone always asks me is yes. He's..." she trails off with a shy but sly grin.

"Big everywhere?"

She nods. "Yes. Big, and...not always gentle, but in the best way possible." She covers her face with both hands. "I don't talk about this stuff with others much."

"You don't have to if you're uncomfortable."

"It's fine. I don't, like, gossip, you know? Like talk about our sex life just for giggles with the girls. It's private, and, honestly sacred to me. But this conversation with you, it's different. It's not just for fun."

"No, I guess it's not."

"Bear made it okay for me to not just enjoy sex but to feel confident in expressing my desires. I can be exactly and fully myself with him. I mean, look, we're not into anything weird or kinky. But he makes me feel safe being...a little wild, I guess. It's a part of myself that I can only show him, and it's…" She shrugs, sighs. "It's a vitally important part of our relationship. For the seriously hot sex, yes, but more importantly because of the freedom in it. I can open up the deepest, most uninhibited parts of myself and not be judged. He returns it—he accepts it, loves me for it all the more, and gives it back to me just as passionately and openly."

I swallow hard. "That sounds beautiful, Noelle. Really and truly."

She stops and leans on the concrete railing and gazes down at the rushing river. "It is. And that's what I mean, Ember." She looks at me. "It takes total trust and commitment to open up like that with someone. But if you can, and if he opens up to you like that in return, it's a thousand percent worth it. Because it's…it's a connection of your souls *through* your bodies."

This makes the tears drip down my cheeks. "I want that. But I'm…I feel guilty. Because I loved Dutchie—I still do, in a lot of ways. And it's just hard to accept that my sexual relationship with Felix might be…better, in some ways. More fulfilling. It hurts. It feels like a betrayal of my love for Dutchie, and I don't know how to reconcile that, or…or get past it." I let out a ragged groan, slapping at my cheeks. "*UGH!* So—sick—of crying! And I know I shouldn't feel that way. Dutchie—his last words to me were to extract a promise from me that I'd move on and fall in love again. I'm just…I'm *stuck*. I've been stuck since I met Felix and felt an attraction to him that immediately eclipsed anything I've ever felt in my life."

Noelle leans a shoulder against mine and rests her head on my shoulder. "There's no good or easy answer to that, I don't think."

"No, I don't think there is," I whisper. "So what do I do?"

"I think what I said back at The Alt is still my best advice, assuming you're asking for advice."

"I am," I confirm.

"I'm not sure there's any way past that hangup except through. You know, mentally, that letting yourself be with Felix, letting yourself fall in love with him—you *know* intellectually that it's not a betrayal. If anything, it's you keeping your promise to Dutchie. But it's...I dunno. I think it's just gonna hurt a bit at first. Sometimes in life the only way out is through. I don't mean just sleep with him and get it over with, just..."

I laugh even as I sob a little. "But you kinda are saying that."

"I don't mean just get it over with. I mean..." She throws her hands up. "Maybe I don't know *what* I mean. I guess I just mean you might just have to face that feeling head-on. It's not going to just go away suddenly. If you care about Felix and if you want to have a relationship with him, you're gonna have to face that feeling and deal with it."

"I kinda hate you a little for being right."

"Sorry?" She says, wincing while making it a question.

I can't help but laugh. "No, you *are* right. I guess I'm just scared. I have to give myself permission to move on, and I have to give myself permission to feel what I feel and then be brave enough to actually feel it without running away."

"I do think there's one factor you're maybe not taking into consideration that may change how the whole thing ends up working out for you," she says.

I frown. "What's that?"

"You won't be facing it alone. That's the whole point. You're not really taking Felix into consideration."

I don't know why, but this stuns me. "Oh. Holy shit, you're right." I rub my face with both hands. "God, I'm a bitch."

Noelle rears back, glaring at me in total confusion. "What? I think you must have misunderstood me."

I blink at her. "I'm only thinking about myself. I'm not thinking about him—about how he feels in all this."

Noelle shakes her head, turning to face me and grabbing both of my hands. "No, no, no, Ember. That's not *at all* what I mean. While there may be some truth to that—and that's not for me to say—that's not at all what I meant."

"Okay, then what *did* you mean?"

"That you're not factoring in Felix's understanding and support. You won't be going through any of it alone, in a vacuum. He'll be there with you every step of the way, if you let him. I don't know Felix super well—we're close in age but ran in totally different social circles and I went to the private Christian school connected to the church I grew up in. But I *do* know that he and Bear are pretty close, and Bear thinks a lot of him. And Bear doesn't think much of most people."

"Oh," I breathe. "That's...very different."

"Just a little," she says, laughing. "Just take it one step at a time with him. Talk to him. Be honest with him. Be vulnerable. Put yourself out there." She gives me a side hug. "You have friends, now, Ember. We'll be here for you. So, whatever happens, just...don't run away. Okay?"

I nod, sighing. "Yeah, I...I'm trying." I give her a weak but genuine smile. "Thank you, Noelle. It's...honestly, it's a little weird having girlfriends."

We walk back to The Alt and rejoin the others; I engage in the conversation, which moves on to other lighter and less important fare, but my mind is on Felix.

For the first time since I met him, I'm finally feeling ready to…

Really try, I suppose.

It's time to talk to Felix.

19

Felix

I'M IN A PARTICULARLY SAVAGE MOOD AT THE moment.

Robby, one of my most skilled finish carpenters, injured himself on the job this morning. Fucking awful. Blood everywhere, motherfuckers yelling and screaming. Hours in the ER. Hours on the phone with insurance fucks. Paperwork. Finding someone to replace him until he's back to work, which could be weeks, if not months.

Then someone rear-ended me in the Lowe's parking lot as I was backing out of a spot—his fault, not mine; the damage is minimal, but I'll need a new bumper.

And then, just to top it all off, I stopped at my favorite gas station near the office for a fill-up and a big cup of coffee—necessary at four in the afternoon since I'm not sleeping for shit lately. Get into my truck with my coffee, pull the lid off to let some of the heat escape, seeing as they keep that coffee hotter than the sun itself, and I want to drink it at some point this millennium. My phone rings. What do I do? Drop my fucking phone *into* the fucking coffee, splashing my thighs with scalding liquid...and my instant reaction, of course, is to drop the cup. More coffee on my legs. Coffee all over the footwell, all over my seat—everywhere.

Burned legs, fucked seats, fucked phone.

Which brings me to now. Sitting in my truck with burning yet wet legs, no coffee, and a seriously shitty attitude. For some reason, the Limp Bizkit song "Break Stuff" is running through my head.

"Fuck it," I mutter. "I'm going home."

I leave my truck running and head into the office. Jess smiles at me. "Hey, Fee." Her gaze snaps to my bottom half—wet from crotch to boots. "Um, you good, boss?"

"No," I snarl. "I'm far from fucking good." I grit my teeth and breathe in and out slowly for five seconds. "Not your fault. Just...a massively shitty day."

"Oh god, Felix, I'm so sorry. What can I do?" she asks.

I hate the hope in her eyes. I've known about her feelings for me for years—she's not subtle. And there's nothing wrong with her, at all. She's a great chick—smart, hot, responsible, and hardworking. I just feel no attraction beyond the basic recognition of her attractiveness. I've done everything I can to politely and kindly make it clear I'm not interested. Most of the time she keeps it under wraps—especially since I brought Ember around the office a while back. But every once in a while, I catch a glimmer of that hope.

And I have to crush it all over again. Yay me.

"No," I say, endeavoring to sound…normal? Not like a grouchy shithead. "My phone is fucked at the moment and I'm going home. So yeah, the one thing you can do is call Bear and let him know he's in charge of wrapping things up for the day, and if there's a 'someone else is bleeding or on fire' emergency, call me on my landline at home."

Jess slides her blue-blocker glasses off her face. "You have an actual landline?"

I snort. "Yeah. Came with the house. It's like five bucks a month with my internet, so I just leave it. Mainly for sending the occasional fax to some jackass contractor who still lives in the stone age and doesn't email."

At that moment, just because the universe fucking hates me *and* has a wicked sense of humor, the fax machine starts spitting out pages.

Jess glances at the fax machine, and her face goes red as she tries to keep from laughing. Because I am, in fact, one of those jackasses who still uses a fax machine—only for other fax machine-using jackasses, but still.

The timing, man. The timing.

I can't help but splutter a laugh. "Oh, fuck you! Jesus. How is it not a Monday? It feels like a fucking Monday."

Jess cackles, snatching the sheet out of the fax machine and getting up to scan it. "Just go home and try to relax, Fee. It's after four. What else could possibly—"

"SHUT THE FUCK UP!" I shout, startling her so badly she slams the lid of the copier and almost breaks it. "Sorry. Sorry. But you absolutely *cannot* say shit like that on a day like today, Jess."

She claps a hand to her chest, breathing shakily. "Holy *shit*, Fee, I almost had a heart attack."

I turn for the door. "I'm going home now. And for

real, I don't want to hear from *anyone* unless someone is missing a limb or a fucking house is on fire." I pause in the doorway, looking around at the office. "How well do you know the books, Jess?"

"The books. Like…our financials?" I nod, and she shrugs. "Pretty well. Why?"

"See if you can free up a few grand. We need to update this ugly fuck of an office. It hasn't changed since Reagan was president."

She literally claps her hands over her mouth. "Oh god, please tell me you're serious. If you're teasing me, Felix Crowe, I will quit right now and I'm not even kidding."

I frown. "I'm serious. I'm not talking a twenty-grand rebuild. Just some new carpet, new drywall and drop-tile, and an updated bathroom. A step or two above a realtor special."

Jess hurries to her iPad, opens it, taps and scrolls, and then comes over to me and shows me what's on the screen: a digital mockup of the office after a refresh like I'm talking about—hardwood floors with rugs underneath desks, a siting area, coffee station, bathroom, pale, neutral gray walls with pops of color…everything is updated and professional and comfortable.

"This is great, Jess. You did it?" I ask.

She blushes. "Yeah, I…honestly, Fee, I hate this office. Like, *hate*. It's soul-suckingly awful. I've been tinkering with this design for months. I've even estimated the costs, assuming we do the labor, obviously." She swipes to our invoicing and estimations app, showing me the quote, which is extremely reasonable—none of the materials are top grade, but not cheap, either.

I tap a finger on the door frame, which doesn't match

the rest of the interior since we used a door Riley salvaged from a demo project to replace it after Bear smashed it to fucking smithereens looking for an address for the asshole who assaulted Noelle.

Scanning the office as it is, I go back to Jess's design. Look at her. "You ever design anything else?"

She blushes harder, nodding. "Yeah, I...I just play around. I've always thought about going into interior design, but..." She shrugs. "I'm too chicken to try." She swipes through invoices and photos until she comes to a series of digital mockups. "Swipe left. These are designs I did for my friend Kayla's house when she was doing some updates. The photos are before and after."

I swipe. The before is a *very* dated mid-century craftsman living room and kitchen—dark, dingy, and heavy. The after is pulled directly from her design; it removes a key wall to open the space, making it light and airy. Looks like luxury vinyl to resemble vintage hardwoods, a shiplap accent wall (sparingly used because too much of a good thing is a bad thing), and a totally revamped kitchen.

"Who did the work?" I ask.

She grimaces. "McKay and sons. We quoted for them, but they couldn't afford us."

"Well, it's a great design and looks well executed. Definitely ups their value." I stare outside, thinking. "How about this—you're lead on the office reno. Pick a few guys, buy the materials, and get it done. Do well on that, and we can talk about you doing more design work. I know Eric could use the help."

Eric is our in-house designer. When we were growing and expanding, I did most of the design work as most of our projects were flips or spec—nothing fancy. But now we're doing more and more custom homes and still doing a lot of flip business as well, so Eric is being run ragged. He could use an assistant and-or intern, and if Jess was working with him, I could hire a new office manager…someone who doesn't have a major, years-long, unrequited crush on me.

Jess tears up. "Felix, you mean it?"

I smile at her. "Absolutely, Jess. You're a hard worker. You've been a loyal employee for a long-ass time. I had no idea you were interested in design." I gesture with the iPad. "This is good work. Make this office look cozy and professional and welcoming. Stay within five percent of that budget and get it done in a month, and you're Eric's new intern and assistant."

She flaps her hands in front of her face. "Hooo boy. Okay." She breathes deeply, holds it with her eyes closed, and lets it out slowly, visibly controlling her emotions. "I'll get it done on time and under budget, and it'll look phenomenal. I *promise*."

I squeeze the outside of her shoulder. "I believe in you, Jess."

She laughs. "It'll get me and my silly feelings out of your hair, if nothing else." She doesn't look at me as she says this.

I barely suppress a groan, turning it into a sigh. "Jess… shit. I guess I should've addressed this a long time ago. Your feelings aren't silly. I just…don't return them. And that's not you—you're great. Any man would be lucky as fuck to be with you. There've been a few times I've honestly wished I *did* return your feelings, but I don't. I see you as a valuable employee and a friend, and I hope we can keep things that way."

She nods. "I appreciate you saying that, Felix. Really." She hesitates. "Can I have a totally platonic hug?"

I laugh. "Sure."

It's a quick and—as advertised—platonic hug. When I let her go, she backs up, lifting her chin and pushing away her personal feelings. "Go home, now. Shoo. Go on."

"See ya, Jess. Thanks."

She nods, waving at me distractedly—she's already working on the reno, probably. "Bye, Fee—And thank you for trusting me. I won't let you down."

I head home, finally. And as much as I'd love to just jump in the shower and kick back with a beer, my truck smells like old coffee, so I change out of my soaked jeans, socks, and boots, set the boots out in the sun to dry, and get to work detailing my truck. I've thought about getting a new one on and off for a couple of years now, but I can never convince myself to pull the trigger—I always end up with a new project car instead. Of course, now that the FJ40 is with Nyx getting un-fucked, I have no project.

I also haven't done any work on my build in months— work has been nuts, and then helping Ember with her recovery…whatever. It's not going anywhere.

Finally, my truck is as clean as I can get it inside and out. I'm feeling less like doing a murder, which is nice. That done, I'm sweaty, shirtless in a pair of rather short workout shorts, and ready to chill on the back deck.

I find myself, far from the first time, wishing things with Ember were different. There's nothing I'd love more right now than to hang out with her on the back deck. We don't even have to do anything physical. I just enjoy her company. Lately, though—as in the last week or so—she's been avoiding me in the rare times we've both been home at the same time. Even on the rides to her appointments, she's been stiff and standoffish.

I grab a beer from the fridge, take the Louis L'Amour paperback I haven't cracked open since the last time I picked it up out onto the deck, and...actually read. I'm pretty engrossed in the story, so I don't notice Ember until she sits on the Adirondack beside me.

"Hey, Fee. You're home early." She indicates the book and the empty beer bottle. "And actually relaxing. I didn't know you knew how to do that."

I shrug. "It was..." I slip the gas station receipt I'm using as a bookmark between the pages and let the book flap closed. "A spectacularly, magnificently, catastrophically shitty day. So I gave myself permission to say fuck it, and came home."

She nods. "Excellent plan. Is it working?"

I smirk, gesture around the backyard. "I haven't murdered anyone and buried them in the backyard, so yeah?"

Her eyebrows lift. "That bad?"

I recount the events of the day, and when I'm done, she sits back in the chair, blowing out a surprised sigh. "Damn, Fee, what'd you do to piss off the universe?"

"Um? Existed?"

She holds up a finger. "Be right back."

She returns a minute later with a thin joint. "Yes? No?"

I can't help glancing at her head, where her hair hides the evidence of her fracture. "Is that...okay? For you, with the whole...you know, recovery process?"

She sparks her lighter and puffs to get the joint going. "Actually," she says while holding in the smoke and handing me the joint, "there's a decent amount of clinical evidence that it may *assist* in recovery of a T-B-I by reducing inflammation. So...yeah."

I take a hit. "For real?"

She nods and takes it back, inhales, passes it to me. "Yep. Nothing conclusive. You know how studies are—'studies suggest' blah blah blah, but I've skimmed through several papers on the topic." She grins. "Mainly because cannabis is my one vice and I was worried about that too. Trust me when I say that, I, more than anyone, don't want to do anything to jeopardize my recovery."

"I wasn't judging, Ember, I was just—"

She brushes her knuckles against mine as we pass the joint back and forth. "I know, Fee," she says, her voice soft, her eyes searching and...almost hesitant. "You're worried. Looking out for me."

"Yeah," I say, "Exactly."

She accepts the joint from me, searching me with her gaze. Holds my eyes, inhales deeply, holds it, and then cups my face as if she's going to kiss me. My heart starts pounding, hope blossoming in my chest.

"Inhale," she whispers, a trickle of smoke escaping with the word.

She touches her parted lips to mine, and I breathe in while she exhales—I feel and taste the smoke, but I'm focused on her, her scent, the soft ghost-touch of her lips, her nearness, the exhilaration of her mere presence and the wonder of her touch.

I can't help myself.

I'm still holding my book—I toss it aside carelessly, slide my fingertips along her temples and into her hair, and fuse my lips to hers. Smoke swirls between us, leaking from our lips as they move and mate, trickle out of our noses as we catch our breath.

She lets out the tiniest, quietest, softest whimper as I plunge my tongue into her mouth. And my god, that sound goes straight to my cock like a lightning bolt.

A predatory growl escapes me and I lean forward, snag her by the hips, and lift her onto my lap. She settles onto my thighs, and her arms go around my neck like they've always been there, like they belong there.

"Fee," she breathes.

"Please don't tell me to stop," I murmur.

"I don't want to," she whispers, "but we need to talk."

I'm so fucking frustrated and disappointed that I could cry or hit someone—I'm not sure which. Swallowing a dozen different responses, I slide her off my lap as I stand up. I pace away from her, down off the deck, and across the yard, breathing hard and thinking about prune-faced nuns with yardsticks smacking my knuckles—a memory from that one memorably awful year our mother sent Riley and me to the private catholic school...right before she took off, never to be seen again.

"Hey, why'd you walk away?" Ember's voice is behind me, and I feel her hand rest on my side.

"Needed a minute."

"Are...are you angry with me?"

I shake my head, gripping the trunk of the silver maple in the middle of the yard; sunlight filters through the fluttering leaves in a drowsy dapple. "Not angry. Frustrated."

"Frustrated like..." She tucks her chin around my bicep to glance down at my groin. "All we did was kiss for, like, two seconds."

"Yeah, well, you affect me. That fuckin' whimper." I

shake my head, but this time it's an attempt to get the sound out of my head before my hard-on comes back. "And also frustrated in the other sense."

"I'm sorry," she whispers.

I shrug. "It's fine. I get it." I squeeze the tree trunk to keep the anger and disappointment out of my voice. "I know you asked for space, and I didn't respect that. I'm sorry, Ember. I shouldn't have kissed you."

There's a moment of silence, and it prompts me to look down at her; she's frowning in confusion.

"Felix, no. God, no. That's not—" She ducks under my arm, twisting to face me with her back to the tree. "I shotgunned you. You think that was…what? A tease? I *wanted* you to kiss me."

"Then…" I hold my ground, relishing the closeness of her, the way she's gazing up at me with an open expression, so unlike the shuttered looks I've gotten used to since the accident. "I don't understand."

She rests her hands on my chest. "I had a long talk with Noelle today at lunch."

"Ohhhhh-kay?"

She curls her fingers into my pectoral muscle. "I'm scared, Fee."

I laugh, shaking my head—it's a sarcastic bark rather than any kind of amusement. "Sorry, babe, but I am *not* following."

Ducking her head, Ember snickers a laugh. "I know, I'm sorry—I'm not making any sense, am I? Giving you all sorts of mixed signals."

"I mean…"

She lifts her head to meet my gaze. "Let me start over. When I told you I needed time and space? That was true.

I needed time to focus on healing, and space to sort of...
figure out my feelings. And you gave me that, Felix. You
never pushed the issue, and you went above and beyond
taking care of me. Even when you knew there was nothing
in it for you, you..." she shakes her head, swallowing audi-
bly. "Here we go again with the waterworks. Jesus. Gah!"
She tips her head back, blinking furiously.

I laugh at the ire in her voice. "Hey, it's fine. It's been
a lot and it's totally understandable that you'd have strong
feelings."

She shakes her head, swiping a finger under her eyelids. "I know, I'm just not normally a big crier. But ever since
the accident, it's all just right there on the surface all the
damn time, and I'm suddenly crying at the drop of a hat,
and I'm usually the one to drop the hat. I'm just sick of it.
I'd like to get through *one* conversation without bawling."
She sighs as if to fortify herself. "Felix, you...you did *everything* for me. Gave me a home—my own room, something I've never had. You took my wacky mood swings in
stride. You cooked for me. Took me to my appointments.
Hung out with me. Introduced me to a seriously *great* group
of ladies." She pushes away from the tree to lean into me,
hands on my shoulders and chin on my chest, gazing up
at me. "I will *never* be able to thank you enough, Felix."

My heart is pounding, and my hands itch to bury in
her hair, to slide over her curves, to strip her naked and
take her here in the yard, to hold her, to...make her mine.

Instead, I let my hands rest on her waist just above her
hips—intimate but not sexual. "You don't need to thank me."

She licks her lips. "You said you only did what you'd
do for your friends. But I...am I...am I *just* a friend, at
this point?"

"I don't kiss my friends." I let my hands slip a little lower onto her hips. "Or hold them like this."

She grins. "I dunno. Jess may like it."

I frown. "Jess is a friend, yes, but an employee first and foremost. And I talked to her today. I'm promoting her, sort of, to be an assistant and apprentice for my interior designer. Which will mean I'll see a good bit less of her on a day-to-day basis because I do not now and have never returned her feelings for me, which I *am* aware of."

"I was teasing."

I shrug. "I know, but I wanted that clear." Fuck it, go for broke. "The only way I could live with you and stay halfway sane the last couple months was to friend-zone you. Think of you as a friend and nothing more. But that doesn't mean my feelings have gone away. They haven't. I just…"

Her fingers tease up to my shoulders, trace fiery lines down my biceps, slip over to my belly and sear back up to my chest. "Just what?"

I can't look at her as I say this. "Friend-zoning you was the only way to keep my hands off you. It was the only way to…not think of you as an object of desire."

She blinks up at me. "So…you haven't…"

"No."

She shakes her head. "Fee, just so I know we're on the same page, here…you haven't jerked off? At all?"

"If I went there in my mind, at all, you were the only thing I could picture."

She hesitates, gnawing on the corner of her lower lip, which for some reason drives me fucking wild. "I…even if I did know you were thinking about me while doing that, I wouldn't have minded."

I tug her lip free with my thumb. "If you don't quit biting that lip, this conversation is gonna be cut real fuckin' short."

She frowns. "What?"

"You chewin' on your lip. It drives me nuts."

"Like, annoys you?"

"No, babe. Turns me on."

She snickers. "Why? That's weird. It's not sexual at all."

I shrug. "I dunno. It just does." I let out a breath. "It wasn't so much thinking you'd mind as it was for my own sanity. I had to put you in the friend box completely. I'm too fucking attracted to you. I care about you too fucking much to be able to think about you sexually and not do something about it."

"Oh."

"You know how goddamned frustrating it is to know how fucking hot you are naked, to know how it feels to touch you, kiss you, to make you scream my name while you're coming? To hear the shower going on the other side of the wall and know you're wet and naked?"

Her eyes widen. "Wait…on the other side of the wall?"

"Yeah. Your shower shares a wall with my bedroom. Specifically the wall my bed is against."

"Oh…fuck," she breathes. "So…"

My eyes blaze. "Yeah, babe."

Her eyes close, mortification emblazoned on her face. "Every time I masturbated in the shower…"

"Why do you think I started going to my basement to work out while you were in the shower?" I ask. "It wasn't a fuckin' coincidence."

She leaves the shelter of my arms, hands on her face. "Oh…my…*god*." She whirls to face me, cheeks tomato red. "Fee, I…ohmigod. I am *so* sorry. I didn't even think about it."

I roll a shoulder. "I adjusted when I worked out to give you privacy. You weren't doing anything on purpose. It's fine. It was just…a little rough for a few days."

"And…." she approaches me slowly, almost as if I'm a skittish horse. "You've been totally celibate since you and me…."

I nod. "Yes."

She stares at me for a moment or two. "What about blue balls?"

"I've routinely gone months at a time, Ember. I've never really enjoyed jerking off, to be honest. Maybe that's weird, but it just…it doesn't…satisfy the urge, I guess. I'd rather wait until I can have sex. Or, you know, someone else help me out."

"What did you do before you met me?" she asks. "Don't answer if you don't want to."

"Tinder. Even in the winter, we get enough tourists that I could meet up with someone for drinks and…you know…" I grimace, embarrassed. "Casual hookups. But it was only once in a while, when I really needed the relief. But it had been several months before I met you since I'd done that. And that said, I will help myself out if the Tinder pickings are slim. I just…the casual stuff stopped being fun and started feeling like another form of masturbation, I guess. Up till I met you, it just seemed easier emotionally to focus on work, keep busy and just not…think about it."

"But you didn't have a woman you're attracted to living with you, masturbating in the shower." She covers her face. "Fuck me. The more I think about it, the more mortified I am. I'm…not always quiet."

I can't suppress a laugh. "No, you are not." I let arousal flare in my expression. "The only reason it was so difficult to hear was because it was so fucking hot, Ember. Don't be embarrassed."

"Easy for you to say. You weren't jerking off where I could hear."

"True." I feel my mouth running, hear myself saying stupid shit—and I'm powerless to stop myself. "I could arrange for that, if it'd make you feel any better."

"It just might," she whispers, stepping closer. "Although, if I'm being brutally honest…I'd rather watch." She licks her lips nervously. "Or help."

"Fuck, Em." I swallow hard. "Do *not* fucking tease me."

"I'm not, I swear."

"What did you and Noelle talk about that prompted this whole…conversation?" I ask.

"Wanting you, being attracted to you, our chemistry…none of that was ever the issue holding me back, Fee. The opposite. I'm…I've been mixed up about you because…I…." She looks away, thinking, then back to me, starting over. "It's because of how attracted to you I really am. How strong my feelings are."

"And that conflicts with your grieving process?" I ask.

She tips her head side to side. "Sort of?" A pause. "I just…I miss him, you know? From the day I met him in Oregon until the day he passed, I never spent a single day away from him. I don't know if I spent more than an hour or two here and there apart from him in the eight years we were together. And then he's just…gone."

She backs up and turns around, speaking, facing away from me. "It's so hard to put into words, Felix. It's not just missing him that's messing with me. It's…everything. My whole way of life—he became nomadic with me. That's not an option for you—it's just not, and I'd never in a million years even ask. Your life is here. But I've never belonged anywhere, with anyone but Mom and then Dutchie. And now…everything is different. My whole way of life is… just gone. And I…" she hesitates, her voice wet with tears. "Dammit. Fuck!" Pause. "I don't know if I could go back to the way it was. If I even want to, whether anything happens with you or not. Being on the road, vlogging, I can't do that without Dutchie. That was *our* thing. Our *life*. He's gone, and it's gone with him."

"Ember," I start.

She holds up a hand, still facing away from me. "Just… let me get this out. Or, let me try at least."

This is a thing with her, I think: she stews on things for a while, and then has to let it all out in an uninterrupted monologue.

"Okay," I say. "I'm here, and I'm listening."

She reaches behind herself without looking. "Come closer. Please."

I move closer and take her hand—she pulls me up against her and snugs both of my arms around her middle, leans back against my chest and takes a few slow breaths.

"That's all one part," she says. "Then there's you and me. I told you about my relationship with him. We talked about our sex life a bit too. And…in talking to Noelle what I…well, I knew it, but talking to her was the first time I verbalized it out loud."

"What's that?"

"My physical connection to you is fucking insane. How I respond to you. How I feel about you. How it feels to be with you, even considering the fact that we haven't actually had sex." She tightens her grip on my hands, squeezing harder. "That's hard for me to come to grips with. Because I...I don't know how to feel about it. What does it say about my relationship with Dutchie? He healed me. Gave me the space and safety to heal and feel comfortable in my body, and with my sexuality. I wouldn't be able to be like this with you without what he did for me. But...letting myself just enjoy...you, us? It feels like a betrayal even though I know it's not, even though I promised Dutchie on his deathbed that I'd move on and let myself fall in love again. But it's just not that fucking easy."

"I understand all that, Ember," I say. "Not from personal experience, obviously, but I get it. It makes perfect sense. And I'm willing to wait until you're ready. If you find out you're never ready, I'd understand that too—I won't lie and say that I wouldn't be hurt if you decided you couldn't be with me *ever*, but I'd get it. I wouldn't hold it against you."

"I'm not saying that."

"What *are* you saying?"

She doesn't answer for a few moments. "When you said the thing about only doing what you'd do for a friend, I sort of freaked out a little bit. Or a lot a bit."

"I just meant—" I start.

"I know that *now*," she interrupts. "But it just...I guess it made me realize that I don't want to lose you."

I feel my heart slam against the prison bars of my ribcage, hear my blood roaring in my ears. "You're not going to. You haven't."

She turns in my arms, keeping hers pinned between us, hands flat on my chest. "Ever."

"I'm here, Ember. I've got you. Just...say the word and I'm yours."

"What's the word?" she asks.

The germinating seed of hope sprouts, blooms. "Figure of speech, babe. Just tell me you're ready. And for the record, this is still on your terms and at your pace—whatever it is."

"I'm just scared, Felix."

"Of what?"

"Everything. That I'll...I'll somehow end up loving you more than him." She buries her face in my chest. "That I'll forget him. I'm scared that I won't—that I'll never be able to love you fully, the way I did him. I'm scared that if I—if we—*when* we have sex, it'll be...better, and I'll freak out."

"Ember," I whisper into her hair. "Hey. Listen to me, okay? I'm no expert on this stuff. But I really don't think either of the first two scenarios is gonna happen. What we have, or what could have, or will have...it's *ours*. It's unique. I'm not him—for better and for worse, I'm not him. You had your life with him. You won't forget it, or him. Sure, memories fade with time. I don't always have the clearest memories of my father, but I haven't forgotten him. He's gone, several years now. I miss him. He was a bit of a bastard at times, and not always the best husband or father, but he did love Rye and me, and he did his best. Especially considering that his father was a real piece of shit. But I remember him, good and bad. He was my dad." I cup her face, tilt it up to mine. "You won't forget Dutchie. I don't want you to. I won't *let* you. He's part of you. I'll *never* be jealous of the parts of you he had that I won't. So...you won't love me more than him, because it's not...I dunno, apples to apples. I'm not him. I'm me."

She touches her forehead to my chest and nods. "I like how that sounds."

"As for sex?" I tip her face up. "I don't think comparisons

are fair to anyone—you, me, or him. But I think you know that. You said it yourself, sort of—where you are now in terms of your sexuality is because of your relationship with Dutchie. If he hadn't passed away, I think you would have found a way forward with him that satisfied you. But he did pass, and now you have to decide what you want to do." I pause and stare into her silver eyes. "If—*if* you decide you want to pursue things with me, then we'll take things however you're most comfortable. And if you do freak out, that's okay. I promise I'll understand and do whatever you need to get through it, even if that means backing off and giving you more time and space."

"You wouldn't resent me or think I'm being a cock-tease?" she whispers.

"No, Ember, absolutely not. You're not that type of girl. You've been very clear about where you are with your feelings on this stuff, and if you have an issue and need to back off, that's a totally different thing than playing games with me. I've never thought you're playing games."

She lets out a relieved sigh. "Thank you, Felix."

"For what?"

"Being so understanding." She rolls her head back and forth on my chest. "I'm sorry I'm such a mess."

"I'm no expert, but I think that's just called welcome to being a person."

She snickers. "You're not an expert on being a person?"

"Nope. Still figuring it out, and rarely successfully."

Ember slides her arms up around my neck, trailing her fingers up and down through my hair from the back of my head to my nape. "I can't make any promises about how things will go, Felix, I just know that I want to try."

She searches my face, showing me with her expression

the depths and complexity of her emotions: fear, uncertainty, and desire all tangled up in a Gordian knot.

I decide it's time to push her, just a little bit. "Do you trust me?"

She nods without taking her eyes off of mine. "Yeah."

I dip at the knees, scoop my hands under her ass and lift her—she immediately and instinctively hooks her legs around my waist, keeping her arms around my neck, fingers toying and teasing through my hair. I walk with her across the yard, up onto the deck, and inside. She rests her forehead on mine, taking slow, deep breaths.

She twists to glance down the hallway at my open door, then back to me, frowning. "I don't know if I'm ready to—"

I nip her lower lip in my teeth, silencing her. "Ssshhh. Just trust me, Ember."

She hesitates, and then nods. "Okay." A breath. "Okay. I do. I trust you."

I sit on my couch, and now she's straddling me. I frame her face, pull her down.

Touch her lips with mine.

"We'll just start here," I breathe. "Just a kiss. Nice and slow."

I feel her lips curve against mine. "This...I can do."

20

Ember

HIS LIPS ARE DIVINE.

I focus on physical sensation, blocking out the war of thoughts and feelings in my mind and heart. Focus on the soft, wet slide of his lips on mine, the heat of his mouth, the tender delicate probe of his tongue. His hands in my hair, thumbs on my cheeks, temples. His powerful, thick thighs beneath me, brawny arms around me.

I close my eyes and lose myself in the kiss. Breathe his breath. Taste his tongue. Relish the hungry power in his hands as they scrape down my neck, clutch my arms, scour the line of my spine, grip my ass.

Guilt tries to make a break for it, bubbling up in my throat and threatening a panic attack.

I break the kiss and rest my forehead on his. "Sorry, I...I need a second."

Felix pulls back and carves a loose tendril of my hair behind my ear. "Okay." He tilts my head up, exposing my throat. "Can I do this?"

He ghosts his lips against my jawline, breath huffing hot over my skin, kisses my throat in a dozen different places, each kiss softer and sweeter than the last—and more arousing.

"Yes..." I breathe. "That's good. I like that."

He tugs the neck of my shirt aside and kisses my collarbone. The base of my throat. Up one side of my neck and then down the other.

"Felix," I breathe.

"Tell me what you want," he whispers. "Tell me what you need."

"Just...a little more."

"Where?"

I know what I want, but I'm scared to ask for it—scared I'll panic and bolt...and I do *not* want to run away. I want to be with him. I want to make love with him. Fuck him. Have sex. Whatever phrase you wanna use, that's what I want. And I will *not* let my fear and irrational, but understandable, guilt stop me.

Felix reads my hesitation for what it is. "Say the word and everything stops," he murmurs. "And the word in this case is 'wait.'"

He tilts me away a bit, creating room between us. Works his fingers under the hem of my shirt. His eyes find mine and search me, waiting, assessing.

He lifts my shirt a few inches, and the slow, hesitant way he slides it up triggers a memory:

Dutchie and I in the bed in the back of Pumpkin, parked in an RV campground in Bozeman, Montana, his fingers hesitantly guiding my T-shirt up.

Felix's gaze holds mine, waiting for my objection.

I squeeze my eyes shut. "Fuck."

His hands vanish, rest on my thighs. "Hey, it's fine."

I shake my head. "No, it's not. It's not fair to you."

"Fuck that noise, Em. All I give a shit about is you. I want to make you feel good. But only if you're okay with it. If it's too hard, then we wait."

"The problem is that I'm pretty sure it'll always be too hard. I don't *want* to wait. I want to do this with you. I just..."

"What, Ember?"

"I'm having...I don't think flashbacks is the right word. Just...memories." I seize my courage. Exhale sharply. "I want this. I'm not going to let the past dictate the future. I promised Dutchie I'd let myself move on, and I'm going to keep that promise—for him and for myself." I reach for him, find hot skin and hard muscle. "I just have to...face my feelings. Stop running from them."

"Tell me what you need from me, Ember." His eyes are serious, intense.

"Just...kiss me. Kiss me and don't stop."

His answer is a rough, ravenous growl that sends goosebumps shivering over my flesh, sets my stomach to flipping and my thighs to clenching. He frames my face and claims my mouth, rakes his tongue through my lips. I open for him greedily and whimper at the fury of his kiss; I glory in the firm swell of his bulging biceps and the hard slab of his abs. Devour his tongue, let desire well in my core, give myself over to it.

My whimper sets him off—when he hears it, his hands tighten in my hair and he tilts his head to deepen the kiss. I explore the round hardness of his shoulders, the rippling field of his broad, muscular back. My fingers dive up into his hair. Down to the waist of his shorts, dip under the elastic…discovering he's commando under the shorts.

And god, those shorts. They're short and tight, barely containing the tremendous girth of his thighs—yes, I said girth. His thighs are girthy. It's fucking hot.

The shorts cling to the boulders of his ass.

There's nothing under them but him. All of him.

Raw, feral need for Felix boils in my veins.

More—I need more.

I need him. Need skin-to-skin contact.

I need an orgasm I didn't give myself.

I need to feel him lose control, knowing I brought him there.

I need him to take me. To make me his.

I need to make him mine.

You don't deserve this. Dutchie was your husband and he's dead. You should be in mourning, still. Where's your grief? How can you move on so fast? The voice is cruel and nasty. The voice is my own.

I grip Felix's sides and push the voice away, shove my tongue into his mouth—his surging growl of desire scorches the voice into nothing.

With his mouth on mine, his tongue dancing with mine, Felix sweeps his hands under my shirt to explore my back, skipping over my sports bra strap. Under my shirt, up to my shoulders, back down to my waist. To my belly.

Up.

I lean back without losing his mouth on mine, lift my

arms over my head—he grants my request and removes my shirt. I break the kiss only as long as necessary—the second the fabric is past my face, I slash my lips over his again, fuse them to his, whimpering and then gasping as his hands rush roughly up my stomach to cup my breasts over my bra.

I gasp again at this touch, mouth hanging open as he grips the weight of my tits, thumbs brushing over the bumps of my erect nipples. "Fee," I breathe. "I love how you touch me."

I hope he reads this as the encouragement it is—more. *More.*

"That works out," he whispers, pulling away from the kiss, "because I love touching you."

His fingers slip under the strap at my back, pause, his eyes on mine. My response is to trail my fingers down his abs, shimmying backward on his thighs so I can hook my fingers inside the elastic of his shorts. He scrapes his hands up my back, taking the strap of my bra with them, palm calluses rough on my skin. The bra snags and strains at my breasts as he tugs the strap upward, and then with a sudden rubber band snap, the bra slips up past my breasts, which fall free with a swaying bounce. His eyes follow their movement greedily.

"Fuck, Ember," he breathes. "you're perfect."

"Touch me," I whisper. "Please."

I do not have to ask him twice. He cups them in his big work-roughened hands, kneading and squeezing them, letting them go so they fall and sway before lifting them again. My nipples are hard and erect and aching and his thumbs scrape over them, eliciting a gasp from me.

Felix leans into me, kissing my breastbone, the slice of

skin between my breasts. Lifts one and kisses underneath it where it joins to my torso and then the underside, and then my nipple is in his mouth and I'm clutching at his head and arching my back as he trades one breast for the other, licking and suckling and then kissing and teasing around the circle of my areolae. I feel his arousal beneath me, a hard ridge sheathed behind his shorts and my leggings and underwear.

I want it.

I play with the hair at the back of his head as he continues to worship my tits, tipping my head back and just... wallow in the wonder of this, of his mouth on me, on the swell of arousal in my core. His hard cock beneath me begs for my touch, teasing me with each shift of our bodies.

Felix pulls away from my boobs, cupping them and gazing up at me with his palest blue eyes blazing with arousal. "Need more of you, Ember," he murmurs. "Need to watch you come apart for me."

"Please," I whisper. "*Please*, Felix."

It's all I can manage—my throat is tight with nerves and hot with desire, my flesh tingles and my nipples are so hard they ache, and my core is pulsing and drenched.

Felix stands up, twists to deposit me on the couch, sinking to his knees in front of me. Leans between my splayed-apart knees, wedging his big body between my thighs, cupping my tits and kissing my diaphragm, my belly. My navel. Nerves sing inside me—you'd think this was my first time, I'm so nervous.

He curls fingers inside the waistband of my plain, tight, black leggings and the black thong beneath them. His eyes go to mine, silently asking permission. I press my heels into the floor and lift my ass.

He strips my leggings and thong off inside out and tosses them away, and I'm bare for him, nipples hard, sex exposed and dripping desire, thighs wanting to close, breath coming in short, sharp gasps of nervous excitement.

He runs his hands up my thighs, burying them in the tender creases where legs meet hips, thumbs pressing in just above my sex. His touch carves over my hips and behind me, gathering my ass and pulling me to the edge of the couch. My legs hook over his arms and he holds me like that, ass hovering off the edge of the couch, thighs splayed wide. Touching soft, ghostly, questing kisses up my inner thigh, Felix teases me, kissing nearer and near my pussy before kissing elsewhere instead, until I'm crazed with need.

"Fee, please, fuck, stop teasing me."

He rumbles a laugh. "Mmmm...no. Not yet."

More teasing—kisses to my thighs, my belly, my pudendum, the delicate silk where my thighs meet my pussy, his beard scratchy in the most amazing way.

"Please," I whisper.

"Please, what?"

I push him toward my pussy. "Eat me out, Felix. Make me come. *Please.*"

He snarls, an eager, muffled sound as he fuses his mouth to my pussy, tongue swiping up my seam to flick against my clit. He lets out another hungry rumble, tongue delving between my nether lips, sweeping through the drip of my desire.

"Fuck, I love the way you taste."

"Mmmm," I breathe. "Fee!"

I feel a tremor building already—I give myself to it, trying to convince myself to relax into it. His tongue is quick and busy, flicking and probing, swiping and circling.

The tremor builds into heat behind my navel and spasms in my thighs, an arching of my spine and contortions of my abs. I cry out as he sucks my clit between his teeth, and then the tremor cracks apart inside me and becomes a full body shudder; I drape my thighs around his neck, rest the backs of my knees on his shoulders, heels hooked over each other behind his neck, toes curling as he devours me to level after level of heady, delirious ecstasy.

"Oh fuck—*Felix*!"

I clutch at his head, dig my fingers into his hair and knot them in the silky, cool locks, hips helplessly rocking to the rhythm of his tongue. He runs his hands up my belly, toying with my tits as he plies me with his mouth, and all I can do is hold on to him as he works me into a frenzy unlike any other.

Yet, the moment before my climax bursts, he pulls his mouth away, grinning up at me with a mischievous glint in his ice chip gaze, beard soaked with my essence and glistening in the afternoon sun.

"Felix!" I hiss through gritted teeth. "Please, fuck, please—don't stop now! I was about to come."

"I know."

It's all the answer I get.

Grinning at me, he trails a fingertip down my seam. Fits it between my lips. Delves inside me. Withdraws. Traces down my slit again. Delves inside again. Withdraws again. And again—a single push of his finger into me.

"Fee!"

He turns his hand palm facing up, dipping his long middle finger inside me, curls it, withdraws until just the tip of his finger is snugged between my pussy lips, and then presses in again. I gasp at the delicious intrusion of just his finger, and now I'm craving the fullness of his cock inside me.

The memory that plays in my mind as he toys with me and teases me with that one middle finger, is me on my knees in front of him, his thick hot hard cock sliding into my mouth, and the wonder on his face and in his voice as I give him pleasure.

And I want that again.

I want to taste him.

I want to make him wild. Make him lose all sense, all control.

I want to ride him.

I want to lie beneath him and take him inside me.

I want to be on my hands and knees for him, screaming as he pounds into me from behind.

I want to be taken. Owned. Set free.

For now, though, all I can do is shudder and shake as he ever-so-slowly builds me back up the mountain of ecstasy to a shuddering, shaking, tremulous orgasm, all with a single finger.

And…stops.

Again.

"Felix! Goddammit!" I whimper, hips bucking, every part of me—mind, body, and soul—desperate for the rush and relief of release. "Please, for the love of god, Fee, let me come, please!"

"You're not ready yet," he grumbles, words whispered against my sex.

"I am!" I snap. "I'm ready. I'm *so* ready. Please!"

"I love it when you beg."

Irate, desperate, and delirious, I grasp at his face. Stare

into his eyes. "Felix Crowe, I swear to fucking god. Don't play with me!"

He just grins, nipping the sensitive skin of my upper inner thigh sharply enough that I gasp in shock. "Felix!"

"You wanna come, Ember?" he asks.

"God, please!"

"Then trust me."

I growl in frustration. "I'm trying."

He slips that finger back inside me, and then adds a second, and then his thumb presses against my clit and his mouth is questing beneath my navel, dipping kisses lower and lower, and then his thumb is gone and his mouth is there suckling my clit and his fingers are plunging in and out of me with a come-here curl that does something insane to me, makes my belly flutter and my blood burn and my skin tingle and my pussy tighten around his fingers.

I can't keep still, now. I clamp my thighs around his ears and lift, quaking as an orgasm like no other mounts within me. It's titanic and wild, sun-hot even in this growing, nascent form. My hips buck and dip, my thighs quake, and small breathless screams rip out of me as Felix plunges his fingers in and out of my clamping, pulsing channel while suckling and tonguing my aching, throbbing clit.

"Fee! Oh god, Fee! *FEE*!"

He growls wordlessly as he thrashes my clit with his tongue, the sound one of pure male aroused enjoyment, eager and hungry. His left hand slides and stutters over my flesh on its path to my breast, squeezing it with delicious, ungentle aggression while his right hand squelches inside me and his tongue swirls and flicks my clit.

This time, as I quiver and gasp my way to the edge of climax, Felix doesn't stop.

He sustains the pace, fingers drilling and slicking in and out of me, tongue flicking and circling, hand squeezing my breast and pinching my nipple just this side of too hard.

"Fee!" I whimper. "Oh—oh—oh, fuck, fuck, fuck, Fee! *YES!* Oh god, yes, oh god, yes!" I writhe and arch off the couch, crushing his face to my sex and clamping down on him with my thighs as I detonate.

My scream is loud in my own ears, a wild shriek of ecstasy, utterly without reservation. There's no holding this back, no keeping it in. Felix keeps me going, pushing me to a second climax hard on the heels of the first, and my scream dissolves as my lungs run out of air, and then all I can do is gasp for breath and thrash and buck and mewl.

"Fee!" I push him away, or try to. "I can't— I can't…"

"One more, baby. Come for me one more time."

"Oh god oh fuck—" I tangle my fingers in his hair and hold on so savagely it's a wonder I don't rip his hair out by the roots, but he only growls again, feasting on my clit like a starving man at a banquet. "Felix, I…oh god, ohmigod, I'm—I can't, I…oh *FUCK!*"

Another throat-searing scream tears out of me as a third orgasm shatters me completely, every muscle tensing and contorting as the climax boils me alive from the inside out, white heat occluding my vision and sizzling in my veins, forcing me to curl in on myself as my scream goes ragged and trails off, tears streaming down my face, sobs wracking me.

Felix guides me through the last of the orgasm, slowing me to panting whimpers with soft kisses to my clit and gentle caresses of my breasts and delicate thrusts of his fingers, until I'm boneless and limp.

Darkness rises up and snatches me, pulls me under.

21

Felix

T HE AMOUNT OF PRIDE I FEEL WHEN EMBER passes out is ridiculous. Her eyes roll back in her head and then close and she lets out a tiny, quiet gasp and then she's dead weight, arms and legs going slack.

I let her feet down to the floor and scoop her up into my arms and carry her to my bedroom. Settle on the bed with her in my arms and get comfy, holding her on my lap, her head on my chest. My hard-on is at an awkward angle, pinned in place by her hip, but I stay still, accepting the discomfort.

Nothing matters but her.

Less than five minutes later, she stirs, nuzzling my chest with her nose and lips as she rouses. Blinking up at me, she wrinkles her nose. "Wha—? What happened?"

"You passed out."

A slow, hot smirk curves her lips. "You made me come so hard I passed out?"

I can't help a cocky grin. "Seems that way."

She moves her hip against my hard-on. "And you enjoyed yourself, did you?"

"Making you scream my name? Making you come so hard you pass out?" I brush a thumb over her lips. "Yeah, sweetheart, I enjoyed myself." I bend and nip her lower lip. "More to the point, I enjoyed *you*."

She grins at this. "I think that means it's *my* turn to enjoy *you*."

She shifts to straddle me, grinding her pussy against my cock, leaning over me so her big soft tits brush my chest in tantalizing, swaying circles as she presses kisses to my breastbone and pecs, pausing to run her tongue over my nipples. Down and down she kisses until she reaches my shorts. Looks up at me. Grins.

Tucks her fingers into the waist at my hips and tugs the shorts down an inch and then another, until the tip of my cock is peeking out. She flicks it with her tongue, making me jerk and gasp. Grinning eagerly up at me, she parts her lips, moving with slow intention toward my erection. Pulling the shorts lower, she fits the tip of my cock inside her mouth, slowly lowering my shorts while taking more of me in her mouth. The shorts reach my knees and I hook them with my toe and kick them off. Her hands slide up my abs, reach my nipples and pinch until I gasp, cock pulsing in her mouth.

"Em," I breathe.

She hums in response, the vibrations shivering through me. Backs away until her lips reach my glans, her tongue sliding against my frenulum; back down until I hear a soft gag, and then her tongue tickles and slides against my length on the way up. Ember's hands scour and carve over my body, exploring me.

When I feel my climax start to rise, I pull her away. "Ember, wait."

She frowns up at me, wiping at her lips. "Why'd you stop me?"

I haul her up my body, settling her astride me—her sex slots against my cock, a soft damp tease of what I need more than anything else in this world. I cup her glorious ass in one hand and palm her cheek with the other. "Because I don't want to come in your mouth this time," I say.

Her cheeks go pink. "Felix…" She rests her cheek against mine, lips near my ears. "I'm scared."

"Of what?"

"I don't know. I just am." A short pause. "Of really and truly falling in love with you," she whispers, her words barely a breath in the golden afternoon light.

I free her hair of the messy, loose, coming-apart braid, feather my fingers through the platinum locks so they curtain in kinky waves around her shoulders. Touch her chin with a fingertip, keeping her face tilted to mine. Kiss her— soft, slow, and gentle. Pull away, touch my lips to her ear. "I'm already really and truly in love with you."

Her arms snake around my neck and cling hard, her face going to my throat. "Fee."

The way she whispers my name like that, a breath, a mewl—as if she doesn't know what to say, so she just says my name…

I love it.

"Say my name again."

"Fee." This time it's breathier.

"I'll wait for you to be ready. You don't have to love me back yet." I cup her cheek, brush her hair away from her eyes. "It's okay. I'm here. I'm not going anywhere. Not ever."

"I…" I hear her swallow hard, feel her twitch her hips, teasing a slide of her sex against my cock. "I'm not on birth control."

I reach to my bedside table and open the top drawer, pull out a brand new box of condoms. She takes the box from me, eying it and then me. "I…"

"Ember, there's no pressure. *None.* I'm in love with you. I'll wait." I take the box back and toss it into the drawer.

Her eyes fill with tears. She blinks them away. Shakes her head. "I don't *want* to wait. But I…I know it's silly, I'm just…I don't know why I'm so scared to do this with you."

"You don't have to. Not if you're afraid."

"It's the last thing. The gateway to fully moving on for real."

"And that's okay. I understand." I sit up all the way, settling her sideways on my lap. "I'm not in a hurry. I fucking want you more than my next breath, Ember." I touch her lips to silence her so I can finish. "But even more, I want to be with you *only* when you're completely ready for it."

"I don't want to be like this, Felix. I just want to be yours. I'm all over the place. One second I'm thinking about how badly I want you to take me from behind as hard as you can, and the next I'm…like this." She gestures at her tear-streaked face.

I let out a ragged sigh. "Can't say shit like that to me, babe. I'm barely keeping it together here." I lean in and kiss her wet cheeks. "It's *okay*. You hear me? *It's okay.* You have to feel what you feel."

She searches my face. "You're in love with me? For real?"

I snort. "Ember. C'mon. Of *course* I am. What do you think all this is about? I fell in love with you the first time I saw you."

She frowns. "The first time you saw me, all you saw of me was my ass."

I shrug, grinning. "Yep."

She rolls her eyes, huffing. "That's so sweet," she deadpans, sarcasm ripe in her voice.

I grin all the more. "It was love at first sight and only got better the more of you I've gotten to know."

Her expression softens. "Fee, god. That actually *is* sweet."

Heart pounding, I go for broke. "I fucking love you, Ember James. I'll do anything for you. Including keep waiting."

At my words, she tears up again, but this time it's with a smile. "When you say that, I'm a little less afraid."

"Then I'll say it a thousand times." I kiss her lips. "I fucking love you." Lips to her left ear. "I love you so fucking much." Right ear. "Ember James, I am *so* fucking in love with you it's crazy."

She shudders all over, whimpering. "Fee." That breathy utterance of my name again, fraught with emotion. "Again."

She twists on my lap to straddle me, sliding back so my subsiding erection angles between us, pointing at her navel. "Tell me how much you love me, Felix. Please?"

"With all my fucking heart."

She grasps my cock and strokes it. "Yeah?"

"Yeah." I gasp. "It's scary, sometimes. I look at you and I can't remember life without you."

Both hands caress my length. "That's what's so hard, Fee—I sometimes have a hard time remembering life without you, too."

I put my hand over her heart. "He's here, Ember. Always."

She nods, watching her hand slip down my shaft, twist, and slide up again in a slow, sinuous stroke. "Fee, I…"

"You don't have to say anything," I tell her.

"Can you promise me one thing?" she asks.

"Anything."

"Don't hold back." She reaches into the drawer and grabs the box of condoms, opens it, tears one packet free, tosses the box back into the drawer, and rips the foil open with her teeth. Withdraws the ring of latex. Meets my eyes, hers serious and deep and swirling with a universe of complicated emotions. "Don't be sweet all the time. Don't be gentle. I'm not made of glass and I'm not…I won't—"

I clutch her face in my hands, cutting her off, my forehead against hers as she caresses my cock to full erection. "I promise, Ember. I will never hold back."

She rolls the condom onto me hand-over-hand, making me shudder and hunch forward. Rises to sit up tall on her knees in front of me, straddling my thighs. Balancing with one hand on my shoulder, she reaches between her thighs and grasps my cock, guides me to her entrance. Once I'm notched between her lips, she hovers there, touching her forehead to mine, arms locked around my neck.

"Fee?" she breathes.

"Yeah, baby?"

She sinks onto me, impaling herself to the hilt on my cock in one slow, smooth drive. "I love you."

I gasp as her hot wet pussy wraps around me, tight and slick. "Ember—fuck. Oh my god, you feel *incredible.*"

She pulls back to look into my eyes, her mouth hanging open and trembling, eyes wide. "Fee!" She circles her hips, taking me deeper yet, even though that should be impossible, since I was already so deep inside her it ached. "Fuck! You feel..."

"Tell me," I growl, grabbing a handful of her amazing, perfect, full, round, plump, glorious ass in each hand, pulling the cheeks apart so she settles even lower on me. "Tell me how I feel inside you, honey."

She sinks her teeth into the meat of my shoulder, groaning as she lifts her ass off my thighs, sliding my cock almost out of her. "Fee—fuck! You feel—oh god...*so* fucking good." She slams back down with a guttural shriek. "Oh my fucking god—*FELIX*!" My name is a ragged, disbelieving female snarl.

"Talk to me, sweetheart." I dip to suckle her tit into my mouth, biting her nipple hard enough to make her shriek and jerk, slamming down onto me hard. "Tell me what you want. Tell me how it feels."

"Your cock," she whispers, resting her elbows on my shoulders with her hands in my hair, holding me to her chest as she sets a slow, grinding rhythm on me. "It's so fucking big, Felix. It's perfect inside me. Made for me. So big and it hurts so good."

"Your pussy is so fucking tight, Ember," I growl. "Like a vise."

She clenches around me. "Feel that?"

"Oh fuck, yes, I feel it. Do it again."

She squeezes me again, even harder, and I nearly come

right then. "Feeling you inside me is…it's so much better than I could ever have imagined or fantasized."

"Did you?" I ask. "Fantasize about me?"

"Of course," she breathes. "What do you think I was thinking about when I was masturbating in the shower every morning? You, Felix."

"Me what? Specifically."

She doesn't answer immediately, lost in gasps and whimpers as she rides me faster now, my cock slicking through her folds with wet squelches that only fires me up all the more.

"This," she gasps. "Us. I fantasized about all the ways I want to fuck you."

"How, Ember? Tell me everything."

"I want—" she whimpers as her pace stutters, her belly spasming as a climax starts to ripple through her. "I want to…oh fuck, I'm gonna come already. I want to ride you just like this. I want to be beneath you, watching you fuck me. I want you to fuck me from behind and I want you to slap my ass until it hurts. I want to make love in the shower. Out on the deck. In your truck. At the office. In a house you're building with your workers a floor below. I want to suck your cock when you least expect it. I want you to take my ass—I've never done that and I've always wanted to. I want *everything*, Fee. Everything with you. All of it." She hooks an arm around my neck and fits the other hand between us to press a finger to her clit, wailing abruptly as her climax ramps up to set her to shaking all over. "Oh fuck oh fuck oh fuck oh *fuck*!"

I lean back to give her room for her hand, then lift her so I can get my knees beneath me, giving me better leverage to thrust. Her eyes close and she hangs onto my neck and fingers her clit and rides me as hard as she can, her ass slapping my thighs loudly—but even that sound is drowned out by her screams as she finally lets go.

"FELIX!" My name is a wail, and then it becomes a series of wordless, ecstatic, breathless shrieks as she bounces on me, tits shaking and swaying and jiggling beautifully, her ass slapping my thighs and flattening as she smashes herself down onto me with every thrust.

She comes, and her pussy squeezes my cock so hard it makes it difficult to thrust into her, and still she comes, shrieking and screaming and wailing with sensual, erotic abandon.

I don't dare even blink, wanting to soak up and memorize very second of this, of her, a goddess made flesh fucking me to wild climax, her white-blond hair a long curtain around her waist and shoulders, head thrown back, breasts high and huge and proud and shaking with the vigor of our lovemaking.

She can't even form words as she comes apart, hunching forward over me as her climax rips her to pieces.

Her eyes snap open. "Fee, baby."

"Yeah, Em."

"Come for me." She lifts so I slip out of her, and then she lays backward on the bed. "Come fuck me. Come inside me, Fee."

Her eyes are hot and wild, the conflict and the pain and the fear gone, replaced by need and by desire and by love.

I move over her and she reaches for my cock, eagerly fitting me to her slit and taking me back inside her, eyes rolling back in her head with pure ecstasy as I fill her.

"Oh my fucking *god*, Fee, the way you feel inside me,"

she claws both hands into my ass and pulls at me. "So fucking good. You fill me. You complete me. You make me whole again. You make me whole in a way I've never been."

I start slow, one hand braced beside her ear, the other caressing her breasts, pulsing slow shallow thrusts into her.

She pulls at me, encouraging me to go faster, to go harder. "More, Fee. Harder. Please."

I dip to kiss her. "Not yet."

She growls in frustration. "I want it, Fee. I need you. I need you to come. I need you to fuck me."

I go slow and sinuous. "Not like this?"

She whimpers. "No! *Hard*. Fuck me as hard as you can, Felix. *Please*."

I cup her cheek, still moving slow and gentle. "Look at me, honey."

Her eyes fly open, wet and fraught. "What?"

"Don't look away, Em. Don't close your eyes. Stay with me."

"I'm with you."

I push deep. "You feel me inside you?"

She shrieks as I thrust again. "Yes! I feel you, Fee. I feel you."

Her eyes start to close. "Keep your eyes on me, honey. Don't look away."

Tears flow. "Fee, I can't. It's too much." She shakes, trembles, weeps.

"Stay with me," I command, moving slowly, still, soft and gentle and smooth and sinuous. "Eyes on mine."

She gazes up at me with fierce determination, tears streaming even as she meets me thrust for thrust, wantonly, desperately, needing me to let loose. "Fee! Oh god, Fee. It's too much. Too much."

"Look at me, baby." I cup the back of her neck and gaze down at her as I move.

"I am," she sobs. "I'm looking, Fee."

"You feel us?"

"I feel us."

"I love you," I whisper.

She lets out a cry, tears flowing freely, spasms overtaking her. "Fee! Oh god, Felix. I love you! I love you!"

"Come for me, sweetheart," I murmur. "Right now."

"I—oh! Oh! Felix! I—I'm coming! Oh god, Felix, come with me, please god, come with me!"

I let myself go, finally. I let my control snap; I give myself to her completely. Burying my face in her throat, her legs wrapped around my ass and pulling me to herself and thrusting into me, I give her everything I have.

"YES!" she screams, clawing my back so hard it burns, definitely leaving marks that I'll be tempted to turn into tattoos. "FELIX!"

I bellow and roar, guttural and going hoarse as I fuck her with all of my strength and passion, driving into her as hard as I can. She takes every ravaging thrust and screams for more, using her legs to pull me deeper.

I feel her coming, and as I come, she squeezes around me and shakes, and then she lets out a raspy, shocked whimper, head thrown back as her orgasm wrenches her to a new peak of ecstasy.

I feel wetness gush out of her and soak both us and the bed beneath us at the same time that I reach my own climax, hunched over her, pounding into her—as my orgasm leaves me shuddering and panting and gasping, she's still coming and coming, spasming and squirting.

Slowly, I float back to earth, sagging to give her some of my weight.

She caresses me everywhere her hands can reach as we breathe together.

"I love you, Ember."

She pushes my face up to she can look at me. "I love you, Felix." She dissolves into giggles. "We made a bit of a mess."

22

Ember

ELIX ROLLS US TO THE SIDE, OUT OF THE gigantic wet spot I made on his bed, placing me prone on his body. Mortified, I know my face has to be beet red—it's hot and burny.

I cover my face with both hands and bury my face in his chest. "I'm sorry about your bed," I whisper.

He laughs. "Oh hell no, Ember. I *know* you're not apologizing right now."

I lift up and peek at him through my fingers, all my weight on my elbows, which are digging into his pecs… not that he seems to notice or care. "You're gonna need a new mattress. I just peed everywhere."

"You didn't pee, you squirted. And it was hot as fuck."

I put my face in his hot hard muscle again. "Which is peeing."

"No, it's not. I...never mind."

I roll off of him and curl into the sheltered nook of his arm and body, my cheek on his heartbeat. "No, say it."

"It's not the kind of thing you say in bed with your girlfriend after the best sex of your life," he says.

My heart stops beating for a second. "Wait, hold on. Two things. One...girlfriend? And two, best sex of your life?"

"Yes." There's no question or hesitation in his voice. "Unless you have an objection, then yes, you're my girlfriend. I don't go around telling random hookups that I love them and from what you've told me, you've never had a random hookup. I really doubt you'd tell me you love me if it wasn't true." His long, strong arm cradles me to him, his hand resting on the swell of my hip. "And yes, best sex of my life. Hands down, not even close."

My heart is pounding. "I..." Now that I'm no longer consumed by the most wildly intense and all-devouring sexual desperation for all things Felix, it's harder to ignore the gut-churning panic in my belly.

I told him I love him.

I search myself, terrified at what I'll find when I knock down the last of the walls around the emotions that I've been compartmentalizing for so many months. The guilt is there—I've moved on. I don't really count *him*—my actual first—as a sexual partner; that was...something else. Dutchie was my first. My first love and my first lover. The first man I gave myself to fully and truly and willingly. And then he died, and now I've taken another lover. But the guilt is...tolerable. I know I haven't betrayed Dutchie.

This is what he wanted for me. What he made me promise I'd do. So the guilt is just…what?

Why do I still feel any guilt at all?

Because I'm scared of moving on. I'm scared that I have, and that Dutchie will eventually just be a memory.

But…he already is. He's my past, now. Part of me—an integral, vital part. One that Felix understands and accepts without reservation or hesitation.

What else do I feel?

I glance up at Felix; his eyes are closed, but I know he's not asleep. "Fee?"

He only lets out a long, happy exhale, a small smile on his face, his hand cupping my hip, caressing my ass, my thigh, and my side. "You need a minute." It's a statement, not a question.

"I just…I've got a lot of complicated feelings."

"I know." He pats my butt. "So take your time. I'm not going anywhere. I'm not asleep. I'm just chillin.'"

I settle into his chest and close my eyes, letting the steady drumming of his heartbeat lull me into a Zen-like state of drowsy thoughtfulness.

I told him I love him. Is it true? Or was it just the intensity of the moment? The heightened madness of my sexuality? Because it did feel like craziness. Not mindless, just…wild. Not out of control…just a frenzy that demanded release. A ravenous hunger that demanded satiation. And Felix gave me what I needed. What I've needed for so very long.

He gave me space to express my sexuality without being threatened or intimidated by it. More, he craved it. He got off on it.

So was it just sex?

No.

That was love. That was months of pent-up sexual tension between us and months more of sexual tension built up inside me—years of it, perhaps. A year, year and a half? When did I begin wanting things in bed that Dutchie couldn't or wouldn't give me?

"You know," Felix says, apropos of nothing. "You can tell me what you're thinking and feeling. Even if you just need to get it out and don't want any, like, man-fix-it re-actions from me. I can be your sounding board." A pause. "Even if it's about your husband and your relationship with him. I'm not threatened by that. It won't hurt me."

"I was just trying to figure out if I do really love you or if that was a heat-of-the-moment thing." Before he can react, I continue. "And it was real. I do love you. But it was more than that. What we just shared, Fee, it was…a lot of things for me. And that's why this is a complex moment for me, trying to figure out what I'm feeling because it's all tangled up and confusing."

"It's okay if it was a heat-of-the-moment thing, Ember. Don't ever give me the easy-to-hear lie, okay?"

I sling my thigh over his groin, palm his cheek, gaze into his eyes. "Fee, I meant it. I mean it. I *am* in love with you."

He searches me, and I see relief wash over him. "Thank fuck. Had me scared for a second."

"You know," I say, echoing him from a moment ago, "you don't have to be understanding about everything all the time, Felix. You can be scared, too. You can share your negative feelings with me. I want you to."

"I just want it to mean as much to you as it does to me." He brushes a lock of hair behind my ear. "Just now, and this relationship, however you want to define it or not define it. If you don't want to label it…I mean, it's not what I want, but I'll get it and I'll be okay with it if you need more time to be able to put us in that box."

I let my head droop down to his chest again. "I'm still trying to wrap my head around the sex."

"How so?"

"You said it was the best you've ever had."

"It is—you are. By several orders of magnitude."

"That's tricky for me, Fee. Because on one hand, I feel the same way. I've only had multiple orgasms a few times before. Like, just to be clear, sex with Dutchie *was* good. He was…attentive. Generous. He took care of me. I always felt loved and…wanted. But…it wasn't always intense. Or wild. We've talked about this."

"We have."

"And…" I let out a shaky breath. "Now that we're on the other side of having sex together, it's even more…real, I guess. What I was worried about."

"Which is?" he asks. "I mean, I know, but I think it may help you to put it out there again."

"It was the best sex of my life, Felix," I whisper, struggling against tears of overwhelmed, mixed-up emotion. "And that's complicated for me. Like, I really, really, *really* fucking loved Dutchie. I loved our relationship. I loved being with him. But I…I wasn't always satisfied, especially in the last…I dunno—that's what I'm trying to sort out. How long did I feel that way? How long was I wanting more sexually that Dutchie couldn't or wouldn't give me? And what are those things?"

"And?" he prompts. "Come up with any answers?"

"Trying to." I slide my thigh off of him and trace the

grooves and slabs of his absurdly shredded midsection. "It was about a year and a half before he died that I tuned in to my feelings of wanting to—for lack of a less cliché term— spice things up. I mean, in an eight-year relationship, things get…habitual. Comfortable. And that's okay. That's life, that's long-term relationships. But I wanted…" I sigh.

"You can say it."

"I wanted him to take charge more. To initiate more. Not necessarily be more aggressive, let alone more 'alpha' or anything toxic like that. Just…I…I didn't always want it to be sweet and loving, and that's just how he was."

"Did you talk to him about this?"

I nod. "Oh yeah. Of course. A few times. And it was— he tried. But he felt awkward, like he was pretending to be something he wasn't. So we went back to how things were. And I just…I can't help wondering what would have happened if he hadn't died. Would that low-level discontent have built up inside me to become a problem? Like, I wasn't unhappy—I swear I wasn't. And don't get me wrong, I *do* want to be treated like that sometimes, too. Sweet. Gentle. Loving. Careful. Tender. All that. I love that. But…"

He doesn't fill the space. He lets it stand, lets me take my time filling it.

"You gave me exactly what I needed, Felix." It's a small, careful whisper. "Obviously, the physical pleasure was off the charts, but emotionally? I…you gave me the space to express myself. You took charge when I needed you to without restricting me."

"And that's a super confusing feeling," he guesses.

"Very." I let the question percolate before I ask it. "Do you have any fantasies, Felix?"

"Yeah," he answers immediately. "You."

"No, Fee, for real. No bullshit. Do you?"

He swallows. "Um. Yeah, I mean...of course. But there are fantasies that are just for fun and fantasies that you might actually want to experience. Which are you asking about?"

"Both."

"Like pretty much all guys, I've had fantasies of being with two girls, but in reality? No way. Sounds better than it is. I know that for a fact—Riley, unsurprisingly, told me as much. Fantasies that could come true? Minor things. Outside under the stars is one." He hesitates, glances at me. "Um. I dunno, Em. To be totally honest, you really *are* a fantasy come true. Your body is my fantasy."

I blush hard, covering my face with my hands. "Fee. C'mon."

"For real. When I would fantasize and jerk off before I met you, your body shape is what I would envision. I'm *not* making this up."

"Yes, you are," I mumble.

He rolls into me, snatches my hands away from my face and pins them over my head in one huge, powerful hand. "No," he snarls, eyes blazing with fiery need. "I am *not*."

He grabs a breast and squeezes it, nuzzles it.

"These." He bites my nipple suddenly and sharply, and I gasp, writhing in his grip. "I fantasized about giant, perfect tits like these."

"Fee," I whisper.

Keeping a firm, unbreakable hold on my pinioned wrists, he rolls me to my stomach. Puts his lips to my ears. "Can you leave your hands there if I let go?"

I nod. "Yeah."

He presses my hands into the mattress above my head. "Then leave them there. Do *not* move."

"Okay," I breathe.

"This is a fantasy," he whispers into my ear. "This, right here. You, spread out for me. Helpless."

"Fee," I breathe again. I fight instinct, keep my wrists crossed as if tied together over my head, stretched out on my belly. "Please."

"Please, what, honey?" he asks. "What do you want?"

"You. Whatever you want. Do it to me. Please."

He kisses between my shoulder blades, growling. "Whatever I want?"

"Just don't hurt me. I'm not into pain. Spanking, within reason, is fine. Biting is fine, obviously. But...no real pain."

"Never," he growls. "I'll never, ever hurt you."

He nips the sensitive skin at my side, licks the hollow at the base of my spine. Frames my ass in his hands and kisses the left cheek all over, the right. Nips here, licks there. Bites hard enough that I gasp, writhing, pushing my hips into the bed to escape the bite. Stretched out on my belly, I'm helpless to resist anything he wants to do to me, and I love it. Because I trust him. I love him. And...this is fun. I love not knowing what he'll do next.

He slips a hand under me, and then his fingers are inside me and I'm drenched with need and panting before he's done anything. I lift my hips, pushing my ass into the air to make room for his hand, but he presses his other hand on the small of my back, pushing me down into his touch, leaving me nowhere to go, no way to escape the intensity of how I know he's about to make me feel.

And oh god, it's incredible. He takes his time, slowly driving one and then two and then three fingers inside me until I'm shaking and whimpering and on the cusp of coming, and then he presses those slick fingers to my clit and brings me right back the edge again—back and forth, back and forth, finger-fucking my channel and then my clit, never letting me actually come until the hot pulsing need is a hurricane in my core, my channel pulsing around his fingers, my clit swollen and throbbing, my nipples aching, my every muscle tensed. I can't breathe, too fraught with the need to come to be able to suck in a full breath—there's no room for both my breath and the titanic immensity of the orgasm he's building inside me.

And then, just when I think he's going to finally let me come, his fingers plunging in and out of me hard and fast—

He stops.

Guides me so my knees are under my belly and spread apart, ass high, core exposed, breast and belly and face in the bed, arms extended. I feel him moving, feel his absence, and then his hair tickles my thighs and then—

"FUCK!" I scream, jerking as orgasm threatens to blow open inside me—he's beneath me, his mouth on my sex, lips fused to my clit, tongue driving inside me.

I'm utterly powerless to hold back. All I can do is come—shaking, crying, screaming as he devours me like a last meal. His hands clutch my ass and hold me in place, encouraging me to grind on his mouth, ride his face. I have no control. There's only wild abandon. I fuck his face, screaming until my throat is sore as he licks and tongues and suckles me to climax so potent I feel almost paralyzed by the intensity of it.

Which is when he pulls away and flips me to my back,

working his fingers inside me with his palm pressed to my clit and ravages me like that, fingers inside me, palm pressing on my clit—and his touch hits something inside me, something that breaks me, shatters me, destroys me. I have nothing left—no more screams, no more breath, no more thrashing or contorting. The world is all white heat and pulsating glory, blazing and wild detonation, heels in the bed, hips high, clutching his shoulders with clawed fingers until I know he'll have bruises, and yet he doesn't relent, keeps me on that runaway train of colossal climax.

The shattering becomes a dissolution of self, and I feel another layer of my being come apart, another layer of resistance snap, and I feel that same rush at my core as my resistance is utterly eradicated. The wet gush floods out of me as my mouth works silently, my whole body spasming, jerking, shuddering, twitching, thrashing, and I still can't scream or cry or breathe.

Pulse after pulse, each one more intense than the last until I'm wrung out and jellied—as weak and helpless as a newborn kitten.

When he lets me stop coming, I collapse to the mattress, and my lungs expand, and I greedily gulp oxygen.

I hear a crinkle, and then Felix is kissing me—his beard smells like me. He rolls me back to my stomach, and I can't resist. Not that I would. He helps me get my knees under me again, like I was before, and he's behind me. I can't move, can still barely breathe, and I'm still coming, still shaking with the viciously intense quaking madness of my orgasm. And now I feel his fingers at my entrance, and then the head of his cock nudges me—I lift my ass higher for him, and then he's sliding into me. Filling me. And like this? Fuck. So full.

His cock is perfect.

His hands grip my ass cheeks and pull me apart so he drives deeper, and now I can't breathe all over again for how deep inside me he is, stretching me to glutting, glorious burn, and he's thrusting into me hard and fast, fucking me furiously. Our noises are the most beautiful music I've ever heard—my cries, his grunts, the slap of his hips and thighs against my ass, the wet squelch as he plunges into me. The scent of our sex fills the air. Sun streams golden, bathing us in light. Dust motes dance in front of my eyes.

He leans back, pushing on my ass, and drives into me, and now his cock hits that place inside me that makes me combust, screaming as the orgasm that never quite stopped breaks apart all over again, and I'm a spastic, shuddery, weeping mess as he pounds into me, chasing his own release. His hand cracks across my ass cheek, sending a sudden sharp sting through me that makes me squeal with shocked pleasure, and he growls in his chest—does it again on the other side, and it makes my orgasm splinter to new heights of delirium, so my muscles spasm and go jellied and boneless.

Only, as the orgasm wracks me, I lose control of my limbs and cannot stay upright, can't stay on my knees.

I collapse to my belly and lose him in the process.

"Felix!" I wail. "Oh god, I need you. Give it back!"

I'm on my back suddenly, and he's above me, fumbling with a condom packet.

"It came off," he snarls, his voice tight with frustration.

I grasp him and pull him to me. Fit him inside me.

Bare.

I whimper. "Oh my fucking god, Fee. You feel…oh god."

He isn't moving—frozen, stunned. "Ember. I'm not wearing a condom."

I pull him down to me, lips to his ear. "I know."

"You're not on birth control."

"I know." I thrust against him. "I don't care. I need you."

"But—"

I open my eyes, find his. "Do you love me?"

"With all that I am."

"Do you know I love you?"

"Yes." There's no hesitation.

"Will you take care of me?"

"Always."

I cup the back of his head, whisper in his ear. "Then give me this. Make love to me." I thrust again, whimpering at the feel of his cock bare inside me. "I've never had sex without one."

"Me either."

"I want to give you this. A first. Just for you. For us."

He puts his face in my neck. "Em, honey." He pushes into me. "Oh god. It feels so fucking amazing."

I weep. "More than amazing."

He rolls again, and now I'm on top of him, straddling him, and he's filling me to overfull, his hands full of my breasts as I sink lower on him, braced on his chest. "Make me come for you, Ember." He stares into my soul. "Take it all from me."

I lean over him and take his face in my hands, touch my forehead to his, and fuck down on him. Take him into me. Just once.

He bucks into my thrust, groaning into my open, shaking mouth.

"Em!" He grunts.

Again. another thrust, slow and deliberate—I whimper, glorying as I focus on the sensation of his cock sliding into me; I memorize the way each inch stretches me, time distorting into an infinity of instants, each vein stuttering past my stretched-thin lips.

I cry out, feeling him pulse inside me, now, his cock swelling thicker as he prepares to come.

No condom, no birth control.

I don't care.

I want this.

Need it.

With Felix.

NOW.

Something I've never done, never had.

This moment, right now—Felix, my love, my lover, my soulmate, giving himself to me so utterly that there's not a shred of himself held back.

Soul to soul.

Another slow slide of my pussy around his cock.

His growls go ragged, become breathless as he thrusts, instinct making him want to fuck harder and faster, but I'm in control now. And I want it slow.

I gather his hands, tangle our fingers, stretch our arms overhead. He tucks his heels against his ass for leverage and thrusts deep, holds there.

Giving me space to take him.

Relinquishing control to me.

Helping me take what I need.

This moment.

Flat out on him, I whisper to him. "Don't look away."

"Never."

I roll my hips on him—it's all I can do. The only motion available to me is a sinuous roll of my hips, taking his thick, slick, throbbing length through me, taking him deeper and deeper until he's bottomed out inside me and I can't breathe from the fullness.

He grips my hands hard, trembling. "Em!"

"Come for me, Fee," I beg. "Give it to me. Let go."

"I—ohhhh," he gasps. "Oh *fuck*."

"Don't look away," I demand, gazing down into his glacier eyes, so wild and fraught, hazed with intensity, blurry with need, hot with love. "Look at me while you come inside me. "

"Ember—I'm…" he shudders, buck up, and then goes tense all over, mouth hanging open and shaking, and I feel it in him, feel his cock pulse madly. "Oh god, Ember. I'm coming—I'm—oh…oh god, oh fuck, Ember!"

"*YES!*" I cry, releasing his hands as he begins to come. "Take me!"

He grabs my ass and lifts me, slams me down on him while fucking up into me, arched off the bed, and I brace against his chest with my hands and fuck him back as hard as I can.

Screaming.

Coming with him.

A hot, wet flood fills me, and he goes still, buried deep, and I can't move either for a moment—and then I can. I have to. I push back against him as he comes, slam down and bury him to the hilt.

Deeper.

Deeper.

Crying.

Aching around him.

Full of him.

He fills me with his cum, floods me to overflowing.

The hot rush of his cum spreads through me and I come around him, spasming and slamming onto him.

He's grunting and groaning wordlessly, shattering and coming and coming.

Finally, he finds words. "Ember!" My name is all he can manage.

I feel him coming inside me for an eternity, and I feel it slipping out of me, trickling down his shaft as he slides through me—our thrusts are slow and gentle now, love-making rather than fucking.

I find his mouth, demand his tongue. Pull away, whispering. "I love you, Felix."

"Ember…oh god. Oh my god." He gasps helplessly. "God, I love you."

I rest my elbows on his chest and gaze down at him. "That was everything, Fee. Everything."

He's teary-eyed, overwhelmed, and overcome. "Ember, I…" A shake of his head. "That was…"

I kiss him again. "Just promise me forever. Promise me this kind of love until we grow old."

"I promise," he breathes. "Forever."

I put my lips to his ear. "Then take me to the shower, my love."

And so he does.

Where he fills me again.

Maybe it's reckless. I don't care.

I realized at some point today that I want this life with Felix. Here, in Three Rivers.

With him.

With Riley, Cole, Nyx, and Bear.

Noelle, Raina, Layla, and Lainey.

Lazy days at home.

Busy days.

Storms.

Arguments.

Make up sex.

A home.

A place where I finally belong.

Maybe even a ring on my finger and a swollen belly—a life growing.

Felix puts me in the nook again, rolls me to my back. His hot palm covers my belly. "I love you. And if this happens, I couldn't possibly be happier."

"Promise?" I ask, searching him for the truth I know I'll find.

"Promise."

I put my lips to his ear. "Because I'm pretty sure it did."

"Pretty sure?" His eyes find mine again.

I nod. "Pretty sure."

He stretches out an arm, fumbles in the drawer, and comes up with a red velvet ring box—the velvet is crushed and faded and dirty.

Old—very, very old.

I stop breathing. "Fee?"

"When my parents divorced, Mom gave me this. It was her engagement ring. Before her, her mother wore it and hers before her. If you accept it, you'll be the fourth woman to wear the ring."

"Fee," I whisper. "You have to ask the question."

"Ember James." He slides the ring around my first knuckle, then pauses. "Marry me. Be my wife—my forever. Please. Marry me, Ember."

I push my hand to take the ring, and, impossibly, it fits perfectly.

"Yes," I whisper. "Yes. I'll be your wife."

"You belong now, Ember," he whispers. "To me. With me. To my family. To my friends. To Three Rivers. You *belong*."

He holds me as I cry tears of joy.

Of relief.

Of belonging.

I found my light in the dark.

I found my home.

With Felix Crowe.

Epilogue

Riley

ANYONE HAVE A HOT FORK? BECAUSE I'D RATHER shove one into my fucking eyeball than be here right now.

Look, I am legitimately over the moon happy for my big bro, okay? For really real. He deserves the sparkly hearts joy he's finally found in Ember. The dumbass put himself through a decade and almost-a-half of loneliness and guilt for something that wasn't even remotely his fault. He was nineteen and at a party, he's not gonna get obliterated? Of course he was. Cassie fucking Miller was the problem. Fuck that bitch. She got what was coming to her, too—last I checked, she's gotten herself knocked up by three different guys over four years, none of whom stuck around longer than it took to blow their load. She lives in a trailer—which there's nothing wrong with, just to be clear—and makes ends meet stripping at The Fuzzy Muffin. Yes, it's really called that. And yes, it's as skeezy and grody as you're probably picturing. I only know because I lost a bet and had to...well, never mind. No one wants to hear that story.

Point is...I love Felix to bits. I owe him fucking *everything*. I'm happy for him. Ember is a goddamned miracle; she puts the biggest smile on his face. Which has taken some getting used to, after twelve years of him being Mr. GrumpyPants. I mean, how can you *not* be happy when monster tits like those are yours to play with every day?

Bad Riley—bad. Don't think about your about-to-be sister-in-law like that.

She's got an amazing personality.

I mean, she's very sweet.

Lots of great qualities.

Good fuck, I'm an asshole.

I scrub my face, hoping the scrubbing action will transfer to my hopelessly horny brain—someone needs to scrub that filthy motherfucker clean.

Cole elbows me. "The fuck is your problem, Rye?" he whispers.

I shake my head. "Nothing."

He rolls his eyes. "Jealous?"

I stare at him like he's grown a third head. Y'know, cuz he's already got two? Haha. I know, I know. Lame.

"Yes, Cole, I'm jealous. *So* jealous. I crave the stability and responsibility of a wife and child. Yes, yes, you found me out." I say it all in a monotone.

Felix, standing at the altar, glares at me to shut the actual fuck up. So, out of love, I shut the fuck up.

He looks good, though, my big broski. His tux is impeccable, and Ember finally got him in to see Noelle for a long overdue haircut, so the shaggy, almost-mullet he was rocking for the last few years is gone, replaced by a nice, clean Superman side part and a short, neat beard. His eyes betray his happiness, as does the eager, nervous, shit-eating grin on his face. Lucky motherfucker.

The queasy feeling in the pit of my stomach is just because I drank too much last night. It's not jealousy.

I'm a bachelor. Lifelong, committed. A lone wolf.

I almost laugh out loud at myself for being such a fucking dork.

The crowd gathered in St. Michael's Lutheran Church is restless, whispering and shuffling as we wait for the wedding march song to play. St. Michael's was the only real choice for a wedding venue, according to Felix. Ember took one look at it and just knew, and I get it. It's a gorgeous church, a classic white clapboard building with a bell and steeple, front steps with original wrought-iron railings, pointed arch double doors, and original pews and flooring from the mid-1800s, the whole thing set against a backdrop of flowering cherry trees.

I pull at the tight collar of my dress shirt, trying to loosen the stupid fucking tie without looking like I'm loosening it. What the hell is taking so damn long for Ember to come down the stupid aisle? Come marry your man already, for fuck's sake.

On the other side of me, Nyx nudges me *with* his knee. I glance at him, and he surreptitiously hands me a THC gummy. Cole notices and gives us both his Cop-Glare-of-Disapproval, which he has perfected over the years.

Nyx puts them away, and we both roll our eyes.

Finally, the doors to the sanctuary open and the organist—a 500-year-old woman named Ellen Montgomery, who has played the organ here since the church was built back in 1854—strikes up the iconic song: *Bum-BUMMM-bum-BUMMMM…*

We all stand and partially turn to watch the bride do the slow glide down the aisle.

She's beaming. Noelle outdid herself on Ember's hair, braiding all 75 feet of the white-blond tresses into an elegant crown on top of her head, which was then wreathed with baby's breath and white roses. Her dress is custom— it has to be, seeing as she's 437 weeks pregnant. Her belly leads the way, with a long train trailing behind her, a slit in front showing flashes of her short, muscular legs. Her unique silver eyes are bright and watery and emotional as she approaches Felix, her smile brighter yet.

I know what you're thinking: *why is Riley not his brother's best man?* Followed by: *Why are his two best friends not standing up in the wedding?*

Felix and Ember decided not to have a best man, groomsmen, maid of honor, or bridesmaids. It's just them up there with Reverend Vickers. Felix's reasoning for not picking a best man was that he couldn't choose between the three of us, so he didn't. Did it sting a little? Meh, some. I'll get him back at the reception when I tell an embarrassing story.

Ember reaches the altar, and Noelle—also extremely pregnant—waddles up to take the bouquet from Ember and dab at her eyes with a napkin.

The honorable Reverend Vickers has us all sit down and he launches into a twenty-five-minute homily on the enduring power of love, which includes the obligatory reading of First Corinthians chapter thirteen.

Then, the vows. Felix goes first.

"Ember, I love you. I must've written at least fourteen different versions of these vows—"

"TWENTY-ONE!" Nyx shouts. "I counted!"

Everyone laughs.

"Thanks for that, Nyxie. Is it too late to un-invite you?" Felix clears his throat. "So yeah, twenty-one versions. I'm not an eloquent man, and I'm sure as heh—um, heck—no writer. I just know that you're it for me. You're my forever. I was so lost when I met you, Ember. I'd been drifting in the dark for years. And then you showed up, parked—sorry, *stalled*—in the middle of the road, half out of the engine bay of a violently orange 1967 VW Type Two, and I was gone. You have lit up my life every single day since then. I can't imagine life without you and I have no intention of finding out. My vow to you, Ember James, is that I will spend the rest of my life figuring out how to love you better. How to be the man you deserve. I'll probably get it wrong more than I get it right, but you'll always have every single part of me until the day I die, and then some."

Ember blinks hard, tips her head back and blows out a breath through pursed lips. Shakes her hands out and then takes his again. "Felix." She waves a hand in front of her eyes. "There's no chance I'm getting through this without crying, but I'll do my best."

"You got this, Sparky!" Nyx shouts.

Ember laughs tearfully. "Thanks, Nyxie." She breathes sharply a few more times and then starts over. "Okay, here we go. Felix. I really struggled with what to say to you. I could promise to honor and obey you in all things, but let's be realistic, here—I'm not good at doing what I'm told. Except when—well, never mind. That's for later." The crowd laughs, and the Reverend suppresses a disapproving frown. "I love you. You saved my life in *so* many ways." She glances this way. "Cole, you literally saved my life, but I can't marry you. Sorry."

Cole just laughs, looking like he wants to bury his head under the pew.

She returns her attention to Felix. "I'm lucky—so, so lucky. I mean, who gets a second chance not just at love, but life itself? When Dutchie died, I thought my life was over. I didn't see a point to anything. And then I met you, and you were…well, to be honest, annoyingly charming. I didn't *want* to like you. I didn't *want* to fall in love with you. Goodness knows I tried hard enough not to. And it's not that you're unlovable; it's that I doubted I could ever feel that way again. And I almost died. I should have died." Her voice cracks, and she glances at Cole again. "If not for Cole, I *would* be dead. He…oh god, this is hard. He talked to me. Showed me pictures on his phone. Kept me awake until Chelsea and the firemen showed up—-Rob, Marcus, Ellington, Marek." She glances at the four burly men in the front row, where she insisted they sit with Chelsea and Mike, Three Rivers' finest paramedics. "You all are heroes. I know, I know: you hate that word. But this is my day and I get to use it."

The firemen are pulling at collars and clearing throats, and Chelsea is trying like hell not to sob. Mike is stoic, but if I could see his face, I know he'd have red eyes, too.

"I owe you all my life," Ember continues, and then looks at the Black woman sitting next to Mike at the end of the front row. "Connie. You taught me how to walk again.

Bullied me into getting stronger. Refused to accept 'I can't' for an answer."

Connie waves her off, but her shoulders are shaking, too.

Dammit, I've got something in my throat. And who turned on the allergies in here? My eyes are scratchy.

"I couldn't get up here and not honor all of you—Chelsea, Mike, Connie, Rob, Marcus, Marek, Ellington, and Cole. Thank you." She turns back to Felix. "They saved my life so I could be in yours. They didn't just keep me alive, they gave me my life back." Another pause. "You know, in a way I'm thankful for the accident. I'm thankful, because in order to heal, I had to stay put. I had to let you take care of me. And you did. Day in and day out for months, you took care of me. And you did so without knowing if I'd ever come around to letting myself love you. You did it because you loved me. Selflessly and patiently, you took care of me because that's just the kind of man you are."

Yeah, not a dry eye in the house. Even Nyx is intently studying the weave of his jeans.

"I love you, Felix. And the vow I'll make above and beyond anything else is that I'm done running. I'm a Three Rivers girl for good."

There's a chorus of female cheers from the girls—Noelle, Raina, Lainey, and Layla.

Then comes the exchange of rings and the promises to love, honor, and cherish in sickness and in health till death do them part.

A very long, very wet kiss.

The walk down the aisle hand-in-hand. A rain of rice.

Photos in the cherry blossoms while the crowd heads

to Noelle's parents' property—they're hosting the reception. There's an hour or so of milling around their backyard in suits and dresses, chatting with…well, most of Three Rivers is here.

Raina, Noelle's best friend, corners me at one point and flirts pretty blatantly with me.

God, I wish. She's gorgeous. But she's good—inherently just a good person, like Noelle.

And I'm…well, me.

After a few minutes of Raina doing her best to make sure I don't miss the fact that she's hitting on me—she even leaned on the table with her arms bracing in and propping up her magnificent rack—she lets out a frustrated sigh. "This isn't gonna happen, is it?"

I wish I had Nyx's gummy in my system right about now. I cover her hand with mine. "Raina, to say I'm honored and flattered that you're interested in me is a massive understatement. You're gorgeous, sweet, and funny. But trust me when I say you don't want any of this mess."

She frowns at me. "Shouldn't I be the judge of what I want?"

"Yeah, maybe. But I just…" I sigh. "I *can't*. Okay? I respect you…a *lot*. And the reality is, I'm just not cut out for what I know you want."

"Which is what?" she asks, her voice a little cold. "Since you're the expert on what I want."

I spend a silent moment gazing at her, wishing. God knows I've had a little crush on her for years. Who wouldn't? All that beautiful brown skin, that killer body, that thick black hair? I fucking wish.

"A commitment," I answer. "Loyalty. Honesty."

"Rye," Raina murmurs. "You're short-changing yourself."

I shake my head. "I'm not. I'm really not. See, deep down, I know the truth: I'm a piece of shit. I'd only hurt you in the end and you deserve a hell of a lot better than that." I clear my throat. "Than me."

"You're not a—"

I move around the table and do something, recklessly, that I've wanted to do for a long fucking time: I kiss her.

No tongue—I'm not that much of an asshole. It's just a kiss.

I pull back. "See? Only an asshole would do that at his brother's wedding." I tug on a tendril of glossy black hair. "Find a man who deserves you, Raina. And he ain't me."

I walk away, then. Find Nyx and Cole hiding at the edge of the pre-reception cocktail hour party, surreptitiously sharing a flask.

Cole hands me the flask. "So. You and Raina."

"Nope." I take a slug.

"You kissed her."

"Yep."

"But…you're not…"

"Nope."

Nyx takes the flask from Cole, shoots a slug from it, and hands it to me. "He was proving a point."

"And what point would that be?" Cole asks.

"That he's the kind of asshole who'll shoot her down, kiss her, and walk away."

"Oh."

I take the flask but before I can take another hit, Cole snatches it and gives it back to Nyx. "You have a speech to give, Rye. Once you've done that, I'll get you clobbered. But you gotta stay with it until you've given your speech."

"Why do you think I need the whiskey?" I mutter, but don't fight him on it because I know he's right, the responsible fuckstick.

"Oh, shit, gotta go, boys. I'm being summoned." Nyx shoves the flask at Cole and hurries away.

Cole and I watch, bemused, as Nyx hurries over to Barbie, who presses him against a fence post, cups his groin, and then hauls him double-time toward the barn.

"You think those two will ever be more than fuck-buddies?" I ask Cole.

"Nah. At the end of the day, Nyx is just as fucked up about relationships as the rest of us." Cole tucks the flask in the inside pocket of his suit coat, glancing at me. "You alright, buddy? Don't think I don't see you."

"You see me? I'm right here. Of course you fucking see me, douchebag."

Cole slaps me upside the back of my head. "Don't be a dumbass. You know what I mean. *Are—you—alright*?"

I sigh. "Fuck off. I'm fine."

"Rye."

"Fine, you pushy ass bitch," I grumble. "Yeah, I'm a little…I dunno. Upside down. I dunno. I dunno!" I shrug expansively, slapping my thighs. "I don't fucking *know* how I am, okay? I'm happy for Felix. I love Ember. I'm excited for a little niece or nephew. I'm happy for Bear and Noelle. I don't know what my goddamn problem is."

Cole sighs. "Little bit of jealousy mixed in with a little bit of *I wish* mixed in with a little bit of knowing there's no way in hell that kinda goodness is ever coming your way."

I nod. "Yeah, pretty much." I glance at him. "You too?"

"Yep."

"Wanna talk about it?" I ask.

"Nope."

"Good," I say. "Me either."

Finally, the bride and groom show up and we all take our seats at the long rows of white-cloth-covered picnic tables lined up in the backyard near the barn. It's late evening by now, a beautiful late spring day. Fireflies wink. The sunset stains the sky pink and purple. Crickets sing as the band goes quiet.

Salads are served by catering company servers.

The band leader speaks into the microphone, unclipping it from the stand and bringing it to me. "Riley Crowe, the groom's brother, will give the first speech."

I stand up and accept the mic. Wipe my hands on my slacks, one and then the other, and try to ignore the hammering of my heart.

"Uh, okay. Whose idea was it to let me have the mic?" I grin. "Too late now, bitches. Oops, probably shouldn't say that, huh? Well, I am who I am. So, Felix. Bro. Remember back in tenth grade?"

Felix drops his head to the table with a thunk the whole audience can hear, and everyone laughs. "Do *not* tell that story, Riley Crowe."

I scan the crowd, grinning. "Oh yeah, I'm telling that story. Mainly because I bet Ember hasn't heard it. So, it goes like this…"

And I launch into a greatly embellished version of a real event in our lives involving cow tipping, a rogue tractor, a shotgun full of rock salt, and Felix only avoiding arrest because Cole's dad was the sheriff at the time.

I've got everyone howling with laughter, wiping tears away, and doubled over by the time I'm done.

"So, that story is about eighty percent true," I say. "And only we know what's not true. You'll all just have to wonder." I turn to Felix. "I *do* have a serious side, though. It's very small, and you only get it for the next thirty seconds, bro, so enjoy it."

I pause, breathe out my shaky nerves.

"I fucking love you," I tell him. "You are the *only* reason I'm where I am in life, Fee. You let me crash on your couch when I had nowhere else to go. You gave me a job when no one would hire me— not even people who knew me my whole life. You took a chance on me after I blew up my life. I owe you *everything*, brother, and I couldn't possibly be happier that you found Ember. Enjoy the life you're gonna have, because you deserve it." I turn my attention to Ember. "Sparky. I'm sorry you're saddled with my asshat of a brother. Good luck." I pretend to sit down, to much laughter. "No, for real, I think Heaven is missing one of its angels, because that's the only explanation for a girl like you taking on the gut job project that is my brother." I sigh a laugh, knuckling my forehead. "I'm trying to be serious, I promise. You put a smile on his face, and pretty much everyone here can attest to the fact that for a very, very long time, that was a rare thing. So, instead of any more tasteless jokes, I'm just gonna propose a toast to you two." I lift my glass of champagne. "To a life of happiness, laughter, lots of kids, and all the love in the world. To you guys."

I sip champagne and take my seat. Fake laughter and eat food. Drink too much. Dance with my friends and avoid Raina like a plague-ridden rat…for her own good.

Finally, I can take no more.

It's midnight and the party shows no signs of slowing down. The old folks and married-with-kids couples have long since taken off, and Ember is holding court under the tent while Felix cuts loose as I've not seen him cut loose in a long, long time. Apparently, Ember gave him permission to party for the both of them, since she can't.

I cruise through the crush of dancers to find my brother. He's at the center, black bowtie loose around his neck, shirt unbuttoned to mid-chest, coat long since abandoned, hair sweaty.

I clap him on the shoulder, and he turns to me. "Hey, Fee." I pull him into a hug. "Congrats, man. I'm happy for you and proud of you."

He hugs me back with rib-jarring slaps. "Love you, bro."

"Hey, I'm gonna bounce, okay?"

He pulls back, holding onto my shoulders. "You good?"

I bury it all, because no one can see through my shit like him. "Yeah, I'm good. Just partied out."

He cackles. "Okay. Pussy."

"Oh shut up."

He sees it, of course, the insightful bastard. "Rye, promise me you're good."

"I will be." I shake him. "Enjoy your day. Take that beautiful bride of yours home."

They went on a two-week vacation to the Bahamas a few months ago, before she got too pregnant to fly—a pre-wedding honeymoon, since she'll be having the baby any day now.

He searches me. "I worry about you, you know."

I shove him playfully. "I'm good. I'm good. I swear."

"Don't make me sic Cole on you!" he shouts after me.

I flip him off as I walk away.

Hop into my truck and leave the farm.

But I don't go home. I can't. I just can't bear that empty fucking place.

Maybe I should get a dog or something.

I end up cruising through town, my windows open to let in the cool spring night air. I love Three Rivers at night—it's quiet, dark, and peaceful. No summer crowds jamming the sidewalks. No block parties, as cool as those are. Just the streets and the shuttered businesses, the trees with their skirts of flowers rustling around their feet, the stoplights flashing yellow, and the silence.

Whoa—hold on. That's unusual.

I squeal to a halt, mentally reminding myself to have Nyx do my brakes soon.

At the far north end of town, sitting on a bench by herself, is a woman. Or a girl. Not sure. Her head is down and her shoulders are heaving. She's sobbing, like, bad.

Fuck.

I'm the last moron that should be trying to comfort her, but god knows no one else is gonna come by, so it's me.

I shove my truck into park and cut the motor right in the middle of the street—the sheriff is my best friend and he's at the wedding, three sheets to the wind.

I sit on the bench near the girl—close but not creepy or in her space. "Hey."

She lifts her head. Sniffles. Looks at me. "Hello."

I'm dumbstruck.

Strawberry blond curls—a wild, untamable profusion of them in bouncy ringlets. A perfect heart-shaped face. Big green eyes the color of holly leaves. Exactly that shade. Pale, creamy, freckled skin.

My tongue sticks to the roof of my mouth, and my heart palpitates. Hands go clammy. Stomach flips.

What am I feeling?

Why can't I breathe?

"Um." I close my eyes. Shake my head in an attempt to clear it of the nonsense. "What's...um. What's wrong?"

"Nothing."

I snort. "Yeah, okay. You're a shitty liar, beautiful."

She frowns at me. "You are not very good at this."

I laugh. "No, I'm not. Do I get credit for trying?"

She sniffs. "Yes. Two points extra credit."

"Sweet. That brings me all the way up to zero."

This gets me another sniff. "That bad?"

"Let's just say school wasn't my strongest suit." I hold out my hand to her. "Riley Crowe, at your service, madam."

She puts her hand in mine—her hand is tiny. I could wrap my fist around hers, and it's not like my hand is as big as Bear's. Big, deep, sad green eyes find mine. "I'm Cadence Cresswell."

"Cadence?" I repeat. "Wow. That's...a really beautiful name."

She tries to smile and doesn't quite make it. But hey, it's the thought that counts. "Thank you."

"So, Cadence. What has you crying alone way up here at this hour?"

She shrugs. "I am certain you do not want to hear about my silly problems."

"Sure I do. Beats the hell out of what I was doing."

She sneaks a look at me. "What were you doing?"

"Driving around thinking about *my* problems." I

realize, belatedly, that I never let go of her hand—I'm holding it as if we're trying out a new extended-duration handshake. So, I keep it. See if she notices.

"It is silly."

"I dunno," I say. "I feel like if it's got you crying alone at the ass end of a two-stop-light town like this, it's something." I shrug. "You don't gotta tell me shit, though. I'm just not very good at minding my own business. you can tell me to fuck off."

"Oh, I could never do that."

"Sure you can. Won't hurt my feelings. Mainly because I don't have any."

"No, I just...I do not speak in that manner." She lifts a slender shoulder. "I am glad you stopped, however. It is nice not to be alone." She looks at me curiously. "What... what did you mean?"

"About?"

"Not having feelings."

"Oh." I laugh, wave a hand. "Just being an idiot. Most of what I say is bullshit, just F-Y-I."

"So you *do* have feelings?"

"Well, sure. I just don't know what they are." I beat my fists against my chest. "Ook-ook, caveman tough. Caveman not self-actualized."

She giggles—and it's the most musical sound I've ever heard. "Caveman know big words."

I laugh with her, and it...it feels amazing. I dunno why.

I steal a longer look at her—she's sitting down, so it's hard to tell how tall she is, but she's not tall. Not short either, just not tall. She's slender. Willowy. She's wearing an ankle-length dress, white with little blue flowers on it.

Not much by way of cleavage showing—the dress isn't cut for that, so I can't really tell what's rocking under there; the neck scoops only a few inches below her elegant ivory throat. She has the most delicate hands I've ever seen. They flutter on her lap constantly, fidgeting, drumming, like restless birds.

"You don't wanna talk about it?" I ask. "If I'm being nosy, please tell me off."

She shakes her head, her strawberry-blond ringlets bouncing. "You are not being nosy, you are being sweet and kind." She levels those huge green eyes at me—and I swear, her face is 75% eyes. Mesmerizing green eyes. mossy pools. "My funding got cut."

"Funding for what?"

She sighs. "I am a medical doctor. I've spent the last six months putting together a mission trip to South Sudan to provide emergency medical care. I raised almost half of the required funds from private donors, but I was relying on a big grant from a corporate sponsor, and I just found out that they pulled out of our agreement. I am supposed to leave in two weeks. It is too dangerous, they said. I will never raise the funds now, and I will have to return the money I raised, and…I…I do not know what to do, now."

"You're a doctor?" I ask. "I'm sorry if I sound surprised, you're just…you seem pretty damn young to be a doctor already."

She smiles, nods. "I am twenty-four."

"And you're a fully licensed doctor?"

She nods again. "I was rather precocious. I graduated high school at fifteen and received my medical degree at twenty-two. I have spent the last two years doing medical missionary work all over Africa. This trip was very important to me."

"You can't—I dunno, take out a loan? Borrow it from someone?"

A shake of her head. "No. With the war breaking out again, no one will fund me. I have tried, believe me. I am crying because I have exhausted every possible option to salvage the mission. I was up here begging the last people I know with enough money, and they refused to help. The risk is too high."

"I mean, shit *is* gnarly there, isn't it? I don't really follow politics or whatever, but I know the war is not good."

"Yes. It is very dangerous. And that is exactly why I have to go. The people there are suffering. They need help and I am called to help them."

"How much do you need?"

"Eighty thousand dollars."

"Oof."

"Yes. I have to buy and transport all of my own supplies."

"I don't have that kinda cash, or I'd give it to you."

She shakes her head. "I appreciate that thought, Riley, but I am merely going to have to recalculate the vector of my life." Her stomach growls, then, noisily and extensively. She grimaces in embarrassment. "I am sorry. It has been a very long day and I have not eaten in quite some time."

'How long is a while?" I ask, starting to pick up on her unusual speech patterns.

She looks up to the left. "Since yesterday afternoon. I took the bus here from Chicago and then walked to my meeting with the Caterhams and then walked back. I could not walk anymore. My feet hurt too badly. I…I just sat down and started crying and discovered, much to my dismay, that I cannot seem to stop."

I frown at her. "Wait, wait, wait. You *walked*...where?"

"The Caterhams live in Grand Lafayette."

My stomach twists. Grand Lafayette is a tiny little town about thirty minutes' drive from here. Which is a good two hours of walking...*one way*.

"Jesus shits, woman. You took a bus from Chicago to Three Rivers and then *walked...by yourself...at night* from Three Rivers to Grand Lafayette and back?"

She just nods.

"You're mucho loco, sweetheart."

She just stares at me again, and I can see her brain working but I couldn't possibly comprehend what she's thinking. "As I have previously stated, the mission is very important to me. I believe that one does what is necessary without complaint when something is important."

I stand up and hold out my hand to her. "Well, come on, then."

She frowns up at me. "Where are we going?"

"I'm gonna feed you."

The frown deepens—and only makes her more beautiful, somehow. Although a smile would be better. I'll just have to work on earning a smile.

"All the restaurants in town are closed."

"Yup."

"Then...where are we getting food?"

I grin. "Well, see, they have these things called houses. And in these houses are refrigerators, which contain food. And I, madam, happen to be the proud owner of just such a house with just such a refrigerator."

She gives me a long, blank stare. "I understand the concept of houses and refrigerators."

I grin, waiting. "Well? You comin'?"

"I do not know you."

"Yes, you do. I'm Riley Crowe." I sit back down. "Listen, Cadence. I'll shoot you straight. Okay? I'm an asshole. I'm a player. Y'know? I'm *not* a good guy. You can't trust me with your heart or anything. But you *can* trust me to keep you safe and feed you some good-ass food. So, if you want, I'll take you to my house and I'll feed you. And then I'll take you anywhere you want to go. Chicago. Detroit. Lansing. Wherever home is for you. A hotel. Mrs. Abel's B-and-B. Or you can crash at my place. And I promise you—I *promise* you—you're safe with me."

"If it is good food, then why do you call it good... *ass*...food?" She blushes, whispering, when she says "ass."

I snicker a puzzled laugh. "Just a figure of speech, babe."

She looks at me, examining me closely. "You do not seem like a bad person to me."

"I'm not a *bad* person. I'm just not a *good* one."

Another long pause. "I do not know where else to go. I cannot walk another step."

"Who are these Caterhams that let you walk all the way there and back by your fuckin' self, anyway?"

"They are friends of my parents, and they offered to drive me here. But after they refused to fund me, I..." She blushes pink. "I became angry and...well, I fudged the truth somewhat, I must confess, to my shame."

"The word here is *lied*," I say.

She bites her lip. "I know! I feel very guilty about it. I *never* lie. But I was so angry and disappointed. I could not spend another thirty minutes in an automobile with them, so I told them a lie and walked away. It was very, very foolish of me."

"I'll say." I take her fluttery-bird hand in mine—it's soft, and tiny, and warm, and it tries to flutter inside the cage of my fingers. "C'mon, Cadence. Let me do something nice for you. It'll make me feel better about myself."

She blinks owlishly at me. "It is all about you after all, then." I can't tell if she's teasing or not, since her expression is unreadable.

"Now you get it. I'm all about me, baby."

She inhales, filling her lungs, and then turns to face me. Takes my other hand in hers and meets my eyes.

Her stare is serious and probing.

It hurts, meeting that powerful green gaze.

This woman is unlike anyone I've ever met.

Quiet.

Reserved.

Good.

A little odd.

Shockingly, stunningly, beautiful.

Tiny.

Delicate.

Strong.

Her eyes are wise. Mature. Insightful. Intelligent.

They search me. They see my soul. Read my secrets.

The longer she examines me, the more stripped bare I feel…and the less I like it.

I'm the one to look away first.

She nods. "Very well. I will allow you to feed me at your home."

"Okay?"

She smiles—and it's as stunning as I'd imagined. It transforms her face and literally steals my breath right out of my lungs.

Cadence Creswell squeezes my hands and lets go. "I believe there is more to you than you think, Riley Crowe. And I am choosing to trust you."

What the *fuck* am I getting myself into?

ALSO BY
Jasinda Wilder

Visit me at my website: **www.jasindawilder.com**
Email me: **jasindawilder@gmail.com**

If you enjoyed this book, you can help others enjoy it as well by recommending it to friends and family, or by mentioning it in reading and discussion groups and online forums. You can also review it on the site from which you purchased it. But, whether you recommend it to anyone else or not, thank you *so much* for taking the time to read my book! Your support means the world to me!

My other titles:

Forbidden Fruit

Wild Ride: Biker Billionaire

Delilah's Diary

Big Girls Do It:

Big Girls Do It
Married
On Christmas
Pregnant
Rock Stars Do It
Big Love Abroad

The Falling Series:
Falling Into You
Falling Into Us
Falling Under
Falling Away
Falling for Colton
The Ever Trilogy:
Forever & Always
After Forever
Saving Forever

From the world of *Wounded*:
Wounded
Captured

From the world of *Stripped*:
Stripped
Trashed

From the world of *Alpha*:
Alpha
Beta
Omega
Harris: Alpha One Security Book 1
Thresh: Alpha One Security Book 2
Duke: Alpha One Security Book 3
Puck: Alpha One Security Book 4
Lear: Alpha One Security Book 5
Anselm: Alpha One Security Book 6
Sigma
Gamma

Goode Girls:
For a Goode Time Call...
Not So Goode
Goode To Be Bad
A Real Goode Time
Goode Vibrations
Dad Bod Contracting:
Hammered
Drilled
Nailed
Screwed

Fifty States of Love:
Pregnant in Pennsylvania
Cowboy in Colorado
Married in Michigan
Christmas in Connecticut

Billionaire Baby Club:
Lizzy Goes Brains Over Braun
Autumn Rolls a Seven
Laurel's Bright Idea

Club Sin:
Rev
Kane
Chance
Silas
Saxon
Solomon

Blood Heir:
Blood Heir
Blood Bonds
Blood Reign
Blood Bonds

Three Rivers:
Into the Light

Standalone titles:
Yours
The Cabin
The Parent Trap
Wish Upon A Star
Big Hose

Non-Fiction titles:
You Can Do It
You Can Do It: Strength
You Can Do It: Fasting

Jack Wilder Titles:
The Missionary

JJ Wilder Titles:
Ark

To be informed of new releases, special offers, and other Jasinda news, sign up for Jasinda's email newsletter.

www.ingramcontent.com/pod-product-compliance
Lightning Source LLC
Chambersburg PA
CBHW021122260626
47169CB00005B/1406